FRONTIERS

FRONTIERS

a novel

MICHAEL JENSEN

POCKET BOOKS

NEW YORK · LONDON · TORONTO · SYDNEY · TOKYO · SINGAPORE

POCKET BOOKS, a division of Simon & Schuster, Inc.
1230 Avenue of the Americas, New York, NY 10020

ISBN: 0-671-02720-4

First Pocket Books hardcover printing April 1999

10   9   8   7   6   5   4   3   2   1

POCKET and colophon are registered trademarks of Simon & Schuster, Inc.

Printed in the U.S.A.

For Brent
Without you it wouldn't have happened.
Without you it wouldn't have mattered.

FRONTIERS

PROLOGUE

I COULDN'T STOP TREMBLING, THOUGH WHETHER FROM FEAR OR THE blood-numbing cold I didn't know. For the thousandth time I touched the worn flyer carefully folded and tucked into my shirt pocket. Soon I'd know if I'd been right in coming here or if I'd made the worst mistake of my life.

I'd waited anxiously in the Major's chamber for so long now that I swore my rigid body was dissolving into the freezing darkness. Such a sensation was familiar to me—I often lost my sense of self in the Major's formidable presence. An unbidden image of him softly singing came to me, bringing with it not a little solace, and I smiled wistfully.

No matter what manner of misfortune might be about to befall me, I would never regret having shared my bed with him these past few weeks. One of his shirts hung to my left, and I buried my face in it, inhaling the piquant but soothing smell of his body mingled with the scent of his comfrey soap.

Except for the soft sound of my breathing, the room was as still as a tomb. The cold from the fort's earthen floor seeped through my thin leather shoes. I wiggled my toes, but my feet were already so frigid I could barely feel them. The numbing chill only intensified the dark, the room's sense of menace, and I felt my resolve waver. No wonder the soldiers called this place Fort Friggin' Frigid.

How much time had passed since I'd first entered? A quarter

hour? A full hour? I couldn't be sure, but at last the harsh sound of iron heels striking stone echoed from the corridor.

My mouth went dry. Even if it was the Major, I feared almighty how he'd react upon finding me in his quarters, much less under these circumstances.

The footsteps halted just outside. Two voices began conversing—one being the Major's distinctive baritone, the other a gruff, angry growl that deepened my fear. If the Major came in with someone else, I was done for. He'd deny ever knowing me, turn me over to the townsfolk, and I'd spend twelve months fettered in bilbos and at hard labor with the wretched English convicts local wags called the King's passengers. This was if I was fortuitous—and I wasn't feeling lucky.

The voices ceased, followed by the sound of footsteps moving away, then a moment of silence. Even though I knew hiding to be futile, I pressed myself against the back wall. Swinging open, the door squealed, spilling in light, and I couldn't help myself—startled, I jumped and banged into a table.

The squealing ceased. A bar of tremulous torchlight from the corridor lay wavering on the floor. A silhouette stood motionless in the doorway. He had heard me, and I barely dared breathe.

Without warning, the door shut, plunging the room back into darkness. The sudden rasping of flint against flint cut through the silence. Light from the oil lamp leapt up, and even as weak as it was, I had to cover my eyes from the brightness.

"What the bloody hell?" cursed the Major.

"It's freezing in here, Colin. No wonder we always met at my place."

"What the devil's deuce are you doing here, Chapman? Are you insane?"

"Aren't you—"

"Answer me. *Now.*"

I took a deep breath to steady myself. "Some of the townspeople know about us. They're looking for me now."

"Fires and fagots!" He pressed his hand to his forehead. "What exactly do they know about us?" he demanded.

"That we spent the night together."

"So you came here? Are you trying to get me killed?"

"I came to *warn* you. I risked getting caught doing this."

"How did they find out?" he demanded.

"I don't know. Someone saw something—or someone told."

"Told? Unless *you* said something, nobody else could . . ." His voice trailed off as he glanced toward the door.

"Did *you* tell someone?" I dared to ask.

"Stop your mouth while I think. Who exactly is looking for you?"

"The constable. Coming into the barn, I overheard him asking Mr. MacMurria if he'd ever seen me alone with a British soldier. If I'd gotten there five minutes earlier, he would have found me for sure."

"Damnation. Did the constable know I was the soldier?"

"I don't think so. It sounded as if whoever saw us together recognized only the soldier's uniform, not you."

"But they recognized you?"

"Apparently."

"And that dolt of a Scotsman must have told the constable your name, that you're not even British."

I nodded.

"How did you get in here?" he demanded. "Who did you talk to?"

"Two guards out front."

"You used my name?"

I hesitated before answering. "Yes."

"By all the devils, Chapman! You've less brains than a drunken Dutchman! Do you realize how badly you've botched things?"

"I didn't mean to, Colin. I didn't know where to go."

"I know. I'm sorry," he said, his voice on the edge of panic. "We've got to get you away from here." He reached over and touched my face. "They know who you are—you're done for if they catch you. I think I can talk my way out of this by telling them you used my name as a ruse to get inside. Once you're gone, maybe I can even send them looking for you in the wrong direction."

I took the flyer from my pocket. "Come with me," I said softly, handing him the precious paper that promised free land and supplies.

"Do what?" he asked incredulously. "Why?"

"So we could be together. Read the flyer."

He quickly did so. "John, I've no more desire to settle western Pennsylvania than I do to bed King George's wife. And I've never heard of this Warren."

"Right now it's nothing but a frontier outpost, but next spring they're giving away land and supplies to those willing to stake a claim. We could be together. I know it's where things will finally be right for me."

He studied me, then laughed. "Good bloody God. You're actually serious, aren't you?"

I said nothing.

"John, be serious! Together, indeed. I'm a *major* in His Majesty's army. I go back to England in less than a year, where I'm to be married. I've got my station to think about." He put the flyer back in my pocket.

"But, Colin, what if—"

"John, I'm sorry, but I'm not going anywhere with you." He went to a trunk, hurriedly pulling out pieces of old uniforms. "Get shucked and put these on. If anyone sees me with you dressed like that, they'll remember and ask questions later. Hurry!"

I studied the uniform. "Father always wanted me to join the military," I whispered, joking to hide the pain his refusal had caused.

"I'm glad you didn't. We might have faced each other in battle if you had. At least this way, we had a few weeks together."

Shivering in the cold air, I yanked off my shirt and pants and shoved them into my pack with my few other belongings. I wriggled into the tight-fitting clothes he gave me.

Wearing the uniform, I tried to stand differently, with more confidence—more like the Major. Father had fought the British twenty years earlier and raised us on stories of how cruel and cowardly they were. On the other hand, Father had been accused of being a traitor, so I had no idea how true any of the tales were that spilled from his drunken mouth. Still, it felt more queer to wear a British uniform than it had to lie in the arms of one of their officers.

"There's an embrasure in the back wall that's hardly used," the Major said. "It's only a few hundred yards from there to the woods. Now, if we run into anyone, by Saint Christopher's whiskers, keep your fool mouth shut."

He slipped outside, then motioned for me to follow. Given my height, the ceiling of the corridor was barely high enough to allow me to walk without stooping. Like the Major's quarters, it, too, was dark and dank.

He signaled me to stop as we came to a corner. A soldier, picking his nose, rambled down the corridor but exited to the right before he reached us.

Again trailing behind the Major, I whispered, "What am I supposed to do, Colin? Where am I supposed to go?"

"What about that flyer you showed me? Go there."

"Alone? I can't, Colin. I don't have supplies or money or even a good sense of direction. I get lost between the cabin and the outhouse."

"Stop making jokes, for God sakes!" He turned to face me. "We'll get you supplies on the way out. You'll go to this Warren, stake a claim, start fresh. Nobody there will know you. And that's better for the both of us, isn't it?"

"If you say so."

"I say so. Now you have to go, and you can't come back. Not ever. It's too dangerous. Do you understand?"

"But it's dangerous for you, too. I still think you—"

"Never mind what you think. Just follow me."

For five minutes, we wordlessly made our way along various corridors until a ladder hove into view. We climbed ten feet up to an opening that led to the fort's back entrance. One at a time we stepped out into the warmth of the late-August afternoon. Colin anxiously cast his eyes along the embankment.

Birches and elms dotted the hillside beyond the fort, the long shadows of their trunks stretching across the field like bars. Farther up the hillside, the forest grew thick and wild and dangerous. I doubted it would take me long to pass into Indian country or stumble across a she-bear and her cubs foraging in the blackberry bushes.

"What about a gun and supplies?" I asked.

"Damnation! Why didn't you say something before?"

"I did!" I snapped, surprising myself. "And *you* said you'd get them. How the hell was I supposed to know where to stop?"

"You don't really need—"

This selfish, callous tone angered me. "Now who's being as dense as a Dutchman? Forget it, Colin. If you want me gone, then you damned well better get me supplies. Otherwise, we can wait and talk to your superiors."

"Of course. Forgive me, John. Stay here, and don't move. I'll be right back." He ducked down again, vanishing from sight.

Nervously I waited, fidgeting and tugging at the ill-fitting uniform. Once someone passed overhead, walking along the fort's upper perimeter. Thin to start with, I tried to make myself even smaller as I wedged against the log wall. In the tiniest of whispers, I practiced a British accent in case I was spotted. The accent was terrible, and I was unspeakably grateful when the sentinel passed out of sight.

The Major, clutching a burlap sack, appeared at the bottom of the ladder. At first I didn't realize anything was wrong, but when he leapt up the ladder in three bounds, I knew we were in trouble.

Excited voices echoed up from the corridor.

"They're coming!" he said, wild-eyed. "They know about me! They know everything! I'm coming with you!"

"But how—"

"Just run! Go! Go!" He shoved me hard, sending me stumbling forward as I jumped down to the ground. If captured now, I knew the punishment administered would be far worse than hard labor. Sodomy was bad enough; sodomy with a British officer would get me a flogging till I passed out, then clapped in leg irons in the shit-hole that passed for their gaol. I would never survive the twelve months I would spend there.

I didn't want to guess what fate would befall Colin.

Regaining my balance, I sprinted as fast as I could for the forest. We'd covered perhaps a hundred yards—a third of the way—when I glanced over my shoulder as two soldiers vaulted onto the top of the fort. Another fifty yards had vanished under our fleeing feet when the first shot rang out. Stunned, I stumbled to a halt.

"Are you hit?" the Major cried out.

Before I could answer, the second soldier fired. Not five feet away, the slight trunk of a pepperidge sapling, its leaves already a bloody scarlet, splintered into dozens of pieces. Without a word, I took off running again, but by now more soldiers had joined in the shooting. Twenty feet from reaching the first line of trees, I stumbled and fell as another shot rang out. At the same moment, the Major, just behind me, leapt upward, as if suddenly taken by a fit.

Hot blood speckled my face as he crashed down, face-first, into the soft purple heather.

"Colin?" I called out. I scrambled on my belly to where he lay. Rolling him over, I moaned at the sight of the gory wound in his chest. I could've reached into the ragged hole with my hand. Blood issued forth in pulsating spurts, soaking his shirt before being drawn into the dark earth.

His green eyes—the very first thing I'd noticed about him—were wide open as he stared up at the azure sky. He labored to breathe, giving rise to terrible sucking sounds that arose from the bloody wound. A pink bubble formed between his lips, shimmered in the light, then softly popped. He inhaled once more, then his mouth went slack. His eyes glassed over, as dead and lifeless as a pond in January.

Voices clamored in the distance. Glaring back, I saw soldiers racing across the meadow. The sight came near to overwhelming me. Panicking, I scrambled to my knees. I grabbed the bag, racing forward, reaching the sanctuary of the woods in a matter of moments. The sound of my ragged breathing coursed through my ears as I ran wildly, tripping and stumbling my way through wealds of dense timber that alternated with sun-drenched meadows. Breathless and as panicked as a hunted deer, I at last paused in one of the meadows. Wiping stinging sweat from my eyes, I looked backward, forward, then left and right, trying desperately to decide where to go.

Overhead, the flat, hot disk of the sun tracked steadily west.

I followed it.

ONE

My first memory is being lost on a cold December night when I was four. Behind our run-down house, I'd spotted an injured blue-wing duck flapping in distress. Wanting to catch it and take care of it, I chased it far into the woods, but the duck vanished into a thick row of gallberry bushes. I spent a few moments searching and calling out for the bird, but it was gone.

I don't know how long I wandered amongst the forbidding trees pointlessly calling for Mother or Father or my sister, Elizabeth. Mother was dead since summer, Father was probably drunk, and Elizabeth was only seven. I started to cry.

When night finally fell, I found a dry space under a log, crawled into it, and lay there shivering until the sun came up. Hungry and freezing, I staggered about the next morning until I was nearly trampled by cows being driven to pasture by a farmer.

"Whoa, there, little fella," the farmer said to me. "'Tis awfully early for you to be out. Where's your pa or ma?"

I was in such a daze, I could only look up at him.

"You're lost then, aren't you?" he said, sliding off his horse. "I'll have you home in no time. What do you call yourself?"

Ma called me her "Chappie," Pa called me his "Woe," but I didn't know what I called myself.

9

November 1797

SNOW SPEWED FORTH OVER MY SHIVERING FORM AS I GLANCED BACK-ward one last time at that hellish region of western Pennsylvania known as the Allegheny Plateau. For the first three days of November, I'd battled across the plateau's stony, windswept heights, surviving only by some miracle. Thank God, it lay behind me.

Peering ahead, I tried to make out the yawning valley stretching ahead of me, but it was quickly lost in the swelling gloom of night. My only hint of the best way down appeared to be the faint scoring of some animal's hooves upon the steep rocks descending beneath me. Even that trail would soon be lost in the dark, leaving me to find my way down the precipitous route by feel. I felt dizzy just looking at the descent. It was far too easy to imagine the fatal slip that would send me careening onto the rocks far below.

My name was John Chapman, though I would gladly have been anyone else if given the chance. Two months had passed since I'd watched the Major die. Once again fingering the now tattered flyer upon which I'd foolishly pinned so many hopes, I smiled grimly at my appalling circumstances. I felt certain I was to follow in the Major's steps before morning.

At least I was ready to do so.

For hours I clambered downward over icy snarls of shattered stone, razorbushes that rent my clothes, and twisted, tangled roots that snagged my feet. I was more than exhausted by the damnable wilderness; I was being overwhelmed, crushed like a snail under the iron heel of a marching soldier. By the time I reached the bottom, I literally counted it another miracle I hadn't broken my neck.

At some point as I pushed along the valley floor in a haze of delirium, the storm passed on. Without even realizing it had stopped, I found myself in a clearing staring upward at the unex-pectedly cloudless sky. Above me arched a panoply of brilliant, sparkling stars that would've taken my breath away if the cold hadn't already done so. And in front of me, not more than fifty paces away, stood a cabin.

I turned and fled back into the woods.

Here I was, frightened, confused, and dangerously close to dying, and upon being offered a reprieve, I *hid* in the woods. No wonder, as Father had oft pointed out, I would never achieve more than keeping myself alive—and I was barely doing that. Shivering, I sank against the trunk of an enormous tree, wondering what to do, when any fool less timid and shamed than I would simply have gone up and asked for help.

A thin ribbon of white smoke, barely visible in the early-morning light, streamed up from the top of the cabin's chimney. The sharp, pungent scent of a fire reached my nose, sending pangs of hunger sweeping through me like brushfires across sun-baked fields in summer.

This was absurd. Gathering my courage, I rose and stepped into the clearing, common sense telling me to call out a warning before approaching. Otherwise I risked startling someone who would bestow me with a belly full of lead instead of soup. However, before I could utter so much as a syllable, the barrel of a gun bit deep into my neck. The strong stink of whiskey assaulting my nose only frightened me all the more. Without being told, I walked forward, being certain to keep my hands open and at my sides.

"I'll say this once," said the bearer of the gun. "Whether you live or die is up to your own sorry self. Drop your pack and tomahawk and step away."

At least whoever stood behind me didn't sound as drunk as he smelled, though his intent was unquestionably clear: do as told or die. I slid the leather straps off my shoulders, letting the nearly empty pack pitch to the ground. The barrel of the stranger's rifle stayed flush with my neck as I crouched to lay my tomahawk next to it, then stepped away.

"By the devil's accursed soul, who are you?"

Certain this man would just as soon shoot me as not, I tried to speak but found my voice had fled as surely as the summer sun.

"Not talking? You don't value your pitiful life much, do you?"

Anger and distrust radiated from him like a fever. "I said, 'What's your goddamned *name?*'"

"It's John. John Chapman."

"Who sent you here?"

"Sent me? Nobody."

"You're a beshitted liar, that's what you are. It's the Company you're with, ain't it?" He jabbed me with the gun. "Ain't it?"

"No, I swear I'm not. I've no idea what you're talking about."

"Maybe. Maybe not." He pressed the barrel harder against my flesh. "Perhaps you're a brigand preying on decent folks. I'd probably be better off killing you now and being done with it."

"Please," I begged. "I'm nobody. I'm not with anyone. I'll leave right now, and you'll never see me again."

"Where's your horse?"

"I don't have a horse."

"Bullshit."

"It's the truth."

"Then how in hellfire did you get here?"

"I walked."

"Walked?"

"Yes."

"You make as pathetic a liar as you do a brigand. Where are your supplies?"

"In my pack."

He kicked the pack where it lay by my feet. "It's empty."

"I ran out a couple of days ago."

"You mean to tell me that you have no supplies and no horse?" The gun slid down my neck to my back.

"That's right."

"You're not just a liar, you're a liar who takes me for a fool."

"Please, I'm not a liar. I'm lost and hungry."

I felt his eyes on me. "You do look as if you've taken more than one meal with Saint Anthony."

"You're right—I haven't eaten in three days. I swear I intend you no harm."

"So said Judas to Jesus." He jabbed me again. "I'm supposed to

believe that you show up here on the heels of a blizzard—goddamned weeks from nowhere—with no supplies, no horse, and all
by yourself?"

I started to shrug again, but he jabbed me so hard in the back
that I stumbled forward. If I lived until tomorrow, I knew I would
find a bruise there. Furious, I nearly spun around and charged him.
Only knowing that I would surely die held me back.

Then the anger drained away as quickly as it had come. Now the
only feeling I could muster was despondency—after all, who wants
to die alone, unmourned, and having done nothing in life but run?

"Answer me!"

Not ready to die, I snapped back to the present. "What did you
ask?"

"You must think me as dull-witted as the Indians who traded this
valley for a barrel of whiskey. Well, I ain't buying what you're sell-
ing." Before I could speak, he grabbed me by the shoulder, then
spun both of us around so I was positioned between him and the
woods.

"It's a trap, ain't it?" he whispered, his mouth pressed next to my
ear. He had wrapped his arm around my chest as if holding me in a
lopsided embrace. His face felt warm, rough, unshaven, and the
scent of whiskey-saturated sweat emanated from him. "You *are* a
brigand, ain't you? Your friends are hiding and watching us right
now."

For a moment, all was silent, except for the crunch of snow
under his feet as he shifted about. "I know you're out there, you
shits!" he bellowed abruptly. "If you try anything, I'll splatter your
friend's guts from here to the Allegheny River!"

Already half out of my mind with cold and fear, I had to suppress
an insane desire to yell "Get him now!" just to see what he would do.
Instead, I said as evenly as possible, "I'm alone. I swear it."

"I doubt it, you filthy bunghole," he snarled. Without warning,
he shoved me away. Before I could run or even fall to the ground,
his rifle exploded from not more than two feet behind me. Petrified
I'd been shot, I staggered forward, my ears ringing as I frantically
searched my torso and arms and stomach.

I hadn't been hit, but missing from that distance hadn't been by accident. He must have been firing into the woods, hoping to frighten my nonexistent companions.

Weak-kneed and nauseated, gagging on the choking smell of gunpowder, I finally dared to look at the lunatic who might yet be the last person I ever saw. He retrieved a second rifle, then began pacing along some unseen border like a dog defending its territory. I half-expected him to stop and piss on one of the tree stumps.

In the dark, I could only make out his silhouette—short but broad-shouldered, and as solid-looking as the trees that ringed us. Pausing, he drank from a bottle he took from his pocket, then stood facing the Cimmerian woods. Though he mostly struck me as a foolish drunk, there was also bravery in the defiant way he stood there ready to face the unknown.

"All right," he said at last. "So maybe you are alone. But where are your supplies then?"

I all but threw up my hands. "I told you before—I ran out."

Raising the rifle, he stepped toward me. "Unless you want to see how interesting your insides look spattered all over the snow, you better watch your uppity tone. Understand?"

Wide-eyed, I nodded.

"Christ. You must be telling the truth about not being with the Company. Even they wouldn't hire someone this incompetent. You get lost, is that it? Been wandering around out there like some goddamned pudding head? What must your father think?"

At first I'd only felt humiliation, but at the mention of my father a wild anger swept over me. "Yes, I'm lost like some wretched pudding head! Is that what you want to hear? I can't do anything right, damn you! So if you're going to shoot me, you whoreson, then just do it! I don't give a twopenny damn anymore! Just get it over with! Go on!"

He stared at me a moment before lowering the gun. "I think I get it now. I've seen the likes of you afore."

My tirade left behind a throbbing in my head akin to a hangover. "The likes of *what?*"

"You're a fugitive from one thing or another. God knows what you're running from. Probably only God that cares."

Hoping this drunk, ignorant frontiersman's keenness went no further, I said weakly, "I'm not running from anything."

"Suit yourself. What's your name?"

"I already told you. John Chapman. What's yours?"

"None of your goddamned business. You ever even been on the frontier before, John Chapman?" He rolled his eyes. "I might as well be asking if you ever been to the moon."

Shivering again, I tried to respond, but couldn't. The longer we stood there, the more disoriented I became until the tall trees behind the man began to sway. First they tilted right, then as I tried to adjust, they swung back to the left. A strange look came over the man, and for some reason I tried to smile.

Then everything disappeared.

Somewhere nearby an owl called out. Looking up toward the heavens, I saw a shooting star arc its brief and brilliant path against the slowly lightening horizon. My breath, I realized, was drifting away into the frigid night.

I wasn't dead. Not yet. Either that or heaven was nothing like what the preachers had preached. On the other hand, not much about anything was what the preachers preached.

Coughing, I forced myself to sit upright. My legs were numb, despite my thick linsey pants, and I tried to massage some warmth into them. I wondered how long I had lain there like some ginned-up inebriate. Passing out wasn't the most auspicious start to my stay here—wherever here was. Sprawled on my ass in the snow, I probably resembled my father more than I cared to admit. What a grand day this was turning out to be.

With a sigh, I rose and tucked in my shirt.

The cabin stood not more than twenty yards away. The open doorway, a lonely rectangle of light in an ocean of dark, put me in mind of the Longmeadow lighthouse. Fetching my pack, I trudged across the clearing but hesitated before entering. Warm air, redolent with the smell of frying and spices, flowed over me. My mouth watered, my body trembled.

"Are you going to come in, or should I just bar the door and let you freeze out there?"

The sudden' sound of the man's voice made me jump. I half-expected to feel the cold bite of his gun on my neck again. I entered.

An old oil lamp on the table threw a small circle of feeble light onto the floor. A log burned low in the fireplace while several rush-lights—dried rushes dipped in grease and then lit with an ember—burned weakly and smokily in various cracks of the cabin walls. A large metal cross—simple, barely more than two bars nailed together—hung over a bed, the flickering flames dancing on its somber surface. Whatever else constituted the rest of the cabin lay swathed in quivering shadows.

After being cold for so long, the warm embrace of the cabin felt unnatural. The man sat at the table, just on the edge of the lamplight, his back to me. Next to the lamp sat the bleached skull of a horse, giving the entire tableau a somewhat ominous air. I watched the man's head bend downward as he scooped something into his mouth, then he nodded at a spot on the table across from him. "On the off chance you'd come to afore you froze to death, I dished you up some mush. A few more minutes and I would've eaten it myself."

I stepped around the table so that I could face him. "That there pitcher is filled with cider, and as soon as the griddle is hot, I'll fry up some johnnycakes." In the dim light, all I could see was that he had black hair framing a dark-complected face. "Or maybe you ain't hungry," he added sarcastically.

"What if I hadn't?"

"Hadn't what?"

"Come to."

He touched a large plate in the middle of the table. "There's chestnuts and apples as well. I haven't had much luck hunting of late, so you'll have to make do without any goddamned meat." He lifted one of the apples, its dusky skin reflecting the lamplight, and took a crisp bite.

It was everything I could do to keep from rushing to the table.

Wiping his sleeve across his mouth, he said, "Well, by all the devils, are you going to eat or not?"

"You're fond of maledictions, aren't you?"

"Mallie-what?" He looked at me from under raised eyebrows.

"You like to curse."

"If you don't want to eat, it's fine by me." He reached for the mush.

"No, I do." I lowered myself into a chair. But I still hesitated until he shoved the bowl of mush toward me.

"You look like you haven't had a proper meal in weeks. Don't be so proud, you fool. Eat."

Actual pain rose from my stomach as steam curled from the warm mush into the cold morning air. My fingers shook so badly I had trouble gripping the wooden spoon. Unable to steady it, I gingerly lay the spoon down and resorted to using my fingers to scoop up a mouthful of mush.

Wasn't I just doing myself proud?

I ignored the derisive voice in my head and rolled the hot pulp on my tongue, savoring the sweet flavor. Food served in King George's court itself couldn't have tasted better.

Still not looking at the man, I greedily ate the rest, sucking each bit from my fingers. When I finished, I stared forlornly at my empty bowl and said, "Thank you."

"Refined one, ain't you?" Shaking his head, he wrinkled his nose and slid his half full bowl across to me.

If not for my hunger, I would have felt even more humiliated. Never in my life had I imagined I would be reduced to such circumstances. Desperately I devoured the rest of his mush. When the mush was gone, I grabbed a handful of nuts and an apple, from which I took such a large bite that I was almost unable to chew it. Still, I thought I'd never fill the hunger that gripped me.

The stranger grimaced. "I do believe you're the most pitiable thing I've ever seen. I hope your pa didn't live to see how bad you turned out."

Not only had Pa lived to see, I'm sure he would have found this man's judgment of me just. I wiped my sleeve across my chin. My eyes met his as I chewed, but I said nothing.

Shaking his head, he stood, took the horse's skull, and set it on a shelf by his bed. Going to the fireplace, he began frying johnnycakes that were hot and sweet and glistened with a beautiful golden glaze of fat. I ate them ravenously between gulps of cider.

"Where did you come from?" he asked.

"Back east."

"And you looking so much like an experienced trapper and all, I figured you'd come from trading with Indians out west. *Where* back east?"

"Longmeadow."

"Longmeadow? Never heard of it."

"It's in Massachusetts."

He sat the griddle down with a bang. "Are you stupid or are you just purposefully being bullheaded? I meant where did you *just* come from, fool. And don't tell me you just goddamned walked here from Massachusetts."

His anger brought me up short, reminding me to tread carefully. "I don't know the name of the last place I was. I really don't. It was a small place on the other side of the plateau."

"The other side of the plateau?" He paused. "The *Allegheny* Plateau?"

I nodded as he handed me another johnnycake.

"You're telling me you crossed that plateau in a blizzard, dressed like that, with no horse? *You* did all that?"

Some shred of dignity welled up within me, and I slammed my hand onto the table. "For the last time—yes!"

Narrowing his eyes, he carried the sputtering pan to where I sat. I flinched as a drop of oil spattered my cheek. "Do you like my food? From the way you're wolfing it down, I'd say that you do."

I nodded.

"Fine. Then you damn well better answer all of my questions until I'm done asking. You understand that?"

I nodded again. "Sorry."

He went back to the stove. "You're either lying like there ain't no tomorrow, or you're the luckiest bugger I ever met. I ain't so certain which to believe." He sat down across from me.

"I'm not lying."

He stared at me with an unnerving intensity. "You may be lost and you may be a fool, but you must be tougher than you look." For the first time, his voice carried a hint of—what? Warmth? Admiration?

I took another bite of the apple.

"By the way, it's Daniel McQuay."

"What is?"

"My name."

"Is that Irish?"

"Why do you ask?" The warmth in his voice vanished, replaced with cold suspicion.

"You sound English, that's all."

"Well, I've never even been to England."

"My mistake." I'd asked because he neither sounded nor looked Irish, though I still hadn't got a really good look at him. "You probably hate the English even more than I do."

"What are you going on about?"

"I just meant that the English are enemies for us both, but given all that they've done to Ireland, you probably loathe them even more than me."

"Right. Only good Englishman is one split from his skull to his breastbone."

He really didn't like them. "These are good," I said, nodding at my plate.

When I said I could eat no more, he removed several armfuls of straw from his bed that he heaped into an empty corner. I gathered I would be sleeping alone, rather than our bundling together for warmth. From a box, he yanked a large black bearskin that he threw over the straw.

"We won't be bundling until it gets colder and I know you better," he said, sounding as if he expected me to complain. "I don't expect you're the type to slit my throat whilst I sleep, but make no mistake—I'll be keeping an eye on you."

Shared body warmth or not, I was both too exhausted and grateful to even consider arguing. I stumbled to the corner and tried to pull off my boots. My feet were so swollen and painful that at first the boots wouldn't come free. I considered sleeping with them on, but with a final tug they popped loose. I fashioned a rough squab for my head and settled down into the straw. No bed had ever felt more agreeable.

A shadow dropped across me as the man appeared above me.

"Thanks again for everything," I said, pulling the bearskin over me. My body was so exhausted, I knew it would take only moments to drift off to sleep.

"You're welcome. Get some sleep, and we'll talk more later."

As he walked away, I let out a deep breath and began to believe that maybe everything might come right after all.

The man paused, turned back to me, and said, "If I catch you messing with my gun, my tomahawk, or damned well anything else you haven't been given liberty to touch, I'll kill you. You understand that?"

I nodded.

Sleep didn't come as easily as I'd thought.

TWO

I was seven when I got a new mother.

"Elizabeth, John," *Father said sternly to my sister and me,* "when I return tomorrow, I'll be bringing back your step-mother. This place is to be spotless. I know not how you feel about a new mother, but you're to do as she says and treat her with respect. Understand?"

Wide-eyed, Elizabeth and I nodded. Our mother had died three years previously, and since then, Elizabeth and I had, for all intents and purposes, been orphans. True, we had Father, but given that he lavished far more attention on his still than his children, the result was the same.

Nor did we have much in the way of friends or neighbors to look after us. Not only was Father a drunk, but he was a petty thief and rumored to have been a traitor during the war. Hence, we were mostly shunned, and Elizabeth and I had come to rely almost exclusively on each other. During those three years, I don't think either of us ever heard a kind word except from each other.

As promised, Father returned home the next afternoon. A short, red-haired woman stood next to him in the doorway.

"Children, this is your stepmother. You mind her or you'll soon feel the sting of my belt."

21

Elizabeth and I stood stock-still, each clutching the other's hand. Our stepmother knelt down, smiled, and said, "You can call me Lucy if you like."

"They'll call you 'Mother' and be glad of it!" Father snapped. He advanced menacingly toward us. "Well, don't you have something to say to your mother?"

Without a word between us, Elizabeth and I both burst into tears and threw ourselves into Lucy's arms.

November 1797

SURROUNDED BY WARM, ENFOLDING DARKNESS, I WOKE TO THE RUSTLE of something softly snuffling not more than a few feet from where I lay. At first I thought some animal—a carcajou or a stoat—had nosed its way inside. But inside *where*? My groggy mind couldn't place where I was. No matter my location, I knew carcajous were vicious cusses, so I lay still to avoid drawing its attention. Despite my unease and confusion, I tried to recollect how I had come to be here.

In an instant, everything rushed back, and I knew I was in the cabin of the drunk Irishman. And what I heard wasn't the nocturnal foraging of a dangerous animal but the snoring and thrashing about of the Irishman—the man who had saved me.

I peered around, trying to locate him. I'd no idea how long I'd slept, but my dick was so hard it hurt—piss-boners, my father had called them.

Yawning, I rolled onto my side to relieve the pressure on my bladder, wondering if there was a piss-pot in the cabin or whether I'd have to go out into the freezing darkness. Hadn't the sun been rising when I'd arrived? If so, I must have slept through the entire day and into the next night.

I sat upright, cold air pouring over my skin, goose bumps

swarming over me like ants after sugar. In the inky dark, I couldn't see the floor, much less anything like a piss-pot. Stealthily, I searched for my shirt and boots, found them by the foot of my makeshift bed, and pulled them on. Careful not to wake the cabin's irascible owner by stumbling around, I crept forward, my hands held in front of me. I found and lit a lamp, keeping the flame as dim as possible. I hung the lamp on a hook near the door. Grasping the heavy beam that barred the door, I eased it upward and stepped outside.

The wintry air hit me like a slap, actually bringing tears to my eyes. There had to be a necessary nearby, but it was too damned cold to bother looking for it now. Instead, I ducked around the corner of the cabin and gratefully pissed into a snowbank. The brilliant stars I'd followed the night before were gone now, hidden by slow, lumbering clouds skirting the treetops. Up on the plateau the world had seemed endless and exposed. Here, under the sky's gray cover, it felt small and sheltered.

Finished pissing, I hurried back to the warmth of the cabin; however, when I tried to close the door, it refused to budge. Worried that the cold air might awaken and anger the man, I braced my shoulder against the thick oak plank, shoved as hard as I could, and with a horrible screech it finally slid halfway shut. Cringing, I turned as the man exploded from his bed.

"Who's there?" he shouted. "Who is it?"

The rifle materialized from nowhere, and before I could answer he had it aimed at me. Dropping to my knees, I scrambled out the door—banging my head—and into the snow. The sound of the rifle firing ripped through the night as the lead ball smashed into the door.

"Who's there?" he bellowed again, stumbling across the floor. "I've got another goddamned gun already loaded, so you better get the hell out afore I kill you!"

"Don't shoot! Don't shoot!" I hollered. "I'm the one you took in yesterday! You fed me mush and cooked me johnnycakes!" His name—what the hell was his name? I looked toward the shadowed woods, gauging how long it would take me to reach them. "Remember? You called me pathetic!"

The door jerked inward; I scrambled backward through the snow like a crab searching for the safety of the sea. Weak lamplight spilled out onto the snow. Naked, the man held a pistol aimed at my chest. He, too, had an erection. Despite everything, I couldn't help but notice the fine, black hair that covered his chest and stomach, or that his cock was dark and thick and curved to the left like a wood-carver's adze.

As warm air rushed out, I could all but taste the smell of alcohol that clung to him.

"Who are you and what do you want?" he demanded, swaying slightly as he brandished a pistol at me. His erection swayed back and forth as well, and I tried not to stare.

"My name's John, and I don't want anything."

"Then what are you doing here?" he demanded.

"I couldn't find the piss-pot. I went outside to go."

"Where'd you come from? Who are you?"

"I'm John Chapman," I repeated slowly and clearly. I had to penetrate whatever drunken fog he was in before he decided to shoot me and be done with it. "I was lost. I stumbled onto your cabin. You found me and took me in."

He lowered the pistol to his side, a puzzled look on his face. "Oh." He nodded. "I remember." He still looked confused, and I noticed his cock had already begun to sag.

He turned to go back inside, but stopped. Facing me again, he raised the pistol, his eyes narrowing as he asked suspiciously, "You with the goddamned Company? Did they find out already? Did that bastard Jackson send you?"

"No!" I shook my head emphatically, momentarily wondering what there was to find out. "Nobody sent me. I swear."

He studied me a moment, then lowered the pistol to his side. "All right then. Shut the door. It's goddamned cold out here." He staggered back inside, dropping the pistol on the table with a clatter. As he climbed into bed, he called back out to me, "And the damned mingo's in the corner."

"The what?"

"The mingo! The piss-pot! Use it next time, you stupid sod."

Trembling, I lay in the snow. A single drop of sweat rolled down
my scalp and onto my cheek.

I was no longer cold.

The next time I woke, weak light seeped through greased paper
covering narrow slits barely wide enough to be called windows.
Now I needed to do more than piss, and I wondered where the necessary might be. When I looked around the dim interior, I saw I was
alone.

To be certain, I hesitantly asked, "Anyone there?" Only the still-
ness of an empty cabin echoed back to me. A thin square of light
shone through a narrow peephole in the closed but unbarred door.
Crouching down, I peered through the slit out into a large clearing
covered with snow. From the angle of the light, I judged the time to
be near midday.

Black scorch marks ringed the hole marking last night's close
call. The edge of the cavity felt rough to the touch. A dark smudge
smeared my fingers, leaving them reeking of sulfur, and I thought
fleetingly of the Major. Only the door's thickness had kept me from
sharing his fate.

"Hello?" I called out as I opened the door. "Don't be alarmed.
It's just me. I'm coming out if that's all right."

No one answered.

Several inches of velvety powder cloaked the trees and ground.
Soft light filtered through the gray clouds as a few tag-along
snowflakes wafted from the sky. Dozens of small stumps dotted a
clearing dominated by the enormous stump of what must have been
a remarkable tree. Scattered about were what I assumed to be my
benefactor's footprints, although their outlines had already been
softened by the falling snow. I couldn't make sense of what he'd
been doing or which way he'd ultimately gone.

I found the necessary behind the cabin. Like most privies, it was
crude and cold and encouraged one to be quick about one's business. Despite my alacrity, when I came back out, the few falling
flakes had given way to a steady stream. Even the wind had stiffened, whirling the powder around my feet as if to show its serious

intent. It wasn't hard to imagine what was happening up on the plateau, and I thanked God I was no longer up there.

In the daylight, I got my initial look at the cabin. From outside it looked much larger than it had inside. I wondered if it might not be partitioned into one or more rooms. Dozens of different animal skins covered the cabin's walls like a bizarre quilt run amok. The furs ranged in size and color from tiny gray ones taken from easily killed squirrels to large black hides that I imagined were only grudgingly given up by the previous owners. Most impressive was a huge brown one that must have come from something called a moose, a supposedly enormous creature that I'd yet to see.

The second thing I noticed was that the cabin wasn't really a cabin at all. Instead, its thick walls, narrow, paper-covered windows, and numerous slits for rifle barrels suggested a fort. Such a design, the Major had explained to me, allowed the defenders ample opportunities for defense while affording the attackers little chance to shoot anything other than logs. It struck me right away that one man, or even two or three, could never have built the place alone. I wondered who had helped and where they were now.

Curious to see more, I meandered around the cabin's perimeter. Rounding the corner, I had expected only to see another wall. Instead, I came face-to-face with a lone cow, yelped once, stumbled backward, and fell on my tailbone. I was grateful I was alone.

The cow, apparently as startled as I, lurched away, mooing anxiously, her head bobbing as her haunches banged into the sides of her stall.

"Shh, it's all right," I whispered from where I sat on the ground. Little by little, I approached the startled creature, my hand held out for her to sniff. "Shh, now. It's all right. What a pretty cow you are. Didn't expect to find you out here." When I thought she wasn't quite so afraid, I rubbed the spot between her honey-brown eyes all cows love to have stroked. Calmed, she lowed her contentment, so much so that when I moved to take my hand away, she pushed her head forward, letting me know I wasn't through.

"Well, at least you're friendlier than your owner." Beginning to shiver from the cold, I patted her a final time and said, "I'll see you later."

Beyond the cow's stall, I came across stacks of firewood piled high under an overhang where it would stay dry. Another small building—a smokehouse, I guessed—stood out in the clearing.

"Chapman!" bellowed a voice from the other side of the cabin.

Startled, I jumped.

"Chapman!" came the voice again.

So, despite having been drunk, at least he had remembered my name. I had yet to recall his. As inconspicuously as possible, I came around the corner hoping to reach the front door before he noticed me. Given his temperament thus far, I didn't want him thinking I'd been snooping. For if he did, he might very well turn me out before I was prepared to go, and I wouldn't blame him.

I needn't have worried. Wholly unaware of my presence, he stood in the middle of the clearing inspecting two large bundles that he held in a way that could only be called triumphant. I spied a long, thin pipe of a sort I'd never seen before clenched between his teeth. His red hunting shirt shone like a brilliant splash of blood against the white backdrop of the clearing. He stood on the short side, but his massive forearms, the clear contours of a solid chest, and the broad shoulders visible under his hunting shirt gave him the presence of someone taller. His long black hair, drawn into a ponytail much the same way I wore mine, gleamed in the morning light.

I thought him quite striking.

He swept clean part of the huge tree stump, then laid the bundles down. At last he looked up and saw me.

"There you are," he said, shaking snow from the fringe of his shirtsleeve. He gestured at the thick, stolid bodies. "Beautiful, aren't they? Goddamned beautiful."

Two large beavers, their thick, glossy pelts glistening in the frigid air, lay sprawled across the stump. Looking closer, I realized that each animal had been shot rather than trapped, as even I knew was typical. Why would anybody shoot a beaver, whose fur, after all, was only valuable undamaged?

"Hand me my hatchet and hold this," he ordered, giving me the pipe in exchange. "Finally some fresh meat. Been tracking these two for weeks. Once the ponds freeze over they pretty much stay put in their lodges. But not always, and I keep my eyes open." A strong, rough-looking hand caressed one of the sleek, black pelts, and I briefly wondered how his touch might feel on my skin. Then, just as quickly, I shoved the thought from my mind.

He touched the corner of one eye with the blunt end of the hatchet. "Daniel's always watching. Remember that."

Daniel! That was his name. Daniel McQuay.

He spread the stout, black bodies over the stump so that their heads and small, dark forepaws hung limply over the edge. With two smart chops, the heads tumbled into the snow, their dark, glassy eyes staring into the distance. Viscous blood welled up from the necks, slowly running down the side of the stump like the sap that had once flowed through the tree.

Unable to help myself, I shuddered. I'd always been too fond of animals not to feel sad when they died. Yet another of the many ways I was at odds with most folks.

"What's the matter?" Daniel asked. "Little blood bother you?"

"No, I'm just cold, that's all."

"Better get used to it, Chapman."

I nodded, but I wasn't sure if he meant the cold, the blood, or both. Either way, he was right. That's who I was now—Chapman. Someone who lived on the frontier and wasn't bothered by blood and killing. Someone who wouldn't get cold or too involved with people—especially men who caught my eye.

Someone no one knew.

Daniel took each body by the tail and held them up in the air. Bright red splashes of blood bloomed in the sparkling snow.

"Is this an Indian pipe?" I asked, quickly looking from the blood to the half dozen intricate figures etched onto the pipe's gleaming surface.

"It's a peace pipe. Seneca. I've smoked them afore with the Senecas, and let me tell you—it's nasty stuff they put in there. They believe the smoke goes up to the Great Spirit or something asinine like that. This particular pipe they smoke during religious ceremonies welcoming back the spring. Hell, they got pipes for everything—negotiations, greetings, probably even when they take a piss. Speaking of which, unless you want me to cut your ears off, don't take another piss in the snow around the blockhouse. Come the middle of winter, when we can't get to the creek and have to melt snow, I won't be pleased to find myself drinking your piss. You understand that?"

I nodded.

"Fine then. Goddamn it," he swore as a gust of wind splattered blood on his moccasins. Angry, he flopped the headless bodies back on the stump. They looked smaller now, deflated, sad.

"Were they hard to get?" I asked. "The beavers, I mean."

He finished wiping off his moccasins, then smiling hugely, he pulled a large knife from his belt. I observed his moods were as changeable as a two-year-old's. "Not once I spotted them," he boasted, "but like I said afore, *that* wasn't easy since they don't venture out much in winter. But when they do, I track them to their lodge, bust up the roof with an ax and maul, and . . ." He pointed his finger at the two lifeless bodies. "Pow, pow."

I wondered, as I often did, if animals felt fear. If God was merciful, they didn't.

Daniel smiled, satisfied, as he flipped a beaver onto its back. The blade sliced easily through the sleek black fur; ruby-red guts spilled out like the insides of a ripe raspberry.

Grunting, he slipped his hand inside the beaver. Wrenching his arm back and forth, he twisted his hand until, with the sound of gristle and muscle tearing free, he pulled out a dark red organ.

"Liver's a slippery little bugger," he said matter-of-factly. He bit a piece off and, as he chewed, offered the rest up to me. When I shook my head no, he tossed it into the snow.

"Too bad, Chapman. Nothing better to keep your roger good and stiff for flourishing the ladies." When I blushed, he burst out laughing. I wasn't surprised by his crudity, but I could have done without it.

His attention returned to the beaver, affording me my first opportunity to study his face from up close. I tried to decide how old he might be, what kind of life he'd had. He looked like no Irishman I'd ever seen, but in truth I'd seen one, maybe two. Back in Longmeadow, the few Irish and Scotch around were considered lower than even my family and had kept mostly to themselves.

Daniel's tanned skin was badly scarred—he'd obviously had the pox, which probably explained why he'd grown such a full beard. Even then I could see the scars as they faded into his cheekbones. His features were generally those of someone youthful—he'd probably been called "boy" long after he was sixteen—but he looked weathered as well. He could have been as old as forty, or maybe he was younger and life had been especially rough for him. And something about his expression, the tight line of his mouth—in fact, his entire carriage—made him look angry.

Still, all in all, he was attractive, and I didn't need any liver to make my roger stiffen.

With a start, I realized I was staring at him. Tearing my eyes away, I rebuked myself, though whether for the staring or for the arousal I had allowed to stir within me, I couldn't say.

The snow had once again tapered off, but when I looked up the clouds had grown even darker, thicker, like blood pudding beginning to set. Daniel saw me watching the sky. "Big snow coming. It's only goddamn November, and it's already been a bitch of a winter. There's salt inside. By the chimney. Get it."

Inside, along the back wall next to the chimney, were two rows of narrow shelves. Tins of various sizes along with deerskin bags packed the shelves, but in the dim light of the cabin I couldn't tell what each tin or bag held. Using a pair of tongs, I took a glowing ember from the fireplace and lit several pieces of candlewood—dried, resinous bits of pine cut into strips that had been stuffed into cracks along the walls. Both the rushlights and candlewood burned smokily but gave off enough weak light that I was able to locate the salt.

When I came back out, both of the beaver tails lay in the snow, their shape and size reminiscent of the oriental fans wealthy city women used in summer to keep cool. "Here's the salt, Daniel," I said, using his name for the first time. I wondered if I shouldn't call him McQuay instead. I thought not—coming from me, it would sound forced and phony.

"Hold it," he said, spreading a pelt across the trunk. "I'll tell you when I need it." A just-skinned beaver's body sprawled across the snow, flakes of snow already speckling its slick, red flesh.

With deft, precise moves, he slit the fur around the second

beaver's legs, and as he peeled the skin away from the body, he asked, "Who did you come out here looking for, Chapman? A girl who was supposed to marry you but changed her mind? Or maybe some whoring rascal who got your sister with child?"

"I'm not looking for anybody."

He began to sever the deep red meat from the bones as casually as I turned the pages of a book. "Well, if you ain't looking for someone, you must be running from someone. Or something."

"No."

Cartilage and gristle snapped and cracked as he cut the animals apart, and I wanted to walk away. At some point, he'd absentmindedly wiped his hand across his cheek, leaving a scarlet streak. It made him look as if he were bleeding, as if one of the beavers had managed, if ever so briefly, to fight back and wound him.

"Then what the devil *are* you doing out here?"

"I'm a settler. I've come to claim land."

He burst out laughing. "And this is Bethlehem and I'm one of the three wise men! You ain't daft or cracked, are you? You do know who you are and what year it is?"

"I'm as sane as you, Daniel." His questions didn't offend me. He was right, after all. I was as unprepared for the frontier as the Delaware had been for the white man's diseases.

He laid the strips of beaver flesh over the stump, held out his bloodstained hand, and said, "Salt."

I poured it into his hands, and he began vigorously working the rough granules deep into one of the strips of flesh. "How about you give me a hand?"

I hesitated.

"You fancy yourself something special? This work beneath you?"

"No, Daniel. I don't think I'm anything special." Father had made sure of that.

"Don't know what's bothering you, Chapman. Don't much care. But my goddamned hands are getting cold, and I want to get this finished."

The meat was cool and slick to the touch, and despite my qualms, I was intrigued by its feel. Still, as I rubbed the salt into the flesh, I avoided looking at the heads perched in the snow.

Experience had made it clear to me almost no one understood or shared my feelings toward animals. Only Elizabeth, my oldest sister—and one true intimate—knew how I felt.

Not that it mattered now. As Chapman, I no longer felt that way. As Chapman, I would think of animals only in terms of what use they were to me. At least I would try.

"Put some backbone into it, Chapman. You ain't some dotard playing with your roger whilst reminiscing about poking some doxy's oyster basket thirty years ago."

I blushed again, and he roared with laughter.

"Only joshing with you, Chapman. You don't really expect me to believe you're a settler, do you?"

"Why wouldn't you?"

"Because hatchlings look less bewildered than you did that first night. Because at the mention of flourishing some two-bit doxy, you turn redder than an Iroquois." He gestured around us. "You look faint at the sight of a little blood and guts. You've no supplies and, I'd wager, no money. The way you talk is like an educated person, and I bet you can read. Am I right?"

"What does all that prove?"

"That you ain't a settler. Maybe I can see you buying some farm after it's been a going concern for a few years. But what I can't picture, no offense intended, is you wrestling a claim from wilderness as unbroken as this."

"But I can," I insisted.

"Have you ever raised crops?"

"No."

"Can you tan leather?"

"No."

"Build a cabin, make soap, smoke meat, sew?"

I shook my head.

"But you're a settler? Hell and the devil confound me, Chapman, you know as much about being a settler as an Indian knows about being civilized."

"Fine. I *want* to be a settler then. I can learn those things."

"Maybe. Maybe not. But where were you headed when you turned up here? Were you planning on wintering over with somebody you know? Some uncle or brother who already staked a claim? Is that who you were looking for when you got lost?" He set down one strip, then picked up another. "If so, you ain't need be discomfited. Hell, I've gotten lost out here myself."

"Have you ever heard of the Holland Land Company?"

He paused for a long moment. "Maybe. Why?"

"Well, I have a flyer of theirs advertising a giveaway. To get more folk on the frontier, they're offering free land and supplies to settlers. I've come to stake a claim for myself. They're in a place called Warren."

I continued working, and it took me a moment to realize how quiet Daniel had become. When I looked up at him, he stood motionless, staring at the raw strip of meat he held in his hand. Without warning, he flung it at the stump, stomped into the blockhouse, and slammed the door behind him.

Oh, shit, I thought to myself as I stared after him wondering what had happened. Was it something I said? If so, what? Something about the Holland Land Company? Not knowing what else to do, I picked up another strip and began working in the salt. My eyes wandered up to the gray sky, pregnant with all of winter yet to come, and I fully understood how completely vulnerable I was to the mercy and moods of this man I knew nothing about.

Turning to pick up another strip of meat, I nearly stepped on one of the beaver heads that Daniel had left on the ground. Suddenly furious, I drew back my foot, preparing to send the head flying across the clearing with a kick. Instead, I knelt down, scooped out a hole in the snow, and buried it as best I could.

Twenty minutes later, carrying the strips of beaver, I hesitantly entered the cabin. I'd been afraid to leave them outside for fear they might be eaten by only God knew what. I had no desire to find out how that would infuriate Daniel.

The gloom of the cabin enveloped me as I entered, and it took my eyes a moment to adjust. When they did, I saw Daniel standing shirtless by the fire, stirring a large pot. He'd unbuttoned his shifting, pulling the top half down to his waist. For a moment I just stood there, watching his back flex each time he stirred.

"Daniel," I said at last. "Where do you want these?"

"There, on the table," he said without turning.

Cold, I wrapped myself in a bearskin, then sat and watched him move about the fireplace, its flickering light reflecting off the dark pots, and once, when he turned to look at me, his eyes. Even his black hair shimmered in the firelight. His pants were tight across his ass, and remembering his nearly shooting me, I wondered when I would see him naked again. Despite the crackling fire, I sat shivering at the table, due not just to the lingering chill but to the sensations watching him aroused in me.

"It's all in your mind, you know," observed Daniel.

"What's that?" I asked nervously. Had he known what I was thinking?

"Being cold."

I laughed. "Well, my mind would like a bigger fire."

"Then your mind will have to help cut the wood."

Instantly my laughter evaporated. "Of course." I cursed myself for such stupidity. He'd been sheltering and feeding me, and here I was whining. I took a deep breath. "I've no predilection toward being a leech, Daniel. If you'll tell me which way it is to Warren, I'll take my leave tomorrow. I do have one favor to ask. If you can spare them, I need a few supplies. I'll pay you back, I promise, as soon as I can."

He said nothing as he stopped stirring the pot. Taking the strips, he began to hang them from a rope strung over the top of the fire. Finished with that, he took a large bowl from a shelf, filled it with hot water from a kettle, and set it on the table. Unfolding a cloth, he dipped it into the steaming water. A sigh escaped from him as he ran the cloth over his face.

"There's a bar of soap by the bed," he said. "Get it."

As I handed it to him, he seemed to be studying me.

"You've got blood on your face and hands and arms," he said. "Take off your shirt. Your shifting as well."

He wanted me to do what?

Daniel dipped the soap into the water, lathered it up, and rubbed it over his forearms and chest.

"Come on, Chapman. Didn't your mother teach you to wash up afore you ate?"

She did, but I usually wasn't half naked. Hoping he couldn't see I was trembling, I did as he said.

"Sit," he instructed as he continued to wash himself. The soap smelled sweet, balmy, as if some herb or flower had been added when it was made.

I sat. "Where are we, Daniel? Are we far from Warren?"

"This is upper-northwest Pennsylvania, not too far from the Allegheny River." He motioned with his head. "About a mile that way is a tributary, Conewango Creek. It runs fairly shallow and is frozen over already. It flows into the Allegheny, and that will take you just about anywhere south." He rinsed off his arms, wrung out the cloth, and advanced toward me.

I reached to take the cloth, but he pushed my hand away. Suddenly gentle, he washed my face, leaving the soap's sweet smell lingering on my skin. What the hell was going on?

"Are we close to anything?" I managed to ask.

"Depends on what you mean by 'anything.'" His voice was low, sonorous. It reminded me of a gentle zephyr on the hottest afternoon of the year.

"Outposts, forts, Warren," I replied.

His hands were warm and tough and gentle all at the same time. I prayed he didn't know I was quivering.

"There's some Indian villages not too far from here," he said, rinsing out the cloth again. "Sometimes they're friendly, sometimes they're not. Mostly not, these days. Otherwise the nearest white settlement is Franklin."

I didn't care about this Franklin. I wanted to know where the hell Warren was. Had I become even more lost than I'd realized? "Then there's no other white settlements besides this Franklin?"

"Ain't a one." He lathered up the soap, then knelt in front of me as he washed my chest. Rivulets of water slipped down my stomach.

"Sorry about that," he said, running the cloth leisurely along the waist of my pants. For a moment I forgot about Franklin and Warren and anywhere outside of these walls. Was Daniel like the Major and me, or was this a trick, some sort of test?

Desperate to avoid betraying myself, I asked hoarsely, "How far away is that?"

"What?" he asked, beginning to wash my hands with the cloth.

It was all I could do to sit still, but I managed to stammer, "Franklin. How far is it?" Was he *intentionally* trying to have this effect on me?

"A long ways, I expect. Twenty leagues or more. It's southwest of here. Finished," he said, standing.

I sat there unmoving, desperately wanting him to continue, greatly relieved that he'd stopped.

"Feel better?"

Feeling nothing other than utterly bewildered, I managed to nod.

"Good. By the way—welcome to Warren. You can stay as long as you want."

THREE

I killed a rabbit when I was seven—not for food, but as a way to fit in with the other boys at school.

Joss Kendrick had cornered the rabbit in a hollow behind the schoolhouse. Soon eight raucous boys, frenzied to see blood spilled, gathered around, torturing the creature with sticks and stones. I glanced over at Helmut, who was my age, and the only boy I knew who got picked on more than me. We were friends, though I kept that secret.

The glassy-eyed rabbit lay sprawled on its side at the bottom of the hollow. White foam speckled its mouth and whiskers as its bloodied chest heaved up and down.

Someone pressed a stick into my hand.

"Come on then, John," said a boy named Bryce. "It's only you'n 'elmut that 'aven't 'ad a go. Ya ain't afraid of a little rabbit like 'elmut, are ya?"

I glanced over at Helmut. He didn't seem to care about the taunts.

Closing my eyes, I feebly poked at the gasping rabbit, which set the other boys off into fresh gales of laughter. Angry at being mocked, I jabbed the rabbit so hard it squealed.

"Good on you, John," said Joss, slapping me on the shoulder. With that the other boys leapt down into the hollow,

pushing and shoving to strike at the rabbit. Before I realized it, I was in their midst, yelling and swinging my stick.

When I looked up, Helmut was gone and I knew he'd never be my friend again.

November 1797

OF COURSE, THERE WAS A PRICE TO BE PAID FOR DANIEL'S OFFER THAT I could stay in Warren as long as I wanted. The next morning, he had me out of bed at daybreak to clean out the cow's stall.

"You don't mind doing this, do you, Chapman?"

"No, of course not," I said, exhausted and freezing as we trudged through the snow toward the stall. Now that I knew I had stumbled onto Warren, all I had to do was to locate the Holland Land Company and, despite having arrived six months before the date on the flyer, request my supplies, then establish my claim.

Perhaps I could move mountains as well.

The cow stood in her stall, eyeing me warily as if she knew I'd come to drag her out into the cold. First, I tried to talk her out. I might as well have tried to talk a baby out of its mother's womb. As I continued to plead and cajole, Daniel leaned against the blockhouse whittling a stick. No matter how imploring the look on my face, he offered no advice on how best to induce her outside.

"What did you say her name was?" I asked.

"Whose name?"

"The cow."

He snorted once. "It's a goddamned cow, Chapman. It ain't got a name. Now get on with it."

"Oh." Back home, I'd always named our animals. Giving up the reasonable approach, I squeezed past the cow and tried to shove her out of the strangely warm stall. Since her legs looked quite capable of inflicting a serious blow, each time I shoved I also jumped backward to avoid being kicked. However, the only aggressive thing she did was to fart loudly.

Daniel laughed. "Bet it smells nice in there now, Chapman."

Pinching her hard—really hard—finally did the trick, and with an irritated moo, she staggered out into the cold air.

"Here's a shovel," Daniel said. "Dump the manure in this box and haul it over to that pile of straw. Under the straw is more manure that I'm saving for spring. I'll milk her while you do that."

The day was clear and cold, but I quickly warmed as I shoveled, then hauled the manure. The smell inside the stall was both ripe and redolent, making me think of warm summer days, blue skies, and green meadows. As I worked, I tripped, catching myself against the side of the stall to keep from falling. To my amazement, the wall was hot to the touch, and immediately I realized why the stall was so cozy. Daniel had cleverly built the small stable so that the wall it shared with the cabin was also the wall into which the fireplace had been built.

A short time later, Daniel reappeared, grimly shaking his head. He sat the bucket down, and I could see that not even two fingers' worth of milk were in it. "Hope you don't mind taking your mush with just water, Chapman. At least I made a lot of cheese earlier in the fall when she was still producing." He glanced portentously at me. "I *had* planned on the cheese lasting through the winter."

I shrugged. "I don't much like cheese anyway. Say, Daniel, if this is Warren, then the Holland Land Company must not be too far away, right?"

He looked at me oddly, and I recalled how he had stormed away the last time I'd mentioned that name.

"Your pa had to explain everything real slow for you, didn't he, Chapman?"

"When he could be bothered with me at all."

He arched an eyebrow. "You and he may have been kin, but I'd wager a Dutch pound you weren't kith."

"Figuring that out doesn't exactly make you clever, Daniel."

"True. Your sentiments about your pa are as obvious as the stink on an Indian. By the way, who put the pepper in your pottage this morning?"

"Sorry. I didn't mean to—"

"Don't go apologizing. I didn't say it was a bad thing. To answer your question, Chapman, Warren *is* the Holland Land Company." He gestured to the blockhouse. "This is it. There's nothing else here. I thought you understood that. And by the way, I'm the manager."

I stood there staring at him, dumbfounded by yet another revelation. What would he tell me next—that he knew I'd been coming and cleared my claim for me?

"Chapman, anytime you'd like to finish would be good."

Getting the cow back into the stall proved to be far easier work then getting her out. As soon as I pushed her toward it, she eagerly backed in, flopped up against the wall, and mooed so contentedly that I had to laugh. It was then that I decided to call her Bliss.

Next Daniel had me help him chop and maul wood. As we worked, he removed his shirt, and with a tingle in my stomach, I recalled the sight of his strong hands soaping the black curls of his chest. Cursing my weakness, I shook my head to drive the vision from my mind. I still didn't know what he'd intended the day before with his near-bathing of me.

The cold morning gave way to a surprisingly mild afternoon. Once we'd finished stacking the wood, we set about patching the blockhouse. For patching, water, manure, straw, and bear fat were all boiled together into a sticky, fetid mess that we then plugged into holes and chinks. "We won't see no Indians today, Chapman," Daniel said as his eyes watered. "This mash stinks even worse than they do."

While we worked, Daniel explained that when the cold weather had arrived, he had used a piece of coal to mark an X wherever he had felt cold air seeping in. That way, when the weather warmed above freezing, he was all set to patch up the leaks. "Otherwise, Chapman, you end up waiting till January when you can't take it anymore because your balls are like two chunks of ice. Then you try and patch up the holes and end up freezing your arse off."

Despite the warmth of the thick goo, my hands quickly became cold. The thought of trying to do this in January horrified me.

Since I was taller than Daniel, he held the bowl for me as I stood on a crate to patch the chinks near the ceiling. I, too, was bare-chested in order to keep my shirt clean.

"You're really the manager for the Holland Land Company?" I

asked, still not able to believe my good fortune of having stumbled onto the place.

As it had on the occasion with the beavers, Daniel's mood completely flip-flopped. He slammed down the bowl, grabbed his shirt, and stomped away.

I stood there holding a handful of smelly muck. After a moment, I went back to work, pondering how to proceed regarding Daniel. I told myself that no matter how odd and volatile he might turn out to be, I had no other choice but to stay here. Even more, I had to get, and stay, on his good side. After all, as the manager, it was Daniel who would parcel out the land and supplies come spring.

Pausing, I again envisioned the small cabin I would build on a small piece of land where I could be alone and at peace. That was all I hoped for anymore.

Daniel returned a few minutes later. He crossed his arms and said, "Yes, I am manager of the Holland Land Company. Why did you ask me like that? Like you were surprised that it's me?"

"You misunderstood, Daniel," I said, choosing my words carefully. "I wasn't surprised because you're the manager. I'm surprised that I stumbled onto this place at all. And that it turns out to not only be Warren, but also the Holland Land Company. As if that weren't enough, the only person I meet takes me in, feeds me, *and* turns out to be the manager. If a Gypsy predicted such a future for me, I'd call her a fraud and take my two bits back."

Mollified, he uncrossed his arms and said, "Oh, well, in that case." He took off his shirt and went back to work as if nothing had happened.

This winter was going to be like wearing new shoes for church while crossing a meadow full of cattle—I was going to have to be very, very careful about where I stepped.

Daniel again stood beneath me, holding up the bucket of muck. Despite myself, each time I looked down, my gaze sought his massive arms and dark, hairy chest.

"I know," he said. "I'm as hairy as a bear."

Taken aback, I all but jumped. "What?"

"I see you looking at how hairy I am. It's all right, Chapman. I best be used to it." He scanned the ceiling. "I don't see any more marks. I guess we're finished. So now that you know this is the out-post, aren't you curious where all of the supplies are?"

Still rattled at having been caught staring, I stepped down from the crate and asked, "All right—where are all the supplies?"

"Can't wait to get your hands on them, huh?" He burst out laughing and threw his arm over my shoulder.

The shock of his bare flesh against mine momentarily stunned me.

"Remember, Chapman, the giveaway ain't till next spring. If you're going to winter over here, you're going to have to work for your keep."

I managed a feeble "I know."

"See that opening in the corner by my bed?" His arm moved away, but his fingers fell down to the small of my back, caressing my skin. "Are you listening?" he asked.

Shivering again, I nodded. I no longer harbored any doubt as to whether he was trying to inflame me on purpose. What I still didn't know was why, though whatever the answer, I worried it only bode ill for my chances of succeeding out here.

"The supplies are up there," he continued. "And this room that we're in? It's only half of the blockhouse. There's another room on the other side of the wall, so the second floor is twice as big as this and is completely filled with supplies."

Despite his fingers wandering over my skin, I forced myself to focus on what he was saying. I realized it was no wonder the place had seemed so much bigger on the outside. "How many settlers are you expecting in the spring?"

"I don't know." He reached over and gently wiped some muck from my face.

"Do you think you'll have enough supplies?"

"All business, huh, Chapman?" Laughing, Daniel stepped away and said, "Don't worry. You're first in line. You'll get everything you could ever want."

If only I could be certain what that might be.

For lunch we ate strips of dried raccoon, a bowl of mush, and drank apple cider. The raccoon had an overwhelming, gamy taste, not to mention being so tough and fibrous that I could barely chew it. But not wanting to send Daniel into another of his moods, I said nothing.

His mood shifted anyway. "Look, Chapman, I don't much like raccoon either."

"Daniel," I protested, "I didn't say a word."

"I didn't mean to snap at you. Remember how I said there were plenty of supplies upstairs? Well, there is, except for food, contrarily enough. For some goddamned reason, the last shipment—the one with the food—never made it. That's why we're eating something that tastes like the inside of an Indian's breeches."

I looked distastefully at the raccoon meat.

"I'm going to go hunting," he said. "Do you want to come?"

"Maybe."

"You don't know how to hunt, do you?"

I shook my head.

"Course not. You may be long on aspiration, Chapman, but when it comes to practical skills, you've got one fewer than a belt has buckles." He grimaced at the remaining strip of meat, then sourly shoved his plate away. Slipping out of his linsey shirt, he hung it on a peg above his bed. Before I realized it, he'd slipped off his pants. My eyes were riveted by the sight of his firm ass, creamy white except for two splashes of red on each cheek. Naked, he walked to the table, his thick cock swaying with each step. He picked up a cup, took a swallow of cider, and said, "You sure you don't want to come along?"

Wrenching my eyes away, I said, "I'm sure."

With a shrug, he went back to his bed and pulled on his hunting shirt. The fringe just covered his ass. "I should be back by dusk. Have supper ready."

"Sure, Daniel."

He pulled on his pants and boots and grabbed his already loaded rifles. He smiled as he left.

No matter how hard I pulled and yanked, I couldn't work the stiffness out. Whoever had salted this conner—a type of dried perch—had known what they were about. I paused, glanced toward the darkening window, and wondered how long until Daniel returned. I also wondered if he'd change clothes again before we ate.

Frustrated, I tried adding another dollop of oil and a splash of water to the fish. Then, by clutching it between my legs with one hand, I began applying long, hard strokes with the other. Making pottage for dinner had been a good idea; trying to do so with dried, stringy fish a foolish one. Again and again I massaged the perch's tough flesh.

How much more pleasurable this would be if this were Daniel's back I were kneading. I imagined rubbing his shoulders, then working my way toward his hips.

"Stop it!" I exclaimed aloud. Disgusted with myself, I slammed the fish onto the wooden trencher. Had I no self-restraint?

Standing, I checked the samp steaming in the kettle. After tossing in another handful of ground corn, I stirred it slowly. The milk gave it a pale hue similar to the color of Daniel's ass. And what a fine ass it was. The way it had filled out his breeches made me harder yet.

I dropped the spoon into the kettle. No, no, no! No more thoughts of Daniel naked! I grabbed a handful of pignuts—there couldn't be anything arousing about seeds and roots—and thrust them into a wicker basket for steaming. I hung the basket from a cottrel positioned over a pot of boiling water. Steam wafted around my face, dampening my skin. It felt soothing, and before I knew it, I was recalling a hot springs the Major had taken me skinny-dipping to one night.

I groaned out loud. I gave up.

Almost angrily, I yanked my already hard dick free. Leaning against the wall, I stroked myself, allowing images of Daniel to rake through my mind. How ironic it was, I thought, picturing Daniel striding toward me naked, that even in the middle of nowhere I found myself caught up in the very situation I sought to avoid.

Now I pictured his cock bobbing just beneath the fringe of his hunting shirt. Tension began to build in my loins. What I didn't know about Daniel was whether his actions were a tease or if he actually planned on following through with his advances. He wouldn't be the first man I'd encountered who liked to taunt me.

Most men who teased were vicious and taunted only to prove that I desired them. Some men, I suspected, were simply afraid to face the fact that we desired the same thing.

Which did I want Daniel to be? I wasn't sure.

In my imagination, I allowed myself to kneel before Daniel. The black hair along his stomach felt soft to the touch as my hand slid downward. His fat cock weighed heavily in my palm. I let go and massaged his balls.

Furious with myself for being so weak, I stroked harder and harder even though I knew this sordid release wouldn't bring permanent relief, only more disgust and anguish.

Breathing deep, I imagined pressing my bare flesh against Daniel's hot skin, and that sent me over the edge.

Groaning, I filled my cupped hand with sticky jism.

It had been so long since I'd done that, the sensation was almost more than I could bear. Opening my eyes, I slumped against the wall, where I might have sat for an hour if something hadn't immediately banged up against the blockhouse. Rubbing the jism into the dirt floor, I sprang to my feet, pulling up my pants as Daniel strode back inside.

"Hello, Daniel," I said, attempting to discreetly secure my pants.

Daniel looked at me oddly. "Everything all right?"

"Fine. Just cold, so I was sitting by the fire for a bit."

He sniffed the air.

"I see you've shot something," I said hurriedly. "Pheasant? A rabbit?

Scowling, he flung a bag on the table. "Bloody hickory nuts from a squirrel's nest." Chocolate-hued nuts scattered across the table. "I figured we at least could roast them."

"Sure," I replied, unable to help wondering what the squirrel was going to eat.

"Dinner ready?"

"Soon. No more than half a wick."

He picked up a nut and looked at it for a moment. Without a word, he dropped it onto the floor, then relentlessly ground it under his heel. "I need to fetch something from upstairs," he growled. "Do you want me to show you around up there?"

"All right," I said, more eager than I cared to admit.

From behind his bed, he removed a ladder that he positioned under the opening. "A word of advice, Chapman. Never let a man know more than you absolutely have to. Now turn around." He made me face the other way so I wouldn't see from where he got the key to open the padlock.

"All right, come on." He mounted the ladder, and I clambered up after him.

The entry from below opened up into the center of the room, though Daniel's flickering circle of light was too weak to reach to either end. He hadn't exaggerated when he'd said the Company had supplied everything. As far as I could see in the dim light were stacks of boxes, rows of barrels, bolts of cloth. The sight of that room in the middle of nowhere was simply amazing.

"By all the saints in heaven, I've never seen so much stuff, Daniel."

"I recollect I couldn't believe it the first time I saw it all together either."

As we walked from one end to the other, Daniel showed me rolls of twill and bark, stacks of blankets in dozens of weights and sizes, barrels of flour, salt, sugar, pepper, and lard. There were boxes of scissors, spyglasses, whetstones, lead bars, bullet molds, and on and on. Except for the cate—store-bought provisions—Daniel said hadn't arrived, the room seemed to have everything a settler could need.

Picking up a finely crafted knife, I marveled at the affluence of those who could afford to give away this much wealth. What in God's name must they stand to gain in return?

"And you're to be in charge of handing this out?" I asked.

"That's right. Lucky for you—assuming you stay on my good side all winter."

Annoyed, I turned away.

"I'm only kidding about the supplies. You can have whatever you want. But here's what I came up here for." He handed me the lamp, then hoisted a ratty, stained saddle onto his shoulder. Had the Company sent this?

Once back downstairs, he padlocked the door; then, apparently forgetting to make me turn around, slipped the key into one of the tins on the shelf. Facing me, he said, "You weren't watching, were you?"

"No," I lied.

"Doesn't matter if you were. Not as if you could get very far with much stuff." Taking a tin of bear fat, he sat at the table and began working the foul-smelling stuff into the saddle. The leather alone was such a mess, I wondered why he bothered.

"Daniel, can I ask you something?"

He nodded, a look of distrust darkening his features.

"Where are the others? You look like you're as strong as anybody I've ever seen, but this place is huge. Surely you didn't build it all by yourself?"

He eyed me warily, then said, "No, I didn't. We had federal troops to help us build it."

"Federal troops? Really?"

"Given all of the supplies upstairs, you might guess the people behind this little undertaking wear a finer cut of breeches than sods like us. They also got themselves enough pull in Philadelphia to get federal troops to escort a private venture onto the frontier. They say one of William Penn's shiftless descendants is one of the Company's biggest backers. And that," he added archly, "explains that."

"When did the troops leave?"

"That would've been the end of June. The Senecas attacked almost as soon as they were gone."

"The Senecas attacked! You're kidding."

"No, I ain't."

"But I thought they lived northeast of here?"

"That's right." He looked at me suspiciously. "How'd you know that?"

I knew because the British at Fort Niagara, including the Major, had been friendly with anyone opposed to the Americans. And the Seneca around the fort were definitely opposed. Not that I would be telling Daniel about my sojourn back north.

"I met a few people on my way out here," I said. "I guess I heard it from them."

"I see," he said, still suspicious. "It's true their original hunting grounds are back toward New York, but the Americans finally forced them to sign a treaty three years ago saying they promised to settle down and lived civilized like. Indians being Indians, that's not damned likely."

"Why not?"

"Lord, Chapman—you're greener than the inside of a gooseberry. An Indian's nature keeps some—most, if you ask me—from honoring their word. Those that didn't like the treaty they signed have wrongfully taken over land farther west, including these parts."

"Are they as ferocious as I've heard?"

He nodded. "Even worse. A half dozen of them descended on us like French soldiers on English whores. Being thieving heathens, they coveted our supplies, and once the soldiers were gone, they attacked. They trapped me and Abe and Martin. And Zach."

"Who were they?"

"Just the other fellows hired to help out. Pretty much a good-for-nothing bunch."

"So you've been attacked by Indians." Despite myself, I was impressed.

Daniel nodded. "May God piss on their heathen souls. Usually Senecas creep up on you as silent as morning mist, striking quick to try and surprise you. Then they're gone afore you know you've lost your hair. Even prepared for them, they nearly caught us off guard. When their first assault failed, they settled in to wait us out knowing there was no one to come to our aid."

"Sounds like you were in a hairy spot."

"That we were. See that skull over there? It's from my horse. Those malformed degenerates killed her."

It was the one that had been on the table when I'd first arrived.

"That's her," he said.

"Oh," I said, wondering why he'd kept the skull.

"I tried to set her loose in the woods afore we barricaded ourselves in the blockhouse, but one of the sons of bitches threw a spear through her throat afore she got two feet from the front door. This was her saddle."

I glanced from the skull to the saddle. "I'm sorry," I said before I could stop myself. Such sentimentality wasn't worthy of Chapman. "What about Bliss—why didn't they kill her?"

"Who?"

"The cow."

He sniggered. "Bliss, huh? I don't know why they didn't slit her throat. Probably too stupid to know she'd taste a damn sight better than those disgusting pig eels they eat raw."

"What was her name? Your horse, I mean."

Absorbed in his work, he seemed not to hear me. Just when I'd assumed he found horses no more worthy of naming than admittedly dumb, docile cows, he said, "Joy."

Joy wasn't quite the name I would've expected him to choose—something more like Bloody Beshitted Devil From Hell would've been more in character.

"We ate her," he said.

"You what?"

"We ate her. We had to. We had almost nothing in here, and the Indians had us pinned in. Martin and Abe covered me while Zach and I dragged the body inside." He picked up a knife and began trimming bits and pieces from the saddle.

They'd eaten his horse? Then he'd kept the skull? Every time I began to feel comfortable around Daniel, he said or did something unsettling.

I looked at the floor, half-expecting to see bloodstains.

"What about all the sugar and flour upstairs? Why didn't you eat them?"

His face twitched. "We couldn't get to them."

"Why not?"

"Because that white-livered idiot the Company hired to run this place had forgotten to build an entrance into the supply room from this side."

"Idiot? I thought you were in charge."

"I am now. It was Zach who was supposed to oversee construction." Daniel took up a thick, hefty-looking needle, ran a strip of thong through it, and forcefully drove the needle through the saddle's tattered edge.

I cast my gaze around the blockhouse. "The opening we just used hadn't been built yet?"

"That's right. The goddamned Senecas attacked afore we got to it. We barely had enough lead and powder to keep them at bay when they hit us. Thank God, they wanted the supplies. Otherwise they would have burned us out. On top of everything else, all of our saws and big axes were in the other room, so we couldn't cut our way to the supplies. All we had was one hatchet that Martin tried to use to hack out an opening. The blade was duller than mud afore he came close to getting through."

"So what happened?"

"Late on the third night of the siege, Martin tried to sneak around and get in the other side of the blockhouse to where the weapons were. I swear we watched all night and we never heard a thing after he left, but the next morning, we looked out into the clearing and saw him hanging naked from a tree. Bloody bastards had scalped him. Even worse was that they'd cut off his roger and balls and shoved them in his mouth. Next day, his body was gone."

Horrified by Daniel's graphic description, I just sat there.

"Don't you want to know what happened next?"

I nodded.

"Take a guess."

"What?"

"Guess what happened."

"I've no idea."

"Two days after the Indians killed Martin, they disappeared as swiftly as they had appeared."

"You mean you didn't kill them or drive them away?"

"Nope, they just left."

"Do you know why?"

"Not for certain. One of the fellows, Zach—did I mention him earlier?"

I nodded.

"Well, Zach was a real little bastard." Daniel abruptly yanked the needle through the leather and waved it at me. "As Zach told anybody who'd listen, he'd spent a *little* more time on the frontier than any of us, and he couldn't get the stupid idea out his puny little head that his extra experience meant he was so much smarter than us. Goddamned, cloven-footed little prick—let me tell you, I knocked some sense into him." He jabbed the needle so hard into the saddle that only a quarter of it remained visible. Flushed, he paused and looked at me. "What was your question?"

"Why did the Indians leave?" I said, taken aback and not sure I wanted to hear any more.

"Oh, yeah." He pulled the needle free and resumed his stitching. "Like I said, we didn't know for sure why they left, but Zach thought maybe they'd had a sign from the Great Spirit that told them to leave."

"Why did he think that?"

"The whole reason the Company hired him was because he'd spent some time among the damned Seneca traveling from village to village, and, he *claimed,* befriending their chiefs. Since the less peaceful ones lived hereabouts, the owners wanted someone who knew how to deal with them." A strange smile crossed Daniel's face. "Although to tell you the truth, the thought crossed my mind that maybe the Senecas didn't consider him a friend and in fact were after the goddamned bastard. But he was too crafty, even for them."

Hadn't Daniel just said that Zach was an idiot? "Why were they after him?"

"Two things." Daniel paused to wipe his watery eyes. "One, he'd told me he had this habit of kidnapping little Seneca girls, fucking them, then tying them up and leaving them in the woods. He especially liked the ones that wore their hair braided with the strips of beaded leather intertwined. He'd cut off their ponytails and keep them."

Horrified yet again, I stared at him. "He didn't really tell you such a thing?"

"He most certainly did."

"Did anybody find the girls?"

"Sometimes, I guess." Daniel laughed. "Zach was as morbid and heartless a beshitted cur as I ever met. Or heard of for that matter." A peculiar look settled across his face. "Strange thing, though, he was sort of charming. Handsome, too." He went on fixing the saddle. "Anyway, he would always go back to check on the girls. He liked watching them suffer, I guess. Sometimes he'd go back with food and water, and then sit eating it in front of them. Sometimes by the time he got back, they were already dead, having been attacked by bears or panthers or whatnot. Occasionally they were gone— either somebody had found them or they'd escaped."

Could Daniel be lying? I wondered. But why would he make up such an awful story? "Why didn't the ones that escaped tell who had done it?"

"They never saw his face. He always wore a burlap sack with the eyes cut out."

"But if he raped them, they must've known it was a white man. Didn't they suspect—what was his name?"

"Zach."

"Didn't they suspect Zach?"

"He claimed they didn't."

"Why the hell not?" Could the Indians be as stupid as Daniel said?

"He said they mostly believed it was an evil spirit. Remember, he traveled among a lot of villages, not just one, and the girls' families really didn't want people knowing what had happened. But mostly they didn't suspect Zach because he was a preacher, and he brought them sweets and medicines—the fools trusted him, you see. On top of that, Zach was pretty damned smart. Even I learned a couple of frontier tricks from him."

My stomach recoiled at what Daniel was telling me. "What was the second reason you thought they were after him?"

"Because Zach refused to let himself be seen by a single Seneca."

"But he was hired to deal with them, right?"

Daniel laughed. "Every time we needed to treat with a chief, or even a lone brave, he'd tell us what to do ahead of time and then hide in the woods."

"Why did he hide? I thought you said nobody saw his face, that they believed it was a spirit killing the girls."

"They didn't. But Zach said that one little girl he kidnapped told him that an old man in her village had used—get this—his *medicine* to enter the spirit world where he had a vision to find out who was raping the girls. Indian prattle. Old fart probably got drunk and had nightmares. I didn't believe any of it for a minute. I think someone followed Zach once and seen him take off his mask."

I was still a little confused.

"So if this Zach was in such danger from the Indians, why did he even come back here?"

"You like this story, do you? Four years ago he learned a woman he'd raped seven years previous had survived to bear a child that was half white and had to be his. Zach swore no son of his would be raised by savages. Finding that boy was the only thing I ever saw him truly care about."

"What happened? Did he find him?"

Daniel shook his head. "Afore Zach could grab his son, the ignorant red fools finally realized Zach was the one kidnapping the girls. They would've killed him if he hadn't scuttled his way back east. He reckoned returning with the Holland Land Company would give him the protection he needed to find his boy. Only he hadn't figured on the military garrison leaving so soon."

"So he'd never even seen his son?"

"That's right."

"Surely his wasn't the only white child out here." Even I'd heard foulmouthed white men callously extolling the virtues of "dark" meat. "How would he know which was his?"

"His was different somehow."

"Different how?"

"Zach wouldn't say. But he put out word he was offering a reward for the boy's whereabouts, and that he had a way of knowing for certain if the boy was his."

I'd heard enough about this demented man. "You never told me what the sign was that caused the Indians to leave."

"Don't know for sure. Zach said they had all kinds of crazy notions and rituals about some Great Spirit that they followed rigidly. Things like, a shooting star means a baby had died. A fox with three pups helped protect a tribe. An albino animal was a sign of death. Stupid things like that. Like I said, they're savages."

"So, have the Senecas ever come back?"

"Nope. Never."

"What happened to Zach?"

"Let's just say I decided he and I had too many differences and that he should leave. I'll never forget the sight of that sorry bastard slinking out of here."

"Did the Indians get him?"

"Does it matter?"

"Yes."

"Why?"

"Because he sounds despicable, and I'd like to hear that he came to a horrible end. I hope the Senecas ripped him apart limb by limb."

Daniel laughed. "Chapman! I'd no idea you could be so bloodthirsty. Sorry to say I don't know what became of him." He lay down the needle and rubbed at his red-rimmed eyes.

"What about the other fellow? Why did he leave?"

"Abe? He didn't leave exactly. He died from the fever about a month after Zach left." Daniel tied off the last knot. Picking up the cloth, he dipped it into the tin and began rubbing it over the saddle again.

"This all happened last summer?"

"Thereabouts. We arrived with the troops in late April. The blockhouse was built by the end of June—that's when the troops left. The Senecas showed up a week later, laid siege to us for a week. Then Abe died at the end of July."

"What did you do with his body?"

"Proper Christian burial, of course. His grave is on the edge of the clearing back behind the blockhouse. But I wouldn't go messing with it, if I were you. Might get the fever if you do."

"I won't."

"Won't what?" he demanded.

"Mess with the body."

"Damn right. Well, that's finished."

The saddle sat perched in the center of the table. Where it had been stained and dull before, it was now burnished and lustrous.

Where it had frayed and tattered, it was now neat and trimmed. I found it hard to believe I was looking at the same saddle.

"Daniel, it's amazing. I can't believe how completely different it looks. I thought it would be impossible to alter something so much."

"Oh," he said, smiling enigmatically. "You'd be surprised how far a little ingenuity goes toward changing things."

FOUR

When I was eight, I asked the minister in Longmeadow if animals felt fear and love and happiness the way we do. His eyes widened, and he asked me if I understood what heresy was. I didn't and said so. He warned me sternly that only humans could experience the exaltations of love, especially love in its highest form—the love of God. Any other notion was heresy, and such beliefs condemned one to burn in hell forever. As for fear, he said, animals about to be butchered felt no more fear than a row of corn facing the farmer's scythe. What about cats and dogs? I'd asked. Surely they showed more sincere affection for their masters than some husbands did for their wives. The minister slapped me across the cheek, said I was impertinent, and then went to find my father—which only made me all the more certain I was right.

November 1797

A BLIZZARD DESCENDED THE FOLLOWING DAY, AND WITH IT CAME A melancholy that blanketed us as thoroughly as the snow did the trees. If Daniel's reaction to the storm—getting drunk and staying in bed—was at all typical, I faced a lonely, trying winter. I passed the time dozing, whittling a little, and daydreaming about my plans come spring.

On the third morning after the storm began, a sober Daniel woke me before dawn.

"Come on, Chapman," he said, nudging me with his foot. "Get up."

"No. Go away." I pulled my bearskin up over my head. Either the weather still hadn't become cold enough or Daniel still didn't trust me, because I continued to sleep alone.

"Right now," Daniel said, jerking the bearskin off me.

"What the hell do you think you're doing?" I barked as I sat up. "It's dark, and it's freezing."

"Well, well, so Chapman does have more chine than a possum. Good for you. Now get up afore I thrash your scrawny ass."

Daniel's remark about my backbone rankled. Father had always compared my backbone—or lack thereof—to the jellyfish that used to wash up on the shore.

"Why should I get up?" I asked.

"We're going hunting."

"I thought you said the hunting was so terrible."

"I did, and it is, but that doesn't mean we can just give up. I'm not some lazy Englishman, all bluster and swagger and no dirty deed."

I tried to pull the bearskin back. "I told you before, I don't know how to hunt."

He jerked it back from me and said, "A sad thing, too, a grown man who doesn't know how to hunt. That's more blasphemous than a woman who doesn't know how to screw. I figure it's time to learn you then. So get up, or I'll chuck you out into the snow buck naked."

Wearily, I stumbled to my feet and buttoned up my shifting. Directly I sensed Daniel watching me.

"What are you looking at?"

"You," he said matter-of-factly, his eyes traveling deliberately down my body.

Turning away, I pulled on my clothes.

"I wouldn't suppose you'd be practiced in snowshoeing?" he asked.

"Then you would suppose wrong."

"Aren't you full of surprises this morning!" He tossed me a pair of snowshoes. "Strap these on."

"I think I liked you better drunk and asleep," I mumbled.

"What was that, Chapman?"

"I said, 'I'd like to get a skunk and a sheep.'"

"Sometimes I wonder," he said, shaking his head, "if your brain didn't suffer frostbite up on that plateau. Now let's go."

Groaning, I followed him out into the frigid darkness.

The most difficult snowshoeing occurred almost right away. Daniel led us through a modest copse that ended at the foot of an ascent not exactly hospitable to snowshoes. As if that weren't enough, the trail proved to be quite icy, and what would've taken us a few minutes to walk in summer took in snowshoes a full twenty minutes. Another ten minutes of trudging passed before the brilliant edge of the sun finally slipped past the mountains into the thin strand of rose-smudged clouds stretched across the horizon.

As the sun glided higher with each passing moment, the blue shadows of dawn beat a hasty retreat before a world of brilliant white where every rock, every tree, and every surface had vanished in a flood of gleaming snow. Everything had been softened, blurred, molded together so that I couldn't tell where a tree ended and a boulder began. This realm had no edges or corners, and I felt as if I were moving in a dream.

In the early-morning silence, the only sound was the crunch of snow beneath our feet. It felt cold enough to freeze a man's nuts. To get by, I concentrated on putting one foot in front of the other.

Eventually, we reached some sort of trail—Daniel called it a trace and explained it had originally been made by elk, but was now used by all kinds of animals as well as Indians, although, he told me, the latter weren't as numerous as even a year before.

"Not that that's particularly a bad thing," he chortled. "Besides, the Seneca don't much hunt or do anything outside this time of year besides piss, so we needn't worry about running into them." He sounded convinced, yet a fleeting shadow of concern crossed his face.

I hadn't been worried, but I nodded anyway. Daniel carried one rifle; I held a second he'd given me when we left. He didn't expect me to actually shoot, but since each took more than a minute to reload, I was to hand him the second in case he missed the first time. He never mentioned what to do if he missed again.

The trees grew closer together here, as if huddled together for protection from the cold. Their tops were so intertwined that they looked more like tree roots than tree crowns. Even now, only patches of blue sky were visible between the tightly woven branches, and I wondered how any light at all got through the dense canopy of leaves that would fill the trees come summer.

As we marched on, I noticed that despite the recent snowfall, I spied plenty of signs of game along the trail—both tracks and droppings. Judging from all of the skins drying on the walls of the block-house, I'd assumed Daniel's difficulty finding game stemmed from his having already killed everything. Kicking a clump of deer shit, I wondered what other explanation there might be.

"Daniel, have you tried hunting here before, or are we going someplace new?"

"I've scouted here lots of times. Why?"

"Curious, that's all."

"Do you know your trees, Chapman?"

"What do you mean?"

He stopped and pointed at a tree. "What's that?"

"An ash."

"And that?"

"Cedar."

"And that?"

"I don't know."

"You should, Chapman. If you're going to be a settler, it's important you know each tree and how they're best put to use."

He began to move on.

"Well, aren't you going to tell me what it is?"

He turned and smiled at me. "I would, but I don't know either."

Laughing, he continued on.

Up ahead, the trees thinned, and Daniel held up his hand, motioning for me to slow down. Quietly, we crept forward until we came upon a white-swathed meadow surrounded by slender gray trees.

"Damn," Daniel swore, seeing nothing as he looked from side to side. When we crossed the clearing to pick up the trail again, I nearly suggested that perhaps elk and deer were too smart to come out when it was this goddamn cold. Judging from the frustrated scowl on his face, I expected he might not appreciate my humor.

Daniel asked, "Do you know what part of an elk or deer to aim for, Chapman?"

"The biggest part?" I offered, thinking it didn't really matter as long as you hit the thing.

"Don't try and be funny. It's the neck or the chest," he said, pointing to the appropriate places on himself. "If you shoot them in the neck, they bleed to death afore they get very far. If you get them in the chest, you either pierce their heart or shatter their shoulder blade so they can't run away. Got it?"

"Got it," I said, envisioning an elk stumbling along, collapsing in a heap before bleeding to death. Stop it, I told myself. Only John would think about that—not Chapman.

Daniel continued, "Your biggest worry is wounding them only enough so that they escape and die somewhere where you can't get at them."

Maybe that was his biggest worry. Mine was missing and pissing off some elk that would try to gore me to death.

"Do you know what to do if you corner an animal—say an elk or a bear?"

"Corner them where?" I asked, intending to avoid any such thing.

"Anywhere. A cave or against the base of a cliff."

"Negotiate a treaty?"

Daniel spun around. "Goddammit, Chapman! Don't be wasting my time!"

"Sorry. Should you wait them out?"

"No! Never do that. Don't give them the time to rest or find a way out. Charge them, flush them out while they're still confused and on edge. Press your advantage as long as you have it. Same goes for fighting Indians, or white folks, for that matter."

We snowshoed for another half hour before we came upon the next clearing. Again, we saw nothing but bare trees, snow, and empty space, and again Daniel swore at his luck. He was getting ready to leave when, across the clearing, I saw a solitary deer step from the shadows. Saying nothing, I watched the graceful ripple of the animal's muscles under its dusky brown fur. Even at a distance, its large brown eyes reminded me of Bliss.

As Daniel walked into the woods, John wrestled Chapman inside my mind.

"Daniel!" I hissed. "Come back! There! A deer!" I was surprised at the tingle of excitement that surged through me.

"Where?" he asked, excitedly hastening back.

I pointed.

"Good job, Chapman." He put his hand on my neck and squeezed. His unexpected touch quickened my blood and I blazed inside, as if all along I'd been standing next to a roaring fire without knowing it.

In a blur, the rifle materialized against his shoulder. Daniel lined up the sights. Seemingly unaware of us, the deer circumspectly high-stepped through the snow and into the meadow. There it paused, as motionless as any of the trees behind it; only its ears flicked this way and that while its liquid brown eyes scanned the woods where we stood.

Satisfied no immediate danger was present, the deer lowered its head as it began to paw at the snow.

My whole body tensed as I waited for the blast of the rifle. I briefly wondered if the deer's body would leap upward as had the Major's, but that was another of John's thoughts, and I forced it from my mind.

Glancing at Daniel, I saw the rifle weave about unsteadily as he aimed at the deer. Beads of sweat dotted his forehead. The deer took another step closer.

Why the *hell* wasn't he shooting?

Seconds slipped past, each bringing our quarry a few feet closer.

Several times it stopped, twitched its ears back and forth, then moved on. At some point, I'd stopped breathing, and I thought my chest was going to burst when the sound of the rifle finally ripped through the air like a shriek. Two things happened at almost the same instant—a cloud of snow erupted ten feet in front of the deer, and the deer burst from the spot where it stood as if it had felt the very hand of Satan clutching for its heart. I stared in amazement as the animal, despite the waist-deep snow, bounded back over the meadow.

"The rifle! Give me the other rifle!" Daniel bellowed, yanking it from my hand. Already the deer had nearly crossed the clearing, but Daniel still managed to get off a second shot. A small dogwood on the other side of the meadow shuddered as the lead ball slammed into it. The deer vanished as the sound of the rifle echoed around us.

In the ensuing silence, I stood there staring at the empty clearing.

"Maybe we'll—" I started to say.

Daniel exploded from where he knelt, swinging the rifle wildly about his head as he ran forward. "You buggering whoreson!" he yelled, sending the weapon flying out into the clearing. All except the stock knifed deep into the snow. Without pausing, he rushed out after it, grabbed it by the barrel, screamed, "You accursed, lily-livered, Indian girl–fucking prick!" and proceeded to smash it against a protruding rock. Only when the stock splintered in two did he drop the shattered gun. Wheezing, he sank to his knees.

I'd seen people get angry before, but this seemed something more, something dark and out of control. Thinking it best to leave him alone, I crept back along the trail to wait and ponder just what I'd got myself into.

Please, God, I prayed as I sat on a stump, don't ever let him get angry at me.

Twenty minutes later, Daniel snowshoed past me as if I weren't there. He carried our remaining rifle with him. Scrambling to keep up, I followed as fast as I could until he stopped and spun toward me.

"I ain't completely insane, Chapman."

"All right, Daniel."

"It's just that . . ." He let his voice trail off.

I waited.

"I'm having trouble seeing."

"What kind of trouble?"

"Things are blurry of late. It makes it hard to aim. I just wanted you to know why I missed back there. And why I got so angry."

I nodded. That explained a lot, though I still thought his anger extreme. I wanted to say something reassuring, but all I could think of was my father putting down our dogs when their vision became suspect. I kept that memory to myself.

I wondered if Daniel was going to get drunk once we got back home.

We shambled along in silence for nearly an hour, the first half of which I compelled myself not to undress him from behind. Weak as ever, my resolve melted like snow in April, and I peeled off his wool coat. Next came his hunting shirt, jerkin, and shifting. As I reached to caress his chest, my snowshoe caught on a rock, and I stumbled forward.

"Careful, Chapman," Daniel said.

Regaining my balance, I nodded, then proceeded to mentally flog myself. I had to stop these lust-filled thoughts! I had to think of something else. I settled on trying to find a way to help Daniel with his eyes.

From all of the skins on the blockhouse, I surmised Daniel was probably proud of his hunting skills. It would be tough to lose them, especially since a frontiersman who couldn't see wouldn't last long. At least my knowing his eyes were going bad made him more sympathetic. Maybe I could help him, be his eyes, and we'd make a sort of team. Maybe he'd squeeze my shoulder every time I helped him.

I remembered the feel of his hand and felt a stirring inside at the memory. Images of him washing himself followed, and I quickly felt myself stiffen. So much for thinking of something else.

We were almost home, snowshoeing around a bend, when we came face-to-face with something enormous and brown and hairy blocking our way.

"Get back! Get back!" Daniel hollered, stumbling backward. A god-awful, eerie bellowing like nothing I'd ever heard emanated from whatever we'd stumbled upon. My first thought was that we had stumbled onto a bear and I was about to die horribly.

Since I'd been snowshoeing right behind Daniel, we collided immediately and tumbled to the ground in a tangle of arms and legs and snowshoes. Both of us hollered like sinners facing our final judgment. Tussling to untangle ourselves, we struggled to avoid being trampled or mauled by whatever it was bellowing in front of us.

As I flailed about with Daniel on top of me, I noticed something odd: whatever it was, the animal didn't seem to be charging us.

"Daniel, wait a minute," I said, catching him by his ankle as he crawled away. "I think it's trapped."

He stopped struggling. "What?"

"It's stuck in a snowdrift. It's an elk, I think."

Rolling onto his back, Daniel wiped the snow from his eyes. "I'll be an Indian's cock and balls. You're right. It's a big whoreson, too."

In the vastness of the forest, the three of us stared at each other in an unlikely tableau. Even though the animal had stopped bellowing, it still had a panicked, wild-eyed look about it. Every few seconds, it tried to rear backward with a desperate grunt, but only its neck and head budged. Long, glistening strings of saliva oozed from its twitching mouth, and the animal's nostrils seemed to have a life of their own, opening and closing furiously as lines of phlegm issued forth. I felt bad for it—or, rather, John did.

"Can we get it free?" I asked.

"I don't see why not. The whoreson's going to weigh a ton, but we'll drain the blood first, and it won't be so bad."

"Oh," I said, suddenly numb. "You're going to shoot it."

"Of course I am. Do you want to? It would be your first kill."

"No, you go ahead. Here's the rifle." The creature looked so terrified that I couldn't help but wonder if it somehow sensed we intended to kill it, cut it up, and then eat it. How would I feel knowing such a thing?

Some frontiersman I was turning out to be, worrying over such ridiculous thoughts.

Daniel took the rifle and set about reloading it. "Come here, Chapman. You need to learn how to do this."

"Sure, Daniel," I said, grateful for anything that would distract me from the animal's eyes.

"First off, I should've done this afore we left that clearing. Only someone who's asking to have his scalp pilfered goes around with an unloaded rifle. It was downright asinine of me to have done so. You understand that?"

I nodded.

"Good. First, you measure out a charge of gunpowder using this." He held out a small brass cup. "Then you pour it down the muzzle, take a bullet, and wrap it in a patch with a little bit of grease. Understand?"

Behind me, the elk snorted, then began some kind of moaning that sounded far too humanlike for me. "Yes. What's next?" I knew we had to make this quick, before John opened his mouth and pissed off Daniel.

"Next, you ream the touchhole with a metal pick so as to make sure the spark hits the powder. Then you use the ramrod to shove the bullet to the bottom of the bore—that's the barrel. It usually takes both hands." As he demonstrated, I caught sight of the elk's bobbing head behind me. The moaning continued unabated, and I wanted to cover my ears.

"I thought you were supposed to be fast at this," I snapped.

"Faster than you can ever hope to be. Now shut your mouth. Last you put a little powder on the lock to prime it and—"

Before I could move, he raised the gun and fired. For a moment, I thought he'd shot me. It was all I could do to keep standing. My ears rang as Daniel stared past me. Not wanting to show how badly he'd frightened me, I slowly turned around, steadying myself against the trunk of a chinquapin tree.

The elk's silent, motionless head hung down, its nose just brushing the snow as if searching for something to eat. A ragged, bloodied gash showed where the lead ball had torn through its flesh. Beneath its neck, a florid pool of crimson already soaked into the snow. The animal's mahogany-colored eyes were open, as if helplessly watching its life leak away.

"Are you all right?" Daniel squeezed my shoulder again.

I nodded. Even dead and trapped in snow up to its haunches, the magnificent animal was more physical, somehow more undeniably genuine, than me.

"We'd best get started then," he said, "afore wolves or panthers catch the blood scent and come nosing around like a preacher searching for sin. Let's see if we can push it over, or if we'll have to dig it out."

Benumbed, I snowshoed over to where Daniel stood.

"On the count of three. One, two, three!"

Together, we shoved against the elk's hairy side, but it didn't budge. "Again!"

Grunting, we strained to shift it even an inch.

"Looks like we'll have to dig it out then."

For ten minutes, we worked side by side, clearing the snow from under the animal's fleshy gut. Daniel had just backed away when the elk's massive body began to tip over and slide free from the snow.

"Chapman, look out!" Daniel called out.

I tried to scramble backward, but the snowshoes made it all but impossible. As the elk continued to slide toward me, I had visions of being crushed beneath its massive bulk. The stink of the animal enveloped me as it slid closer, then fortunately came to a stop. But not before it had settled over my left foot and shin. My heart thundered in my chest like a waterfall.

In vain, I tried to pull my foot clear, but it was still strapped into the snowshoe, which had sunk deep into the snow. I couldn't budge. Nor could I reach up far enough to try to dig myself free. "Daniel, I'm stuck."

He came to my side. "Yes, I'd definitely say you are." He made as if to walk away.

"Daniel, could you help me out here?"

"Chapman, what would you do if I weren't here? How would you get free then? I think you should figure this out for yourself." He turned away.

If I were by myself, I wanted to point out, I never would've shot the poor, damned animal. Instead, I made several snowballs, then pelted him in the ass with one.

He spun around to face me.

"Help me."

"Did you just hit me with a snowball?"

"Are you going to help me?"

"No."

This time the snowball caught him squarely in the middle of the chest.

He laughed. "You ballsy son of a bitch!" Before I realized what he'd done, he pounced on top of me and began tickling my stomach.

"Daniel!" I exclaimed, trying to squirm away. "Stop it! Stop it!"

"Hit me with a snowball, will you? You forgot one thing, Chapman. You can't get away, while I can." He kept on tickling.

I was laughing so hard I could barely speak. "Daniel . . . stop . . . please." I managed to get a handful of snow that I threw into his face.

"Now you're done for, Chapman." I felt his hands slip under my shirt. A shiver that had nothing to do with the cold ran through my body.

He began to tickle me again, but now it almost hurt. "You win, Daniel," I pleaded. "You win! I'll do whatever you say."

Still laughing, he collapsed on top of me. His hands were still under my shirt, but now, instead of tickling, he gently brushed his fingers over my skin. I wasn't sure what to do. As we lay there, I caught the scent of whiskey and sweat and burning ash. There was something else as well, something musky and exciting, something I would come to think of over the next several months as Daniel's smell.

Daniel sat up and began to dig my foot free. Maybe this winter wouldn't be so bad after all, I thought.

FIVE

When school began in the fall of my eleventh year, there was a new girl in Longmeadow named Rachel. Rachel had bright red hair, lived not far from my family, and was a year younger than me. Each morning, she walked with me to school, asking questions about Longmeadow or the plants that grew along the path. At lunch, she always offered me an apple tart, a scone, or some other baked thing her mother had made. After school, she followed me home, until we reached her house, where she would stop and call out, "Good-bye, John. Good-bye."

I hadn't many friends, so while I didn't encourage her attention, neither did I discourage it. This went on for a month or so, until one day when she didn't stop at her house but, instead, to my consternation, followed me to our door.

"Is there something you want, Rachel?" I asked.

"You're going to marry me someday, John Chapman," she said resolutely. "You have to because I said so."

I certainly hadn't meant to hit her hard enough to make her cry, but at least I knew she wouldn't say such a thing again.

November 1797

THE LIFELESS ELK LAY IN THE MIDDLE OF THE CABIN'S CLEARING, looking as out of place as I felt. We had only just returned from hauling the damned thing back; the harder task of butchering it still awaited us. Daniel disappeared inside the blockhouse, only to emerge a moment later, shirtless, and carrying a jug of whiskey, a bowl, and a tin.

"Drink this, Chapman," he said, handing me the jug. "Unless my judgment is as bad as my aim, to get through the butchering, you're going to need it more than a virgin taking her first poke."

A ribbon of fire, not entirely unlike the tingle I'd felt when pinned under Daniel, arced down into my chest as I drank.

He held out the bowl. "This here is some nocake. I figured we earned a quick bever."

I quickly ate the ground Indian corn mixed with water.

"Now off with your shirt."

Shivering, I did so. The afternoon had warmed some, but it was still cold.

Daniel picked up the tin. "This is lanolin. We're going to put it on our skin. It'll help keep us warm, but it also makes butchering easier."

"How?"

"You'll see. Now come here. Lift up your arms."

Working quickly, he smeared yellowish lumps onto my face and chest and arms, then began smoothing it evenly. I jumped when his hand rubbed my nipples. He looked up at me and said, "You like that, huh? I'll have to keep that in mind." He handed me the tin. "Now you do me."

Hesitantly, I put some on his shoulder and began working it in.

"Come on, Chapman. This is no time to be shy." He further unsettled me when he pulled the waist of his pants down an inch or so, revealing bright, white flesh. "The lanolin keeps my pants from chafing my skin while I work."

"I see." My hand trembled as I massaged the slippery substance over the fine black hair that covered his muscled stomach. "I guess I'm cold," I muttered when he glanced at my shaking hand. When I'd finished, I took a deep breath to steady myself.

Daniel crouched down by the animal's head, roughly yanking it backward. Puzzled, I watched as he pried its jaws apart, then forced his hand inside. Slowly, he withdrew the animal's thick, stolid tongue, then severed it at the base. "This," he said, handing me the rough-feeling lump, "makes a goddamned good stew, Chapman."

Picking up the jug, I took another swallow of the whiskey, trying to drive John from my mind.

"You all right, Chapman?"

"Yes."

"To gut, you start at the neck," he said, digging the blade into the animal's throat, "then slit it all the way to the tail. But don't go too deep. You don't want to cut into the guts, because then you'll foul the meat."

When he'd finished cutting open the elk, he said, "To actually gut it, we need to pull the rib cage further apart." He stood and gripped the elk along the upper edge of its rib cage, then wiggled his foot inside to step down on the lower half. "Give me a hand."

Gingerly I slipped my fingers inside until I had a grip on one of the ribs.

Daniel counted, "One, two, three!" then grunted as he heaved upward. "Come on, Chapman! Pull harder!"

Digging my fingers in, I leaned into the carcass and pulled. I suddenly felt Daniel's body pressed up against me as he struggled to keep his grip. Glancing at him, I saw taut, swollen veins running down his arms like rivers flowing together and separating again. His whole body was hard and glistening.

Stopping once, sweat rolling down his face, Daniel took a deep breath. With a nod to me, we heaved again. Ribs and bones, tendons and gristle, all tore apart with snaps and cracks that I felt down my back.

Without warning, Daniel let go and stepped back. I sucked in mouthfuls of cold air over my burning throat.

Daniel wiped the sweat from his face, leaving a streak of dark red across his skin. He picked up the jug, took a deep swallow, then passed it to me. He laughed. "What's wrong, Chapman? You look like we're cutting up your sister."

"Nothing's wrong. It's just harder work than I thought." His mention of my sister made me think of Elizabeth. I figured she'd be astonished if she could see her little brother now.

With a mixture of horror and fascination I watched Daniel lie in the snow, then slide his entire arm into the elk's gut. Using a knife, he managed to quickly loosen most of the viscera, which slid free. Taking the knife, he slit open the caul—the membrane containing the intestines and so forth—and set them steaming in the snow.

I found them oddly appealing, their slick textures, translucent colors, and amorphous shapes unlike anything I'd ever seen before. He peeled the caul free, spreading it over the snow. "Some salt, devil's-weed, race, and a few hours' boiling, and we got ourselves supper."

For some reason, I wasn't terribly hungry.

"Next is the heart and lungs," Daniel said. "Lift so I can get in further."

His arm and shoulder again disappeared inside, but this time he continued pushing forward, and with a muffled "Higher, Chapman! Higher!" his head and neck vanished. I struggled to keep the elk's rib cage up. Daniel now lay on his back, his hips arched upward as he tried to push farther in. As he wriggled forward, his pants slid farther down, exposing not just pale, sensuous flesh but the very top of the dark thatch that surrounded his cock. As if taking a breath, he lay flat for a moment, then flexed his back again as he thrust upward. Given the bloody work we were doing, I couldn't believe I found myself wanting to touch him.

A moment later, Daniel slithered free. Panting, he smiled up at me. His skin was slick and streaked with blood so that he almost looked like an Indian who had painted himself for battle. He reached back into the elk and dragged out something resembling a large red rock, followed by a pink, soft-looking organ that looked like an empty bag.

"This is the heart and a lung. We'll eat the heart tonight. Now it's your turn."

"What?"

"Come on, Chapman. If you're going to be a frontier settler, you need to learn this as well."

Shivering, I sank down next to him.

"First, drink," he said, handing me the jug. I swallowed. "Again," he said. After I'd passed the jug back, he reached over and rubbed a spot on my face. By now my head was spinning, though whether from the whiskey or his touch I wasn't certain.

"What are you doing?"

"You missed a spot," he said, gently working the lanolin into my skin. "I left the other lung inside for you to cut free. You've got to get used to this sort of work. Oh, and keep your eyes closed while you're in there," he said, using his knee to force the rib cage apart. At the same time, he guided my lanolin-coated hand, arm, and finally my head up into the elk's wet and still warm gut.

The experience was like being underground in a small, very wet, very slick cave. Moving under the animal's heavy flesh demanded most of my strength. Each of my senses reverberated, overwhelmed by the terrible intensity of the moment. Sweat burned as it ran into my eyes. My own breathing rasped in my ears. Sucking in what little air I managed, I couldn't so much smell the blood as I could taste it. The reek of it—the most base, elemental sensation I'd ever experienced—all but overpowered me, and I marveled at the oddity of feeling so alive while so bound up with death.

Without warning, bile rose in my throat. By swallowing repeatedly, I fought it down. More determined than ever, I sawed endlessly through whatever tied lung to elk.

"Chapman, are you all right?" Daniel hollered.

I opened my mouth to tell him I was fine, but found the side of the elk pressed down on my face so that I couldn't speak. I became dizzy as my nose and mouth again filled with the gagging, ironlike taste of salty blood.

"Chapman?" Daniel hollered again. When I didn't speak, he began to pull me out by my legs.

Determined to finish what I had begun, I began kicking to get him to stop. He quickly let go.

With my strength beginning to give, I sawed and pulled with all the force I had. The lung finally tore free. Little by little, I pushed myself from the dark cavern until my head slid free with a final thrust. Exhausted, I lay on the ground, panting on my back, shading my eyes from the bright sunlight that blinded me. The air outside was cold; between the blood of the elk and my own sweat, I found myself shivering. I held out the lung to Daniel.

John couldn't have done this, I told myself. The bastard I truly wanted to tell was my father. Now who was a worthless sod?

"Strike me blind, Chapman," Daniel said, helping me to my feet. "You did it. Though I was beginning to wonder if you thought maybe you'd found your way back into your mother's womb and weren't coming out. Have another drink to celebrate."

"Very funny, Daniel." I took the jug and drank a deep draft. The whiskey no longer burned my throat as much, but warmth still surged through my limbs. I felt dizzy again, but also a sense of pride. Maybe it was possible that I could be a real frontiersman after all.

"Tired?"

"Christ, Daniel, I'm exhausted."

"Too bad, because now we have to skin it, then we finally start cutting up the meat."

The sun crossed a quarter of the sky as we cut the hide away, then carved up the flesh. When the last of the meat had been cut from the carcass, Daniel ran a rope through the rib cage and around the neck, then tossed one end over a tree limb, and together we hoisted it off the ground. I stood watching as the gory carcass slowly twirled in the evening light. Only the elk's head remained untouched, and it wasn't hard to imagine a stupefied look on the animal's face, as if it were wondering how such a state of affairs had come to pass.

Or perhaps that was just what John was feeling.

Dusk gave way to the creeping night as we finally went back inside the blockhouse. Grateful to finally be done with killing and butchering, I didn't have to wait for Daniel's instructions to set about building a fire to heat up water with which to bathe.

"After we wash up, we eat," Daniel said, stripping off his pants, then wrapping a blanket around his waist. He climbed up into the storeroom. "The way we reek, God Almighty himself must be able to smell us!" he called down from above.

My head was already dizzy from the whiskey we'd drunk while butchering; the thought of Daniel naked, wet, bathing, made it positively spin. I recalled how, after I'd helped him with the beavers, he had washed my face and hands and arms. Look how bloodied I was now. What if he wanted to wash me again?

I took another slug of the whiskey.

A moment later, he called out for me to give him a hand as he lowered down a large wooden tub from the storeroom. Instead of being round, this tub was rectangular, and almost long enough for a man to stretch out in. As he lowered the tub, I glanced up under the blanket he'd wrapped around his hips and nearly lost my grip. Just knowing he was naked under there was enough to make me quiver.

Together, we pushed the table aside, clearing a spot for the tub.

"How's the water coming?" he asked.

"It's hot." The way the blanket hung low around his waist made my heart surge like a river in spring.

"Good. That's how I like it. Get undressed. You can go first."

"No, why don't you? I need to use the necessary anyway."

"Are you sure? I don't mind waiting."

"I'm sure, Daniel. Go ahead."

After filling the kettle with more snow to boil, I went outside. I didn't need to use the necessary any more than I needed to bleed from my ears, but I dutifully wandered over anyway in case he was watching. A sliver of silver moon cast a faint, watery light onto the clearing, but not enough for me to pick out the dangling carcass of the elk against the backdrop of trees. A light breeze rustled the bare treetops, the only other sound being the crunch of the snow under my feet.

Despite the peace and beauty of the night, I could think of but one thing: What was Daniel planning?

Stepping from the necessary, I feared going back inside. The truth be told, the Major and I had only slept together four times, and he'd always insisted on staying partially clothed and my doing exactly what he said and nothing more. Seeing Daniel naked, not to mention the times he had intimately touched me, had scared the living hell out of me. On the other hand, I felt myself stiffening as I remembered those moments.

Catching sight of Bliss's black nose poking out of her stall, I went to her, expunging from my mind the images of Daniel naked. During my time here, it had become a habit of mine to spend at least a few minutes each day scratching her head. She always seemed to welcome the attention, which only made me feel all the worse for her—I thought she must be fiercely lonesome, and I wished she had another cow to keep her company.

Starting to shiver, I reluctantly returned to the blockhouse.

Daniel stood in the tub, rinsing soap from his naked body. Wet, muscled arms and shoulders glistened in flickering firelight. I found it hard to breathe. "Cold out?"

I nodded, desperately trying not to notice the black hair that covered his chest and stomach, or the large cock swinging ponderously between his legs. As he slowly turned away, the white flesh of his ass gleamed in the light.

He sighed and said, "This hot water feels goddamned wonderful."

"Glad to hear it."

"I'm finished," he said, setting down the cup he'd used to pour water over himself. "Your turn."

He was about to step out when I said, "Wait."

He looked up at me.

Unable to believe I was about to do this, I took a deep breath. "You missed a spot. On your back." Taking the soap, I tried not to stare at him as I dipped it in the water, then scrubbed the blood that he'd missed. This was definitely Chapman, and I worried over where he was headed.

Daniel's flesh was wet and hot and hard, and he smelled of soap and whiskey. I could've washed him for hours. Water danced down his body in gleaming rivulets as I rinsed off his reddened skin.

Brushing the hair from his eyes, he turned to face me. "Thanks."

"Sure," I said, my voice trembling slightly. I dared to let my fingers brush over the warm, wet hair on his chest. He stiffened, trembling slightly, then stepped from the tub. "Your turn. Did you put more water on?"

Hastily stepping away, I nodded, worried that I'd gone too far, wishing I could take back what I'd done.

Still naked, he said, "Help me dump this."

Steam billowed into the frigid air as we poured out the warm water. Back inside, Daniel refilled the tub, then motioned for me to come over. Without speaking, he undid my belt and slid my pants down to my feet. Despite myself, my dick was beginning to harden, but he paid no mind.

"Lift your foot."

I did, but lost my balance and had to steady myself by leaning against his shoulders. The touch of my skin against his was so carnal that I would have been satisfied if nothing more had followed.

"Now the other one," he said, and I felt like a child. "Sit."

A moan escaped me as I sank down into the hot water. My eyes fell shut. Little by little, the tension began to dissipate from my stiff muscles, my aching arms and sore back. At least until Daniel spoke.

"You know what I really like?"

I didn't open my eyes. "What?"

"To have my back scrubbed with a brush. Once I knew a girl in Boston who could scrub my back like nobody else in the world—*if* you know what I mean."

Not knowing what he meant, I said nothing.

"Look here, Chapman."

His hands were by his sides. In one, he clutched a wire scrubber, the cake of soap in the other, while his slowly stiffening cock hung in between. He made no attempt to hide what was happening.

"How about I scrub your back for you? If your muscles are half as stiff as mine, then you won't be able to do it yourself."

Even the scalding hot water couldn't keep me from shivering now. "That's all right, Daniel. You don't have to."

"Of course I don't *have* to. An Indian doesn't have to get drunk, but he always does anyway." Before I could say anything else, he sauntered behind me, knelt down, and dipped the soap in the water.

I would've jumped from the shock of being touched except at

that very moment every muscle in my body had locked into place. I'd gone from shivering to frozen in an instant, and I wouldn't have cared if Indians had come crashing through the door—I simply could not have moved to save myself.

"Lord, Chapman," he said, making me jump as if the act of speaking broke the spell that bound my muscles. "You're stiffer than the trunk of a hundred-year-old oak. You all right?"

"Fine," I croaked.

"Good, good. Just relax." His hands had a surprising gentleness as they worked the soap into my skin. Embarrassed by how hard I was, I tried to lean forward to cover myself with my hands, but he pushed me back.

"That girl in Boston I mentioned? She was a real Irish beauty," he snorted. "Course, she wasn't really Irish at all, but English and uglier than what lies twixt a cur's hind legs. She'd suffered the pox and had so many pockmarks that it would've taken half a day to count them all. Not to mention the two black eyes her employer usually left her with—all that's what made her an Irish beauty."

Daniel paused and I hoped he was through. Each cruel word he blithely uttered about this poor woman turned my stomach.

He continued, "Now maybe her face was no treasure, but the rest of her? Let me tell you. She had red hair—beautiful hair—that she wore in a ponytail that I thought quite fetching. And the *curves* that tart had. There were more curves on her than in a bowl full of cherries." He traced his finger along the curve of my hip, and I forgot about the woman.

My dick had become so hard that it now rose up out of the water, as rigid as the barrel of a gun. Everywhere he touched tingled. Too much was happening at once, too much that I couldn't control. Fear and loathing, excitement and curiosity, all coursed through my mind, confusing me.

"That girl," he said, his voice deep and throaty, "could do the most astounding things to my roger with the tips of her fingers. Makes me shudder just to recall them. Like this, for instance."

He leaned forward, his fingertips just brushing the tip of my dick. It felt so intense I had to grit my teeth. Even the Major had never, ever touched me there.

"She used to fondle my roger like this all the time," he said, idly doing it again. This time a ragged gasp escaped me.

My breathing waned so shallow, I felt light-headed, almost as if I were starting to float.

His hands returned to my shoulders, massaging as he continued to talk. "I would come into Boston after a month of working in the coal pits. All filthy and grimy—just like us today—and she'd draw me a hot bath, then wash me as gentle as if I were a newborn baby." He worked his way down my body, scrubbing, massaging, until his hand disappeared into the soapy water. "Her name was Sarah, did I tell you that? Came from a small village in north England called Greenhead. Beautiful country up there." His slick hands slid over my stomach, across my thighs, and along the inside of my legs.

"Comfortable?" he asked as I struggled to sit more upright. Before I could answer, he cupped my balls in the palm of one hand, while the other eased back and forth over my rock-hard dick. Gasping audibly, I closed my eyes as I gripped the sides of the tub. The floating sensation multiplied over and over. Even though I could feel the tub beneath me, I felt as if I were tumbling through the air.

"Do you like that?"

Too lōst in the experience, I could only nod.

"Me, too. No one could do that like Sarah." Daniel let go, and when I unlocked my eyes, he had stepped around in front of me so he now stood in the tub. His dark, fat cock bobbed inches from my face. Without being asked, I took him into my mouth. The heat and hair of his groin pressed against my face, and he moaned as I caressed his weighty balls with one hand. Looking up, I took in the sight of his narrow hips and flat stomach, all rising upward in an arc that culminated in his hairy chest. My left hand slowly teased his nipples.

Daniel slipped from my mouth as he crouched down in front of me. To my amazement, he began kissing me roughly, his beard scraping against my skin, his tongue tangled with my own. A hand gripped me by the neck as he pressed his mouth ever harder against mine, and I felt utterly in his control. His other hand kneaded my shoulders and arms; he became rougher and rougher, but I didn't mind and, in fact, rather liked it. Again I felt his hand grip me, then he did something extraordinary, something I'd never even contemplated, much less done.

He lowered himself down, and at first thinking he was just going to sit on my lap, I tried to move my rigid dick out of the way. Grunting, he pushed my hand away as he continued to sit. I felt myself press up against him, bend a little, and before I realized it, slip inside.

Eyes closed, moaning, breathing heavily, he gripped the sides of the tub and froze.

Stunned, I sat there unmoving, my dick throbbing with a newfound intensity I'd never imagined possible. Unlike jacking off, where the pressure moved with my hand, this squeezed my entire dick at once. The sensation was unbelievable, unreal, like seeing a new color I'd never even imagined existed.

And *then* he began to rise up and down on me. Flexing, he gently bounced once, twice, then slowly lowered himself until he was actually sitting in my lap with all of me inside him.

It felt so bloody wondrous, I thought I would die; dumbfounded, I barely felt coherent.

Leaning forward, he again began kissing me. I kissed him back every bit as hard, which only served to excite him all the more. My hands wandered over his entire body, massaging his chest, his ass, slapping him once, then again. His nipples were already hard, and when I squeezed them, he moaned, then began moving up and down more vigorously. When we stopped kissing, my mouth moved to suck on his nipples, biting and pulling on them. He only moaned louder, bounced harder.

Sitting up straight, I gripped his hips tightly, trying to pull him as close as possible. He buried his face against my neck, and with each movement upward, he tightened, then relaxed as he thrust back down. An exquisite pain suffused my dick, my body, and I realized I was about to climax.

"Daniel," I said, fearful he'd be angry if I came inside him. "I'm going to—"

He pulled his head away from me, pressed his hand over my mouth, and began to bounce so hard that his cock and balls slapped against my stomach with each hop. He began to stroke himself, his face a tableau of ecstasy. Softly stroking his balls, I watched in amazement as the head of his dick swelled just as spouts of white jism erupted from him onto my chest and stomach. The sight of his swollen cock, his jism on my chest, and the knowledge that my own dick throbbed inside him sent me over the edge. Grinding against him, I gripped his hips as hard as I could while savage, guttural grunts and moans escaped from both of us.

"Oh, God, Daniel," I cried out, pumping into him. I felt overwhelmed as my dick swelled, then exploded inside him over and over again.

After I'd finally finished, he slumped against me as I collapsed back against the tub.

It took me a few moments to catch my breath as I came back to my senses.

I couldn't believe how great life as Chapman was turning out to be. If this was what winter held, I hoped spring would never come.

SIX

By the time my parents had moved to Longmeadow, whatever Indians had once lived there had long since left. In fact, I never saw a single Indian until I was ten and an old Indian man staggered into town. He shuffled down the main street, stopping in front of the town mill, which sat along the creek and beneath a lone soaring cedar tree that had been allowed to stand because it was so magnificent. For hours the old man stood rooted to the ground, staring directly ahead of him, seeing something we couldn't. Someone who spoke a little Wampanoag finally approached him and learned that he had grown up beneath that cedar tree.

No one saw what was laid first by the old man's feet—a blanket, food, a Bible—or who placed it there. All day I watched as people left things for him, though they neither spoke nor looked him in the face. By the end of the day, an amazingly large pile of offerings surrounded the man. Yet he seemed to be aware of none of it. I, and all of the others, had finally gone home at sunset, and therefore no one could say for sure whether it was he, or someone else, who lit the fire that consumed him and all that we'd given.

February 1798

THE BLOCKHOUSE DOOR SQUEALED OPEN AS DANIEL SLIPPED INSIDE. The candle on the table sputtered in protest of the draft. Half-melted snowflakes speckled Daniel's hair and beard like morning dew.

"Still snowing?" I asked.

He smiled as he slammed the door shut behind him. "Heavier than yesterday."

At this rate spring was never going to arrive. Groaning, I tried to recall a single day in the past three weeks that snow hadn't fallen. Though he denied it, Daniel's mood often seemed dependent on the weather, but not the way I would've expected. The worse it was outside, the better he felt. During the past four months, he'd often had reason to feel good.

"Don't start fussing, Chapman," he said, wiping his beard dry, then slapping me on the shoulder. "How are those lead balls coming?"

I shrugged and made a feeble attempt to hide the misshapen ones I'd finished.

Daniel lit our brightest lamp, which, in addition to not being especially bright, gave off a thick, acrid smoke that made my eyes burn. Carrying the lamp, he sat down next to me to inspect my work.

"If you ever get a chance, Daniel," I said, shifting away from him imperceptibly, "you'll have to buy some spermaceti candles." Despite the fact we'd slept together every night since the day we'd killed the elk, I wasn't entirely at ease around him—something I felt guilty about. After all, not only had he taken me into his bed, but he'd been teaching me almost everything he knew about being a settler.

"*What* kind of candles?"

"Spermaceti. They're made from whales and burn bright without giving off any smoke. We used to have them in Longmeadow."

"Longmeadow again?" A tinge of harshness was in his voice. "Was there anything Longmeadow didn't have? Tell me, if it was such a wonderful town, why did you ever leave in the first place?"

This was exactly the reason I never completely relaxed around Daniel. His moods were more erratic than the path of a bee's flight.

"Damn it, Chapman!" he said, snatching the lead-ball mold from me without warning. "You're still not squeezing hard enough." He held up one of the balls I'd made. "Look at this. I've felt smoother chunks of sandstone. The mold has to shut *completely*, or the balls won't be uniform." He fell silent as he demonstrated, his larger muscles making easy work of it. "Understand?"

Nodding, I took the mold and tried again. Squeezing as hard as I could, I managed to get it closed.

"That's better," he said.

Over the course of some days—sometimes even hours—I would've sworn he was two different people.

"Do you remember how to make turkey wings like I showed you?"

"Yes." The brooms made from tree branches were time-consuming, but simple to make.

"Then make a couple extra so we won't have to come summer. I'll tend to the still."

The still. If anything else in the world ranked higher in importance to Daniel than his precious still, I'd yet to hear word of it. I had no taste for whiskey, but Daniel consumed so much of the stuff that keeping the fat drops flowing was his primary occupation. The only person I'd ever seen lavish more care on his still than Daniel was my father. If only he'd been half as fond of his children.

Daniel knelt in front of the shimmering copper kettle. With great concentration, he fiddled with the tubes and valves that languorously dripped golden elixir into a malt-scented tub. Satisfied, he sat back on his heels as if lost in thought.

"My father had a still," I said.

Daniel's eyes flickered. "That so?"

"He even taught me how to run it."

"How exciting for you, Chapman."

"Granted, it was only so as to make sure it kept running when he was too drunk to tend it himself." I regretted mentioning my father. It only made me feel more like John than Chapman. I hesitated before I spoke again. "Did your father teach you?"

Daniel's eyes narrowed. Without warning, he rose and said, "Get started on those turkey wings. We've done enough dawdling for one day."

This was typical Daniel. Every time I tried to either tell him about my childhood or ask about his, he changed the subject. "In a minute," I said gruffly, Chapman reasserting himself. "I've got to use the necessary."

Twilight air nipped at my exposed flesh, but to my surprise the snow had stopped falling. Even better, the sky had cleared for what seemed the first time in weeks.

"Guess what, Daniel?" I said upon my return.

"King George has come to pay us a visit," he said tersely.

"It's clear out. Maybe it will warm up some tomorrow."

Daniel pushed past me to see for himself. A thin line of azure hugged the horizon, while above it soared a beautiful curved swath of deep blue shot through with twinkling stars. "Bugger that," was all Daniel muttered.

Passing by me, he trod hard on my foot and said nothing in the way of an apology. Annoyed, I shut the door, then set the bar across it with a thud. Liking Daniel—much less getting along with him—wasn't the easiest task in the world. Did I, in fact, like him? If so, was it worth it?

I wondered.

Daniel took a gully from the shelf, fetched up by the table, and began to whittle with it.

"Aren't you looking forward to spring, Daniel?" I asked, trimming the branch I'd carve into the turkey wing.

He looked at me sharply. "Are you saying I'm not?"

"No, not at all." I felt as if I'd touched the wrong end of a hot iron poker. I decided to change the subject. "What are you making?"

"Why?"

"I'm just curious, for Christ's sake. Never mind."

"Instead of wasting time being curious, why don't you stoke up the fire? It's getting chilly in here."

In more ways than one, I thought as I stirred up the coals. Sparks and embers popped and pulsed angrily as I added another log. Outside, the wind had picked up, rattling around as if angry at being shut out.

"If you must know, Chapman, it's a pipe," Daniel said when I sat again. "A corncob pipe."

"Really!" I pressed closer for a better look.

"Really," he mimicked. "Why do you say it like that?" he asked, leaning away.

I didn't rise to his taunt. "Because my father used to whittle those all the time. I never got tired of watching him do it."

"So you were poor, too, were you?" he asked.

"Eleven brothers and sisters. And a drunk rumrunner who drank most of what he made for a father. It was impossible not to be poor."

Small white shavings flew into the air before settling around his feet. He worked in silence for a few moments, then said, "I hated being poor. Hated it more than being short or the youngest. I *hated* it. I left as soon as I was old enough to hire on as a farmhand."

This was more than he'd said about himself all winter. "How old was that?" I asked hesitantly.

"Ten."

"You left home when you were *ten?*"

Nodding, he poured himself a cupful of whiskey.

"Ballsy, weren't you?" I hated that I'd never be as fully Chapman as Daniel was, well, Daniel.

"Damn right. By the time I was nine, I'd decided that God could boil me in a blood pudding, but that I wasn't going to be poor or helpless anymore—no matter what it took."

"So what did you do?"

"Like I said. Whatever it took."

"I see."

We worked in silence, the only sound that of the wind outside and the hiss of relentless flames working their way through the protesting wood.

"Do you miss Ireland?" I asked.

"Ireland?" He sipped his whiskey as he studied me. "Yes. Of course. But we left there when I was very young, so I don't remember much about it. Nothing in fact. Sailed straight from Dublin to here."

That explained why he had no accent.

"How about you?" Daniel asked, interrupting my thoughts. "Do you miss Longmeadow?"

The question caught me off guard. "No, not at all. I wouldn't go back if John Adams himself asked me."

"Well, you needn't worry about that."

As the cabin grew warmer, I began to doze while Daniel worked. At some point, he had finished his pipe, because I woke to a pall of tobacco smoke hanging in the cabin. It was strong and sweet with an earthy aroma reminiscent of the longhouses in which I'd worked as a boy laying out tobacco to dry. Thankfully, it was nothing like my father's bitter tobacco; it had reeked something fierce. I think Father had chosen that particular tobacco precisely because it was off-putting to so many people.

Through half-open eyes, I watched Daniel alternate long puffs on the pipe with sips from his cup. He was such a handsome man, I thought. If only we had more in common, or if his moods weren't so mercurial. Even then I wanted to go to him, to touch his black hair, his face with its ruddy complexion.

The still made a wheezing sound; yet another plump, glistening drop fell from the tube, but after that the flow ceased.

"Shit a turd," cursed Daniel as he knelt unsteadily in front of the boiler. He again fiddled with tubing that rose from its top like some bizarre copper snake. Orange candlelight reflected off the boiler's ruddy surface, wriggling and dancing eerily in front of him.

"Can I help, Daniel?"

"Keep your filthy bunghole away," he muttered, and I realized he'd indulged heavily while I dozed. "You get near this still, and I'll break your bloody legs."

"Sure you will, Daniel. Christ, you're so drunk I doubt you could even find your legs."

He grumbled as he continued to work.

The logs in the fire hissed and spat; a throbbing, orange spark arced up through the air before landing at my feet.

I ground it out so hard with my heel that I twisted my ankle.

∧ ∧ ∧

Cooking the next night—a chore I'd taken over—I lifted the lid of the roasting pan to check on dinner. Spitefully, I jabbed the sputtering elk shank; golden brown fat bubbled as clear juice drizzled down the side of the joint, and I knew it was almost done. After weeks of practice, I'd become quite adept at the varied ways of preparing elk.

I'd grown so tired of eating the same thing, I felt myself growing angry just looking at it. I fantasized heaving it out into the snow or tipping the pan over into the fire and watching it burn. I could only imagine Daniel's reaction to that. It mystified me how he ate elk every day and never appeared to tire of it. On the other hand, Daniel, I thought, had all the refinement of a lump of iron ore.

"Dinner's ready," I called out, letting the meat fall onto the platter with a thud. From the other pot, I dished out Boston baked beans, then lowered myself down to the table.

Weariness settled over me as I ate. Despite—or perhaps because of—all of the sleeping I'd done of late, I was exhausted. Or maybe the monotony was taking its toll.

Daniel struggled from bed and sat across from me.

"Hand me your plate," I said, cutting off a huge slice of the roast.

He set the plate in front of him and looked at it unsteadily. "The meat smells funny."

I leaned forward, sniffing. "Smells like it always does—disgusting."

I noticed Daniel's faced was flushed, his eyes glassy. It was bad enough that Daniel shared none of my interests, but did he have to turn out to be an inebriate as well? I'd already had enough of that for one life. "Have you been drinking again?" I demanded.

"No."

Liar, I thought to myself. "Well, do you feel all right?"

"No." He pushed his plate away from him. "I feel hot."

Reaching over, I placed my hand on his forehead. "Lord, Daniel, you're burning up."

He pushed his plate completely out of the way and slumped onto the table. "I'm so dizzy."

Allowing myself to be John for a moment, I filled a bowl with cool water, dipped in a cloth, and began wiping his face.

"Don't," he said, trying to brush my hand away.

"Knock it off, Daniel." I rinsed the cloth out in the bowl. Next I tried to do his neck, but he grabbed my wrist.

"I said *don't*, you damned cur. You're not my mother."

"And you're not my father," I said irately. To hell with being nice—with being John. "You're hurting my arm, you son of a bitch. Now let *go!*"

With a shove, he did just that, and I nearly tripped over my chair as I stumbled backward. Daniel was turning out to be far too similar to my father. Disgusted, I threw the cloth to the ground as a stricken look intruded upon his face; he retched several times, and the pemmican he'd had for lunch splattered onto the floor.

Now angry *and* revolted, I stepped away from him. Cold air flooded the cabin as I opened the door to relieve the stench. Damn him for being so stubborn.

Daniel wiped his hand across his mouth. "I want that closed," he ordered.

"Then close it."

Not only was he stubborn, but he was asinine as well. He made as if to cross the room, but was quickly overcome by exhaustion and dizziness. He sank to the floor, gagged violently again, but nothing more came up. Ignoring me, he began crawling toward his bed.

Still angry, I only watched as he struggled to pull himself up. Halfway there, he slipped and slid back onto the floor.

I was sorely tempted to leave him there.

"Listen, Daniel," I said, going to his aid. "You're not feeling well, and that's made you cranky, but don't you push me away again, or I'll damned well leave you lying in your vomit."

This time he offered no resistance. Gripping him under his shoulders, I heaved him into bed like a sack of oats. It took only a moment for him to fall deep asleep.

As to how I felt about Daniel, the answer had grown more apparent each day. I couldn't escape that, frankly, he had become as brutish and unpleasant as the mythological Caliban.

Without thinking about it, I reached over and pinched his cheek as hard as I could; a welt like a bee sting, angry and red, rose up on his face.

^ ^ ^

Even after I'd cleaned up his puke, a sour odor lingered in the air, killing what little appetite I'd had. Taking both plates, I decided to live out at least a small part of my earlier fantasy; while it wasn't the whole roast I sent sailing out into the clearing, there was a certain gratification in flinging hunks of meat as far as I could.

As long as I had my boots on and was already displaying a fine array of goose bumps, I decided I might as well make a trip to relieve myself.

As soon as I stepped out of the necessary, I saw the fox. It was reddish brown, quite small, and therefore a female, I surmised from what Daniel had taught me. She froze as soon as she saw me, the larger piece of elk firmly clenched in her jaws. Even from where I stood, I could see her ribs showing through her fur. Her eyes were black, like chips of coal, and she looked so much like a small child caught stealing a sweet that I wanted to laugh. For a long moment, I stood there studying her as she stood motionless, watching me.

"You're not a deer, you know," I said softly. "You don't blend in at all standing there like that."

Her small, tufted ears twitched.

"I'm not going to take the meat from you, I promise. In fact, if you can carry it, I've got a hundred pounds inside that I'd love to give you." Growing colder, I took a step toward the blockhouse.

With her eyes still fixed on me, she immediately broke into a lurching trot—she could go no faster carrying the meat—and vanished into the woods. I could've sworn there was almost a look of longing on her face when she passed by the second piece of meat.

After that night, I began to cook portions that I knew we couldn't finish and then, knowing Daniel would be furious if he found out, discreetly placed the leftovers on the edge of the clearing for the fox to find. Fortunately, these days Daniel was usually too drunk to notice much at all. Sometimes I caught a glimpse of the fox darting out of the shadows, seizing whatever it was that I'd left her. Two weeks later, I spotted her gliding into the clearing. Not only could I no longer see her ribs under a newly glossy coat, I thought she looked positively pregnant.

^ ^ ^

The following day, a blizzard began that raged for three nights. Outside, the wind howled, piling great drifts in the clearing. I'd prayed for warm weather, some brief respite from the snow, but instead it felt as if an army had laid siege to us. Depressed, I took to the bed.

As I lay next to Daniel, all of my frustrations and ennui and boredom accreted on my soul as surely as the snow on the trees. I wanted to get on with my life! Having seen limbs of overweighed trees snap off, I wondered how much I could bear before some part of my mind gave way with a terrific crash.

Daniel, too, stayed in bed during the storm, no longer ill, but so drunk he could barely stand upright long enough to refill his flask. For some reason, he kept singing the same inane drinking ditty— how he rogered Miss Plover from Dover out in the clover—again and again, until I thought I would go mad because of it. I'd thought long and hard about returning to sleeping by myself, but in the end I decided even a drunk man's body heat was worth the price.

Lying there all but catatonic for hours on end, I dreamt of green summer fields unencumbered by fists of snow; of soft spring air brimming with the scents of wild roses, forget-me-nots, and crab apple blossoms; of days and days of endless sunshine where cool grass tickled the soles of my feet while magpies and killdeers and warblers called out greetings and courtings and warnings. Even a cow mooed in some unseen pasture. But then I heard a strange, ominous sound that I'd never heard before.

It was a low-pitched keening, rising and falling in the distance, somewhere far away from my Edenic meadow. I tried to ignore it, but it grew louder, came closer.

I felt Daniel stir next to me. He sat up. Opening my eyes, I watched him suddenly lurch from the bed, abruptly sober, staring intently at the fireplace built into the back wall. "Bugger my mother," he whispered when the sound welled up again. "Chapman, get up! Something's wrong with the wall!"

"What, Daniel?" I mumbled.

"Listen. The cow. I think I hear the cow."

"Bliss?" I asked, now interested. "What's wrong with her?"

"I don't know," he said, pulling on his clothes. "But get up. *Now!*"

Confused, I stumbled from bed. I pictured wolves or panthers terrorizing Bliss.

"Get dressed!" He pulled open the door. Cold and snow swirled around his feet. "Hurry!"

Half-awake, I stumbled as I dressed, then followed him outside. Snow whipped by the wind scoured my face and I couldn't find Daniel.

"Chapman! Back here!" he called out. His voice, barely loud enough to hear, came from the other side of the blockhouse.

Struggling through waist-deep snow, I found him, panicked, standing next to Bliss's stall. "Thunder, furies, and *damnation!*" he cursed.

I looked up and gasped. Two yards of snow towered over top of the stall. Unlike the inclined roof of the blockhouse, designed to send snow sliding off as it piled up, the roof of the stall had been built level. Sensing the danger, a panicky Bliss skittishly swayed from side to side, mooing so loudly that Daniel had heard her inside.

"I told that ugly, shitting howler this would happen."

"Who?"

Daniel started to speak, then stared at me blankly. Maybe he hadn't been as sober as I'd thought.

I peered in again at Bliss. The roof of the stall sagged dangerously above her, especially where it joined the back wall of the blockhouse.

I stepped forward to try to soothe her, only to be shoved roughly back by Daniel.

Sick of his pushing me around, both literally and figuratively, I became irate. "If you push me again—even once—I swear I'll cut your damnable heart out and feed it to you whole!"

He looked at me with surprise. "Aren't you full of piss and vinegar. Not that I give a beshitted damn, Chapman, but I was trying to protect you, fool. The snow could collapse the whole stall and back wall anytime and bury you under it."

I opened my mouth to apologize, but no words came out. I looked away.

Daniel pointed to the blockhouse. "Look at the back wall."

Wiping the snow from my eyes, I took a step back. At first, I didn't see anything unusual, but then, to my horror, I spotted what Daniel saw.

"Sweet Jesus!" I exclaimed.

The whole back wall bowed inward like a stick about to snap. The snow not only bore down on the stall, but pressed against the back of the blockhouse as well. If that wall collapsed, not only would Bliss and the fireplace be crushed, it was damn likely that the entire second floor would come crashing down as well. I didn't fancy our chances trying to live out the rest of the winter in the rubble.

"What do you want me to do?" I asked, swallowing my panic.

"We have to get the snow off the frigging stall afore we lose the whole blockhouse!" Daniel's eyes frantically searched the sides of the blockhouse. "There should be some goddamn shovels lying around here somewhere. I used them to dig out some wood for the still last week, but I don't goddamn remember where I left them."

He began wading through the snow, plunging his hands into the snowdrifts that clung to the walls of the cabin. I searched the opposite direction, desperately wishing I had my gloves as crusty snow scraped and stung my hands. A moment later, I heard Daniel calling.

"Thank God," he said, handing a shovel to me.

"Shouldn't we let Bliss out?" I asked. He nodded, and together we struggled to pull the gate open, but three feet of snow was piled against it. Each time we tugged on the gate, the whole structure groaned.

"It's too dangerous!" Daniel wiped snow from his spattered face. "She'll be all right, I think. Follow me." We went to the other side of the blockhouse where the roof came closest to the ground. First I boosted Daniel up, then he reached down and hauled me up.

A foot-wide ledge ran the length of the blockhouse. It, too, was buried under snow. Carefully we edged our way along the narrow track until, at last, we stood above the stall. Daniel studied the roof, then turned to me. "I'm too heavy, Chapman. You're going to have to climb down onto the stall itself to dig it out, but by the devil's deuce, make sure you stay on the edge and off the roof itself. The edge is the only place where the roof is supported underneath by a wall. Even one more quartern might be enough to collapse it."

Holding my breath, I stepped onto the edge of the roof. Daniel watched apprehensively to see if the stall's wall would, in fact, support my weight. The groaning intensified, and I froze. Panicked, I edged farther off the roof so that only the balls of my feet remained on the edge. I fought to keep my balance in the buffeting wind. How the hell was I going to shovel snow standing like this?

As the groaning died away, I relaxed a little, and then, with a crack I'll never forget, the stall collapsed beneath me. For a moment, I found myself floating in a sea of white, stunned and amazed, then the earth belted the breath out of me as I slammed to the ground. Before I could even gasp from the impact, a sheath of snow swallowed me whole, pinning me as easily as I might a field mouse. I couldn't move an arm, a hand, not even a finger. My mouth had been open in surprise when I'd crashed down, and cold, grainy snow clogged my throat and nose. Desperate, I struggled to turn my head, but it was locked into place.

I tried to breathe, but only gagged.

How much time passed, I didn't know. Twenty seconds. Forever. My body convulsed with tremors. Without warning, something punched me. The next thing I knew, Daniel was yelling at me.

"Breathe, Chapman! Breathe, goddammit!" His voice was muffled, distant. Fingers scooped the snow from my mouth, but the rest of my body was still encased. "Oh, Jesus. Oh, Jesus," he kept repeating while he frantically dug me out. When I was finally free, he rolled me over to pound on my back. "Come on, you son of a bitch—breathe!" He flipped me back again. "Chapman, you have to breathe now," he pleaded, shaking me. "I can't do anything more. Come on. Please, don't leave me."

I felt as if I were trapped underwater, struggling to surface, but clad in cumbersome clothes weighing me down. Only Daniel's faraway voice countered the pull of the water. I gasped and opened my eyes. Immediately, I began coughing and tried to push Daniel away, but my arms wouldn't move. I couldn't see, and I wanted desperately to vomit.

"That's right, Chapman! That's right!" Daniel pounded me on the back as he pulled me up into a sitting position. "Thank God."

Again and again I coughed as I fought to pull air in over my ragged, burning throat. Daniel wrapped his arms around me as he rocked back and forth. With each passing minute, my breathing became less labored. As I calmed, my eyes focused on the scene in front of me.

The whole stall lay collapsed, leaving only a pile of white snow spiked through with snapped timber. It was a wonder I hadn't been impaled or crushed by one of the logs. I started to shake.

"We've got to get you inside, John. Come on."

He reached under my armpits and helped me struggle to my feet. I leaned against him. "The blockhouse?" I rasped. "Did it collapse?"

He shook his head. "Just the stall. When it collapsed, almost all of the snow slid off the blockhouse and onto you."

"What about Bliss?"

He opened his mouth as if to speak, then slightly shook his head.

Shoving him away, I staggered to where the front of the stall had been. Crouching down, my desperate eyes roamed the snowy rubble of broken planks that lay scattered about like a shattered dream. At first I didn't recognize Bliss's black nostrils poking up through the rubble, twitching erratically as she struggled to breathe. I fell to my knees and began digging her head out. "Help me, Daniel. I know it's just a cow, but please."

Together, we uncovered her head and neck, but her neck twisted from her shoulders in a terrible way.

"Oh, Bliss," I murmured, stroking her face.

"Go inside, Chapman."

"Why? What are you going to do?"

"Just go inside."

"Don't do it, Daniel."

"She's as good as dead, Chapman."

"She's alive, Daniel! She's breathing!"

"You'd rather she freeze to death slowly?"

"No," I whispered. I crawled away.

From the corner of my eye, I watched Daniel pick up and discard several snapped planks until he found one that satisfied him. As he raised it above his head, I turned away and buried my head in my hands.

Bliss never made a sound.

I felt weak for caring about a stupid cow. I felt like John.

"Come on, Chapman, afore you freeze to death."

"You liked doing that, didn't you, Daniel?" I asked, wiping my eyes.

"What the blazes are you talking about?"

"You knew I cared about Bliss, so you were glad to kill her."

"You better stop your hole, Chapman, afore I stop it for you."

"Are you actually sober enough to do it? *That* would be a change."

"I warned you, Chapman. Stop your hole or I'll stop it for you."

"Don't threaten me, Daniel."

"I'll do as I damn well please and don't you forget it. You're blaming me because it's all your fault."

"My fault!" I sputtered. "How the hell is it my fault?"

"You bewitched and beguiled me with your unnatural acts, that's how."

"I bewitched *you?*" I couldn't believe what I was hearing.

"That's the truth of it." He gestured to the shattered stall. "If you hadn't, I would've prevented this from happening, and we wouldn't have nearly died. If you hadn't come here, things would be fine. In fact, if you'd never been born, the world would've been a better place."

Daniel's words hit me as heavily as the snow I'd nearly been crushed by. I'd come so far, struggled so much, and yet this could've been my father standing before me.

How far did I have to run?

After the disastrous collapse of the stall and the bitter words that had followed, Daniel and I stopped sleeping together, stopped speaking, and began to all but behave as if the other had ceased to exist.

On the last night of February, halfway between sleep and waking, I lay curled in the straw that passed for my bed. A loneliness as profound as the winter was cold deepened its grip on me. At some point, I finally slept, but only fitfully. I shivered, then shook until the shaking drove away the chance of any more sleep. Why was it so damned cold?

Upon waking, I guessed maybe an hour or two had passed since I'd finally drifted off to sleep. A light still flickered in the corner of the blockhouse, which I thought odd until I spied Daniel sitting by the half-open door. As peculiar as the open door was, it explained the cold. What it didn't explain was why Daniel sat by it in the middle of a bitter February night.

He poured whiskey from a jug into his cup and took a deep swallow. Fear made me stiffen when he picked up a rifle; a second leaned nearby against the wall.

"Daniel, is there something outside?" I whispered, thinking fearfully of Indians.

"Shh," he said, acknowledging me for the first time in a week. "Puts more fire on the wood," he muttered, "but keeps it quite—I mean, quiet."

Christ, I thought, he was drunk, *and* there probably were Indians outside.

Shivering again, I pulled the bearskin around my shoulders and went to the fireplace. I added wood, then watched the flames lurch and snap as they devoured the log, all the while wondering what Daniel was doing.

Daniel stiffened like a cat spotting a mouse.

"Daniel," I whispered. "What is it?"

Ignoring me, he unsteadily raised the rifle to his shoulder, the barrel weaving about as he tried to follow whatever it was in the woods.

Little by little, I rose enough to peer out the window. I'd slept longer than I'd realized, for dawn had begun to spill down from the plateau. In the diffuse light, I could at first only make out the dark, mute trees, their shadows laying blue-black on the snow. Then at the edge of the clearing, I spied something darting between the trunks of two trees.

The fox. My fox. There had been no Indians.

"Daniel, don't shoot. It's just a fox. I've been feeding her."

Daniel didn't look at me as he said, "I know what you been doing, you sotted cretin. I'm not as blind as you think."

The reddish brown animal paused, took a step forward, sniffing the air intently as if suspecting something. I spotted the meat Daniel

had put out, but instead of being at the edge of the clearing, it lay
farther in: far enough in that he would have a clear shot.

Daniel tried to steady the rifle. "You make a sound, Chapman,
and I'll throws you out of here faster than a nigger runs for the
north. No supplies, no food, no claim—no *nothing*."

Hunger overcame the diffident fox's fear. She trotted forward.

"Daniel, don't," I pleaded again. My hand darted out to push the
rifle away. Then swifter than I would've thought possible for someone so drunk, Daniel struck me in the gut with the butt of the rifle.

Gasping, I sank to my knees, but kept my eyes on the fox.
Please, let his eyesight keep him from shooting her.

Halfway to the food, probably having heard the click of the flint
being released, the fox froze. Gunpowder exploded almost simultaneously with her head, which vanished in a burst of red.
Decapitated, she actually remained upright for a moment before
toppling onto her side.

Too stunned to react, I stared into the dark.

"Yes! One shitten shot!" Daniel exclaimed. "One goddamned,
shitten shot." He rose to his feet, swung around, and struck me
across the face with the back of his hand. "Don't you ever, *ever*,
cross me again," he slurred. "'Cause if you do, God rot your soul, I'll
gut you like an oyster."

Stunned and frightened, I clutched my stomach.

My name is Chapman, I told myself again and again.

SEVEN

Father wasn't much for playing with his children.

He would, on each of our birthdays, play draughts with us, using an old set carved by his father. Other times, when the haphazard mood struck him, I remember him playing King George Is Hiding with me and the other children. But one game in particular he did like to play, especially with me. It was a guessing game he called simply Pick. When he wanted to play—not playing was never an option—he would approach me slyly, his hands behind his back, a smile more like a sneer on his face.

"Pick a hand, John," he said as my stomach sank like an anchor.

I always chose without hesitation, and for a long moment, he would only stare at me. No matter how hard I tried, I never learned to read his face well enough to know if I had chosen correctly or not. Only when he whipped his hand out from behind his back did I know.

If I'd chosen the correct hand, I would receive a sweetmeat, a pretty stone, or maybe an Indian arrowhead.

If I'd chosen the wrong hand, he would slap me so hard that the shape of his hand might be visible on my cheek for hours.

March 1798

THE WEATHER IN EARLY MARCH PROVED MORE CHANGEABLE THAN THE wind in a dust devil. The first week, it snowed four days in a row, followed by a warm spell that melted it all in half that time. The pattern repeated itself the following week, and as usual, Daniel and I couldn't have had more antipodean responses. Where I became hopeful as the weather warmed, he sank into despondency and drunkenness.

One afternoon, I finally got up the nerve to broach the subject of the supplies for my claim. His killing the fox had been the final straw. As soon as I thought the weather bearable, I had to get away.

Wanting Daniel to be as sober as possible, I'd waited until snow again fell, though it only snowed lightly and barely felt cold enough to do so at all. Though only two weeks into March, the weather had been so warm the day before that I hoped this storm might be winter's final act.

Daniel stood in the doorway watching the wet, heavy snow plunge to the ground as if it, too, were in a hurry to be done.

"Daniel," I said, coming up behind him. "Can I ask you something?"

He didn't react, and I wasn't sure he'd heard.

"Daniel—"

"Look at it snow, Chapman. It's coming down so hard I can barely see the trees."

I glanced outside at trees as clearly visible to me as was Daniel. If he couldn't see them, perhaps he wasn't as sober as I'd thought. "Daniel, I wanted to ask you about something. About the supplies. When do you think I could have them?"

"Supplies?"

"Yes. The supplies the Holland Land Company is giving away."

"But that's not until spring."

"It's March, Daniel. Spring is almost here." My new life was almost here.

He shook his head. "Spring's a long way off, Chapman. Look at the snow."

"Nonetheless, Daniel. The other settlers will be here soon. And I just want to be sure—"

"No," he said, shaking his head. "No, there won't be anybody here soon. It's snowing too hard. Spring's far off. You're mistaken. You understand me?"

I wasn't getting through to him. "Fine, Daniel. I'm mistaken."

And I was.

Two days later, the temperature plummeted again. Huddling by the fire, I struggled to keep warm while Daniel lay in bed.

Without a word Daniel got up, dressed, and left, going, I assumed, to use the necessary. When after fifteen minutes he still hadn't returned, I began to wonder where he'd gone. After another five minutes passed, I pulled on my boots and went outside. The door to the necessary was shut, but then it always was, whether occupied or not.

"Daniel?" I called out, but no one answered. I crossed the icy clearing. "Daniel?" I repeated when I reached the necessary. "Are you all right?" Reluctantly, I knocked on the door, waited a moment, then pulled it open. A lone piece of corn husk fluttered out with the biting wind.

Where the hell had he gone?

"Daniel?" I called out, turning around, but no one answered.

Searching the clearing, I found his tracks headed off on a trail into the woods. By now I was trembling in the cold, and I tried to recall whether he had taken a coat. I didn't think he had. Was he so drunk when he left that he'd gotten lost going to the necessary and wandered off into the woods? Despite everything he'd done, if he'd wandered off drunk, I felt I owed it to him to fetch him back. Going inside, I grabbed my coat and gloves, then hurried down the trail after him.

After a half hour of slogging as fast as I could along the muddy trail, I caught a glimpse of Daniel's red shirt moving through the gray trees. For another twenty minutes, I trailed after him, keeping out of sight.

All of a sudden, he stopped. I halted as well, waiting to see if he had only paused to catch his breath. He made no move to go any farther, staring at something out of my sight. Like a rapt dog—I could practically see his ears straining forward—he had his head cocked at an angle as he listened to something I couldn't hear. Unsure what to do, I rested against a tilting chestnut tree, watching him stand there listening. Gradually, I began to shiver.

Without warning, Daniel turned and jogged back down the trail. Panicked, I looked the way we'd come, but knew I could never be out of sight before he would spot me. With no other choice, I plunged into the woods to my left and found myself sliding noisily down a steep, snow-covered slope. Frantic, I grabbed a tree branch to stop my slide seconds before Daniel passed by.

Despite standing waist deep in snow, I no longer felt the least bit cold.

After I felt certain Daniel was out of earshot, I hauled myself back up the embankment. Brushing snow from my legs and arms, I made my way to where he had stood. It was an embankment over-looking a frozen creek that wound its way past the forbidding, sentinel-like trees. Scrutinizing the woods, the embankment, the twisting course of the creek, I tried to determine what had so riveted Daniel's attention.

Seeing nothing, I was about to leave when movement on the opposite side of the creek caught my eye. A good-sized hare, winter white except for the black buttons of its nose and eyes, clawed at the bank. The animal found a root or a bud, then chewed furiously, its eyes darting to and fro. A sudden shadow slid along the surface of the creek. The hare froze instantly.

Glancing up, I caught sight of an eagle gliding above before it vanished from sight. The hare had escaped this time.

Funny, I knew just how it felt.

Then the eagle struck without warning. Streaking down from above, it sank its talons into the hare's back. A struggle ensued as the hare, pathetically bleating like a sheep, tried to scramble away. Both eagle and hare slid down the bank and onto the creek. For a moment, both creatures skittered along the ice, looking for all the world as if the eagle only wanted to ride piggyback. But soon the eagle's powerful wings beat strongly enough to lift the hare from the ground, and the poor hare could do nothing but dangle helplessly.

After they vanished, all that remained was a bloody streak smeared across the ice.

The rains came two days later. Almost overnight, the clearing transformed into a mud-filled morass. But while the snow melted, the temperature remained quite cold due to the cutting March winds. For two days, rain drummed unbroken on the roof of the blockhouse as Daniel lay in bed, glaring at the ceiling. The rain filled me with hope, for in it I saw the promise of coming warmth, and green crops flowering and blooming across my soon-to-be claim. As I looked outside—even at gray, chilly skies and mud—anything seemed possible.

The only burr in my shifting was the issue of my supplies, which still pervaded my every thought. I was reluctant to broach the subject again, though I decided to try a different tact.

"Daniel?"

"What?"

"Could I ask you something?" When he said nothing, I plunged ahead. "With spring coming—eventually, I mean—I wanted your advice, to know where you thought I might be best off staking my claim."

"Your claim?"

I nodded.

He laughed. "Chapman, you're no frontiersman. When are you going to give up this sham of yours and go home?"

Only John would give up, and I was no longer him. "I'm not giving up. I *am* going to have a claim. And there's nothing you can do about it, Daniel."

"Really. What about supplies, Chapman? How are you going to stake a claim without supplies?"

"Would you really do that to me?"

"If you keep pestering, I just might."

My stomach tightened. Angry and confused, I went to the window, looking outside. The rain finally slackened off to a fine mist that shrouded the tops of the tallest trees. Instead of green rows of corn and my own cabin, I saw only gray slush and muck, and nothing seemed inevitable anymore.

Two days later, Daniel ventured back to the creek. While I didn't want to risk angering him any more than I had, I sensed it might be important to understand what he was doing.

Warm weather had followed drenching rain; some of the trees already had small blossoms dotting their branches, and following behind Daniel, I became lost in thought planning what fruit trees would eventually occupy my claim. I'd finally settled on a combination of apple, pear, and wild plum trees when I realized Daniel had stopped. A few more steps and I would've given myself away. Backtracking, I slipped behind the pungent branches of a savin to wait for him.

"I know you're there, Chapman," he called out. "You might as well come the rest of the way."

Caught off guard, I remained motionless, wondering how he had spotted me.

"Chapman, I said get your goddamned arse over here."

Sheepishly, I came out from behind the tree. Coming up behind him, I climbed onto the steep bank. While the weather had warmed, a blanket of cold air, spawned by the ice, still lay over the creek and its banks.

"Listen," he said. The odor of whiskey hung around him as heavily as the cold air hovering above the creek.

I listened, but heard nothing.

Expressionless, he glanced over at me, then turned back to the creek, his bloodshot eyes darting back and forth to different spots along the ice.

"This is Conewango Creek," he said. "Not far from here it flows into the Allegheny. It's the way to Franklin."

"Franklin?"

"The closest settlement to us. I told you about it when you first arrived."

"I guess I forgot." But now that he reminded me of it, I wondered what it was like, how hard it would be to start a claim there. "How long a trip to—"

Frowning, he held up his finger to shush me. "Do you hear it?"

I shook my head.

"Well, *listen,*" he said again.

Annoyed, I closed my eyes and strained to hear. To my surprise, I did hear something—a low, unearthly groan, almost a lament. I opened my eyes. The sound seemed to come from nearby, but I couldn't pinpoint where. Instead it seemed to roll across the landscape, then back again.

Taking several steps toward the Conewango, Daniel crouched down, staring intently at its frozen surface. The moaning rose in pitch, then abruptly stopped, as if someone had choked off the sound with his hands. Just as abruptly, Daniel rose and turned to me as if he knew the noise wouldn't resume.

He reached over to a tree branch, wrapped his palm around it, then pulled his hand toward him; small green buds popped off, flying away in all directions. "You didn't really think I wouldn't know you were following me, did you?"

"I didn't want to bother you, that's all."

"I see. Mighty considerate." He plucked the solitary bud he'd missed, tossed it onto the snow, then ground it under his heel.

"Are you checking to see if the creek is thawing?"

"Maybe." He released the now naked branch, and it sprang forward, narrowly missing my face. "Why?"

Frowning, I stepped backward and said, "Just curious."

He looked back toward the creek, snapping the buds off another branch. "If the weather stays this warm, the ice should be breaking up soon."

He didn't sound the least bit happy about it.

By now the days were undeniably lengthening, and even the wind had moderated in both temperature and temperament. White blossoms bloomed along knobby tree limbs, while hundreds of herons and cranes and scarlet tanagers began to pass overhead from the south. The washed-out, gray sky of winter was gone, replaced by a bright blue sky. The air was filled with a hundred new scents along with the euphonic dripping of snow splashing to earth from hundreds of trees. Something about the sight and sound of snow melting from the forest put me in mind of a large, shaggy dog shaking its coat dry.

One morning, as I slogged my way to the necessary through cold muck that pulled and sucked at my boots, I noticed splashes of red in a melting snowbank. It looked as if something had been killed or injured there. Apprehensive, I approached. It was the remnants of a dozen or so crocuses stomped into the ground.

I turned and looked for Daniel.

Upon exiting the necessary, I again stared in annoyance at the sea of mud that now necessitated a thorough wiping off of my boots every time I returned from outside.

Suddenly, I had an idea.

Instead of going back to the blockhouse, I picked my way to where Bliss's collapsed stall lay. What I was after were the planks that had formed the roof and walls of her stall; it had occurred to me that some could be lined up to form a crude walkway over the mud. For an hour, I worked, separating good planks from the unusable, then laying them end to end. There were barely enough for two walkways: one to reach the necessary and one the woods.

I thought Daniel would be pleased, if for no other reason than he would no longer get muddy using the outhouse.

"Daniel," I called out as I entered. "Come see what I've done."

He sat by the fire, smoking a pipe. "And what might that be?"

"Just come and see."

"I don't want to go outside, Chapman. It's winter out there."

"Once you see what I've done, you won't mind coming out."

"I don't much care *what* you've done."

"Please, Daniel."

Uttering his usual litany of maledictions, he rose and shuffled to the front door.

"See?" I said, pointing at my handiwork. "They're the planks from Bliss's stall. I've made two trails for us. One goes to the necessary and one to—"

"Get out of my way, you sodding meddler." I stumbled backward as Daniel shoved me aside.

Bewildered, I watched him grab an ax leaning against the blockhouse and, grunting like a boar, begin to hack away at the planks. Again and again, he wildly swung the ax above his head, then smashed it down with a guttural grunt. Once he lost his balance; swearing, he stumbled and fell into the mud. Uncowed, he rose and continued shattering the boards into pieces.

Was everything I tried to do destined to end this way?

I watched for a moment, then stepped into the cabin and shut the door on the sound of splintering wood.

The third and final time Daniel and I went to the Conewango, I again trailed behind him, but this time I wasn't trying to hide. He'd been drunk and agitated when he'd left, and I'd simply thought it wiser to try to avoid incurring his wrath by following behind.

More bright red crocuses were scattered along the trail, while hundreds of pale green leaves unfurled like banners on outstretched limbs. A gentle breeze blew, fluttering the delicate leaves in the lemon-colored sunshine. Daniel reached the creek ahead of me. When he glanced back, spotted me, and reacted only with indifference, I decided it was all right to approach.

As I came up the steep bank, the cold air hanging over the ice enveloped me. Where the sound of the Conewango shaking free of the ice had been soft and barely audible before, the groaning was now impossible to miss. Shivering, I stood beside Daniel, his grim eyes scanning the frozen twists and turns of the creek.

I started to speak once, but he shushed me, his eyes flitting from place to place along the creek. The eerie groaning gave way to a grinding noise, and Daniel's intense gaze sought out the spot from which it welled up. For a full minute, the grinding increased, until, without warning, a sound like the sharp report of a rifle pierced the air, then echoed along the banks of the creek. Startled, Daniel jerked in surprise and staggered several steps backward. A large crack burst into the center of the ice.

Daniel's face blanched a shade almost as white as the remaining snow.

With the pressure bled away, the eerie groaning ceased, and a silence settled over the cool afternoon. Except for the rupture in its center, the creek looked as immobile, as bound by the ice, as I by my uncertainties. Yet I knew it to be only a matter of time before the creek would break free.

Daniel never spoke, barely moved, and after another few minutes, I left him standing there. Returning to the blockhouse, I was almost inside when the sound of grunting and snorting reached me from the far side. Curious and fearful, I crept along the blockhouse and peered around the corner, but saw nothing.

The loud, determined sounds repeated themselves. My eyes probed the woods bordering the clearing until I spied spouts of dirt erupting from between two trees. As I watched, the white rear of a wolverine lurched into the clearing while more clods of earth flew from between its paws.

About to turn and leave the animal to its foraging, I recalled Daniel saying one of the men—Abe, I thought—was buried back there. Even though I wasn't particularly religious, the thought of the body being dug up and eaten by a wolverine didn't sit well with me. I felt an obligation to at least try to protect the fellow's grave.

Taking a busted plank from the wreckage of the stall, I marched toward the grave. Before I'd even got within twenty feet, the bloodthirsty bugger spun around to bare its razor-sharp teeth at me. Chapman or not, I didn't fancy getting close enough to those teeth to land a blow.

Dropping the plank, I dug the tip of my shoe into the muck until I uncovered several good-sized stones.

My first throw went wide to the left, but the second caught the damned creature square in the back. Instead of fleeing, however, the bugger—a good thirty pounds at least—yelped once, spun around, and to my consternation, lunged toward me uttering a deep-throated, quivering growl.

Picking my way through the mud, I fired off rock after rock. The snarling wolverine, its thick, coarse hair bristling furiously, stood its ground until one large rock careened off its left eye with a sickening thud. Yelping piteously, it finally turned tail and scrambled into the woods.

Keeping a rock at the ready, I apprehensively approached, ready to turn and run should the little demon charge me. It didn't, and I looked where it had been digging. The first thing I spotted was a black cross. It was crude—two branches hastily nailed together—but it was a cross nonetheless. It occurred to me that Abe had been the fellow who had died from the fever, which explained the color of the cross. Black was used to warn others to grave-rob at their own peril.

Knowing nothing of fevers, the wolverine had uncovered the tip of a boot, from which it had already gnawed a sizable chunk. Recalling Daniel's admonishment to stay away from the grave, I took a step back. The fever wasn't something to be taken lightly, even if the body had been buried for nine months.

Standing near his grave, I wondered what Abe had been like, what his reasons for coming to the frontier had been. Was he as moody and peculiar as Daniel, or had he been a more easygoing person that I might have got on well with? I wondered how he'd caught the fever, if his death had been a painful one, and—recalling the collapse of the stall—if it might not yet happen to me.

The cross leaned to one side so that the horizontal branch almost touched the ground. Staying as far away as I could from the actual grave, I kicked dirt over the exposed boot, then circled around to the cross. Crouching down, I straightened it, then happened to look into the shadows just beyond.

Two empty eye sockets stared back at me.

Hollering, I stumbled backward and fell right on top of Abe's grave. Repulsed and frightened, I scrambled away, furiously wiping off my hands and pants. Could I catch the fever just by coming in contact with the grave? It was doubtful, I told myself. Abe had died almost nine months ago, and the body had sat out here all winter. Most likely, the fever was gone.

I shuddered as I stared at the skull. Apparently the wolverine had dug up more than just Abe's boot. Ignoring the fact I was neither Catholic nor religious, I crossed myself. Looking into the shadows, my eyes picked out other bones scattered nearby. Hesitant, but curious, I edged closer. I spied the intricate, pointed bones of an upturned hand attached to a broken forearm. Glancing at my own hand, I made a fist then opened it wide, imagining it stripped of skin and flesh. Doing so left me feeling queer—as if I'd seen something unnatural, something not intended for the eyes of the living.

As my vision continued to adjust to the gloom, I saw strewn all about bits of bone, pieces of cloth, a shoe, and even a buckle.

Something didn't make sense.

Puzzled, I glanced back at Abe's grave. Studying it for a moment, I realized that except for the tip of the one boot, his grave lay undisturbed. I wasn't looking at Abe's skull.

There were two bodies here.

If that first grave was Abe's as Daniel had said, then who the hell was this? I shuddered, quickly stepping away from the half-dug-up corpse. Judging from the shoes and the belt, I figured this to have been a white man. Besides, I had a hard time imagining Daniel taking the time to bury an Indian. Maybe it was one of the soldiers who'd helped build the blockhouse? That made no sense either— none of the pieces of clothing looked at all military, nor could I believe that soldiers would have left one of their own so poorly interred. That only left the three fellows Daniel had said he'd come here with. Abe's fate I knew. Martin, Daniel said, had been taken by Indians and never seen again. And that nasty piece of work, Zach, had left after some sort of disagreement with Daniel.

Unless either Martin or Zach hadn't left the way Daniel told me.

Curious if there were any more graves, I scoured the surrounding woods, but came across nothing—at least not until I gave up and came back. What I saw then wasn't another grave, but the skull that had startled me. Only now, I saw it from behind.

This unfortunate soul hadn't died from the fever. From the fractures radiating outward from the back of his skull, I knew whoever hit him had intended to kill.

Daniel emerged from the woods just as I came around the corner of the blockhouse. As I approached, he paused, narrowed his eyes, and watched me warily like a cat weighing the threat posed by a nearby dog. I knew he wondered what I'd been doing, for if I'd just used the necessary, I would've come around the other corner.

"What are you up to, Chapman?" he asked suspiciously.

"Nothing. See anything interesting at the creek?"

He ignored my question. "Did you just come from the necessary?"

What he really wanted to know was if I was going to lie.

"No," I said as indifferently as possible.

"What were you doing back there then? And how come you look so spooked? You look like you just saw an Indian."

"I don't look spooked. And I didn't see any Indians."

"You saw something though."

"I just stopped by what's left of Bliss's stall, that's all."

"I see," he said, derision replacing suspicion. "Still mooning over that stupid cow?"

Content to let him think that, I shrugged.

"And you think you're a frontiersman."

Two days later, the cross had been knocked over again. Or so I thought at first. I'd gone to check whether the wolverine had returned. It hadn't been there again, but someone—it could only have been Daniel—had. I not only discovered the cross had vanished, but that Abe's grave was now covered with rocks and vines as if to hide it. Even more unsettling, though, was that the skull, the bones, and the pieces of clothing from the second body had vanished entirely.

There had to be an innocent explanation, a logical reason, for what Daniel had done.

I just couldn't think of it.

I returned to the cabin, but hesitated before going in. Taking a deep breath, I tried to make my face a mask of boredom.

"Shut the goddamned door, Chapman," Daniel said drunkenly as I entered. "Window, too."

"But, Daniel, it's so stuffy in here. Do you really want the door shut?"

"Gotta build up the fire as well. Gonna be damned cold t'night," he mumbled, slurring his words. He staggered over to the window, pulled it shut, then wrapped his bearskin around him. With a thud he flopped down by the bubbling still.

Concerned that I do as little as possible to make him suspicious, I said nothing else as I handed him his plate.

"What you doing out there anyway?" he asked, waving the plate away.

"I went to use the necessary."

"Seemed like you were gone a long time."

"My stomach's acting up."

"Oh," was all he said, taking a swig from the flask of whiskey. Morosely, he stared at the flickering flames under the still. "So you're really not going back east, Chapman? You really think you can make it here?"

"I do."

"Well, that's your business, but I got something to tell you. I don't want you settling around here."

"Daniel, I—"

"Not gonna argue with you. This is company property, and I'm in charge no matter what nobody says."

"Fine. I'll leave. I'll go to Franklin. But I still need the supplies."

He shook his head. "Might as well ask me to turn lead into gold. Someone from the goddamned Company will be coming out here this spring. Matter of fact, that's who I thought you were. Sooner or later, somebody got to come to make sure things is going right. Too much damn money involved not to. They check supplies 'gainst who's livin' around here, they'll know stuff's missing."

"Daniel, I don't need much."

"Sorry, Chapman. Got to think of me. Make sure they don't get no more suspicious." He huddled deeper into his bearskin. "Made too many mistakes already. Just know they're gonna be asking questions when they get here."

All I wanted to do was escape. "Then tell them I lied to you, Daniel. That I said I was going to stay, but then I left. How's that sound, Daniel?" He didn't answer me. "Daniel?"

The son of a bitch had passed out again.

For a long time I sat there watching him, trying to think of ways to change his mind. Reason, begging, and threats seemed doubtful. Other than splitting his skull like the one out back, I couldn't think of a way.

To hell with him and his toying with me, I decided then and there. My mind was made up. I'd take what I needed and go.

Daniel had said the way to Franklin was to follow the Conewango to the Allegheny, and the Allegheny would go straight there. All I needed to know now was when the creek would be free enough of ice to be navigable. Checking that Daniel remained passed out, I pulled on my shoes and coat and hurried outside.

A short time later, I stood on the bank of the creek, listening to the ice groan relentlessly. Large cracks now ran from side to side, cold, gray water swirling under the ice. I thought the creek would break up soon, but how soon I didn't know.

Returning, I entered the cabin, surprising Daniel, who wore his coat and held a pistol in his right hand; it happened to point right at my gut. For an instant, he looked at me with an expression of such unadulterated malevolence that I considered turning and fleeing. I thought he was going to kill me where I stood.

"Thought you'd gone, Chapman."

"I went for a walk." I stared nervously at the gun. "What do you mean 'gone'? Where did you think I'd gone to?"

He shrugged. "I wasn't sure."

"You look like you're about to leave yourself."

"I was. To look for you." It sounded more like a threat than a profession of concern.

"With that?" I asked, nodding at the pistol.

"You never know what you might bump into out there, Chapman. Spring coming on, there's a smart chance of running into bears that could kill a man and not leave a trace. A man's family might never know what happened to him."

I thought it possible, even likely, I might vanish out here, but I doubted it would be a bear to do me in. "Seems like you need more than a pistol to stop a bear, doesn't it, Daniel?"

"I reckon I wasn't thinking clearly. Just shows how worried I was—about you."

"I see." I wanted to believe him, but I didn't. "I appreciate your concern. I'm also starving and want to fix something to eat for supper." As nonchalantly as possible I pushed past him, hoping he couldn't see I was trembling.

He watched my every twitch.

"Are you hungry?" I asked.

"No. No, I'm not." At last, he shut the door, propped his pistol on the table, and sank into his bed. He pulled a long swallow of whiskey from his jug, stared vacantly into the ether, then said softly, "I goddamned hate spring."

By the time I had dinner finished, he'd drunk enough to fall into another stupor. I almost made my move then, while there was still at least a little daylight and Daniel was as torpid as a bear in January.

But I was torn, even a little scared. The Conewango wasn't clear of ice, and it wasn't even yet April; I'd no guarantee more snow wouldn't fall. And all I knew about reaching Franklin was to follow the creek. I didn't know how long it might take, how dangerous it might be, or even what I'd find once I got there. I knew this was John talking, and I tried to stiffen my resolve.

Soon it was dark, and I lay curled on my straw in the corner listening to Daniel wheeze in his sleep. Outside, the trees creaked, their branches swinging back and forth, buffeted by winds that had sprung up just after sunset.

What would Daniel have done if he'd found me down by the Conewango? Every time I looked at my hands or closed my eyes, I saw my bones, white and stripped of flesh, like those of the hand the wolverine had dug up. I thought of the graves out back, and then of Daniel sneaking up behind either Martin or Zach and caving in his skull.

I knew what I had to do.

As quietly as possible, I slipped from my bed and edged over to Daniel's. The embers in the fireplace burned low, throwing off barely enough light to make out his face. Satisfied he was still out cold, I lit an oil lamp and silently stole to the shelf where he kept the key to the storeroom. Grabbing a burlap sack, I crept over to the ladder that rose to the opening in the ceiling. The ladder creaked faintly as I climbed, but Daniel slept on, oblivious. Nervous and fumbling, at first I couldn't force the key inside the lock. Finally I did. With a hard twist, the stubborn padlock sprang open and leapt from my grasp. Aghast, I nearly dropped the lamp as I struggled to trap the lock against the wall. I failed, and it tumbled to the floor, where it landed with the softest of thuds. Leaning down, I held out the lamp and saw that it had fallen on a bearskin in the corner.

As Daniel might say, my beshitted nerves were already shot.

Quickly, I clambered up into the storeroom, positioning the

lamp back from the edge of the opening. Closing my eyes, I leaned back against a crate to take a moment to steady myself. Lamplight flickered off the walls as I stared into dim corners. In the weak light, I mostly saw shadows, sharp-cornered boxes, and the curves of barrels disappearing into the dark. Even though I knew I was alone, I felt uneasy—I half-expected Daniel to leap out from the shadows.

Taking the burlap sack, I threw open the nearest box from which I grabbed a handful of short, stubby candles. As fast as possible, I went from box to barrel to sack, taking whatever looked to be useful—soap, twine, flints, and flour. The farther I moved from the lamp, the harder it became to see what was in each.

Inside a small box I came across five or six items the size and heft of a short length of rope, but they felt much silkier than any rope I knew of. Thinking I'd found especially fine thread for sewing and therefore useful for trading, I took several, then heard a creak come from the other side of the room.

It was all I could do to keep myself from calling out Daniel's name. Rigid, I listened for any other noise but heard nothing. Finally, I let out my breath. My imagination was getting the best of me.

The storeroom plunged into darkness.

Despite myself, I took two hurried steps toward the ladder, only to noisily collide with a crate. I cursed myself for my clumsiness. I stopped and squeezed my eyes shut to calm my mind. Realizing I still held the bundles of thread, I jammed them into my pockets. Motionless, I waited in the pitch black, listening for footsteps or someone breathing. I tried to recall if any of the closest crates had held a hammer or pot with which I could defend myself.

Then it occurred to me—the black devil of a lamp had probably run out of oil, that's all. I should have checked how much remained before I'd come up. When after another minute had passed and no other sounds drifted up from the dark, I relaxed a little.

Carefully this time, I made my way back amongst the crates. As I drew close to where the opening should lie, I slowed and began probing the floor ahead with my foot. At last my foot found nothing but open air. Relieved, I crouched down to retrieve the lamp.

It wasn't there. My mouth went as dry as three-week-old johnnycake.

My hand bumped against the base of the lamp.

God Almighty, John, I thought, calm down. You don't remember exactly where you left the lamp and you fall to pieces.

I found the ladder, and using one hand to hold both the sack and the lamp, I made my way back down. Once at the bottom, I listened for the sound of Daniel's snoring, but heard only silence. Had he been snoring before? I struggled to remember. My heart pounded so hard, I almost fancied that it hurt.

I again felt my way around in the dark, trying to find the peg from which my coat hung. Beneath that I would find my pack. My hand had just touched my coat when the room flared into light.

Daniel stood by the fireplace holding a lamp.

Speechless, I stared at him.

"Looking for something in particular up there, John?"

I shook my head.

"Maybe you got lost on your way to the necessary again?"

"No."

He took a step toward me, and my mind's eye foresaw my caved-in skull. "Then what were you looking for?"

"Supplies, Daniel. I was just getting a few supplies."

He looked at me blankly. "Supplies?"

"Yes, supplies. The ones I came here for, but you won't let me have."

A look of understanding crossed his face, and he smiled slyly. "I see. You're a thief then."

"I would've paid you back."

"So you say. I'm not sure the law would see it that way." He laughed. "Out here, I suppose I *am* the law."

"Daniel, all I want is a chance to make it on my own. You can make or break me, we both know that. So I'm asking you, won't you please let me take some supplies?"

"Chapman, you should see the look on your face. You look like a mouse that's been halfway swallowed by a cottonmouth." He wiggled his fingers in front of his face. "I can practically see your little whiskers twitching. Relax. You can have the damned supplies."

"You're serious?"

He shrugged. "I'm tired of looking at you anyway."

I hesitated, disbelieving what I heard, but when I saw that he really seemed to mean it, some of the tension slipped away. I even smiled a little. "I'll leave tomorrow then," I said, my voice filled with relief. "Do you think winter is really over?"

"Probably not. Usually snows at least once in April. Mostly it rains, though. With time, you might decide rain is worse than snow."

I nodded. "I'm exhausted. If you don't mind, I think I'll turn in." A sheepish smile spread across my face as I began undressing for bed. I'd no proof Daniel was responsible for the body that I'd seen. Maybe Abe had caved in the other fellow's skull before succumbing to the fever. Who knew what the truth was? All that mattered was that I would soon be on my way.

Slipping off my breeches, my hand brushed over something lumpy in my pocket, and I pulled out one of the bundles of thread I'd taken from upstairs. In the light, however, it didn't look at all like thread. Puzzled, I held it closer, and then I recognized it. It was glossy black hair—hair with a strip of beaded leather woven into a ponytail that had been hacked off someone's head.

I nearly dropped it.

This could only be one of the ponytails that bastard Zach had hacked off an Indian girl.

But what was Daniel doing with it?

As inconspicuously as possible, I pulled out a second bundle. It, too, was a hacked-off ponytail, but it wasn't black. It was red. Where on earth had Zach gotten this from? Daniel hadn't said anything about Zach's kidnapping white girls. In fact, Daniel's only mention of red hair had been that which belonged to the Boston girl who'd done such a good job of scrubbing his back. Something was wrong. Waves of uneasiness raked through me.

I glanced back at Daniel, who again fussed with his still.

There was something about that Boston girl, something Daniel once said that had seemed unimportant at the time but that nagged at me now. But what? In truth, he hadn't said much about her. Just that she'd been a pox-scarred whore who could do amazing things with her fingers. But there was something else, if I could only remember what. The other sole fact I could dredge up was her hailing from some town in England that Daniel had said he thought so beautiful.

It was something about England, and I almost had it. I thought furiously.

Daniel was Irish, and being so, he was sworn to hate England and all things English. In fact, he claimed he'd never been to England. But he had.

Suddenly I understood everything. I glanced from the red hair to Daniel.

Not only wasn't Daniel Irish, he wasn't even Daniel. Daniel was Zach.

Only now did I let the braid fall to the floor. The instant it hit the ground, I knew I'd made a terrible mistake. If he saw the braid, he'd know I'd found him out, and I'd never get out of Warren alive.

As casually as possible, I crouched down to retrieve the hair.

"Something wrong, Chapman?"

"No."

"What's that in your hand?"

"Nothing. Just some rope."

"From upstairs?"

"Yes."

"Odd. The only rope I recall being up there were the big, thick coils. Let me see."

"I'm exhausted, Daniel. I think I'll turn in."

He rose and strode to where I stood. "That's fine, but let me see the rope first."

"Well, it's more like bundles of thread than rope," I said, laying the ponytail on the table.

"Oh, that," he said with a laugh. He picked the hair up and began caressing it. "What's the matter, Chapman? You've got that half-eaten-mouse look again."

"Nothing."

"Good. Because I can explain this."

"Daniel—"

Before I knew what happened, he grabbed me by the back of the neck, spun me around, and smashed my forehead against the wall. Dazed, I tried to stay upright but collapsed to the floor. Blood trickled down my face.

"Had to be a damned busybody, didn't you, Chapman?"

"Daniel, I—"

His foot caught me square in the gut. "Not Daniel, imbecile—Zach. I expect even you have finally figured that out by now. You can't imagine how sick I am of being called by that son of a bitch's name." He crouched down and stared at my contorted face. "Christ, I can't believe I *ever* thought you were someone to fear. I should've just killed you in November and been done with it."

I crawled away from him and used the table to pull myself up.

"When did you figure it out?"

Sucking in air, I said, "Figure what out? I don't know—"

This time he hit me across the face. The blow sent me tumbling over the table and onto the floor. At least now I had the table between us.

He leaned menacingly across the table. "I asked when you figured it out."

"Why does it matter?" I struggled to stand.

"Because, fool, others are going to be arriving soon, and I don't want to make whatever mistake with them that I did with you."

"Why should I tell you? I *want* them to figure out what a bastard you are."

"Because if you don't, you're going to die very painfully and slowly. I might even use you for bear bait. They like their prey alive."

I knew he'd do it, too.

"I realized it only now, when I saw the hair. But I should've known sooner. You look and sound as Irish as I do Russian."

"But I told you I left Ireland when I was four."

"Still, your parents would've sounded Irish, and I've never heard of an Irishman who didn't spend most of his time with his countrymen. You should've had at least a bit of an accent." I moved away as he slowly circled the table toward me.

"What else? I reckon there has to be more than just that."

"There was the whore you visited in Boston."

"What about her?"

"You said she was from England. Greenhead, I think. You said it was beautiful country, and that you missed it. But you also said you'd never been to England, that you sailed directly to America from Dublin."

"Stupid mistake. I won't make that one again."

I wiped away blood that was running into my eye. "Maybe not that one, but you will make others."

"You're going to hell, Chapman, and I'm going to be the one to send you there."

"Haven't you killed enough people, Zach? Even you must worry a little about your soul. I'll make you a deal—I swear I won't say anything. Let me leave tonight. I'll head west, and you'll never see me again."

He shook his head. "That's just what Daniel said. Said he would take his chances and move further west. And you know what? I figure he would have kept his word, seeing as he had a shrew of a wife and a brat back east he didn't particularly care to be saddled with." He circled back the other way, keeping himself between me and the door.

I had to keep him talking. "So why did you kill him?"

"Because," he snarled, "he was a goddamned shitter of a know-it-all." He pounded his hand against his chest. "*I* was the one who had spent years living out here. Me, not him. *I* was the one who should have run this place from the beginning. Daniel McQuay was a fat, fucking, filthy Irishman who wasn't fit to drink my piss." Zach stopped, ran his hand through his hair, and took a deep breath. "Besides, I enjoyed caving in the back of his head, then watching him try to crawl across the clearing. Of course, I had to drag him back from the woods three times before he finally had the decency to stop breathing."

"Zach, I promise I won't say anything."

"Oh, I know you won't, Chapman," he said ominously.

"Zach, let's talk about—"

Before I could finish, he flipped over the table as easily as if flipping the page of a book. The rest of the dishes, the lamp, a tomahawk I'd taken, everything went crashing to the floor. The lamp went out, plunging the cabin into darkness.

Desperate to buy time as I tried to maneuver toward the door, I said, "There are other mistakes you made, Zach."

"Liar. I know what you're trying to do, Chapman."

Moving as quietly as possible, I began singing, "Miss Plover from Dover, I banged in the clover. How often, Captain Grover? Over and over! Miss Plover from Dover I banged—"

"Shut up!"

I listened to the sound of his breathing in the dark. "Sometimes when you're drunk, you sing that same English song again and again. Any real Irishman would rather cut out his tongue than sing an English song."

"To bloody hell with the Irish! A filthier people never soiled God's green earth! I tell you what; scalping that Irish whore felt better than actually flourishing the bitch. And as far as the drinking, I'll watch myself, that's what."

I laughed out loud as I edged farther along the wall. "That's a fine plan. Judging from what I've seen of your self-control this winter, I don't fancy you're going to have much success in staying sober."

I thought the door now stood about ten feet in front of me and a bit to the left. Three steps and I'd reach it. Before I could move, I heard him rush toward me. Despite the dark, he crashed into me, driving us both backward. Slamming into the wall with a grunt, I staggered a moment before sinking to my knees. He must not have realized I'd fallen, for he now flailed about, cursing as he tried to find me.

Desperately, I groped about the floor to find something to use as a weapon.

All sound ceased as he stopped to listen for where I hid. I froze, waiting for him to move. My hand brushed against the upturned leg of the table.

"Now, John, come on," he cajoled. "You know I can make good on my promise—this can be quick and easy, or slow and painful. Ask those girls whose ponytails you found." He paused and laughed. "Or ask Daniel McQuay." He took another step forward, promptly banging into the table.

"Goddamn it!" he shouted. "All right, that's it—where the beshitted hell are you, Chapman? I'll burn the goddamned place down if I have to. Don't think I won't."

He rushed forward blindly. His knee caught me in my side, but it seemed to take him by surprise as much as it did me, and he went stumbling forward. For a moment, we each frantically scrambled around in the dark. Then he grabbed a handful of my hair and yanked hard. Searing pain shot through my head. Howling, I tried clawing at his hand while lashing out with my feet, trying to kick his legs out from under him. Over and over, I hollered, until he smashed his fist across my mouth.

Dazed, I could only gasp as he grabbed me by my shirt with one hand, the waist of my breeches with the other, and sent me hurtling through the air. Stunned, I crashed down onto his bed. Before I could even try to escape or strike out, he scrambled on top of me, pinning me to the bed.

"Zach!" I started to plead but was cut off by a foul-tasting cloth shoved into my mouth; I had to fight not to gag as I struggled to breathe. One at a time, he wrenched my arms above my head, then clutched them there with one hand.

When he first started to undo the waist of my breeches, I didn't understand what was happening. It was only when he began undoing his own that I understood.

Terrified, I wrenched my shoulders and hips back and forth but to no avail. He only squeezed my hands harder until the pain became so sharp that I expected to hear bones break. I stopped fighting. He jerked up my shirt. My stomach and chest prickled at the touch of the cold air.

Making small grunts at first, he began grinding his hips against my body, his hardening cock sliding up and down my belly with each thrust. Each time he rammed against me, his thigh crushed my balls against my body. I closed my eyes as tears came to them, and I longed to cry out. Suddenly, he stopped.

Opening my eyes, I swore I felt him watching me in the dark, quivering with anticipation or rage, or maybe both. I heard him spit into his hand, then I turned away as he forced my legs apart. Several times I'd tried to let him enter me, but it had always been too painful, and he'd stopped. Not now. Grunting, he pressed himself against me, then, as a stabbing pain shot up through my body, he forced himself inside me.

I would've gladly killed him then.

He began to grind and ram into me over and over. With each passing thrust, he moved harder and harder so that my head banged against the wall just behind me. The sweat that began to slicken our two bodies only increased the urgency with which he frantically pumped against me. I felt as if I were being ripped in two. The top of my head began to throb from banging against the wall. As his grunts became groans, I felt his hand loosen around my wrists.

I had an idea.

Driving himself hard against me, Zach's grip continued to loosen the closer he came to climaxing. Just before I thought he was reaching his hateful release, I wrapped my legs around his waist, yanked my hands free to grab his breeches by the waist, and with one frantic motion as he jerked forward, used all of the strength in my arms and legs to propel his body forward as hard as possible into the wall behind me.

His head smashed into the wall with the satisfying crunch of bone meeting oak. He gasped once and slumped against me.

Ripping the gag from my mouth, I flung it away as hard as I could. For a moment, I lay there panting and sobbing, stunned and unable to move as Zach lay on top of me.

Then the anger hit. With a scream, I heaved his unconscious body onto the floor, sprang from the bed, and began kicking his inert form as hard as I could.

Only the sound of a rib breaking brought me up short. Gasping, I stopped, my whole body trembling, but poised to lash out again if he moved at all.

He lay there as if dead.

I pulled up my pants, then scrambled about to find a lamp to light. Once I could see, I gathered the burlap sack, the tomahawk, and for good measure I took Zach's best boots and skinning knife. As soon as I had everything, I looked once more at the crumpled form of the man who had gone from being my savior to lover to would-be executioner.

The oil lamp I'd lit sat on his bed; for a moment, I considered turning it over.

I extinguished the flame, opened the door, and vanished into the night.

Chapman was gone for good. But I knew for a fact I couldn't be John again either.

EIGHT

Ash Hodges thought I hated him. He couldn't have been more mistaken, though it was understandable he thought so. After all, I couldn't bear to be near him.

I was eleven, and Ash thirteen, when being with him first made me understand the other boys' hoarse whispers of the thoughts they had about girls. I had those thoughts about Ash.

Being near Ash all but caused me physical pain, not to mention the fear of giving myself away. Whenever he spoke to me, I mumbled one-word responses and turned away, unable to look into his eyes for fear of what he might see in mine. Ash, unlike so many older boys, didn't pick on those of us who were younger. In fact, he taught two of my brothers how to swim and fish and hunt. Even worse, he seemed pained by my rejection of him.

It wasn't Ash I hated, it was only myself, at least at first. But maybe in the end, Ash was right. Maybe I did hate him. After all, if left too long, the jug of wine turns into the bottle of vinegar.

April 1798

A STINGING SLEET LASHED DOWN FROM THE COLD, GRAY SKY. ZACH HAD warned me I might come to hate rain more than snow. He was right. God only knew how many weeks and leagues had passed since I'd fled Warren and the nightmare Zach had wrought on me. And God only knew how many more might yet pass before I reached Franklin.

Or if I would.

Just ahead the Allegheny funneled into a short but narrow ravine, its rocky sides far too steep to allow me to pass. Along most of the stretch behind me, the river already flowed free, but in this shaded cleft, the sun had yet to sweep away the ice.

High above either side of the river, stony ridges vanished into the mist. Leaving the river to climb them might take weeks and meant facing the very real chance of losing my way, or wrenching an ankle and dying from exposure on their exposed heights. Given my diminishing supplies and strength, I had no choice but to dare the ice.

It would only take a minute to dash across, no more, but if the ice gave way beneath me, I might easily drown.

After enduring a winter akin to an eternity, I found the idea of deciding my fate in a matter of moments oddly appealing.

Taking a fallen limb, I probed the ice as far out as I could reach. It resisted my jabs well enough. Taking a deep breath, I stepped onto the ice.

It seemed to give or bounce a little with each step I took, and I wished it felt more solid. Quickly, I headed downstream, slipping once and nearly tumbling to the ice. Halfway to the end of the ravine, the ice began to groan, then creak. I recognized the eerie sound from watching the ice buckle with Zach.

My heart pounded. Three-quarters of the way across, I heard the first earsplitting cracks as the ice gave way behind me. I broke into a full-out sprint.

My foot caught on a ridge of ice and I stumbled, falling to one knee before I regained my balance. Fissures split the creek's surface to my left. The footing, already arduous, became downright treacherous as water surged onto the ice. I dashed for the shore. Ten feet from the bank, the ice collapsed beneath me. Desperately, I grasped at the slick stones of the ravine, but I couldn't hold on.

I plunged into the water.

As my arms flailed about, my feet sought purchase on the rocky bottom of the river. The cold was such a shock that for a moment I simply stood there gasping. It took a moment to realize the water came no higher than a new candle's length above my waist. The water stung furiously, prodding me to struggle forward, breaking through the remaining ice with my fists. Shaking uncontrollably, I reached the far side and, with all of my strength, heaved myself upward.

Immediately something yanked me back. Wrenching my head around, I could just see a sunken tree limb that had snagged one of the straps of my pack. Panicked, I lunged forward, determined to yank the straps free. Instead, with a sickening rip, the straps tore loose, and my supplies spilled into the water as I crashed onto the bank.

Scrambling upright, I slid back into the river. Desperately, I plunged my arms under the surface again and again, vainly searching for anything the river hadn't swept away. I fought to keep my balance against the urgently flowing current, my arms and fingers so cold that they burned each time I pulled them empty-handed from the water.

My pack had vanished, swallowed by the rushing water, and my whole life seemed a cruel joke.

Stunned, I clambered from the frigid water and stood shivering on the bank. Only the purl of the river broke the cool silence.

Eventually, I realized I had to move or die, but I didn't much care which. Dying soon was beginning to seem more and more inevitable. At last, I started walking, and that at least helped to quicken the flow of blood to my arms and legs. As I passed from the ravine, a knife-edged breeze snapped along between the banks of the river, threatening to freeze my clothes to my skin.

Unable to think clearly, I didn't know where I was heading, only that I had to keep moving until I could go no farther. I had a sinking feeling it wouldn't take me long to reach that point.

Someone kicked my foot, and I opened my eyes. It was night. Thinking it all a dream, I stared up indifferently at the hooded figure standing by my feet. He kicked me again, harder this time, and I realized I was, in fact, awake.

In the dark, I could see nothing of his face, only that he wore a cloak and a cowl like a thief. Or death.

"What?" I mumbled. "Do you want to rob me? Well, I have nothing to steal."

The figure said nothing.

"Do you talk?" I demanded, now half out of my mind with fear. "Say something, dammit! What the hell do you want?"

A small hand darted out from the cape, flipping back the cowl. The round cheeks, small mouth, and dark eyes of an Indian woman gazed back at me. A long braid of black hair fell over her left shoulder. She looked from me to the river, twice motioning with her head in its direction. She took two steps away, repeated the gesture, and stared at me knowingly.

What the hell, I thought as I staggered wearily to my feet.

The Indian woman set a fast pace, and I struggled to keep up. For several hours, we walked in silence, until we stopped without warning. From under her cloak, she produced a pouch from which she removed several pieces of jerky, a handful of dried berries, and mushrooms of some sort. She appeared not to have much even for one, and at first I refused. Thrusting them into my hands, she foraged alongside the trail and in only a few minutes produced several handfuls of plants that I didn't recognize. I gave in and ate.

Our quick pace had warmed me more than I realized; now that we'd stopped, my sweat quickly cooled, and I began to shiver. I offered no protest when the woman rose, took off her cloak, and draped it over my shoulders. Sitting again, she continued to eat, neither the cold nor the rain seeming to affect her tranquil demeanor.

With the moon hidden behind the thick clouds, I could tell neither what time it might be nor get a particularly good look at my benefactor. My strongest impressions thus far were that she was young, but not girlish, and very tough. I wondered where we were going and what would happen when we arrived. Perhaps we were headed for an Indian village. The thought gave me pause—images of whites being scalped alive bedeviled my mind. But since no one else had rescued me and since I had nowhere else to go, I shoved the thought aside.

"Thank you," I said when we'd finished eating. "For both the food and help." I hoped she spoke at least some English.

She glanced at me, but still said nothing.

"Where are we going? If you don't mind my asking."

She drank from a flask, handed it to me, and after I drank the sweet, slightly fermented cider, she returned both it and her pouch to someplace under her dress. Without a word, she rose and resumed walking.

Apparently, I would find out when we got there.

Under the starless sky, I lost track of time, and only the roseate glow of dawn in the east told me morning approached. Sometime shortly after sunrise, we left the Allegheny and descended into a valley bisected by a good-sized creek. At first the tree-covered sides of the valley crowded in against us, but gradually both trees and hills retreated, leaving me to walk through what I imagined would, one day soon, be flower-filled meadows. The valley continued to widen, as did the creek, almost a river by now. Again, I wondered where she was taking me.

When we next paused, she motioned for me to return her cloak. Embarrassed at not having offered to do so sooner, I sheepishly handed it back to her. With a snap, she whipped it into the air, set-tling it over her shoulders as gently as falling snow. Fastening it around her neck, she nodded at something behind me. I turned to look, but in the mist and shadows of the burgeoning dawn, I saw nothing. Then an unnatural shape—a sharp corner—did catch my eye. Tucked up against the darkened hillside stood a small cabin. No lights shone in the windows, no smoke curled up from the chimney. This must be where the woman lived.

When I turned to ask her, she had already begun walking away. "Wait!" I called out, scurrying after her.

Turning, she faced me, her hands shooing me away like a small child.

I stopped. "But don't you live here? If not, who does? What am I supposed to do?" I stepped toward her.

Once more she shooed me back, and I had a vision of her pelting me with rocks the way one did to drive away a stray dog.

I turned and slowly walked back toward the darkened cabin. Even though she had saved me, I cursed her now for leaving me. Had she ever met the people who lived here? Did she know how they might react to a stranger appearing in their midst?

Having experienced Zach's extreme reaction to my appearing from nowhere, my reluctance to approach this cabin was palpable. Waiting to see who lived there, I hid behind a tree, watching, waiting for someone to light a lamp, start a fire, or at least to come outside to relieve himself. No one did.

I knew I had to do something. Bracing myself, I marched up to the door—making sure my empty hands were visible—and thumped on it loudly. Then I held my breath as I waited. No one answered.

"Hello?" I called out, knocking again. "I mean no harm. Someone brought me here." I decided not to mention it had been an Indian. When I still received no response, I pushed open the door, waited a moment longer, then stepped inside. In the near total dark, I peered around, but saw nothing. Fumbling my way forward, I found a table and, after a few more minutes searching, a lamp and flint. It took several tries for the lamp to catch and throw out a smoky light. Turning in a cautious circle, I held the lamp in front of me. All I saw were shadows dancing against the walls.

"Jesus!" I hollered, spotting two figures hugging the wall. I dropped the lamp, snuffing the light. I said nothing, not moving, barely breathing. "I truly mean you no harm," I said at last, but the dark gave no response.

Carefully, I felt for the lamp, made my way back to the table, and lit it again. I laughed out loud. I'd been startled by a man's hunting shirt and a woman's nightgown, each hanging from a peg on the wall. Beneath the shirt stood a pair of boots.

For several minutes, I sat at the rough table in the center of the room, drumming my fingers on the table as I decided how to proceed. Looking about me, I saw shelves well stocked with bags and jars. Firewood sat neatly stacked next to the fireplace. Dirty dishes rested in a wooden tub. Several braids of onions and a spoiled squash—black and collapsed in on itself—were suspended from a hook in the corner. A large black kettle, a ladle resting inside, was perched in the ashpit of the fireplace, while a baby crib sat next to an unmade bed strewn with nightclothes.

A fine layer of dust covered everything. Even the spiderwebs in the corner were dusty and tattered. The owners were gone, and they looked to have left in one hell of a hurry.

Finally hunger overcame my reluctance to take what wasn't mine, and I rifled through the bags, finding cornmeal, flour, salt, pepper, and sugar. Along the wall were numerous bags of barley seeds, corn, wheat, pumpkin, squash, and even a bag of apple seeds. Unfortunately, mice had got into several bags, destroying much, though not all, of the barley, wheat, and squash. The mice, it appeared, had no taste for apple seeds. In the tins were jerky, bear fat, and hardtack. Plus there were dried apples, nuts, and even a bumkin of cider.

Within a half hour, a fire blazed as I prepared pemmican, hominy, and johnnycakes—the first hot food I'd eaten in weeks. When I could eat no more, I crawled into bed, pulled the blanket up over my head, and slept like a bear a month late for hibernation.

The following morning, the coffee had begun to boil, the lid of the pot banging about, when the cabin door burst open.

"Alexander! Catherine! What happened? Where have you . . ."

The cup in my hand clattered to the floor.

A large man stood in the doorway, staring at me with a puzzled expression.

"What the hell? You're not Alexander."

Pressing my spine against the back wall, I stammered, "I . . . I didn't steal anything. I'll replace what I ate. I promise."

As I spoke, the man seemed to deflate. He stepped all the way into the cabin, pulled out a chair, and sat.

"We thought you were Alexander and Catherine. Thomas saw the smoke and he . . ." His voice trailed off as he flung his hat across the room.

I took a deep breath, but immediately regretted it when he looked over at me.

"What's your name, son?"

"Chapman. John Chapman."

"My name's George Chase." He nodded at the fireplace. "Is that coffee I smell?"

I nodded.

"I'll have a cup, if you don't mind," he said, slipping off his coat.

"Of course not."

As I poured the coffee, I got my first good look at him, and all I could think was that he was built as much like a draft horse as anything else. His shoulders were broad and thick with muscle, his neck as solid-looking as a good-sized tree trunk. Massive hands extended from meaty forearms that were nearly as wide. Only his legs were normal-sized, giving him a top-heavy look. And despite his bald head, he sported tremendous white muttonchops and a bushy white mustache yellowed with tobacco smoke. His eyes were deep blue, the color all the more pronounced for the sea of white on top of which they seemed to float.

Handing him the coffee, I said, "I didn't mean to trespass. I was only—"

"I don't care. It don't matter. It's hardly trespassing if a place doesn't belong to no one anymore."

I sat down across from him.

"It's just that I've prayed so hard that they might have made it," he said.

"Alexander and Catherine?"

"And the baby." He smiled ruefully. "Of course, you have no idea what I'm talking about."

"Were you related?"

"No. Just friends, good friends. Such a nice young couple. The kind of people Franklin needs to thrive."

"Did you say Franklin?" I was hardly able to believe it possible.

"Yes."

"This is Franklin?"

"Not here exactly. The town proper is a day's walk south of here, where this creek joins the Allegheny, but I think of the whole valley as Franklin. Have you heard of it?"

"Yes," I said hesitantly, and his entire face brightened.

"So people are already talking about us. That's good, real good."

That Indian woman had led me right to Franklin. If she hadn't found me, I might have missed it entirely. Hell, if she hadn't found me, I'd be dead now.

Aware of George watching me, I said, "Had they been here long?"

"No. They arrived last May, staked this claim. Catherine was already pregnant when they got here. Gave birth to Isaiah in November. He was a sickly child right from the beginning. Course she was near frantic with worry. End of December—when the snows were the worst—Catherine insisted they leave Franklin and go for a doctor. Thomas, Alexander, me—even Gwennie—all tried to talk her out of it."

"How far to the nearest doctor?"

"Hell, as far away as Pittsburgh for all I know. But definitely somewhere back east. Anyway, Catherine threatened to go alone if Alexander wouldn't take her. Most people love their children, but sometimes nature just has to take its course. Catherine couldn't see that, though—no surprise there. You see, they had been trying to have a child for years, and after she gave birth to Isaiah, Gwennie had said there couldn't be any more." He sipped his coffee.

"So despite the cold and the snow," George continued, "they grabbed a few things, took their horse, and went. Thomas rode with them till the end of the first day, then pleaded with them one last time to come back. They wouldn't, and Thomas wasn't no fool—he knows the sun rises whether you watch or not—so he came back alone. A week later, their horse turned up by itself." George sighed. "My thinking they'd come back was a foolish hope, I know, but when Thomas saw the smoke . . ."

"I'm sorry."

He drew himself up, tried to smile, and said, "Enough about what can't be undone. Tell me about yourself, John Chapman."

My shoulders tensed. "There isn't much to tell really."

"Are you here by yourself?"

"Yes."

"Not married?"

"No."

"I understand that all too well—not many women who are prepared to raise a family in the frontier. But don't worry. I can already think of one young lady a fellow looking to marry should meet."

"Oh . . . really?" When he glanced down at my feet, I realized I was tapping my foot on the floor.

"Come to think of it, maybe your being here is Providence."

"What do you mean?"

"First, tell me how you came to this place, and if I'm right, you'll see what I mean."

Quickly, I had to decide how much to tell him. "On my way here, I had an accident and got lost. I thought I was going to die."

"Haven't we all out here? And I admire your honesty in admitting you thought you'd perish. A lot of men wouldn't do that. What happened? If you don't mind my asking."

Recalling how I'd lost my pack in the river, I decided on the spot, if a pack, why not a horse?

"I was trying to ford a river on my horse. I'd thought most of the ice was gone so we'd be safe, but just as we were halfway across, a fair-sized chunk, ten feet or so wide, caught . . . Zach smack in the head. I barely had time to get my hands free of the reins before the poor thing had gone under." I was amazed—and a little distressed—at how easily the lie came to me.

"That's terrible, son. And you lost all of your supplies?"

I nodded.

"How long ago did this happen?"

I thought back to the day I'd fallen in the river. "Three days ago." At least that was true.

"And you found your way here?" He let out a whistle. "That's

Providence—the Good Lord meant for you to be here. Not that you don't deserve credit yourself. A lot of fellows would have lain down and died. You're one tough, capable young man, John Chapman. Exactly the sort we need in Franklin."

We'd only been talking a few minutes, and he already thought I was somebody I utterly wasn't. I realized my foot was tapping again.

"Well, it's clear to see what has to be done," he said. "I've my own claim and plenty of supplies already. You should take over this claim."

"I couldn't."

"Course you could. Like I said before, your being here is obviously Providence—just the fact that you found this place on your own proves it."

I started to speak, to tell him about the Indian woman, but I held back. I didn't know how he might feel about Indians, nor did I particularly want him to think less of me.

"I'm not a Calvinist," George said, "so I don't know if the Lord intended you to have this place from the day you were birthed, or if He is just trying to make something good come of a tragedy. From what you told me, though, it's evident to me that your role here is to make this land productive."

"But, George, I can't just take something without paying for it, and right now I have nothing."

"But don't you see, son? Alexander and Catherine had no other family that I know of, so there is no one for you to pay. This way the land still gets plowed and planted and Franklin keeps growing— that's what's most important to the rest of us. Losing Alexander was bad, terrible even, but having this land sit idle as well would be salt in my eyes."

"Why would that be so bad?"

Rising as he spoke, George became more animated with each word. "Someday, not too many years from now, the Good Lord willing, this area will be organized into a county, and of course, a county needs a county seat. I founded Franklin—that's my father's name, by the way—with the intention that someday it would be that county seat, maybe even more than that. But"—he fingered a gap between two logs in the wall—"there are two other settlements near the same size as Franklin south and east of here, and every settler, every cabin, every acre plowed, strengthens the chance for Franklin to be the county seat." He stopped pacing and stood right above me. "So you see, you have to do this. It's what Alexander and Catherine would want. It's what the Lord wants."

"All right, George," I said, giving in because it was by far the easiest thing to do.

"That's the way, son," he said, pulling on his coat.

So I finally had a claim of my own, though I couldn't help but worry. For if George could decide so easily that the Lord meant for me to have this claim, I had a suspicion George could also decide if the Lord wanted to take it away.

"So where did you winter over?" he asked, disrupting my thoughts.

I almost answered Warren before I caught myself and lied, "Back east." And he'd very nearly left without asking too many questions!

He smiled indulgently. "Well, son, I didn't think you'd come from treating with Indians in the Ohio Territory. Wherever you come from, it couldn't have been too far from here for you to have arrived so early."

"It was a small place, somewhere you've probably never heard of." I felt trapped, as if anything I said might raise suspicions.

"Shit, son, I know western Pennsylvania better than a baby knows its mother's titties. Try me."

"It was called . . . Monroe."

He frowned, then said, "That is peculiar. I've never heard of it."

"I suppose you've heard of every town in Pennsylvania?"

"Course not." For the first time I heard suspicion in his voice. "But as I said, I do know most everything in the western half."

"Well," I said, more sharply than I meant, "Monroe must be far enough east that you don't know it." I knew it was foolish to speak to him this way, but I was tired of being peppered with questions, having to explain myself and fend off other people's notions of what I should be doing.

George stared at me for a moment, then said, "You know, son,

I'm not the one who appeared from nowhere and came unbidden into someone else's cabin. And if I were, I think I'd be careful how I spoke to anybody I just met. See, I wouldn't want them to get the wrong idea about what kind of person I was. Especially if I was planning on staying any length of time. Now if I was planning on moving on soon, I suppose it doesn't matter as much, except that you might find yourself moving on sooner than expected." He opened the door and stepped outside.

"Do you want me to leave?" I asked, following him out.

He looked puzzled. "Didn't say I did. Let me tell you a quick story. Years ago I found myself a starving stray dog that I took in. Now that dog had been hit and kicked by so many unpleasant souls that by the time I got him, it took me weeks before he'd let me get within four feet without his growling as if I weren't Old Scratch himself." George mounted his horse.

"And I suppose I remind you of him."

"For your sake, I hope not," he said, shaking his head as he nudged his horse to a walk. "The mean ol' bastard kept trying so hard to bite me, I finally had to shoot him."

Craving eggs for breakfast the following morning, I found several robins' nests in the trees behind the cabin. After plucking the last egg from a wobbly nest, I lowered myself to the ground, carefully cradling the eggs against my chest.

"Hope those are chevet eggs," said a voice from behind.

The unexpected sound of another person startled me so badly that I yelped and lurched forward, dropping all of the eggs. Annoyed, I turned and found myself facing a man as tall and thin as a white spruce.

"Startled you, didn't I?" he asked, possessing an obvious bent for understatement. He sat astride a decrepit horse almost as skinny and bony as he. I decided on the spot I didn't like him.

"As a matter of fact, you did."

"Sorry about the eggs. You're all right, I hope?"

"I'm fine."

"So were they?"

"Were they what?"

"Chevet eggs. Nasty birds. Every morning I got whole flocks of those big black bastards caw-cawing around my place."

"Well, they weren't. Sorry to disappoint you." Brushing the dirt from my hands, I studied his appearance. He had black, curly hair, a thin, narrow face—once again, not unlike the animal he rode—and a rather dark, olive complexion, as if he spent a great deal of time outdoors. Given that winter had just ended, I wondered how he had gotten dark so quickly.

He slipped down from the horse, which immediately wandered over to the edge of the lush meadow and began to graze. We both watched her, listening to the gentle rip of grass being torn from the ground.

"It's called kwenaskat," he said. "At least that's the Delaware word for it. The Mingo must have called it something else."

"The horse?"

"No, not the horse. She's a nag in any tongue. I was talking about the grass, though white folk call it river grass." He walked to where the horse stood.

"Kwen-a-skat?" I repeated as I followed.

"Kwe-nas-kat. It means tall grass or brokenstraw. It almost fills this entire claim."

"Do you know how much land belongs to this claim?"

"See that bend?" The thin man pointed south to where the river curved out of sight. I nodded. "That's where it starts. And it stops at the north end of the valley. It's a good-sized claim, and like I said, the grass fills almost all of it. It's one of the reasons Alexander knew this claim would be good." He paused. "Of course, I knew it as well."

I reached down to break off a handful of the grass. The blades were wide but thin; a sweet smell exuded from the broken stems. "Do you speak Delaware?" I asked.

"Actually, it's Lenni-Lenape."

"What?"

"Lenni-Lenape—that's what the Delaware call themselves. It means 'original people.'"

"Oh. Well, do you speak it?"

"A few words here and there."

"What about Mingo? Do you speak that?"

"No."

"But the Mingo live around here?"

"Not anymore. With the Eastern tribes—like the Delaware—getting pushed further west, the tribes here either have to live more crowded than they like, fight to keep their land, or move further west. The Mingo mostly moved."

"I see." I hadn't given much thought to the fact that I might be settling on land somebody already lived on, even if they were Indians.

"I'm Thomas Martin," he said, interrupting my thoughts. This then was the fellow who had gone off with Alexander to try to get him to turn back.

"John Chapman," I said, and we shook hands.

He bent down to pluck a blade of grass. "Kwenaskat and new settlers are always one of the first signs of spring." He began chewing on the grass. "Both seem to be awful early this year."

I glanced up at the sky. "Is it always this hot in April?"

"Nah. That's another strange thing. After that terrible winter, I'm expecting an even worse summer. I've got a premonition about this year."

"A premonition of what?"

"You know the saying that dead dogs don't bite?"

I nodded.

"Well, I've a feeling there are some dogs out there that should be dead but aren't."

Was Thomas referring to Alexander? Was this a hint to reconsider taking over his friend's claim in case Alexander had survived?

"Are you expecting to be bitten by one of these dead dogs?" I asked. "Or is it me who should be careful?"

"It's me I'm talking about. I'm just hoping it's a dog I know something about."

"Is that right?" Now he sounded as if he were running from something. I wondered what. What was it about these people and their queer mentions of dogs?

He laughed. "Don't pay me any mind. I expect you probably think I'm as cracked as one of those busted eggs."

"No, not at all. Can I ask you something?"

"Sure."

"Why do the Len . . . ni-Len . . . nipe call the grass brokenstraw?"

He smiled. "It's Len-ni Le-na-pe. Because by fall it turns the most amazing hue of gold as well as getting so tall and top-heavy that it snaps at the base and falls over." He held up his finger, then snapped it downward. "Brokenstraw. Then next spring it does the whole thing over again. It's tough, too—doesn't matter if the creek floods for weeks, or if rain doesn't fall for a month—nothing hurts it. And it grows faster than anything I've ever seen. That's why most settlers hate it, even though it means the ground is fertile."

He crouched down, plucked a blade, and stuck it between his teeth.

"By fall, it'll reach my shoulders," he continued. "And when you stand in the middle, it makes a lovely sound when the wind rustles the blades up against each other. It's like the earth itself is whispering secrets. Or leastwise, it would have sounded like that."

The ardent way he spoke made me suddenly yearn to see this golden grass.

He glanced over at me and grinned sheepishly. "Lord, would you listen to me babbling on like some vainglorious poet."

"You said the grass *would have* sounded like that. Why won't it?"

"Because you're going to plow and plant it. At least that's what George told me."

"You know George?"

"Course I know him. You can't live in Franklin and not know George any more than you can drink and not have to piss." His tone made it sound as if he wasn't exactly happy about knowing George. "I shouldn't have said that," he added quickly with downcast eyes. If he weren't so dark, I imagined I would see him blush. "Don't repeat that, will you?" he implored. "George has been good to me, and sometimes I forget."

"I won't say a word. How big is Franklin?"

"How big did George say it was?"

"He didn't."

"That's unusual," he remarked, quickly reverting to his previous barbed tone. "Well, between you and me, Franklin's barely a town no matter what George says. Ed Hale, the Chadwicks, and George all have claims. George's sister's family—the Baxters—arrived last week. Let's see. In Franklin itself, there's a smokehouse, a barn, and a blockhouse in case Indians attack, but precious little else. Not much for a future county seat."

"George mentioned that."

"I bet he did. That's what he's counting on happening. But I tell you what: Franklin is to a town what a newborn is to an adult—a start, but just as likely to die in infancy as to reach manhood. George Chase dreams big, but I suspect he fails even bigger."

"Given that he founded the town, I can see why he's so concerned." Thomas's bitterness made me nervous. He was like a poisonous plant that I wanted to avoid brushing against.

"You've no idea what concerned is."

"What do you mean?"

He ignored the question. "So George told you he founded Franklin?"

I nodded.

"That's what he tells everyone, and I suppose he sort of did. He founded *Franklin,* what this place is currently called, but the Frenchies were really the first white men here. They built a fort called Fort Venango. What's left of it is south of here—and not more than a healthy piss past Franklin. But since it is a little downstream, George can say he founded Franklin. Before the Frenchies, there was a Lenni-Lenape village, but not even the few Indians left remember what it was called."

"Where do you live, Thomas?"

"Just down the valley. You pass my place on the way into Franklin. You can miss it."

"You mean, I *can't* miss it."

"No, I mean you *can* miss it. It's small, crappy land, not worth much, and since it sits back in a hollow, it's hard to find."

I wondered why he hadn't taken this claim, especially since he admired it so. "Are you farming?"

"No. That's not what *Providence* meant for me to do in Franklin," he said with obvious rancor at whatever role George thought Providence had allotted to him.

"I see." The only thing I saw was that this was an angry man. "How far is Franklin from here?"

"Twelve, thirteen miles, or five leagues, if you like. Full day's walk however you measure it."

"Well, I'm not in any big hurry to go anyway."

"With all the plowing ahead of you, you won't have the time. At least not for a while."

"Maybe. Maybe not. Now that you've told me about the kwe-naskat, I'd sort of like to see it come fall. It sounds beautiful." I suddenly felt foolish, a grown man talking about grass being pretty, but then he'd waxed pretty sentimental himself.

He slowly shook his head and said, "Not this year you won't. Like I said, George expects you to plow." Thomas mockingly held up his hands as if in awe. "He told me God sent you here to make sure that this claim doesn't lie idle and that Franklin moves forward. He said it was Providence that sent you and that Providence wants you to plow this claim." He lowered his hands. "You probably noticed George has some funny ideas about God."

"It's been my experience that most people do."

His eyes met mine, and he smiled a little. "Anyway, since George basically owns Franklin, and he thinks it's your role to plow, you'll plow."

"He doesn't own this claim, does he?"

"No."

"Well, then he can't make me plow it."

He clicked his tongue and his horse trotted over. "A bear may not own the forest, John Chapman," he said as he climbed into the saddle, "but it sure has a big say on what happens there."

NINE

When I was twelve and Elizabeth was fifteen, a tall, fair-haired man named Mason Collier began calling on Elizabeth, walking her to church and stopping by to visit with Father. Elizabeth thought she had found the love of her life, not to mention a way out of Longmeadow and her life of increasing drudgery. Even though I couldn't have articulated exactly what I felt, I was filled with envy and jealousy, for I wanted to be the one to flee Longmeadow with Mason.

After several months of courting, she was certain he was going to propose. Instead, he suddenly stopped coming by, and a week later, we learned he was set to marry Dora Carlisle. Dora happened to be the homely and boring daughter of a struggling merchant, but her prospects were better than Elizabeth's.

I expected Elizabeth to be bitter, but she wasn't, and I didn't understand. I told her if I thought someone loved me, only to find out he hadn't, I would never trust anyone again. "Don't be silly, John," she said. "If a beautiful day turned cold and stormy, would you never venture out when the sun again shone?"

I told her it depended on how beautiful that first day had been.

April 1798

TWO DAYS AFTER GEORGE HAD TOLD ME PROVIDENCE INSISTED I TAKE the claim, I began to settle into the Jacksons' cabin.

After airing out and cleaning the small, one-room structure, I took stock of what supplies they had left behind. The foodstuffs— potatoes, flour, cornmeal—were more than plentiful enough to get me through until I planted a few crops, not to mention the berries and eggs and fish with which I would supplement my diet. They had also left a good stock of tools—a plow, shovels, axes—to work the claim. In a rather morbid bit of good luck, it turned out that Alexander and I were of a remarkably similar size and build, so much so that even his shoes fit. In fact, they fit better than the ones I'd been wearing. Having heard all I could stand about Providence, I hoped to hell George wouldn't notice how well Alexander's clothes suited me.

The following afternoon, I set out to explore the claim itself. Under a hot spring sun floating in a soft blue sky that looked to have never even known rain, I left the cabin, wading through the kwe-naskat, whose rippling blades came halfway up my calf. Walking in the afternoon heat, I found myself surrounded by the thrum of crickets, even becoming mesmerized by their incessant buzz. Upon reaching the creek, I turned to look back at the cabin, which, like an owl in a tree, sat perched up on a hillside amongst the shade of elm and birch and chestnut trees.

From either direction, the lush river grass flowed in from the valley before filling the meadow and washing up against the cabin like a tide. Only the brown scar of the dead truck patch—a vegetable garden cleared, planted, and harvested the year before—marred the carpet of green that rolled down to the creek. The meadow itself was divided in half by the creek as both meandered toward Franklin.

I could see why Alexander Jackson had chosen this place.

Heading north, I discovered a cool, shaded bog at the end of the valley. The Indian woman and I must have passed quite near here, though I couldn't recall doing so. Tadpoles scooted along the rank, spongy shore choked with wild-pea vines, pistia, and skirret. Swaying cattails flourished in the green water, while around the bog itself stood unassuming alders, their green leaves fluttering in the breeze like the flags of a hundred conquering armies.

Hidden in the shade, I spied the deep red petals of Dutchman's-breeches, white-flowered trillium, and despite its name, my favorite plant: skunk cabbage, whose graceful green leaves and single yellow blossom had always looked to me like a pair of delicate hands cupping a flame.

Blue jays and woodcocks flitted from tree to tree, chattering like schoolgirls hurrying home. Warm sunshine bathed me as I stood watching light play on the verdant water of the bog. A royal fly-catcher skimmed gracefully across its water-lily-covered surface. If the best life I could hope for was to be one of solitude, then this valley wasn't such a bad place to be alone.

The area south of the claim was unremarkable except for one odd and disturbing matter regarding the trees. While the trees to the north were cloaked with new green leaves, these trees appeared to be dead, with not even a single bud. Not only did I not particularly fancy looking at dead trees all summer, but I worried that a disease might slowly be making its way up the valley. I made a mental note to ask George or Thomas when I next saw them.

Then it was time to get down to the serious work—work that, in fact, I should have begun right away.

Besides having cleared land for, and built, the cabin, Alexander Jackson had also cleared and planted the truck patch, one of the first things every settler hacks from the wilderness in order to supplement his supplies of dried meat and flour. Therefore, it only made sense for me to take advantage of what he'd already done by tilling and sowing the truck patch.

Lacking a horse, I harnessed myself up to the wooden plow and began the backbreaking, monotonous work of plowing the truck patch. The glare of the heat and the sun made it hard to believe April was only half over. Sweating and aching, I struggled up and down the fifty feet of hard-packed soil. Wheezing, I reached the end of a furrow and struggled to turn the plow around for the next go. How the hell did oxen do this year after year?

Late in the afternoon of my second day of plowing, I struggled the final few feet of the last row, then let the harness slip from my blistered shoulders. Exhausted and thirsty, I stumbled down to the creek. Stripping off my shirt, I toppled into a cool pool, splashing myself as I drank my fill. When I glanced up at the opposite bank, I glimpsed an Indian wearing a headdress.

"Shit!" I hollered, scrambling backward, expecting to hear the evil hum of an arrow whizzing toward me. Banging my rump against a submerged rock, I cried out in pain and surprise. I looked to see if the Indian had come any closer. Not only was he no closer, but I realized he was a she and what I'd thought to be a headdress was, in fact, a bonnet.

She stood there unmoving, naked from the waist up, except for the bright blue bonnet fixed to her head. Perhaps I suffered from heatstroke, and she was a hallucination. I closed my eyes, splashed my face with water, and looked again.

Not only was she still there, but now I recognized her. This was the Indian who had rescued me. At least I thought she was the one. The bonnet cast a shadow across her face that made it hard to be certain.

"You there," I called out. "Are you the one I saw in the woods?"

Like a dog cocking its head to listen, she tilted her head sideways.

As if worried that someone—say, George—might overhear our exchange, I glanced along the creek, then said conspiratorially, "You know, the one who rescued me?"

She said nothing, her face remaining expressionless.

"Well, can you talk? Do you speak English?" Still no response. Not knowing what I intended to do, I rose and began wading toward her.

With an alacrity that belied her short legs, she turned and dashed for the woods.

I couldn't have caught her had I tried.

^ ^ ^

Later that afternoon, done working for the day and as certain as I could be that the woman had gone, I bathed in a pool in the creek. When I'd scrubbed my face and body raw, I floated on my back, my face turned up toward the more mellow late-afternoon sunshine.

For the first time in months, I found myself thinking of the Major. A stab of sorrow pierced me, and I even cried a little. But then, other memories came back: memories of our laughing, the touch of his mouth on my skin, the way his rough cheek felt on my belly. I began to touch and stroke myself, imagining the feel of his whiskers against my face, the touch of his hand, the sound of a horse whinnying.

A horse whinnying?

Thinking I'd dozed off and begun dreaming, I lazily opened my eyes. Disoriented by the sunlight, it took me a moment to register the towering silhouette of a man on a horse looming over me. Mortified at what he must have seen, I panicked, rolled over, and sank under the water. My hands and knees came to rest on the soft, sandy bottom of the creek.

I'm not sure what I thought I was doing. Did I think that if I stayed underwater long enough he would just leave? That somehow I could pretend it had never happened? Whatever I'd been thinking, after about sixty seconds, I had no choice but to reemerge.

Gulping air, I pushed the hair from my face as I scanned the bank. It was empty.

"Huzzah!" said a voice from off to the side.

Startled, I twisted sideways, trying to see who it was. I slipped and sank back under the water. Sputtering, I came back up. "Damnation!" I exclaimed.

The sun still silhouetted him so I couldn't see his face, and my first thought was that it had to be either George or Thomas. But then a voice as genial as the afternoon sunshine laughed and said, "You spend more time underwater than a salamander." I still couldn't make out his face, but I knew it wasn't Thomas. "Sorry about that. I didn't mean to startle you. At least not the first time anyway." He laughed again. "I reckoned the second time was just too good an opportunity to pass up."

"That's all right," I stammered, resenting this amusement at my expense.

"Did you find what you were looking for?" he asked lightheartedly.

"Excuse me?"

"I reckoned you must have dropped whatever you had in your hand and that's what you were doing underwater all that time— looking for it."

This mocking was humiliating. "I didn't drop anything." I paused. "Were you . . . there long?"

"Long enough to know that I wouldn't mind some of that myself."

I felt myself blush furiously, even though I wasn't sure exactly what he meant. I wished he would move out of the sun so I could see him—I wanted to memorize his face so I could avoid him for the rest of my life.

He slid from his horse, knelt, and thrust out his arm. "I'm Palmer." He was no longer silhouetted, but now his face was hidden by the shadow cast by his hat.

Only by wading forward to where the creek rose as high as my knees would I be able to shake his hand.

"You don't reckon I bite now, do you?" From the deep, confident timbre of his voice, I guessed him to be at least a few years older than me.

"I'm John," I said, water coursing down my thighs as I stepped toward him. I thanked God my stiffened dick had dissolved in the cold water. We shook. His hand was rough and strong, and I let go as fast as I could.

When he finally removed his hat, I was taken aback by the smiling, tan face with bright blue eyes that roamed over me. His blond hair, pulled back in a tight ponytail, further emphasized his angular features and almond-shaped eyes. Not only was he handsome, but he looked young, no more than eighteen or nineteen, and my discomfiture deepened.

"Is something wrong?" he asked, fanning himself.

"No," I said, noting how composed and stalwart he appeared, not to mention broad-shouldered. I doubted he would ever be as easily flustered as I was, and I hated that. I started to think of how Chapman would act, but stopped—I no longer thought of myself that way.

"Cooling off, I see," he said, his eyes traveling the length of my body. I blushed again, my resentment at this stranger's intrusion deepening.

"Well, I've been plowing all day," I said, attempting to back up nonchalantly until the water came up over my hips. "I needed a bath."

"I'd heard there was a new fellow up here. Thought I'd come up and say hello."

"Peculiar way of saying hello you've got there," I said sharply.

His smile vanished. "I've gone and done it again, haven't I?"

"Done what?"

"Took my chaffing too far. George reckons it's one of my worst flaws."

"Are you a friend of George's then?"

"Me!" he exclaimed with a short, sharp laugh. "No, I reckon George don't think of me as a friend. Maybe more like a stone he has to carry around his neck." Palmer must have seen the puzzled look on my face because he said, "You know, a curse."

"Oh," I said, becoming wary.

"Reconsidering, I see."

"What?"

"You're reconsidering. You're not sure you want to be talking with a poor nobody that the mighty George Chase might be less than fond of."

He was right, so I said nothing.

"It's all right. I'm used to it. If you're at all a decent fellow, you'll come around to my view soon enough. After all, if it's true that fine feathers don't always make fine birds, then it must also be true that meager feathers don't always make meager birds."

"Meaning?"

He laughed. "Meaning I may only look young and poor, but there might be more to me than meets the eyes. Meanwhile, it was a hot, dusty ride up here, and the water looks more tempting than beef on a spit." His shirt fell to the ground, and I realized I was about to meet the rest of him. "So, John, where are you from?"

"Massachusetts," I said, noting there was nothing wrong with his feathers. He was taller than I, and thin, but well muscled. Golden curls covered his broad chest, darkening as they descended down his stomach. My heart beat faster.

"Never been there myself," he said, pulling off his shoes. "I'm a Kentucky boy." He kicked free of his breeches, stood naked on the bank, and where George had reminded me of a draft horse, Palmer put me in mind of a courser, a lean, ropy mount, but one that was tough and swift and reliable in battle.

Without a trace of self-consciousness, he ran his hand down his body until he cupped his balls with his hand. Naked amidst a copse of blooming dogwoods, he looked completely at ease, as if he were an unfettered otter and this his domain. With a single graceful motion, he sprang from the bank, arcing through the air and into the creek.

Like the said otter, he streaked through the water, shooting under the pool's rippling surface, his white ass flashing in the sunlight; a moment later, he popped back up, blond hair streaming down over his face. Again and again he slapped at the water, all the while jumping and yelling and whooping. I couldn't help smiling. After paddling around for a bit, he found a half-submerged log, climbed up onto it, and prepared to dive again. For a second, he stood there grinning, and the sight of his glistening nude body, rivulets of water coursing over his brown arms and white stomach, burned itself into my mind.

As warm sunlight dappled the pool, I ordered my thoughts from the nearness of this carefree, naked man. In its stead came an unbidden image of Zach on top of me, pinning me to the bed the night I'd fled. Suddenly, all I wanted to do was to get away from this stranger.

The man dove back into the water. By the time he had surfaced and begun to swim back, I'd clambered out of the creek and pulled on my pants.

"Didn't mean to chase you away," he said, leaning back against the half-sunken log, his elbows propped up behind him for support.

"Oh, you didn't . . ." I couldn't believe I'd forgotten his name.

"Palmer," he said, pushing blond hair from his eyes. "Guess I haven't made much of an impression."

"You didn't, Palmer. I mean chase me away, not make an impression. I mean, you have made an impression." Feeling foolish, I paused. "Anyway, I'm afraid I've tarried too long already. I've a lot to tend to."

"Of course. I didn't mean to keep you. Say, perhaps if I find myself hunting up here sometime, I'll come by and visit. Unlessen you mind."

"I suppose that would be fine." Frankly, I hoped I never saw this easygoing, smart-alecky walking complication again.

"Good, good," he said, wading toward me. Sunlight danced off of his hard, shiny body as he held out his hand. I couldn't help but believe he was showing off. "It was nice to meet you, John."

Shaking his hand, I said, "Me, too . . ."

"Palmer," he said with a mischievous smile.

I turned and fled.

Over the past decade, I'd been as likely to remain in one place as a thundercloud was to stay directly overhead. So a week later, after the truck patch was sowed and watered, I set about planting a small apple orchard to demonstrate, if only to myself, that I was serious about staying.

Alexander Jackson had brought a large sack of apple seeds, so I assumed he had planned on having an orchard and that the valley was a suitable location for such. Taking the apple seeds from the cabin, I went outside to scout the most likely location for an orchard, but I had no idea whether that would be along the creek, in the meadow, or somewhere else. Of course, I'd seen apple trees growing in Longmeadow, but I'd paid them no mind and knew next to nothing about raising them. What kind of soil did they grow best in? How much water and sun did they need? Hell, I didn't even know if these particular seeds would produce eating, baking, or cider apples.

Planting them seemed as much a turn of the cards as having children.

After walking once around the cabin, I settled on a likely looking spot just beyond the back wall where the ground sloped upward, and where I'd noted the sun shone for much of the day. The soil was dark and heavy, and when I held a handful to my face, it smelled fecund and, I hoped, like a fortuitous place for apple trees.

For twenty minutes, I worked at clearing away rocks and fallen trees. As far as how deep to plant, I adopted a plan of varying depths. The first seed I planted just under the soil, the next a little deeper, and so forth. At least by experimenting I could learn what worked.

"Never will apple trees grow there," said an unexpected voice from behind me.

"Sweet Jesus!" I hollered, stumbling forward, while the seeds I'd been carrying spilled out onto the ground. As I fell, I managed to twist myself around. Landing on my rump with a tooth-jarring thud, I scrambled backward, crablike, up the slope. This time I recognized the bare-breasted Indian woman right away, and I had no doubt she was the one who had guided me here. "Why the hell did you sneak up on me like that?" I snapped, still rattled.

"I not sneak up on you."

"Not sneak up on me!" I sputtered. "You most certainly did."

She shook her head.

"How can you say that? I had no idea you were behind me."

"That not my fault. You should be more . . . what the word? Awake." She nodded toward the field. "Loudly, I came through kwe-naskat. So you hear me."

"I should've heard you coming through the grass?" I sputtered in disbelief. "And just how am I supposed to hear you walking in the grass?"

She shrugged as if it were obvious. "You listen."

"Well, I guess I didn't listen well enough. And since you do speak English, how about next time you sneak up behind me you say something, such as 'Hello' or 'Good day.'"

"Maybe I say 'Good day' now."

"No, please. Don't go. You just scared me, that's all."

She scooped up a handful of soil, sniffed it for a moment, then began kneading it with her fingers. Shaking her head, she came toward me, holding out the handful of earth and pouring it into my hand. "Too wet will the ground be in spring for apple trees," she proclaimed, wiping her hand on her deerskin skirt.

Her breasts swayed with each movement, making it hard not to stare at the large, dark circles that crowned each one.

"You hear me?" she said, and I looked up into her stern, brown eyes. "I said water all run down mountain to here. Will be big swamp in this place. It will be very much cold, too." She turned around in a circle, seeing or sensing something that I couldn't. "Too strong wet or cold will kill apple seedling. This place is no good for apple trees."

That was the second time she'd said that. "How did you know I was planting apple seeds?"

She stared at me as if I'd asked how she made her legs walk or her ears listen. "I look with my eyes. How else you think? Maybe I smell them?" With that, she laughed at her own joke.

"Do you really expect me to believe that you can tell today how cold it will be in this very spot come winter?"

She shrugged. "I not care what you believe. I only helpful trying to be." She turned and began to walk away.

"Wait! I'm sorry."

She paused but didn't turn back.

"I never thanked you properly for helping me. Before, I mean. You are the one who led me here, aren't you?"

She turned back toward me.

"Thank you," I said.

"You welcome."

"Can you really tell me where I should plant the seeds?"

"If you like."

I nodded.

"Follow me."

Despite her short stride, the woman moved quickly, and as I followed, I again had trouble keeping up. Her shoulders were as wide as her hips, and with her dark complexion, her body would have resembled nothing so much as a block of especially dark garnet if it weren't for the generous curves of her breasts and hips that left no doubt as to her sex.

"My name is—"

"John Chapman," she said, cutting me off. "Already George told me all about you."

"You know George?" It had never occurred to me that they might be acquainted.

She nodded. "I know George very well. You didn't tell him I one who brought you here." It wasn't a question.

"No."

"Why not? You embarrassed that Indian woman rescue you?"

"Well, maybe a little. Mostly I didn't say anything because some white people don't like Indians much. I didn't know what kind of person George might be."

"I see. Well, John Chapman, you can call me Gwennie."

George had mentioned someone by that time. "All right, Gwennie," I said, wondering how this Indian woman had come to be acquainted with George.

We'd gone a hundred or so yards north of the cabin when Gwennie stopped, suddenly turning toward me. I'd been so lost in thought that her abrupt movement caught me off guard. I jumped backward, startled.

She crossed her arms and stared at me. "Think I call you Chahkoltet from now on."

"Chak-el-et?" I asked suspiciously.

"Chah-kol-tet," she said, enunciating each syllable. "It means little frog, or jumpy one." She suddenly jerked backward as if startled, and I realized she was imitating me. She smiled, and I couldn't help but smile back.

She crouched down and pulled up a handful of grass. Tossing it aside, she dug at the dark earth underneath. Holding a handful up to her face, she breathed deeply as she crumbled it between her fingers.

It wasn't the soil, however, that I found myself watching. To my consternation, it was once again her breasts. I'd never been so close to breasts before. In fact, the only ones I'd seen at all were my stepmother Lucy's, and that had only been a brief glimpse when I'd accidentally come into the kitchen while she bathed. Lucy had been old by then, close to forty, and her thin, wrinkled breasts had hung flat against her chest like a pair of drained water bladders. So I was surprised to see that Gwennie's were so full and round.

"Can touch them if you want," she said, interrupting my thoughts.

I involuntarily took a step away from her as my eyes darted to her face. I hadn't meant to stare. What must she think of me? Her dark eyes were unreadable, her expression blank. My gaze slid back down her chest. It was the nipples that fascinated me: fascinated *and* shocked me. I'd never imagined anything like them. Daniel's and the Major's were the only ones I'd ever touched, and theirs had looked nothing like this. The Major's had been soft and pink, the size of the base of a candle. Hers were easily twice that large, covering the end of each breast like a lid, and such a dark brown that they almost looked black. Most unsettling were the tips of the nipples, long, elastic things that seemed somehow unnatural.

I reached out, and my fingertips brushed the skin around her breast, sending a tingling up along my arm. The skin itself was like nothing I'd ever felt, smoother, softer, than I would have guessed. I could've caressed it for hours. Gently, I traced a circle around the dark nipple, then ran my finger along the tip. Slowly I closed my hand around her breast, squeezing slightly, shocked at how yielding the flesh was. I felt stupid for thinking her breasts unnatural. What the hell might she think of my dick? When I looked up at Gwennie, her expression was no longer blank but sympathetic, understanding. I pulled my hand back and, with a loud rush of air, exhaled.

"Never before touch a girl's bosom, have you?"

I shook my head.

"I thought not."

God Almighty, what must she think of me? I felt I should say something—apologize, explain, take it all back. Yet, I saw no trace of anger or guilt or embarrassment on her face. In fact, she looked as if nothing extraordinary had occurred.

Maybe it hadn't.

"Apple seeds you still want to plant?" she asked, changing subjects as abruptly as a hummingbird might directions. "If so, this good place."

Shading my eyes from the bright light, I stared at the ground, struggling to control my voice, to make it work. "What makes this a good spot?"

"It . . . Damn, what's the word?" This time she made a sweeping motion with her hand. "No hills."

"Smooth? Flat?"

"*Flat*. That word I want. Also not crowded with other trees. Apple seedlings need plenty light. Soil is good here, not sandy, not heavy. Even more, it deep. Also other flowering plants nearby so many bees come."

For the next half hour, she lectured me about apple trees. She explained that the trees needed deep soil since their root systems tapped so far into the earth. She also explained at what depth and how far apart to plant the seeds; how often to water them; that if I did plant on a hill or slope, to always go higher rather than lower; and to always plant at least two trees or neither would ever produce fruit. Trying to remember as much as I could, I only nodded after each explanation.

"How do you know so much about apple trees, Gwennie?"

"I learned long time ago." She paused. "When I was younger."

"Was that around here?"

"No. Was what you call the Ohio Territory." Her voice had gone as cold and flat as the Allegheny Plateau in January, but I hadn't the sense to heed what I heard.

"Is that where you grew up?"

She nodded.

"Does your family still live there?"

She seemed to stare past me, her eyes looking as cold and life-less as a piece of coal. She looked the way I felt when I thought of the Major. I mentally kicked myself for being so insensitive. I, of all people, should've known better than to pry into other people's lives.

"Gwennie, I'm sorry. I didn't mean to be nosy."

She shaded her eyes and looked up at the sun. "It getting late morning. We should plant your seeds now. Go ahead."

Staring at the earth, I tried to remember all she had taught me. At last I chose a likely looking spot to plant, although it was more a guess than anything else. One by one, I planted a handful of seeds, hoping that Gwennie would approve of where I'd chosen.

"There," I said, standing when I'd finished. I brushed the dirt from my hands. "How does that look, Gwennie? Gwennie?" I turned to look for her.

She was nowhere to be seen.

Several days later, George sent word through Thomas that I should come to Franklin for the town's May Day celebration.

"You seem disappointed to see me, John," Thomas said as we rode his horse toward Franklin.

His perceptiveness startled me. "I'm tired, Thomas, that's all." But, in truth, I was disappointed, though I was surprised by the reason. When I'd first glimpsed the figure approaching from the south, I'd thought it might be Palmer—the fellow who had come upon me bathing.

"You're sure there won't be too many people there?" I asked. "Throngs of folk aren't my favorite thing."

"Depends on what you mean by 'too many.'"

The way I felt at the moment, "too many" meant three.

"You needn't worry, John. There'll be a dozen people, maybe two dozen, tops."

Five dozen turned out to be more like it, and my first visit to Franklin was nearly my last. There were more people milling around the clearing—sixty or more at least—than I had seen since I'd fled the fort. And as far as I could tell, not one of them was Palmer.

A fit of paranoia gripped me. What if someone else here had come from Lower Canada, and what if they recognized me? It wasn't likely, but nor was it impossible. Even more, people were going to ask me questions, innocuous to be sure, but I'd still have to lie. Watching the people mill about, I wished I'd never set foot south of the damned claim.

Thomas disappeared to tie up his horse. Anxious, I stood on the edge of the crowd until George burst from the tumult.

"John, you're here!" he boomed, shaking my hand with a grip that matched his enthusiasm. "I'm glad you made it."

I smiled, grateful to see someone I at least knew a little.

"Well, come on. Let me introduce you to the others," he said, my gratitude vanishing as swiftly as a startled deer into the woods.

He steered me through the crowd like a sheepdog driving its flock. George was self-assured and boisterous, while I was apprehensive and withdrawn. He knew everyone, nodding at each person we passed, shaking hands, calling out names, introducing me to a blur of faces. Maybe Franklin wasn't yet a full-fledged town, but I could've sworn George was already running for town proctor.

"John Chapman," George said, stopping abruptly to introduce me to yet someone else. "I'd like you to meet Caleb Baxter, our town preacher. Like every real town, Franklin has to have a preacher, something neither of those other backwaters calling themselves towns yet have."

"Hello, Mr. Baxter," I said, thinking he looked familiar somehow.

"Good day, Mr. Chapman," Caleb said stiffly. He was a tall, sharp-faced man who seemed rather restrained and priggish. His blond hair was pulled back in such a tight ponytail, I thought his blue eyes were going to pop out of his head. I recalled something my father used to say about the English carrying themselves about as if they hadn't taken a crap in a month. Mr. Baxter didn't sound English, but otherwise the description seemed apt.

"William!" George called out suddenly to a family that had just arrived. "Over here! John Chapman is waiting to meet you and Sam."

I was? Sam who? I glanced at George.

A short, broad-shouldered man with a wide, squat face came toward us, and I couldn't help but think he looked quite like a badger walking upright. Behind followed a dour-faced woman clutching a robust, red-faced infant who looked alarmingly like the man. Around the both of them, nine or ten children swirled like a cloud of dust.

"William Connolly, John Chapman," said George eagerly.

"Pleased to meet'cha, John," William said, gripping my hand as if desiring to force me to my knees. "Everything we've 'eard about you 'as made us eager to make your 'quaintance. Specially Sam."

Who the hell was Sam? And why was he eager to meet me?

At last he let go of my hand, let fly a gob of tobacco juice, and turned to the woman standing next to him. "This is m'wife, Sylvie," he said, pushing forward the tired-looking woman wearing a jaunty yellow bonnet that clashed with her sallow complexion. She was suddenly seized by a deep, racking cough.

"Mr. Chapman," she managed to mumble, then began coughing again. Both she and her husband wore clean but threadbare clothes, which was rather how they looked themselves. They were what my stepmother would have called poor but respectable—which is what my family had been.

William gently pulled his wife back to his side and took the baby. She smiled gratefully. "And these are some of our young-heads," he said, gesturing to their brood. "Say 'ello to Mr. Chapman."

"'Ello, Mr. Chapman," they said together in singsong.

"Hello," I said wanly.

"Well, I've things to tend to, George," Caleb said abruptly. "Mr. Chapman, I trust I'll see you at the sermon."

"Oh, certainly," I said, despite neither knowing of any sermon nor having any intention of staying for it. I looked from George to the Connollys to their children. I felt as if I'd just been thrown from a cliff and told to fly. I wondered how quickly I could escape.

"Now 'e left in a bit of a 'urry, didn't 'e?" snorted William. "Notice 'e couldn't be bothered to ask us if *we'd* be attending 'is infernal preaching. Stuffed shirt, that one is."

"Show a little respect, William," George said. "He is carrying God's word after all."

"Well, an ass be an ass even if it is laden with gold."

"Don't be so touchy, William," said Sylvie.

"Perhaps, William," George said, "you and John can talk . . . business. John will be planting the upper valley and maybe you can work out an—"

"But I won't be," I interrupted.

George looked at me for a moment before he coolly said, "You won't be what?"

"Planting. At least not anything more than the truck patch."

George fixed his eyes on me. "Really. I thought I'd explained to you how important plowing was, that it was Providence that gave you that claim."

"You did. But Providence hasn't bothered to provide a horse to help with the plowing. It was all I could do to plow the truck patch by myself. My shoulders are still rubbed rawer than uncooked meat."

George softened. "I forgot about the misfortune with your horse. Let me see what I can do." He frowned. "I'd be sorrier than a barrow freshly parted from his balls to see that meadow go unplanted. And beyond that, John, you do know that you have to make improvements to the land in order for the claim to be valid? If you don't, the government has the right to sell the land again. Unless, of course, you can buy it outright."

I hadn't known any of that. "What kind of improvements?"

William answered first. "Plant crops is one. Clear more land, build a barn, start an orchard."

"Really?" I asked excitedly. "Because I've done that. Start an orchard, I mean."

"You did?" asked George. "Bully for you. That's very commendable."

"The Jacksons left behind a bag of apple seeds," I said. "I think Alexander was going to start an orchard. Of course, I didn't know the first thing about apples, but Gwennie's been teaching me."

"That awful, 'eathen Injun woman?" asked Sylvie.

"Well, yes," I said.

"George, I don't understand why you let a filthy, unwashed Injun remain in Franklin," Sylvie said. "Specially that one. She's as cold as a mountain peak in January and about as distant. Talking to 'er is like talking to the moon. It just sits there, all big and round, and stares back at you."

"Well, Sylvie," George said, "there are some that say Indians are actually cleaner than whites. After all, I've heard Easterners complain that settlers reek of bear fat."

"Well, that's an addlepated New Yorker fer you," she bristled. "'Ow else we supposed to keep the duns and gallinippers from chewing us to pieces come summer? And there ain't no way that Injun woman is cleaner than I am."

"Of course not, Sylvie," George soothed. "Now I know you weren't here, but it was Gwennie who helped Catherine Jackson birth her baby even though it was breech."

"It's also true that child was sickly right from the beginning. Maybe that 'eathen witched the baby when no one was looking."

George shook his head. "All I can say is that Gwennie's tonics and herbs have set me right more often than any white doctor I ever met. Gwennie's not like other Indians."

"Pshaw," Sylvie said. "No disrespect intended, George, but you can't turn an Injun woman into a civilized lady any more than you can change a polecat into a 'ouse cat."

"Speaking of young ladies," said George, "where is Miss Sam? I'm sure John would be pleased to make her acquaintance."

Miss Sam? I thought in alarm. Oh, shit.

"Yes," said Sylvie, turning on me as she forgot all about Indians. "I understand, Mr. Chapman, there ain't no Missus Chapman."

"Pardon me?" I asked, not sure I heard her correctly.

"George 'ere told us you ain't married. Is that right?"

"Yes," I said, scanning the crowd, looking for a reason to excuse myself. A forest fire would have been nice.

"Remember, John, the first day we met?" George asked. "I told you I might know a young lady capable of enduring the rigors of the frontier. Sam is her." He grinned at me. "And guess how I could tell she'd be right for you?"

If he said it was Providence, I swore I'd scream.

"It's Providence, that's what it is," he said.

Knowing I couldn't actually scream, I clamped my jaw shut with all the force I could muster. I also fought the temptation to tell George it was Providence that made me picture Palmer when I touched myself and not some silly woman named Sam.

"Now where is Samantha, William?" George demanded. "I told you to bring her. After all, you can't eat the kernel if you don't crack the nut."

William nodded. "She'll be along."

"I hope so," George replied curtly.

This talk of marriage, Providence, and my being a nut to be cracked had me more nervous than a mayfly in a pond full of frogs.

George eyeballed the crowd and said, "Quite a turnout, isn't it? Mark my words—Franklin is going to be bigger than Haas, that sorry piss-pot of a town."

I nodded, grateful that George was changing the subject, even if it was again about Franklin's getting larger. "I'd no idea there were so many people here," I said.

"Well," George boasted, "close to another forty people have arrived in the past two weeks. Can you believe it? Word must have got out about how bad things are up north."

"Were you widowed, Mr. Chapman?" asked William, interrupting George.

"What? What makes you ask if I'm widowed?" More important, what did George mean about "up north?"

"You are twenty-four, after all," said Sylvie. "We figured you musta been married by now."

"No. I'm not widowed." How the hell did she know how old I was? I felt like a panther being pursued by dogs. As obviously as possible, I turned to George. "You were saying that things are bad up north. Where? Bad in what way?"

"Ever hear of a place called Warren?" he asked derisively.

"No," I lied, feeling as if Bliss's stall had again vanished from under me. The subject of my marital status suddenly didn't seem like such a bad thing to talk about.

"It's less of a town even than Haas. Just a pathetic little block-house owned by a mismanaged land company that wants to bring in settlers to solidify their claim. Only problem is that most of the land up there is no good for settling and, according to folks back east, was sold to two different companies."

"They sold the same land twice?" asked Sylvie.

George nodded vigorously, as if we had expressed an interest in moving there and he was desperate to dissuade us from such a foolish decision. "I've even heard tell of three times. Remember William Penn? As upright and honest a man as there ever was. Then there's his gundy-gut heirs. Talk about greedy. They'd sell the stink off their shit if they thought you'd buy it."

George shook his head mournfully, then continued, "Goes to show that it's not always true that muddy streams have muddy springs. How his progeny came by their dishonest ways, I'll never understand. Anyway, they're some of the biggest land speculators in Pennsylvania, and they want to sell the land they own to settlers, but the problem is nobody knows who actually owns it. Mark my words—making a claim up there is going to be a real gamble. So instead, people are coming down here to settle, which is great for us."

"So tell me, John," said William, taking no notice of George's enthusing, "if you're not married, do ya 'ave somebody back east that you're planning on bringing out once you're 'stablished 'ere?"

Before I could answer, Sylvie clucked, "Yes, Mr. Chapman. It must be turrible difficult livin' all by yourself. Specially with no close neighbors."

I found myself speechless. I hadn't seen stones like these since I'd helped geld a neighbor's draft horse.

"We're not far from you, John," William continued. "You'll 'ave to come down real soon, 'ave a spot of whiskey and get to know Sam."

"George?" interrupted a man whom I hadn't yet met, but would willingly claim as a long lost brother if it would've gotten me out of there. "We've about got the pit dug. We need to know when Caleb's gonna preach so we know when to start the fire."

George looked at me. "I've got to go tend to some things, John. But be sure to stick around after Caleb's preaching. We're having a sort of an official town founding celebration along with the May Day festivities. There will be all sorts of food, drink, music."

With that, George was gone, and like a pair of wolves finishing off a wounded deer, William and Sylvie closed in on me.

Feeling trapped, I stepped backward, William and Sylvie matching my every move. William looked like a fitch stumbling upon an unguarded clutch of pheasant eggs.

"John, thank heavens I found you!" Palmer exclaimed, sweeping down on me from out of the crowd.

"Excuse me?" I stammered.

"Is something wrong?" William asked.

Palmer whirled me around so I faced him. "I think I'm in time," he said, seriously studying my face before flashing me a quick wink.

"In time fer what?" asked Sylvie.

"His tonic," said Palmer.

"My what?" I asked.

"'Is tonic," said Sylvie. "Is 'e ill then?"

"Yes, terribly," said Palmer.

"With what?" asked William.

"He has fits," Palmer told them. "Fits and seizures. The tonic prevents them."

"Fits! That's turrible!" Sylvie stared at me as if I'd sprouted horns.

"And who might you be?" asked William suspiciously.

"I'm his brother. Half brother actually."

"You didn't mention any brother, John," said William.

"That's the first symptom," said Palmer. "Forgetfulness. Do you recognize me, brother?" he asked, shaking me vigorously.

"Are they *bad* fits?" Sylvie asked. "I mean, 'e'd still make a good 'usband, wouldn't 'e?"

"I reckon John's fits are one of the most awful sights a man can behold," Palmer said mournfully. "First he gets agitated."

"I thought 'e got fergetful," said Sylvie.

"Right—that's first. Then he gets agitated—all sorts of facial tics, eyes rolling about, his tongue turns purple. Next he thrashes his arms about." Palmer waved his arms wildly above his head. "Gave me a black eye once."

William and Sylvie each took a step backward.

"Then he froths at the mouth."

"No!" said William as my hand involuntarily wiped at my lips.

Palmer nodded gravely. "Yes. And he issues a smell far more rank than any black-and-white stinker I've ever run across."

William and Sylvie both wrinkled their noses.

"Then things get worse," Palmer said, shaking his head sadly.

"Worse?" they asked in unison.

My head was spinning, and I considered kicking Palmer in the shin.

"Much worse. He starts burning up and turns a bright red—almost as scarlet as Satan himself—and gets so hot he tears off all of his clothes and runs around raving no matter whether he be in church or hunting bear."

Gasps escaped them both.

"So, of course, you can see why I've got to get him his tonic."

Palmer gripped me by the elbow and pushed me forward. "We'll beg your pardon now."

The last I saw of Sylvie and William, they were huddled together, staring after us bug-eyed and openmouthed.

"I take my clothes off and run around ranting?" I whispered as he led me through the crowd. "I turn the same color as Satan? I froth—"

"You want to go back and chat some more with those two?" He stopped and turned to face me. "I'll come with you if you like, tell them I'm joshing, and you'd be happier than a dog rolling in stink to meet their daughter."

He resumed walking away. "Palmer, wait!" I caught up to him and matched his stride. Despite myself, I glanced over at him as he marched along, his shoulders thrown back, and I was put in mind of a sailing ship plowing defiantly through the ocean. "Thanks for getting me away."

As we passed the last of the crowd, he touched his hand to his forehead in a mock salute. "Anytime, Master Chapman."

"Knock it off. I'm not that much older than you."

"And not much more experienced, I'd wager."

I glanced at him. What the hell did that mean? And did he have to be so brash in everything he did and said? Of course, that brashness was why I'd thought about him much of the week.

"I spotted you soon as I reached town." He came to a log that faced back toward town and flopped down. "You looked like a rabbit in a snare."

"That's about how I felt," I said, sitting next to him.

"Truth be told, the only reason I even came to this gathering was in case you was here."

That comment brought me up short. I reminded myself that foremost I'd come to Franklin to establish a claim, to finally make something of myself. I would do well to avoid any of the entanglements that had already made such a glorious success of my life. If only this particular entanglement weren't so daring, so different from anything I'd ever known. Could he really be as young as he looked?

"Let me guess," Palmer said. "They wanted to know if you were

married and, if not, whether or not you had anybody back east waiting for you."

"What?" I asked, gathering my wits.

"Watch yourself around them. They have thirteen kids, eight of
whom are girls, and they all need *'usbands,"* he said, mocking their
accent. "Or at least they will. Right now, only one of them is really
old enough to be married, although I reckon you could have your
pick of 'em if you wanted."

"Uh, I don't think so."

He smiled. "I thought not. I had a fair notion the other day that
you weren't much interested in meeting prospective brides."

Uncomfortable, I glanced around to make sure no one was
within earshot. I had the unshakable feeling this man, as young as
he was, could be dangerous. I'd had enough of dangerous men.

"Bet you haven't even seen Samantha Connolly, she's the one
they're trying to marry off."

I shook my head.

Palmer pretended to shudder. "Figures. Her folks probably reckoned they should feed you tipsycakes washed down with whiskey
first."

"Is she ugly?"

"Does a bear stink? There's something not right with her neck.
It's all big and puffy, like she's just been stung by bees. She's got
these big, round eyes, real strange looking, like she's been startled
'cause somebody poked a finger in her oyster basket. Plus they're
such a poor family, I can't imagine anybody desperate enough to
marry the likes of her. And she's an old maid, too. At least twenty
and still a virgin, no doubt. Lord knows who'd want to flourish her."

Poked a finger into her oyster *basket?* I couldn't believe the
things that came out of his mouth.

"I'm twenty-four, Palmer. And I've never been married."

"But you're a man. It's different. Besides, I reckon you've dipped
your wick a few times. Though, I suspect, not where these good
folks might think."

"Palmer!" I exclaimed, glancing up at the crowd.

"Don't worry. Unless it's something they can shoot, eat, or flourish, these folks aren't too likely to pay much mind to what's going on around them."

I thought of George and Thomas and the man who was a preacher. They all struck me as fairly sharp.

Palmer paused as he looked toward the creek bank. "Looks like my brother, Caleb, is gonna be preaching soon. We best head back." He rose, and I fell in beside him as we walked.

"Your brother's the preacher? I met him earlier." No wonder he'd looked familiar, though where Palmer's angular features were appealing, Caleb's were intimidating, aloof.

"Too bad. I wanted the pleasure of introducing you to the insufferable little prick. If Caleb thought he were any closer to God, he'd think he was Jesus himself."

"I'd no idea he was your brother, though he did look familiar."

Palmer smiled. "I bet there's a lot of things concerning me you have no idea about."

Just as the first time we'd met, he continued to throw me off balance with his impertinent comments. Was there any thought he wouldn't risk uttering? I knew I should take my leave, and I intended to—in a moment.

"How old are you, Palmer?"

"How old do you reckon?"

"Nineteen," I said hopefully.

"Eighteen. Next month."

I shook my head, amazed. This brash, confident man was seven years younger than me? The thought depressed me. Still, I was more glad he was here than I cared to admit. "You're seventeen? You don't act like it."

Palmer wrinkled his nose as if he smelled something bad. "You sound like my father. I sure as hell hope you aren't going to give me any of that squiddle about not knowing my place. Father thinks I shouldn't have opinions or do things the way I see fit. Mind you, this comes from a man who doesn't fart without his father-in-law's permission."

"Well, that certainly doesn't sound like you."

"By damnation, you're right about that. If I know what I want, I go after it. When Father decided it was past time for me to be married, I reckoned it was time for me to get out," he said as we reached the edge of the crowd milling about the clearing.

Logs had been rolled down to the creek for the few foolish women who wore dresses made from something other than sensible linsey-woolsey. I noticed one woman in particular who had perched her precious self where she could be seen by the greatest number of people. She wore a satin dress topped off with an enormous hat sprouting a ridiculous assemblage of colored feathers. Most of the other, more practically dressed families sat on the ground or on blankets they had brought with them.

"If you've such a strong aversion to your brother," I said, "then why are you so eager to hear him preach? Wouldn't you rather go somewhere else?"

"And miss the sainted Caleb's performance? Oh, no, I live to watch this. Pomposity like his is scarcer than humility in a Puritan. Hell, it's half the reason I followed him all the way out here." To my chagrin, Palmer waded into the very center of the gathering until he found us a clear spot. Reluctantly, I lowered myself to the ground.

Everyone continued to chatter while Caleb solemnly proceeded to the front of the crowd. He silently stood there for a moment, surveying the gathering, before he abruptly raised his hands high above his head. Another moment passed, and I began to feel uneasy.

"Look around you!" he boomed, and everyone jumped as if a gun had gone off in our midst. He gestured with his hands as he turned in a slow circle. "Look closely and tell me what you see."

Confused and uncertain, people looked tentatively at each other. If the men didn't know each other, they nodded stiffly, while the women at least managed to smile. Brothers and sisters giggled and nudged one another until shushed by their parents. Gradually, as Caleb continued to stand motionless, everyone's gaze wandered along the creek, then to the mountains, and off to the horizon.

Only Palmer kept his eyes locked on Caleb, and I got the distinct impression he was trying to unnerve him. Caleb appeared not to notice.

I myself had yet to look at Franklin, and not wanting the discomfiture of meeting anyone's eyes, I did so now. Under a blazing sky

more suited to the dog days of August than the more mellow April, I
studied my surroundings. The main buildings, and those under construction, that made up the town sat back from the creek in what
looked to have once been a meadow much like my own. But where
on my claim I looked out on swaths of green that rippled in the
wind, here there was nothing left of the meadow but a field of hard-
packed dirt.

Back behind the buildings was a growing pile of refuse—ashes
from fires, rotten food, a discarded saddle, a broken plow—that
slowly spilled outward like pus seeping from an infection. And just
beyond the former meadow, where woods had once begun, stood
row after row of tree stumps looking like nothing so much as a field
of headstones. Past them I noticed that all of the uncut trees were
dead as well, like the ones south of my claim. Had they been killed
by the same thing?

No matter what George might think, Franklin was ugly.

"Did you see it?" Caleb whispered, suddenly wading into the
crowd. "Do you have the discernment, the vision, to *see* it?"

"Oh, brother," whispered Palmer as the crowd murmured softly.
I wondered if I had missed something.

"What you should see is redemption—the redemption of a land
that we have claimed and sanctified in the name of Our Lord! This
land has been redeemed because, until you good folk arrived, it lay
idle, a nursing ground for the devil and his minions, and Jesus and
the Bible were not known here. No, only sin and heathens and sacri-
lege flowed in these rivers, filled these woods, fell from this sky."

As Caleb spoke, I looked around at the crowd. A few of the
smaller children squirmed and had to be hushed by their parents,
but everyone else sat transfixed. Palmer especially seemed so, but
not in the same way as the others. They looked enraptured. He
looked as if he saw something he wanted to stomp on with the heel
of his boot.

"For close to two thousand years," Caleb continued, "the good
words of Jesus have flowed out from Jerusalem until all of the world
basked in His light. His honor. His glory."

"Amen!" said someone in the crowd, and Caleb nodded toward
them.

"But, you may say, you may even insist, that there are still places, still people, that worship false gods and bibles and places. Sometimes they are even part of your own family." For the first time, Caleb glanced at Palmer. "And I say with a heavy, heavy heart that you are right. But know this, take heart in this—even now, this very instant, our soldiers of righteousness are spreading the word, driving out the lies of the false prophets of Satan."

"Praise the Lord!" called out a red-faced woman a few feet in front of us.

"Everywhere that is," Caleb continued, his voice dropping ominously, "except for one place." Like a whirling dervish, he suddenly spun around to the creek, jabbing his finger furiously toward the west. "There! There across the treacherous rivers in those dark, forbidding woods are nests of red-skinned devils who practice fornication, sodomy, and cannibalism. Only there is God's word not yet heard."

"Hallelujah!" called out several voices.

Devils? I wondered to myself, scanning the crowd for Gwennie. I didn't see her.

"But that is changing! It's changing because you, too, are the soldiers of God, doing his work as we push back the dark, as we clear away the woods, as we put this land to its divine, intended use. With every tree cut, we clear the way to let us take another step forward and carry the word of God onward. And that's why Franklin will succeed—not for you or me or anyone else, but for the glory of God!"

A ringing chorus of "Amen"s, "Hallelujah"s, and "Praise the Lord"s filled the air like the cries of so many raucous crows. Caleb's voice had taken on a rhythmic tone along with which people were beginning to sway. "God brought us here to teach the red man what he has done wrong, to have us lead him down the road to righteousness, to give him a chance to repent before it's too late. The red man most certainly doesn't know it yet, but one day he will express his undying gratitude to us for coming and showing him the way!"

Cheering rose up from the crowd, and they began clapping as

well until a cascade of jubilant voices and thunderous applause greeted Caleb's every utterance. Caleb continued speaking, but I had stopped listening because each word made me feel as if I'd fallen farther into a deep, icy pit.

I wondered how it was possible to feel so alone surrounded by so many.

TEN

My brother Arnott was seven when the flux almost killed him. Dozens of people in town were taken ill, half of whom had died. The wealthy ones paid for bloodletting or purges, not that it made any difference as far as I saw. The rest of us made do with what medicine we could afford or home remedies feverishly concocted in kitchens. Especially popular were cures rumored to have been used by the Indians, though judging by the number of Indians left alive in town, we might as well have brewed potions to raise the dead.

When there was nothing more my stepmother, Lucy, could do for Arnott, we prayed. I'd prayed for many things in my fourteen years—for my mother to come down from heaven, for my father to leave, for money to take care of Lucy and my brothers and sisters, especially Elizabeth. Elizabeth worked like a slave to take care of the rest of us because Lucy, frail to begin with, had been worn out from birthing six children.

None of those prayers had ever been answered. Nonetheless, when Lucy gathered us around Arnott's bed, I, too, closed my eyes and fervently prayed to God for my brother to get better.

He did. Lucy said our prayers had been answered, that it was divine intervention, Providence, God's will.

Maybe it was.

May 1798

THE AROMA OF ROASTING BEEF WAFTED OVER THE MEADOW, THOUGH I had long since lost my appetite. As soon as Caleb's sermon was over, he'd been surrounded by men clapping him on the back, boasting about acres cleared, trees felled, and heathen Indians killed, all of it in God's name. I felt nauseous.

Palmer had tried to speak to Caleb, but Caleb had utterly ignored his brother, acting as if he didn't even see him. Palmer grew frustrated and angry, and thus, I noted, Palmer wasn't as unflappable as I'd thought.

"He speaks with passion," Palmer mumbled as we walked away. "I'll give him that."

"Anything else you'd give him?"

Palmer nodded. "How about an iron piggin between the eyes?"

We joined everyone milling about waiting to eat.

The women set out bowls of bonnyclabber; a trencher of smoked gammon; plates of dried and candied fruits; raw, stewed, and pickled vegetables; loaves of bread; quinces, tarts, and jellies.

To my surprise, Palmer stepped a few feet away and began talking animatedly to a young woman. His sweetheart, perhaps? It was fine by me if she was. It wouldn't bother me at all. Truly. Besides, after Zach, I didn't think I had it in me to trust another man.

Palmer brushed a lock of hair from her forehead.

"Why the scowl, John?" George asked, unexpectedly coming up behind me. "You look as if you've found a dead squirrel in your bed."

"No, it's that I—"

"What did you think of the sermon?" he asked, apparently not all that interested in what troubled me. "We need someone like him to bond us together, to let us express what we feel in our bones, but can't always say. Caleb has that gift, doesn't he?"

"Yes," I agreed, nodding weakly.

"More like the curse, if you ask me," said Palmer, joining me again. I tried not to smile.

George eyed Palmer circumspectly. "Well, now, I don't recall asking you, Palmer Baxter. I want to talk to John. Isn't there some other deserving person for you to go annoy?"

"I've had my fill of Caleb for one day, George. So there's just you."

"George, there's something I've been meaning to ask you," I said, uncomfortable with the vitriol of their exchange. "And coming down here today reminded me of it. South of my claim, and the whole way down here, the trees are dead. I've noticed that they're dead here as well, and I'm worried that there's a disease spreading up the valley."

George smiled. "That's no disease, John. We did that."

Palmer snorted. "And you're proud of it, too. Another of Caleb's brilliant ideas, though he actually swiped it from the same Indians he just finished reviling."

"What idea?" I asked.

"It's called girdling," George said, giving Palmer a look cold enough to freeze lightning. "And Palmer's right—it is an Indian trick. You cut a strip of bark all the way around the trunk of the tree, and that kills the tree. Then, without having to cut down the trees, you can plant corn or whatnot without the tree's leaves blocking the sunlight."

"The only difference," Palmer said, "is the Indians only do it to a couple of trees at a time. These fools did the whole damn valley."

"And what business is it of yours, Palmer?" George snapped. "You're lazier than a sow in August. You haven't lifted a finger to improve this valley, to make it habitable. All you do is show up at other people's homes, eat their food, and criticize. If you don't like the way we run our claims, then start one of your own."

"Maybe I don't like claims at all, George. Maybe I think the valley doesn't need improving, especially when it means killing every unfortunate tree, Indian, or animal that crosses my path."

Palmer's temerity took my breath away. George had to be at least twice as old, yet Palmer didn't hesitate to speak his piece.

"Listen, Palmer," George said, "life is hard enough out here without you blathering such nonsense. You're a fit young man who has somehow been led astray, become nothing more than a whifling. God help you. As for you, John, I hope you know better than to keep questionable company or to listen to such foolishness." George shook his head in disgust, then someone caught his attention and he called out, "Hermann! Adam! Come over here a moment. I've someone I want you to meet." George turned to me. "Here are two men you would do well to emulate, John."

Two men I'd never seen before joined us.

"John Chapman," George said, "I'd like you to meet Hermann Mueller from Boston and Adam Penney from Philadelphia."

"Adam Penney, Esquire," the man interjected.

"Ah, yes, I forgot, Adam," said George. Palmer cleared his throat and George reluctantly added, "And this is Palmer Baxter. It was his brother who gave our sermon."

"Ach, fine, fine words," said the man named Hermann, who may have come from Boston, but sounded as if he'd been born somewhere foreign—perhaps Bavaria or the Ottoman Empire.

"Yes, indeed," said Adam Penney, Esquire, bowing slightly toward Palmer, "your brother's words were most uplifting. After all, he whom God steers sails safely."

"Aye, aye, Captain," Palmer said sullenly.

I struggled to keep from laughing. After all, Mr. Penney cut the most outlandish figure I'd seen in a long time. He was small, but enormously fat and dressed in such finery—a silk shirt, ruffled collar, even an ivory walking stick—that he looked as if he had got lost walking between his dining and drawing rooms, somehow ending up on the frontier.

"And that's Mrs. Penney over there, John," said George, pointing at an equally rotund woman sitting stiffly on one of the logs. She was the one I'd noticed draped in satin and feathers.

"I understand, John," Adam said, pointing at me, "that you have a claim that's further north in the valley."

"That's right," I said, amazed by the straining of the vest containing the protuberance that was his stomach. At any moment I expected a brass button to burst free, possibly injuring someone.

"I see, I see," he said, his head bobbing as if his neck were on a spring. "So we all have the same interests at heart. And I think George is just the man to guide those interests to fruition."

"That's for certain," said Palmer. "After all, George practically has King Midas's touch when it comes to business matters."

George glared at Palmer. "Palmer, if you have something to say, why don't you just say it? Otherwise, keep your Scotch comments to yourself."

"Well put," said Adam as Palmer stalked away. I was sorely tempted to follow, but George's probing eyes kept me rooted to where I stood.

"As far as I'm concerned," George said, "Caleb ought to turn that little sod out on his ear. Let's see if the filcher can get by on his own honest labor."

Adam turned back to me. "George tells me that the land up your way is quite fertile. How many acres did you say you have planted?" he asked, but before I could answer, he continued on. "You see, I had thought of making my claim up there, but it's so far from the Allegheny. I'm planning on establishing a *very* large farm, and I need good access to the river. We all know the longest pole knocks down the persimmon."

"Ach," said Hermann, waving his hand at Adam. "I know dis man two veeks and dat all he talk about. Money, persimmons, vill there be enough rain, how big Franklin vill be, how much profit he going to make. Never does he speak about literature or philosophy or art. It da Sabbath, good man. Talk about someting else for a change."

Literature! Philosophy! At last, I thought, nodding appreciatively at Hermann as he spoke—someone who might have something interesting to say.

Hermann paused and looked over at me. "So tell me, John—do you have a *vife?*"

A short time later, one of the women called out that our Sunday repast was ready. A large crowd formed as the branches that covered the cooking pit were removed, allowing great clouds of smoke to billow forth. Almost everyone cheered as two men hoisted the blackened carcass of a cow from the pit. Out on the frontier, it was a luxury to eat beef instead of venison, and I could only assume that George had wanted this to be a truly special day.

The smell of the beef and other dishes brought my appetite back with a vengeance. But was I hungry enough to chance any more conversations regarding my age, plans for my claim, or my state of matrimony? I wasn't sure.

"Did you eat yet?" asked Palmer.

His sudden reappearance startled me, causing me to jump as if I'd been jabbed. Not that I was unhappy to see him.

"Sorry," he said, patting me on the shoulder. "I reckon you're just about the jumpiest fellow I ever did know."

I'd heard that before. "No, I haven't eaten yet."

"You best get to it then, before they eat everything. Bunch of locusts, they are."

"I would, except that Sylvie Connolly is helping to serve the food. And I think her daughter Sam is standing next to her. Though after your little performance earlier, they've probably lost interest in me."

Palmer shaded his eyes. William Connolly had just stepped next to the girl, grabbed her by the arm, and seemed to be berating her in front of everyone.

"That, indeed, would be the fair Miss Sam. And William doesn't look none too pleased with her for missing your big introduction. And by the way, no such luck in throwing them off your track."

"What do you mean?"

"I overheard William querying George about your supposed fits. George looked like he was having a fit himself and told William it was all foolishness on my part."

"Don't you ever worry about getting in trouble, Palmer?"

"Ha! Why should I? Too many people worry about getting in trouble and end up saying nothing about anything their entire lives. Not me. Now come on." He took me by the elbow. "I'll introduce you to Miss Sam."

"Palmer!"

"What?" he said in mock surprise. "You don't want to meet her? I can't hardly believe it." He smiled. "Tell you what. I'll go get you something to eat and meet you in the woods along that creek over there."

"You don't mind? She won't pursue you?"

He grinned evilly. "Nah, I already scared *that* notion out of them. They'd sooner marry their daughter to Lucifer. Now go on before you find yourself unexpectedly proposing to Miss Connolly."

"Nobody asked where you were going with all this food?" I asked as Palmer and I walked along the creek. Famished, I took a huge bite of bread.

He shook his head. "Everybody was too busy stuffing their gullets to notice me at all. You want to stop and eat that, John? I don't mind if we sit for a bit."

Unable to answer with my mouth full, I shook my head vigorously. I glanced behind us to see if George saw who I was with. I worried how he—and Providence—might react to my keeping company with Palmer.

The sound of gunfire rang out from behind us. I almost choked in surprise.

"Relax." Palmer gestured with his rifle. "Reckon they've started the turkey shoot competition. These people aren't having fun unless they're killing something." He nodded at my plate. "Isn't the beef choice? I reckon it's been years since I last had beef."

I nodded, but in reality, I hadn't yet eaten any of the meat. Every time I looked at it, I saw Bliss lowing contentedly as I scratched her forehead. Someone fired again, but this time the sound was more muffled, and I hoped that we would soon be out of earshot entirely. I took a bite of the beef, chewed, then swallowed. It was good, but I didn't care for any more.

We reached the edge of the clearing, passing into the dark domain of towering oak and sumac, and away from the prying eyes of men. We walked in silence as I ate. Finally finished, I wiped my mouth on my sleeve and said, "I can't believe I made such a glutton of myself."

Palmer smiled. "Did George tell you how we came to have fresh-kilt beef?"

"No, but I must admit I was wondering about it." Beef was rare enough back east, but Zach had told me out on the frontier nobody ate cattle as they were far too valuable for breeding and producing milk and cheese.

Palmer laughed once. "You're eating the best milking cow of Mr. Adam Penney, *Esquire.*"

"What?" I looked down at my plate.

"That's right. The ninny shot her by accident." Palmer started laughing again.

"By accident! How?"

"You won't believe this, but he thought she was an Indian." Palmer laughed so hard that he had to stop walking and lean against a tree.

"You're having me on, aren't you, Palmer?"

"No, no, I swear! Last night, Mrs. Penney—her first name is something like Beatitude or Beatrix or Beastly—heard a noise outside their cabin. So she woke Adam, and when he heard the noise, he grabbed his rifle. Being the experienced frontiersman that he is, he crept up to the door, undid the latch, yanked the door open, and blasted away. The poor dumb cow had got loose and was standing right there. He shot her right between the eyes." Palmer laughed so hard that tears streamed down his face. "But get this. It's the second cow he's shot since he got here!"

By now I was laughing so much I couldn't breathe. "Stop it, Palmer! I smell a tall story! You're having me on, aren't you?"

"No, it's God's own truth, I tell you. He was out hunting for deer last week, just south of his claim. There's an Irish family down there named McWhirter. Their poor cow was out grazing in the woods when Ol' Hawkeye Penney mistook her for a deer."

I wiped the tears from my eyes. "No, I don't believe you. You're making this up."

He shook his head. "I swear on my immortal soul 'tis the truth."

"Okay, fine then. But I need to sit for a moment. You've made me laugh so hard I've hurt myself." We'd come to a wide, grassy bank, and we lowered ourselves to the ground, sitting with our backs against the trunk of a fallen tree; a row of large, feathery ferns sprouted from its topside. Palmer placed his rifle within easy reach.

"What is somebody like him doing on the frontier anyway?" I

asked. Using my thumbnail, I dug a pebble from the dirt and tossed it into the water. "I thought I was a greenhorn, but he's so prim and proper looking, I bet he'd have to lean up against a tree trunk just to cuss."

Palmer laughed. "It's George's doing. He's encouraging anybody who can pull up their own pants to settle in Franklin." Palmer picked up a stone and tossed it into the creek. "I give Mr. Penney till the end of summer before he and his missus pack up and head east. Course that's assuming he doesn't go and shoot her first—after all, I could see mistaking *her* for a cow!" We both laughed again.

"Tell me something, Palmer. George said something about you making a Scotch comment. What the hell is that? And why does he dislike you so much? Can't you pull up your own pants?"

"Oh, so John Chapman's not as nice and mildful likes he pretends, is he?" Palmer reached over and punched me on the shoulder.

"Ow." I hit him back. His chest felt hard under his shirt.

Palmer settled back against the tree trunk. "A Scotch comment is a spiteful, mean comment. Sort of like what you just said about me—or what I said about George's business sense."

"Was what you said true?" I hoped Palmer didn't lie for the hell of it.

"It's true all right. George left two failed ventures back east, which he probably hasn't told you, or too many others, about."

"Then how do you know about it?"

"My oldest sister, Beth, is married to one of George's brother's sons. That was how Caleb and George first came to meet each other."

"So you and George are family then," I said slyly.

He elbowed me in the ribs. "Like hell we are. I'd rather be related to Cain himself than that windbag. Anyway, Beth knows all about George, and since she and I are close, she filled me in on everything before I came out."

"I see."

"As to why George doesn't like me—he reckons he has a lot of reasons besides what I know about his past. For one, you heard how I talked about his precious Franklin and what he's done to this valley. Then, when he introduced me to Samantha, I told him I'd rather marry my mother than her. And finally, I think he's an idiot because if Caleb said the sun shone out of his ass, George would stand behind him to bask in the warmth."

"Why is he so enamored of Caleb?"

"He's not really. George isn't even especially religious. He heard William Penn speak once, and he said a town isn't really a town without a preacher. Seeing as there are so few preachers willing to settle on the frontier, George is pretty much willing to pretend to do or believe whatever Caleb decrees."

"And you pretty much do and believe the opposite."

"That's right."

"So why do you live with him?" I wondered how much truth was in George's comment about Palmer's willingness to take from those he criticized.

"Been asking about me, have you? Now why might that be?"

"I wasn't. George mentioned it after you stormed off."

"Figures he'd wait until I'd left," Palmer fumed.

I was digging up another pebble when Palmer grabbed me by the forearm.

"Don't move or say a word," he whispered as he reached for his rifle. "Look downstream."

At first I saw nothing in the gloom, but gradually my eyes made out the alders and birches and blackberry bushes sprouting from the creek bank. What did Palmer want me to see?

"There," Palmer whispered again, "on the far side of the creek by that dead tree."

With a stab of fear, I saw him: an Indian brave crouched motionless in the shade of the woods. Had he seen us? It appeared not. Quickly, I scanned the bank for others, but if they were there, I couldn't spot them. Thank God Palmer had his rifle. The Indian began to creep forward, stopping every few feet, glancing first one way then the other. He sniffed the air as cautiously as a deer leery of panthers.

Reaching the creek, the brave knelt down, dropping his head so his lips touched the water. He was perhaps twenty feet from us now, and I was amazed that he still hadn't seen us. I hoped Palmer wouldn't let him get too much closer without shooting. The brave looked up.

With a start, I realized he wasn't a man, but a boy—eleven or twelve at the most. Bare-chested, he wore only a worn breechcloth with dirty leggings. A long, black strip of hair started just above his forehead, ran over the top of his skull, then down his neck. Otherwise, his head was shaved. He looked weary and frightened, though with an air of resoluteness as well. What he mostly looked, though, was young.

Caleb's words about savages rang in my ears, and I felt like a hypocrite. Even though the boy had yet to make a hostile move, I'd been ready for Palmer to shoot him and wouldn't have uttered a word of protest if he had.

Finally, when the boy had drunk his fill, he turned and dissolved back into the woods. Without speaking, we stared for a moment as if we expected him to reappear.

Palmer made no move to rise. Instead, he set the rifle back on the ground, though still within easy reach.

"What are you doing? Shouldn't we go?"

Palmer shook his head. "I don't reckon we got anything to worry about. He's the one who needs be wary."

"What if there are others?"

"He was alone."

"How do you know?"

"I would've heard our visitor calling to anyone accompanying him with birdcalls. That's how they treat with each other in white man's territory."

I glanced back down the creek. "Should we help him?"

"Help him how?"

"I don't know. You're the one who said he should be wary. Maybe we should warn him. Or get him some food. He looked hungry."

Palmer waved his hand dismissively. "He's an Indian, John. He knows his way about."

I hoped Palmer was right. "What do you think he was doing?"

Palmer shrugged. "Could be a hundred different things. Maybe he's a Huron that got pushed east, and he's come looking for someone who got left behind. Now what were we talking about?"

I thought back. "Why you stay with Caleb," I said doubtfully.

"That's right. I stay because he needs me to."

"He needs you? You wouldn't know it from the way he treats you. I bet English noblemen calling on Philadelphia get warmer welcomes."

"That's Caleb for you, though it's true he's none too fond of me. You saw how fired up he was during the sermon. He saves all of his warmth for his preaching. Just ask his wife."

"What is it he needs you for?"

"Despite everything George says, I'm not utterly useless. In addition to my wit and insights, I'm a damn good hunter and better protection. Caleb's gift is speechifying, and not much else."

"What do you get out of it?"

"Supplies, a horse."

"I see. But you don't want a claim of your own?"

Palmer shook his head. "Nah. Do I act like I do?"

"Definitely not."

"Have you ever thought of heading farther west?"

"Palmer, except for a few foolhardy souls without the sense God gave a titmouse, this *is* farther west. Besides, I have finally got my own claim here."

"Don't tell me you're as eager as the rest to cut down every tree and plow every acre."

"As a matter of fact, I'm going to plant apple trees, not crops."

"Apple trees? I reckon there isn't much profit to be had there."

"I don't care."

"Don't you want to get rich like George?"

"Not particularly."

"What do you want?"

I thought, then said, "Mostly to be left alone, I think. That and to see the kwenaskat in the fall."

"The what?"

I told him about it.

"You mean the river grass. I saw that last year when we scouted the valley. It is quite comely, though I reckon George thinks it no better than charlock."

"What's charlock?"

"A weed. Tends to show up around grain and choke off the roots."

"Speaking of George—he also said something about you being a little sod who should be turned out on your ear."

"He did, did he? Well, a sod I may be, but there isn't anything little about me. As you should know," he said with a wink.

I'd had enough of doing nothing but being shocked by Palmer's mouth. It was time to show I could give as good as I got.

"I don't know. I've seen bigger—sods, I mean."

Palmer laughed. "But I reckon you've not seen finer."

"I never thought of sods as being fine things. I always preferred them rough and a little crude." I couldn't believe the things I was saying! My stomach felt fluttery bantering with Palmer this way.

"Is that the sort you are then—rough and crude?" Palmer asked. "And I'd picked you to be the refined and cultured type."

"Remember your saying about fine feathers not making fine birds?"

"What about it?"

"Then it must also be true that *refined* feathers don't make—"

"No, no!" he cried. "Don't say it! I reckon that's the *worst* pun I've ever heard. And if you make another one, you'll be the one out on your ear."

"What if he does turn you out, Palmer?" I asked, suddenly serious. "What will you do?"

He shrugged. "I'll hoe that row when I get to it. But I reckon it's likely to happen. Even Old 'there's a savage behind every tree' Caleb has just about figured there are fewer Indians around here than there are royals from the court of England."

"But what about the hunting? They have to eat."

"Well, I've gone and about worked myself out of a job. I've done such a fine job of teaching his boys to shoot, he doesn't need me for that much longer neither."

"Where will you go?"

"That depends."

"On what?"

He looked over at me. "If any offers come my way."

A warning call sounded in my head. Palmer wanted to move in with me? Suddenly our joking didn't seem so funny.

"Is something wrong, John?"

"No." After everything with the Major and Zach, what was I thinking by behaving this way? I couldn't even consider acting on my attraction to this man. As if I knew for certain Palmer wanted me to act. Granted, it seemed likely, but maybe it was all joshing for him. I wasn't about to chance finding out.

Palmer silently studied his fingernails for a moment, then said, "I reckon I'll head west not too long from now."

"But that's Indian territory."

"I know. I never intended to stay here though." He paused. "Nothing to keep me."

Closing my eyes, I tilted my face toward the sun. I barely knew Palmer. I didn't care if he left. In fact, I wanted him to.

"You sure you're all right, John?"

I nodded. Memories of Zach attacking me gave way to images of the Major flying through the air after he'd been shot. Then the Major faded away only to be replaced by Bliss lying amidst the wreckage of the stall. All of these terrible things had happened because of me, because of the things I desired. It couldn't happen again.

Suddenly, I felt Palmer touching my arm. Despite myself, I pulled away and demanded, "What are you doing?"

Palmer pulled his hand back. "I'm sorry. It's just that you're crying."

"I am?" I said, genuinely surprised. Sure enough, when I touched my cheeks, they were wet.

"I only wanted to make you feel better. I didn't mean to upset you."

I had to be a complete fool—for this was only the second time I'd been with Palmer, and only a fool could feel so strongly about someone he hardly knew. Smiling at him, I said, "It's all right." Almost without realizing it, I reached out my hand toward him. "I wish that . . . that . . ." As my voice trailed away, I let my hand fall back to my lap.

"You wish what?" Palmer asked so softly I hardly heard him.

"Never mind." I tilted my face back up to the sun. Was it possible, I wondered, to forget everything that had come before today, to start fresh, and believe good things could happen, even to me?

Something warm and wet pressed against my mouth. Startled, I jumped, and opened my eyes just as my teeth clicked against Palmer's.

"Sorry," he said shyly. "Did I hurt you?"

Palmer's kiss removed any doubts about what it was that he wanted from me. I knew what I wanted—him—but I also knew it couldn't be.

"No," I said, "but if you keep scaring me this way, I'm going to die of a heart seizure." I needed to be furious with Palmer, to drive him away before things got out of hand. I tried, but I couldn't do it. If Palmer stayed in my life, I'd be terrified every day. If he left, I'd be miserable. I felt so torn inside I wanted to scream.

"Maybe I should go. Whatever is troubling you, I'm not making it any better. I only want you to know—"

"Palmer, shut up." Since he'd said he was leaving anyway, I figured, what could one time hurt? That way, rather than wondering what one time together would have been like, I'd only have to wonder about what else might have been.

I leaned forward to kiss him. The kiss was chaste at first, but when I slipped my tongue into his mouth, he leaned forward, kissing me eagerly. A glowing warmth spread throughout my body. At least it did until a pain shot through my groin.

"Ow!" I hollered, catching sight of Palmer's hand in my crotch. "What are doing?" I asked, then realized he'd been trying to fondle my balls.

"I'm sorry. Shit. I didn't mean to hurt you, John."

"You're just a little too eager, that's all," I said, gingerly massaging myself.

The brown curves of his cheeks reddened as he stared shyly into his lap. Maybe Palmer wasn't as knowledgeable about everything as I'd assumed.

"You've never been with a man before, have you?" I asked uncomfortably. I'd never before discussed the subject with anyone. Doing so felt fraught with danger.

"No."

"A woman?"

"No!" Palmer said emphatically. "But if you reckon that means I'm not old enough to know what I want, you're wrong. And if you try and—"

"Palmer, I'm not your father or Caleb. Don't attack me."

He let out a sigh that seemed to carry away some of his anger. "Sorry."

"It's all right." I hesitated, then made up my mind. "Now come here."

Nervously he sidled up next to me.

"Let's try the kissing again. But for now, keep your hands above my waist."

I slid my hand behind his neck, pulling him to me. An unbidden image of Zach forced itself upon me, but I focused my mind and told myself that was then and this was now. Palmer watched me intently, but in his face I only saw gentleness and patience and, sadly, a little fear.

First I kissed him on the forehead, his cheeks, and then several times on the lips. I felt him trembling.

"That was nice," he said when I stopped.

"How's this?" I said, again slipping my tongue into his mouth.

He shivered, then pressed his mouth back even harder against mine. His tongue, frenetic and eager, explored my mouth so roughly that I fell backward.

"Sorry."

"No, no," I said, breathless. "That was fine." Clearly able to see the shape of his erection pressing against his breeches, I felt myself stiffen even more. I reached over and began caressing the outline of his bulge. His eyes slid shut as he began to moan until, without warning, he grabbed my hand.

"What's wrong? Was that too hard?"

"No. It was just that . . . I . . . was . . ."

"I see. I'll slow down some." Palmer blushed again. After all of the times I'd felt inadequate around him, I couldn't help but enjoy his discomfiture a little. It was nice to finally have the shoe on the other foot—though I hardly felt relaxed given what we were doing.

Sitting up, I wriggled out of my pants. Before I knew what was happening, my shirt suddenly leapt over my head. It seemed Palmer was eager to help me undress.

"Take it easy," I said, now naked and leaning back against a tree. Palmer stripped off his clothes, first revealing his hard stomach, then the creases that marked where his hips joined his abdomen—the part of a man that never failed to make me hot with desire.

Next came his thick, dark thatch, followed by his cock springing free. The damn thing looked hard enough to bore through rock. Then, the same way he had touched himself the first day I'd seen him, he cupped his balls in his hand and gently massaged them.

"Come here," I said hoarsely. Stepping forward, he kicked his feet free of his trousers. He stopped in front of me, his cock gently bobbing up and down like a boat on the sea.

I took him into my mouth. "Oh, God," he moaned, gripping the back of my head.

My hands slid from his hips to his back, then massaged their way down until I held the cheeks of his firm ass. I squeezed each side, which only caused him to press himself against me with all that much more urgency.

Worried that he would climax too soon, I rose so we could kiss again. My hands played with his nipples. Our hard-ons bumped against each other, Palmer moaning each time they did. I'm sure I did my fair share of grunting as well. I found myself lifting him, his legs wrapping around me as he feverishly kissed me.

I sank back to the ground so that Palmer sat across my hips, though I didn't even think about entering him the way I had Zach. At least not yet.

Reaching up, I took him in my hand and began stroking up and down. Every time I slid my hand along his cock, a little groan escaped him. His whole body rose upward with each stroke so that his balls brushed across my stomach. Harder and harder I stroked him, his moans growing louder each time. Arching his back, he grabbed my shoulders, seeming to lose control as jism shot skyward before landing hot and sticky on my face and chest. Palmer still sat astride me, little tremors rippling through him as he pushed loose strands of hair from his face. Taking a deep breath, he let it out and whispered, "I'd no idea it would be like that."

As he fell backward onto his heels, he looked around us uneasily.

"Do you think someone might have followed us?" I asked, feeling a little uneasy myself.

"Nah." He looked back at me. "Do you want me to have a go at you?"

"Would you like to?"

He nodded slowly.

"You don't have to, Palmer. I won't be upset."

He smiled sheepishly. "Don't reckon I've yet to do a solitary thing I didn't want to do, John. Ask Caleb." Without another word, he knelt forward and took me in his mouth. Several times he went down too far on me and began to choke.

"Take it easy, Palmer."

He nodded.

I watched his head bob up and down as his tongue and lips caressed my dick. The warm, wet sensation of his mouth enfolded me as his hand, gently this time, fondled my balls. The hot pressure that would eventually boil over into my climax built and built. At last the exquisite pain was too much to resist; my hips convulsed, his mouth filling with my jism, and I came so hard it almost hurt. My whole body felt as if it had been skinned, and I half-expected to see blood when I opened my eyes.

Still, he didn't stop until I could bear no more and had to push him away.

"Was that all right?" he asked.

"I think with lots of practice you might get it eventually."

He looked hurt.

"It was a joke, Palmer."

"I don't think this is something you oughten to tease about," he said sulkily.

"I'm sorry," I said, even though I understood it wasn't the teasing that upset him. Unless I was sorely mistaken, he felt guilty for what we'd done. I'd felt bad my first time, too. Hell, I felt bad now.

"It's nearly dusk," Palmer said curtly. "We best be heading back.

"Are you all right?"

He briefly flashed me an annoyed look that gave way to one of chagrin. "I will be. Somehow I keep expecting to hear Caleb or my father or God telling me how awful I am."

We pulled on our clothes and headed back. I walked behind Palmer as we silently wended our way along the creek. I worried how I'd make it back to my claim if Thomas had already left. Palmer had a horse, but asking him was fraught with complications I didn't want to think about.

Halfway back, the unexpected blast of a rifle rent the evening air. I flinched.

"Damnation," said Palmer. "I can't believe they're still trying to prove who's the best shot. I hope they're not drunk. Someone could get hurt."

A second shot rang out, and Palmer shook his head in disgust. We tried to quicken our pace, but could only go so fast—the creek twisted and curved back on itself more times than a maggot marauding through meat.

Finally, we stepped from the oppressive forest into the clearing, and it felt like emerging from a cave. I wanted to throw out my arms and revel in the sense of freedom. The sun had set, and the twilight air felt as cool as the blue colors limning the horizon.

We hurried through the clearing, now empty except for a few low-burning fires amongst the detritus of the day's events. Everywhere I looked I saw dirty plates, cups, corncobs, apple cores, empty jugs, nutshells, bones, and pieces of gristle scattered about between crumpled blankets and logs. I recalled Palmer's words about how ugly Franklin looked.

The picked-over carcass of the cow still hung between the two poles, bits of flesh and tendons dangling from the bones. A half dozen chevets took flight as we passed by, their harsh voices fulminating at us for disturbing their easy meal.

In the distance, among the buildings, I caught the flickering dance of a large bonfire, then a whiff of sweet-smelling smoke, and I knew that was where everyone would be. They were probably gathered inside the cozy circle of firelight, singing and telling stories.

All I wanted was to go home.

As we approached, I heard the voices of the settlers, but louder, harsher, more perturbed than I'd expected. I wondered if someone was having a fight. We paused outside the circle of light and saw, to my surprise, no one sitting around the fire. Squinting, I tried to find the voices, and at last spotted twenty or so people gathered outside George's cabin.

Palmer grabbed my arm. "Look," he said urgently.

"What? Where?"

"The pole. Between the fire and George's cabin."

In what passed for the town square, someone had erected a pole, but it must have been done hastily for it tottered at a crazy angle. Something round was perched on top, but since the pole stood just outside the firelight, I couldn't quite tell what. A gust of wind came up, momentarily stirring the flames higher, and in the flickering light I realized I looked at a head.

The head of the Indian boy.

His expression was frozen in a rictus that said he hadn't died easily. I retched once, then spit and wiped at my mouth.

"By the light of God," whispered Palmer. "What happened?"

"It's Gwennie," I said, suddenly seized by an idea.

"Are you blind, John? It's the fellow we saw by the creek."

"No. I meant it's Gwennie he's coming looking for."

"Why do you think that?"

"I'm not sure. But you said he might've come here looking for someone left behind."

Palmer shook his head. "But Gwennie wasn't left behind. She came here on her own."

"I still think he was looking for her. And someone's got to tell her what happened. I've got to tell her."

"Why you, John? Besides, no one even knows where she lives."

"I'll find out." With that I spun around and headed away.

Even I wasn't sure why I had to tell her—maybe I thought doing so would let me feel less terrible for having done nothing for the boy when I had the chance.

In the end, Gwennie had to find me. Palmer and I asked everyone where she lived, but no one knew. George had claimed not to know either, but the way he hesitated before answering made me think he did know.

Palmer offered to help me search the valley, but I declined. After what we'd done, being with him made me too uneasy. I set out alone the following day, climbing the ridge behind my cabin. It took me most of the morning, and as soon as I reached the top, I knew this was folly. I could search this valley for two months and not find Gwennie. Especially if she didn't want to be found.

So I gave up finding her and went back to tending my truck patch. I hadn't much choice if I wanted anything to eat come winter. For two weeks now, cloudless days accompanied by hot winds from the south had been the rule. That afternoon, Thomas stopped by and ominously told me that steady winds from the south were a sure sign of a drought. I asked him if he knew anything about the death of the Indian boy, but Thomas said he'd left the gathering early and hadn't even known about it.

It was late afternoon on the second day after I stopped looking for Gwennie when she came to me. I had refilled my buckets for the hundredth time when I glanced up and, to my surprise, saw her crossing the creek, as if she had that instant appeared there. How the hell had she made it from the woods, through the meadow, and halfway across the creek before I had spotted her? My frontier skills still needed much work.

"Hello, John," she called out as she approached. The blue bonnet was back, but instead of wearing a skirt and going topless, she wore a beaded, buckskin dress.

"Hi, Gwennie."

"How are crops doing?"

"Fine. Well, rather dry actually." Now that she was here, and I could tell her what had happened, I suddenly wasn't so eager to see her. Turning away, I picked up the buckets and began to walk.

"Would you like me take a bucket for you?"

"No. That's all right."

"Don't be stubborn. Give me bucket."

Handing one to her, I said, "Gwennie, I need to tell you something."

I told her about spotting the boy, about not offering to help him, and that I thought he might have been looking for her.

"He was looking for me. I'd even talked to him that day."

"You had?" I couldn't keep the surprise from my voice. "Where was he going when we saw him then?"

"I don't know."

"Did you know him?"

"No."

"So why was he looking for you?"

"You ask many questions, don't you?"

We reached the truck patch and carefully balanced the buckets on the uneven ground. I'd worked too hard to waste even a single drop. I turned to face Gwennie.

"I didn't mean to pry, Gwennie." I took a deep breath. "Did you know that they killed him?"

"No." Her expression was inscrutable.

"Well, they did. Then they cut off his head and put it on a pole. I don't understand how they could do something so awful, but they did." To my surprise, I felt tears welling in my eyes. "I feel terrible that we didn't warn him. Or offer to escort him safely through the valley." She reached over and wiped a tear from my face.

"What you want to warn him about?"

"To be careful. To watch out for the townsfolk."

"I sure he know quite well need to be careful. It not your fault."

"I wanted to find you so I could tell you in case you had known him."

"You did?"

I nodded.

"You a good man, John. Now why don't I help you finish giving truck patch a good soaking?"

"Aren't you angry?" I asked, puzzled. "Don't you want to know who killed him?"

"Why should I?" she asked, dipping a noggin into the bucket. "I know it a white man who do it, and I know other white people think killing Indian same thing as killing rattlesnake before it strike. Maybe, if white man's God exist, he care and will do something to this man when he die."

For the next hour, we hauled water, then ladled it over the fragile green shoots lined up in their neat rows.

When the red disk of the sun began to sink into the silhouette of the mountains, we stopped work. I asked Gwennie to have supper with me.

"I haven't much in the way of fresh meat, but plenty else."

"You like fish?" Gwennie asked.

"Sure."

"Then you start cooking what else you make, and I be right back."

She returned ten minutes later, holding her skirt in front of her as a makeshift basket. Peering in, I caught sight of a half dozen trout wriggling about, their muscular, silver bodies catching the lamplight and throwing it back.

Inside the cabin, we quickly cleaned the fish, then Gwennie stuffed them with herbs she had gathered down by the creek. She wrapped each fish in the broad, spiky leaf of a plant she found growing under the porch, then buried them in the coals of the fire.

"I not been inside the Jacksons' cabin since last summer," Gwennie said, glancing around.

"You knew the Jacksons then?" I was slicing tonquay, a bread I'd made from roasted roots.

"A little. I help deliver the baby, then seen them once or twice before George asked me to look at baby again."

"You mean when it got sick?"

She nodded.

"I heard what happened. A real tragedy." I glanced at Gwennie, but she only looked back at me indifferently. "I mean it's too bad there wasn't a doctor in Franklin so they wouldn't have had to leave."

"If there doctor in Franklin, then baby would never been sick."

"Why not?"

"Baby being sick only excuse to leave. Catherine not happy here, wanted to go home, but Alexander not hear of it. At least not until baby got so sick."

"So she found a reason to go home. You sound as if you blame her for that."

"I blame her if she want to go so bad, she do almost anything to get her way."

"Are you saying she made the baby sick?"

Gwennie nodded again.

"No mother would do that! Would she?" Gwennie said nothing.

She only stared at me as if I'd claimed no white person would ever harm an Indian. "Did you tell George or Alexander?"

Gwennie laughed. "Indian woman accuse white woman of poisoning her own baby? Ha! People here already barely accept me because I Indian. Only thing happen if I tell is that I accused of making baby sick. Some people already say that about me. Besides, baby no concern of mine, it die no matter what I do. So I say nothing to George, not then, not now. I shouldn't say anything to you either."

"Then why are you?"

She stared at me for a moment, then said, "I think fish done."

I recalled what that otherwise foolish woman, Sylvie, had said about Gwennie—that talking with her was like talking to the moon. Gwennie wasn't unkind by any means, but sometimes there was something a little, well, aloof about her.

We took the food out onto the porch. The trout smelled wonderful, and I was ravenous, which made it all the more disappointing to discover that the fish tasted so awful. Whatever herb she had stuffed it with had a tart, bitter flavor that I didn't care for.

"You not like." It wasn't a question.

"No, it's fine," I said, hurriedly taking another bite.

Gwennie sucked the eyes out of a trout. "You bad liar, John Chapman. You might as well put war paint on face, then say you want peace, for all I believe you."

"Fine. You believe what you want."

"I always do," she said resolutely, and I thought of Palmer.

"Do you think the drought will last long?" I asked, annoyed by her reading me so well.

A quizzical look crossed her face. "Dry-out? I not know this word."

Her English was so good, it hadn't occurred to me that there were words she didn't know. "Um, let's see. A drought is when we don't have rain for such a long time that crops shrivel and die."

She nodded. "I see. I think dry-out will last all summer. My father would say it not rain until Grandmother-in-the-North's luck change."

I thought for a moment about the hot breezes and how they

came from the south, then said, "You mean it won't rain until the wind comes up from the north."

Arching one eyebrow, she glanced over at me, and I felt pleased. "You not like other white people."

"How so?"

"You not just laugh at things Indians say."

"Maybe that's because my father used to laugh at the things I said."

"You not sound fond of him."

It was my turn to laugh. "Is the vole fond of the stoat? I haven't seen him in years."

"What is a vole?"

"It's a small rodent, like a mouse. Stoats eat them like candied fruit."

"I see. Where your stoat, I mean father, at now?"

I laughed. "Dead, maybe. Either that or at Longmeadow, where I grew up."

"What about your mother?"

"She died when I was four, but I've a stepmother, Lucy. She's a good woman, which makes it all the sadder she married my father."

"You have brothers and sisters?"

"Yes, but except for my older sister, they're all quite a bit younger. There are eleven altogether, though Father paid his offspring so little mind that it wouldn't surprise me if he'd managed to misplace a few."

Gwennie smiled, and I realized it was the first time I'd seen her do so. It was only a small smile, like the sun ever so briefly appearing from behind the clouds, but even so, it transformed her face, giving her a warmth I hadn't seen before. It made me want to be her friend even more, but I wasn't sure if she'd let me.

"My father did that once. Lose my brother."

"Was he not a good father either?"

"No, no," Gwennie said, suddenly serious. "My father good man, very hardworking man, but not have strong memory. One day—it fall and the corn was ripe—Father in field picking ears that he put into two big baskets. Mother needed to go into town with Reverend Harris, but not want to take my brother, James, who was only year old. Well, field was very big, many rows, and after a while, Father's back grew tired from carrying James. He not as strong as Mother, you see. He set James down, all swaddled and sleeping in his blankets, in one of the rows. But when he finished picking corn, Father forgot about James and carried the full baskets home to wait for Mother to return.

"I don't think I ever saw her so mad as when she realized Father forgot her baby in field. Ever since we become Christians, five years earlier, we speak nothing except English. In school, if I forgot and said something in Lenni Lenape, the teacher hit with stick. Even at home, we always speak in white man's words, though they not always able to say everything I feel. But that day Mother not speak only English." Gwennie paused and smiled for the second time, but this was a slow, slightly melancholy smile—the kind I had seen as a boy on my great-grandmother's face as she recalled something pleasant from her childhood. "No, that day Mother swore and hollered at Father in Lenni Lenape as if she never stopped speaking it for a day. For fifteen minutes, the three of us ran up and down the rows of corn looking for James, Mother telling Father all the terrible things she do to him if we not find baby. It just started to rain when Father found him, still sound asleep. And he wasn't wet either, because rows of leafy corn had covered him like a tent. Then Father make his big mistake."

"His big mistake? What could be worse than forgetting the baby?"

"When Mother took James from him, he said, 'See, nothing wrong. Look how happy he is. He not mind sleeping outside.'"

"What did your mother say?"

"She furious. She say, 'If it so damned fine sleeping in field, then you going to sleep out there—for a week!'"

"A week!"

Gwennie nodded. "And she made him do it, too—even though it rained that night like God again going to flood earth!" Gwennie started laughing. "Mother felt bad for him, but she a woman who always stand by what she say. But on second night, even though it rain again, she slept out in cornfield with him. Then the third night—the rain had stopped by then—James and I sleep there, too. All the rest of that week we sleep outside under stars thrown over sky like seeds across the earth. At least we did until Reverend Harris found out and chastised Father for behaving like heathen savage." She paused, and her face took on a wistful expression. "Sleeping outside like that reminded me of how things were before we came to Gnadenhutten," she said softly. "I think it reminded Mother and Father, too." When Gwennie realized I was watching her, a ripple of emotion ran across her face until, like a turtle pulling back into its shell, her expression once again became impossible to read. I had a feeling there wouldn't be a third smile.

"So you're a Christian, I take it?"

"No. I was, but not now."

"I see. Is your family still in Gnadenhutten?"

She looked at me blankly, then asked with a voice utterly devoid of emotion, "You ever hear of Gnadenhutten before today?"

"No, can't say that I have."

"It a place built to convert Indians to Christianity—to make them civilized like white people. Indians like my mother and father who took us there when I six and we baptized. We live there peacefully, grow wheat and corn, learn to read Bible, not fight anyone, especially whites who are now supposed to be our Christian brothers. Then sixteen years ago some other Indians—not Christians, not from Gnadenhutten—cross the Ohio into Pennsylvania and attacked a white settlement and kill several people. Soldiers chase those Indians back into Ohio Territory, but can't catch them. Eventually they find Gnadenhutten and say they there for our protection. Say we must gather everyone together in town square."

Gwennie set her plate on the porch, then wiped a few crumbs from her lap before continuing.

"They were led by army man named David Williamson. He decide that we should be punished for what these other Indians did. There were more than eighty men, women, and children in Gnadenhutten. Reverend Harris try to tell them we not to blame, but they knock him to ground and start killing Indians. Soldiers got drunk, kill slow and take all day to kill everybody. They laugh while they do it. I not die because Mother and I argue that morning and when they come, I already hiding from her in woods on edge of field where they kill everybody."

"You saw what happened?"

She nodded and continued as if she were recounting something as mundane as explaining how to grind wheat or sew pants. "I see crying men made to eat their own private parts before they die. I see mothers scream as their crying babies tossed to other soldiers who caught them on bayonet. I see my own father watch my mother raped, then both burned alive."

My plate slipped from my lap. Stunned by what I was hearing, I felt paralyzed and could only peer helplessly down at the spilled food.

"I sorry, John, I not mean to upset you. I didn't mean to speak of such things. Sometimes they force their way out of me."

She picked up my plate, and I stared at her in disbelief. How could she tell the story in such a blasé tone? Or maybe I was confusing blasé with deadened. Maybe that was the only way she could talk about what had happened. Maybe it was her past, not her being an Indian, that made her the way she was.

"I'm the one who's sorry, Gwennie."

"You nothing be sorry for. You not the one who did killing. You even try and save Indian boy you know nothing about."

"Still, I sort of feel—" My words stopped because Gwennie had frozen like a deer in a meadow sensing the presence of danger. I turned and followed her eyes until I spotted the figure on a horse that had emerged from woods just south of the meadow. "It's all right, Gwennie," I said when I was able to make out the figure of Palmer astride the horse. "He's a . . . friend," I said hesitantly as I uneasily recalled all that had transpired between us. We had never had the chance to talk over our having lain together—not that I particularly desired to do so. But I felt I owed it to Palmer if he did.

I turned back to her, but she was already hurrying through the meadow, not caring who it might be. By the time Palmer rode up, she had crossed the creek and vanished into the woods.

I knew from the saddlebags that he was leaving and had come to say good-bye. Only now I didn't want to hear it, even if I owed it to him. Why couldn't being with Palmer be part of George's accursed Providence?

I spied weeds growing amongst the bushel beans in the truck patch. Avoiding Palmer's eyes, I knelt down and began yanking the weeds from the earth with far more exertion than required.

"John," Palmer said softly, "I wanted . . ."

Without looking at him, I shook my head. I couldn't ask him to stay, nor could I say good-bye.

I felt so many things—regret, desire, fear. Lust and shame filled my mind, affection and loneliness my heart.

Sensing Palmer's eyes on me, I glanced up. The sun silhouetted him, and it was only by shading my eyes that I could see his face. We studied each other for a moment. He smiled ever so slightly, and I knew he understood.

He nodded once, tipped his hat, then turned and rode toward the river.

I was alone again.

ELEVEN

Friendships never came easy for me. Perhaps embarrassment over my drunk, traitorous father compelled me to keep people away. Possibly I feared that my longings for other boys would be discovered if I let anyone too close. Or maybe it was because I had nothing in common with people who discussed little other than how the next crop would yield, or whether God approved of this petty act or that questionable thought.

Still, like a flower somehow blooming in the middle of a well-trod road, a friendship occasionally happened anyway.

In my adolescence, one of my few friends, Abigail, was not only a woman fifteen years older than I, but the mother of one of my schoolmates. Not long before I left home for good, Abigail and I began spending afternoons talking seriously about life or laughing as we spun fanciful stories about places with dragons and sea monsters. From the tales she wove for me—most often about ladies-in-waiting escaping—I understood that she, too, wanted to leave Longmeadow.

One afternoon, we arranged to meet for a walk, but she never appeared. When I passed back through town, I discovered why. Her husband, a minister, had long known about our made-up stories—abominable lies, he called them—but that day had forbade her ever to meet with me again. When she still

snuck out to see me he had her arrested and put in the stock-
ade, which was where I found her. I knew I couldn't speak to
her, but when our eyes met, hers seemed to glow for a moment
as if a coal burned from within. Then just as quickly the glow
faded, her eyes fell from mine, and her face seemed to die.

My own spirit wavered, and I knew this place would
suffocate me if I stayed much longer.

May 1798

THE NIGHT AFTER PALMER LEFT, I LAY AWAKE TRYING, AND FAILING,
not to worry about him. How far away was he by now? Was he safe?
I tried to divert my thoughts with plans for my claim, only to find
myself picturing him cooking a meal, or settling down to sleep by a
fire.

Mostly, I tried not to think that, in all likelihood, I would never
see him again.

Somewhere nearby, an owl and a toad hooted and croaked in
tandem as if retorting to one another. Once I nearly jumped out of
bed when a raccoon or opossum dropped from one of the trees onto
the cabin, its tiny nails clicking on the roof as it scampered away.
Shortly before dawn, I finally fell into a restless sleep where I
dreamt that instead of a cow, I had been roasted over the pit and
eaten by the settlers.

A ribbon of bright sunlight fell through the window and across my
face, and I awoke exhausted and morose. Outside, blue jays and
bishop's larks chattered and argued their way through the trees as
they competed for the choicest berries and most succulent insects.
For a long moment, I lay in bed, watching sunlight spill through
chinks in the walls that, from living with Zach, I knew would have to
be sealed before winter. But that was months away; for now I sought

the cool breezes that piggybacked the sunlight through those gaps and into the cabin.

The steps outside squeaked.

Instantly wide-awake, I whispered hopefully, "Palmer?"

The steps creaked again; the sound of muffled voices came from behind the door, and I knew it wasn't Palmer. "Who's there?" I called out, sliding from bed and fumbling around the dim cabin for an ax or one of Alexander's rifles.

Before I could find one, the door swung halfway in, and William Connolly's haggard face poked around the door.

"Good day to you, John." He smiled his yellow, broken-toothed smile and stepped hesitantly inside. "I 'ope I didn't 'larm you none. Per'aps you ought to consider barring your door when yer sleeping. This mayn't be Indian territory no longer, but the infidels still pop up now and then."

My initial panic subsided, replaced by bewilderment. All I could do was stare at him as if he were crazy. He turned and nodded to someone on the other side of the door before facing me again.

"Sorry to 'ave rousted you from bed. I done figured you'd be up by now." When I said nothing, he stepped farther inside and, now less hesitant, glanced around the cabin. "I s'pose per'aps you 'aven't eaten yet?"

I shook my head as his malodorous pong filled the cabin. How had I not noticed such a terrible smell the day we'd first met?

"Good, good," he said. "After all, 'unger makes the best sauce." Emboldened by my passivity, he walked across the cabin to the chair where my pants and shirt hung. "Why don't you make yerself decent then," he said, tossing my clothes at me, "'cause I reckon I got an agreeable surprise for you."

The only surprise I wanted was to find out that I was still dreaming. Already part of my mind chastised myself for not speaking up and telling him to get the hell out. A smile crept across my face as I imagined what Palmer would have said to William.

When I'd finished dressing, William pushed open the door and motioned someone inside. It was no surprise when the young woman whom I had glimpsed at the May Day celebration entered.

"I knew 'ow disappointed you musta been not to make Sam's 'quaintance at the revelry, John. So I took the liberty of fetching 'er up 'ere to meetcha. John Chapman, this 'ere is my daughter, Samantha Rose Connolly. Samantha, this is Mr. John Chapman."

Dumbfounded, I could only stare at the both of them. She, too, seemed too unnerved to speak and stared at the ground.

William looked back and forth between the two of us. "Come on then, Samantha—say 'ello to Mr. Chapman," he ordered at last.

"'Ello, Mr. Chapman," she mumbled so softly that I barely heard her. I disliked such passivity, which I'd often encountered in women. Give me a man, who for all his potential shortcomings, at least wouldn't be as docile as a cow.

She glanced up at me. Her soft brown eyes were unusually large, but comely, nonetheless, and their unusual size only made them more so. Otherwise, she was of average height and weight and, if I properly understood what typically attracted a man to a woman, seemed attractive enough to appeal to the opposite sex. Perhaps her lack of marriage proposals was strictly due to the swollen neck Palmer spoke of. Such defects often frightened off potential suitors, though I saw no signs of hers.

She wore a pale blue dress made of cotton and that looked to have at one time been rather attractive with fancy lace around the collar as well as on the fringe of the sleeves. But most of the lace had long since abraded away, the sleeves were ragged, and I could see where several rents had been stitched. A red ribbon sat atop her auburn hair like a bow on a present.

"Now curtsy like your ma done showed you."

The girl stiffened, her pleading eyes darting to her father's face, but he only nodded sternly. For the first time, I noticed that she carried a burlap sack. After setting it on the ground, she awkwardly placed her left foot behind her, hesitantly held her arms out, and quickly bobbed up and down several times, wobbling as she struggled to keep her balance. I hadn't meant to laugh, but I did and immediately felt like a heel. My sister Elizabeth would have been ashamed of me and rightly so.

"I'm sorry," I said. "That was rude of me."

What Samantha had thought of me before I knew not, but from the furious look she threw at me, to say she now hated me might not have been overstating it.

"She mayn't be the most graceful creature God ever put on this earth, John, but she'll make a sturdy wife. And she's a right fine cook. She's got twelve brothers and sisters, and she done almost all of the cooking since she was ten. She even done made a few things fer you. 'Ere," he said, pulling out a chair from the table, "sit while she gets you something to eat."

"William, that's really not—"

"Just sit, John," he said, cutting me off with an edge in his voice that surprised me. "We're neighbors after all. Why not be neighborly?"

Sitting, I shook my head in disbelief. This man—not knowing, or perhaps not caring, if I was kind or cruel, hardworking or lazy, sober or drunk—had walked all these miles to barge into my cabin to induce me to marry his daughter.

And what about me? This was the frontier, the edge of nowhere for Christ's sake—was I *never* to find respite from such entanglements?

As the girl emptied the sack, then moved about preparing whatever it was they'd brought, William pulled out a chair and sat across from me. "'Tis a terrible shame 'bout what 'appened the other night, isn't it?"

For a moment I was confused, until I remembered seeing the Indian boy's head illumed by the light of the fire. Then I became confused again—William thought what had happened was a shame? Yet he'd cheered and clapped during Caleb's sermon as fervently as anyone. "What exactly do you mean?" I asked.

"The McWhirter girl."

"Who?"

"Don't you know?"

"I guess not."

He let out a whistle. "She was kilt by an Injun in Franklin the night of the celebration. Maybe you 'ad already left by the time it 'appened?"

"We left after we ate," I said in a daze. The Indian boy had killed a girl?

"Pardon me," said Samantha as she squeezed past, but I barely noticed her.

"I'll tell you 'ow it went. After it got dark, we was all sitting around the fire, jus' talking, telling stories and the like. One of the McWhirter girls 'ad left 'er doll back in the meadow where we'd ate, so Ian McWhirter took 'er back to the meadow to see if they could find it. Some of the other kids were bored, so they tagged along as well. What nobody knew was that a sneaky son-of-a-bitch Injun was already there thieving our belongings."

"What belongings?" Palmer and I had walked through the meadow shortly after the gunfire. The only *belongings* had been the refuse—gnawed-on bones, corncobs, and the like—from the celebration.

"Food, whatnot. That ain't the important part. As you must know, Injuns are infamous for snatching white children, and in the dark, this Injun must 'ave thought the kids were alone 'cause 'e decided to grab one of 'em. Turned out it was six-year-old Lizzie McWhirter 'e got, although Ian didn't know it was 'is own daughter at the time.

William paused to clear his throat, spit on the floor, then continued, "Anyway, the kids all started screaming and running around, and somehow Ian spotted the red bastard running toward the woods. That must 'ave been when 'e killed the girl. I figure 'e done it to distract anybody chasing after 'im. Of course, Ian 'ad brought along both 'is rifles in case there was bears that 'ad been attracted to the cow carcass. 'Is first shot missed, but 'is second took the Injun down jus' before 'e got to the woods."

"So Ian shot him?"

William nodded. "Didn't kill 'em, though—jus' winged 'im. Ian took off running to where the Injun 'ad fallen." William shook his head. "The gall of raiding a white settlement like that! Much as I don't care for 'im, Caleb Baxter is right about Injuns being Godless 'eathens."

"What happened then?" I asked, feeling nauseated.

"We all 'eard the screaming and the gunshot, so we came a running. Like I said, the Injun was alive—Ian 'ad shot 'im through the back and 'e couldn't move 'is legs—so we 'auled him back to the campfire so we could see who 'e was."

"And then?"

"And then Ian cut off that fucking savage's 'ead."

"After he killed him."

"No, that was 'ow 'e killed 'im. Couple of men 'eld 'im down while Ian used a knife. Lizzie McWhirter suffered, so why shouldn't 'e?"

My stomach heaved at the image. That boy hadn't looked savage enough to kill a girl, but what did I know about how Indians looked? "How's the family?"

"Upset as you'd expect, but what's to be done? At least it wasn't one of the older, more useful children. Apparently, Caleb 'ad words with that shiftless brother of 'is over what 'appened, so Caleb threw 'im out."

"He did? What did Palmer say?"

"Seems Palmer objected to Caleb's calling Injuns vermin and saying they should be dealt with as such. Palmer said the Injuns 'e'd met were more Christian than any of us, and if 'ell exists, we'd all end up there before anybody else. If that bastard were my relation, 'e'd 'ave a lead ball twixt the eyes by now."

Palmer's audacity took my breath away.

William looked over at Samantha and snapped, "'Bout done, girl? Mr. Chapman is looking awful 'ungry."

"No, no. I'm fine," I protested, trying to get her attention, but she wouldn't look at me.

"It's just done now, Papa," she said, carrying a plate to the table. On it was a slab of some kind of meat, a scoop of porridge, two scones, and a handful of dried apple pieces. "The johnnycakes will be done in a minute, Mr. Chapman."

"Well, go ahead, John," said William. "That's fresh bear bacon, so you best tuck into it before it gets cold."

Between William's reason for visiting and the story about the Indian, any appetite I might normally have had was long gone. But I had to eat—something told me I'd have no peace until I did. With a weak smile, I picked up my fork and took a bite. The food tasted fine, but I wasn't hungry.

As I attempted to eat, Samantha stood by the fire, staring at her feet.

"Samantha," I said, hoping to mollify her, "would you like to sit? Maybe have . . ."

"She's fine where she's at, John," William said. "Sam's a good girl. She knows 'ow a woman ought to behave." He watched me eat for a moment, then cleared his throat. "John, the piece I've come to say needs few words, so I'll jus' get to it. You need a wife, and Samantha 'ere needs a 'usband. What do you say?"

Before I could speak, he stood back, prodding the blushing girl in front of him.

"Now there's no denying she ain't a beauty, but she ain't the 'omeliest woman I've ever seen neither. She's got no scars from pox or measles, still 'as most of 'er teeth, and she's no Scotch bed-warming pan either—I'll vouch that 'er maiden'ead 'tain't never been touched," he said matter-of-factly. Samantha no longer blushed; indeed, her face had gone as white as chalk as she bit down on her lip. Her mortification was obvious and understandable—to have your own father speak about you in such a way!

"She's sturdy, too," William continued relentlessly. "The girl works from sunup to sundown taking care of 'er brothers and sisters. With all that experience, she'll make a right fine mother. And look at 'er arms and legs," he said, pulling up the sleeve of her dress. She flinched, and I caught sight of a purplish bruise. "Why, she can out-lift both of 'er oldest brothers and . . . and . . ." His voice trailed off, and for the first time, I realized that he was as nervous as I.

"Turn around, girl," he ordered, grabbing her roughly by the shoulder. He smacked her hard on the rump and said, "And look at those 'ips, John. She'll bear you big, strong boys." He paused and spun her back around. "Will you 'ave 'er then?" A note of desperation had crept into his voice.

Granted, Samantha was only a girl, but I couldn't believe that her own father would treat her as if she were nothing more than a slave to be sold off at auction. "Uh, William, I don't think—"

"Oh, oh!" he said eagerly. "Don't answer yet. I almost forgot— she sews beautiful as well." He removed a shirt from the burlap sack. "She made this one specially for you." He folded it in half, then pressed it into my hands; I saw that he was sweating. "So 'ow about it, John?"

"William, I don't think . . ."

"I'll throw in a bag of grain."

"William . . ."

"Two bags."

"I . . ."

"A rifle. And a pound of lead." He pulled a handkerchief from his pocket and wiped the sheen from his face.

"Please, William, don't do this."

He walked around the table so that he loomed above me. "It ain't much of a dowry, John, and I know it, but I don't 'ave anything else to offer. I'm a poor man, and this is the best I can do."

Eyeing the door, I wondered if I could escape should William become physical. I glanced at Samantha, who appeared to be trembling.

After a moment, William stepped back from me and took a deep breath. "One of the younger girls then?" he said softly. "You like them young? Their mother reckons they're too young, but what does—?"

"William!" I exclaimed, cutting him off.

He scratched the top of his head as if thinking. After a moment he said, "You know, John, you shouldn't be too picky. You're a little old yerself to not be married, and we all know, unmatched is undone."

"That's *my* concern," I snapped.

"Of course, of course. On the other 'and, George is the one who suggested you meetin' Sam. 'E'll be mighty disappointed if 'e 'ears you weren't interested."

"Are you threatening me? Are you saying you'll get George to threaten me?"

"No, no, John. Not at all. Just an observation. Well, you know, you needn't be deciding nothing right now anyways. Plenty of time for that later." He picked the burlap sack up off the ground, then brightened a little. "'Ow 'bout you two go for a walk then? Jus' to get to know each other a bit."

Before I could respond, he'd already propelled us out the cabin door.

As if we were both eager to put as much distance as possible between ourselves and the cabin, we began walking quickly toward the creek without speaking. Walking next to her, I felt trapped, and all I could think of was Palmer. It wasn't fair that I'd had to let him go without saying so much as a word of what I really felt, and now here I was with this woman, having to pretend that it was at least within the realm of possibility that I might want to marry her.

After so many years of trying to please others or worrying over their expectations of me, I vowed nothing on earth would ever compel me to marry Samantha, or any other woman. At least now I was that much my own man.

Samantha and I hurried onward through the kwenaskat—now stippled with gold—as it brushed against our legs, rustling with a gentle murmur.

I turned my attention to her. In the cabin, I'd been too distraught by what William had been saying to pay her much mind or wonder how she might be feeling. I intended to rectify that now. Unlike her father, I understood she was a real person with feelings and deserved to be treated as such.

As we walked, she pushed her long brown hair back from her face, hooking it behind her ears. In doing so, I caught a glimpse of the swelling Palmer had spoken about. It was there all right, but the sort of thing I wouldn't have noticed if Palmer hadn't mentioned it. I found it hard to believe she remained unmarried because of it. Again I noted the slightly oversized brown eyes that gave her a soft, sensitive air. At least until she opened her mouth.

"Samantha," I said, reaching over to touch her arm, "I just want to say—"

She spun toward me, yanking her arm from my grip. "Take your shitten 'and off my arm, Mr. Chapman, afore I break it."

Stunned, I jerked away as if I'd just touched a hot stove. So much for her being docile and passive. "There's no call to use such language. I was just trying to—"

"I'll use any bloody language I want. And I don't give a twopenny damn what you were trying to do, Mr. Chapman. Just let me be."

Speechless, I walked on. I'd never heard such words come out of a girl's mouth—even one as coarse as she. Although, as I watched her, I realized she wasn't a "girl." She was nineteen, perhaps twenty—a woman—and past the age most women married. No wonder her father was so desperate to marry her off. If anything, I'd underestimated how humiliated she must have been.

"I understand, Samantha. You must be very angry with your father."

She stopped and turned toward me. "Don't try to make me swill your 'ogwash, Mr. Chapman, because you don't understand a thing. My father 'as thirteen children—five boys, eight girls. Despite 'is all but killing 'imself working so 'ard last year, we almost starved during the snows. My father is only doing what 'e 'as to do to get us through the next winter."

We had reached the creek bank and stood side-by-side watching the glassy water slide past. "Even," I said, "if that means all but pointing a gun at me in order to convince me to marry you?"

"If that's what it takes, Mr. Chapman, then so be it." She turned away from me and walked along the bank. "So will you then?"

I hurried after her. "Will I what?"

"Marry me."

"You're not serious?" I stopped, expecting her to turn and face me. She didn't, and I had to hurry after her again. "You don't really expect me to, do you?"

She shrugged. "Why not? You ain't married. You need a wife."

"I don't need anything, except to be left alone."

"We don't always get what we want, do we?"

"No, we don't. If no one wants to marry you, why can't you just stay with your family?"

She spun toward me. "You've no idea, do you? You've no idea what it's like to be no more than a slave in your own family. Thirteen children there are. My own ma died after the fifth. My second ma died when I was twelve, and pa's third wife, Sylvie, nearly died birthing Connor last spring. Sylvie's still ill, might yet very well die 'erself, and since I'm the oldest, the burden of taking care of the other twelve 'as fallen on me. 'Ell, I mostly been doing it the past six years already."

"I do a little."

"Do what?"

"Know what it's like to be the oldest. Well, the oldest boy at any rate."

"Did you feed and wash and wipe the young'uns 'arses till you dreamt you did it in yer sleep? Did you peel potatoes, scrub sheets, cook pottage every meal till the very smell made you want to retch?"

"Well, no. But my father expected me to take any peon job to help support his children. That's part of the reason I left home."

"Hmph. Sounds like you're the walking typification of suffering. 'Ow *did* you survive?"

Coarse and sarcastic—now I understood why she wasn't married. On the other hand, she had a point.

"You were lucky to be able to leave," she said.

"Maybe you could leave. Like I did."

She looked at me as if I were a simpleton. "No, John Chapman, I couldn't leave. If I leave 'ome, becoming a bloody 'ore will be my lot. And I *ain't* a 'ore."

Her crude response threw me, but again, she was right. "So if you do so much of the work, then why does your father want to marry you off so badly?"

"My two next oldest sisters are fifteen now, they're able to do everything I can," she said, her voice growing thick. "My family doesn't need me anymore, and even one less mouth to feed will make life easier. But if I don't get married, then I 'ave to stay and keep working like a damned slave. I won't do it," she said softly. "I won't. I don't care who I have to marry or what it takes to escape, but I will get away." She paused. "Are you absolutely sure you won't marry me?"

"Samantha, I am sorry about your situation. You seem like a good person, and I'm sure things will work out."

"Fine words butter no parsnips, Mr. Chapman." She paused. "Well, I guess neither me nor my family is your responsibility." She drew herself up straight. "'Sides, I don't really want to marry you anyway."

"Why not? Am I not handsome enough?" Turning to show her my profile, I haughtily thrust my nose into the air.

She laughed. "Oh, you're all right, I suppose. But you see, well, there's someone else I want to marry."

"There is?" I said with relief. "Then marry him before he gets away!" I paused, wondering if I'd just said something terribly insensitive. Hesitantly, I asked, "Does he want to marry you?"

She nodded. "But Father would never, ever 'ear of it. That's why I was willing to marry you."

"But that's absurd! If he's so desperate to marry you off, why would he say no to a suitor?"

"I can't tell you. But 'e would."

"Samantha, I think you should tell me who it is and why William would object. I think if I were to talk to your father, I might be more persuasive than you."

"Do you understand 'ow fortunate you are to be a man?"

I supposed I didn't. "Will you let me talk to your father?"

Picking up a twig, she began to scratch into the dirt. "Let me to talk to 'im—my suitor—about it, see what 'e says."

"All right then. You let me know."

"I reckon I should 'ead back. Father's probably getting worried."

Somehow I doubted her father would be worried. He'd probably be thrilled if she came back pregnant.

"You stay 'ere," she said matter-of-factly, "otherwise Father might not give up on you." She began to walk back toward the cabin.

"Is there anything I can do to get him to give up?"

She turned toward me. "Marry someone else."

The relentless sound of a million cicadas somehow seemed to be magnified by the heat that poured down from the midday sun. All week, I did nothing but haul water from the creek that I then ladled over the burgeoning green rows of the truck patch. They looked healthy enough now and were even beginning to take on definite shapes—rows of tiny, erect cornstalks, blunt fists of cabbage, even the first nascent swellings of squash hidden among yellow blossoms.

But I knew without my efforts, they would survive no more than two or three days in this heat. And as if God wanted to mock my efforts, each time I trekked to the creek, it was through the meadow of unwatered, yet lush river grass that already reached past my knees. How the hell did the stuff grow so easily?

Yet again refilling the buckets from the creek, I suddenly felt certain that I was being watched from across the water. I glanced up at the shimmering trees shadowing the far bank.

"Gwennie?" I called out, but she didn't respond. After studying the enigmatic shadows for another moment, I decided the heat was playing tricks with my mind and went back to work.

Returning to the truck patch, I worked my way down the row, feeling as if the sun were turning my skin into leather. Shading my eyes as I watered the squash, I tried to look up at the sky. Christ, I thought, as it beat down on my face—it's only mid-May. How long could this go on for?

"You not get any answers trying to read sun."

"Hello, Gwennie," I said without turning to face her.

"Very good, Chahkoltet. You not jump out of your skin this time—you hear me coming?"

"No, but I sensed you watching me back down by the creek a little while ago."

"I not watch you down by the creek," she said, picking up a ladle and helping me to water.

"Weren't you just on the other side?"

"No, I come from behind your cabin. I have orchard in the next valley over."

"I see." So, the sun was affecting my mind. "Tell me, Gwennie. Is Grandmother-in-the-North's luck ever going to change?"

"Of course it will. It always does. But I not think it change for many weeks."

If I hadn't been so tired, I might have cried. I tenderly ran my finger over one of the delicate yellow blossoms that I hoped would eventually bring forth a squash.

"Beautiful, isn't it?" she asked from across the row.

"Gwennie, can I ask you something?"

She set the bucket down. "Yes."

"Why are you helping me? Why not George or the Connollys or Thomas?"

"George not take help. Connollys, I not help them even if all I have to do is wiggle my finger. They treat me worse than a dog who can't control its bowels. And Thomas not need help—he have no crops to water."

"No crops—not even a truck patch?"

She shook her head.

"What will he live off of come winter?"

She thought for a moment, then said, "Do you like Thomas?"

"He seems nice enough."

"You know Thomas and I are friends?"

"No, I didn't know."

"We are. I think he would like you to be his friend, too."

"He would?"

"Yes, he told me that you seem like a good man."

I thought back to the day he had visited. His manner, I recalled, had been brusque. Certainly, nothing about his demeanor had indicated he wanted to be friends. Even the time we had spent riding together to Franklin for the May Day celebration had passed mostly in silence. "I've only met him three times, Gwennie."

She nodded. "It hard for Thomas to trust people."

"So what do you want me to do? Go see him?"

"No, he have to come to you. I do want to ask you to make me a promise."

"All right."

"If Thomas ever need help, will you do what you can? As return for my helping you."

"That seems fair enough. All right, I agree."

"Good. I appreciate."

"You never did answer my question, Gwennie."

"I help you, John, because I think Thomas is right. I think you a good person."

Embarrassed, I could think of nothing to say. Instead, I picked up my ladle and resumed watering the squash.

When we finished our work later that afternoon, Gwennie handed me the empty buckets, pushed several black strands of wayward hair from her sweaty face, and said, "I see you tomorrow morning."

Through waves of heat, I watched her make her way first through the trembling grass, then hop from stone to stone as she crossed the creek as graceful as a deer. Why or where the impulse came from, I have no idea, but just after she vanished into the woods, I took off across the meadow, splashed through the cold water of the creek, and sprinted after her.

∧ ∧ ∧

For an hour I stealthily pursued her as she made her way up and over the ridge by following some sort of wide animal trail that wound through the dense brush. Despite our continuous climb upward, Gwennie moved at a quick, steady pace, never pausing to rest, and I occasionally lost sight of her as she passed through a particularly dense copse of trees. By now, it was late afternoon, and stripes of soft golden light lay interspersed amongst the exaggerated shadows of the trees that covered the earth.

Up ahead, Gwennie passed behind the trunk of a tremendous oak, and I paused, waiting for her to emerge to see which way she continued. Each previous time I'd lost her, I'd only had to wait a moment, until she again emerged into view. But this time a minute passed, then another, and still she didn't reappear.

Quietly, I crept forward, listening and watching for some sign of her up ahead. Suddenly I caught sight of her to my left, almost behind me. How had she got over there? Afraid of being spotted, I fell to my knees and crawled into the bushes. Thorns and branches scratched my face and arms. I waited until she had again gone ahead of me, then resumed trailing her, but once more quickly lost sight of her.

Trying to stay in the shadows, I edged forward. I spotted her, but this time she was to my right. What the hell was she doing moving about so erratically? And so quickly? Trying to stay out of sight, I turned, promptly tripped, and fell into a pile of elk dung. "Jesus wept," I muttered, trying to catch my breath. Looking up, I saw her heading toward where I lay. Despite the wet, smelly elk dung and having had the wind knocked out of me, I again wriggled into the bushes.

Gwennie passed ten feet in front of me. She no longer seemed to be in such a hurry, and I wondered if she might not be searching for burdock or tubers or mushrooms. Finally, though, she passed out of sight, and I crept out from under the bush where I'd been hiding.

I should've seen what was coming, but I didn't. When I felt a finger jabbing me in the back, my heart leapt to my mouth, my body leapt forward, and I lurched right back into the elk dung.

"Hello, Chahkoltet," Gwennie said from behind.

Slowly I again extracted myself from the scat, then rolled onto my back to face her. "How long have you known I was following you."

"An hour."

"Why didn't you say something?"

"Why didn't you?"

I felt myself blush. "I don't know. I'm sorry. I should have."

"Something more you want from me, John?"

I shrugged and, thinking of Palmer being gone, said, "I didn't want to be alone again, I wanted to talk. But that's no excuse to follow you this way. I really am sorry." I turned and started to leave.

Suddenly I felt a tug on my shirt. "Come on," Gwennie said. "We not far now from where I live."

If it hadn't been for the black cooking pot hovering above the firepit like a hen over her eggs, I most likely wouldn't even have looked twice at the little clearing where we stopped. As it turned out, Gwennie lived in, of all places, a cave, although it was unlike any cave I'd ever seen. The cave opening was hidden amongst a tangle of moss and vines and ferns, and not until she actually pushed the growth aside did I even realize there was an opening. The entrance to the cavern was narrow—I had to turn sideways to fit through—and for the first ten feet, the crevice split the rock in two from top to bottom, leaving a jagged slice of blue sky visible above us. Then the blue disappeared, and I found myself in the dark interior of the earth. Despite the awful heat of the day, here it was cool and comfortable, something my cabin was only late at night or early in the morning; I even felt a breeze flowing out from the dark.

While I waited, Gwennie lit candles, each one revealing more and more of an interior that couldn't have amazed me any more than if I'd found myself in King George's throne room. The cavern was roughly the same size and shape of my own cabin, but although Gwennie was living in what amounted to an animal's den, her quarters were far more nicely furnished than anything I'd ever seen, much less lived in. Against the far wall stood a genuine bed—how the hell had she got that through the opening, much less out here, in the first place?—with two pillows and a satin blanket. Yet on the floor next to the bed was a sleeping mat with a bearskin. On a stand by Gwennie's bed lay scattered an assortment of jewelry, most of it made from feathers and beads, but the two elaborate crucifixes were most definitely not Indian.

Along the wall to my right were shelves filled with ornately decorated clay jars, while next to them was a full set of fine bone china. From pegs on a wall hung a half dozen dresses including a simple one made of deerskin, a second, more elaborate deerskin dress heavily embroidered with hundreds of beads, and then next to those, two beautiful silk dresses that could have come straight from the courts of London itself.

A formal dining table, its dark, rich polish reflecting the light of the candles, sat in the middle of the room with one single high-backed chair perched at the far end. Four stools—really nothing more than three-foot sections of tree trunk—stood where the other chairs would have been. One end of the table was covered with an eclectic assortment of items including an elaborately decorated tomahawk, two brass candleholders, a book, a spyglass, two wooden bowls, several bags that looked to be filled with seeds, a half dozen or so animal pelts, and a small stack of coins. On the floor sat a small cask filled with water.

"Did all this belong to the Jacksons?"

Gwennie turned to face me. "What did you say?"

"I wondered if this all belonged to the Jacksons before . . . well, you know."

In two quick strides, she crossed the room. "Get out!" she said, shoving me with both hands.

Caught by surprise, I nearly fell to the ground. "Hey! What are you doing?"

"I said, 'Get out.'" She shoved me again.

I stumbled back a step. "Gwennie, I don't understand. And stop shoving me." Angry now, I shoved her back; before I could react, she punched me hard in the gut.

"You think I a thief. You think I take these things from Jacksons."

"No," I gasped, "not a thief. And you damned well better think twice before you hit me again, because woman or not, I'll hit back."

"You white people all the same. Think anytime Indian own something, they must have stolen it."

"No, Gwennie, I just meant after they didn't come back, you took some things."

"Oh, you think I steal from *dead* people. That even worse!"

I'd never seen her angry before. While I was genuinely sorry to have upset her, it was interesting to see this other side.

"Gwennie, calm down. You're overreacting. Hell, I'm the one living in their cabin. And this"—I tugged on my shirt—"belonged to Alexander Jackson. So if you're a thief, then I'm one, too."

"That for you to decide. But everything you see here, I buy—not steal. Everything!"

"Really?"

"Why you say it like that?"

"Like what?"

"Like you can't believe Indian woman have these things."

"Gwennie, this is border country, for God's sake. I don't know any women, or men, who have this many nice things. Hell, I've never seen a table that nice in my entire life. These things obviously cost money."

"You think George only person who know how to make money?"

"Well, no. It's just that I've never . . ." Fearing that I would further offend her, I let my voice trail off.

"You never what? See Indian make money?"

"Well, no."

"You ever see bear give birth?"

"No, of course not."

"So you think it not happen?"

"Of course not. Look, I'm sorry, Gwennie. I didn't mean to offend you."

"Sometimes I forget not all white people the same."

"After everything you've done for me, you're the last person I want to anger. Maybe I should go."

Mollified, she said, "No. Stay."

"Are you sure?"

She nodded. "I raise apples that I trade. That how I get things."

"You trade apples? With who?"

"Indians and settlers."

Judging from the items surrounding us, she obviously drove a hard bargain.

She motioned at the assortment on the table that I'd been looking at earlier. "See? I just come back from trading with Miami tribe. Then I trade these things with George or other whites for dresses or gunpowder or something else."

"All this from apples? Good Lord, how many apple trees do you have?"

She shrugged. "A hundred and fifty. Maybe few more."

"A hundred and fifty! Where? We didn't pass any trees outside. I haven't seen an orchard in the valley."

"That because none of them here. I have seven orchards in different places." She sat at the table.

This woman owned seven orchards? "I don't understand. How do you pick and carry that many apples to villages or towns? Do you have a horse?"

"No, no horse. And I don't go to villages. They come to me."

"Indians come here?" I asked, still befuddled.

"No, not here," she said as if speaking to an inordinately slow child. "Where I grow trees."

"I see," I said, even though I didn't. "How do they know when you'll be at a particular orchard? Do you go at the same time every year?"

"I go after other Indians come for apples. Indians who want my apples go to trees and pick them. Whatever they pay with, they leave hanging in tree or buried in cache of rocks."

"But surely you meet them there sometimes?"

She pursed her lips and said, "I never there at same time."

There was still something I was missing. "Are you not there on purpose?"

She nodded.

"Oh."

"Other Indians not want to see me."

"Why not?"

"They call me Apple Woman," she said enigmatically.

"Because you raise apples?" I asked, thinking I stated the obvious.

She shook her head, then said softly, "Because they say I red on outside, but white on inside."

"Do you mean white like I'm white?"

She nodded.

"Because you're a Christian?"

"Because I *was* Christian."

"Have you told them you're not anymore?"

"It wouldn't matter anyway. They never take me back. Besides, even though I not Christian, I not like them either. I not like anyone. I Apple Woman."

Gwennie rose, went to the water cask, and plunged in her hand. She pulled out a turtle perhaps half again as big as my hand. The turtle's grayish green shell gleamed in the candlelight as its four legs slowly twisted about. Gwennie cooed softly as she stroked the turtle's head.

Without thinking, I exclaimed, "I love turtles. I had them all the time as a boy."

I never would've guessed Gwennie would be the type to keep one as a pet.

"Me, too," she said, turning its head toward me. Two eyes slowly blinked, and as always, I marveled at how much like my grandfather turtles looked. Gwennie abruptly changed the subject. "Remember Indian boy who was killed?"

How could I forget? "Yes."

"He came to see me because I Apple Woman. But he thought I called Apple Woman because I half-white, half-Indian like he was." Gwennie again cooed softly at the turtle, then without warning, snapped its tiny neck. I jumped as if I'd been jabbed.

"What did he want?" I asked, blanching.

"His mother was a Mingo—that very unusual—and she die last winter. He alone now and want to find his father. Since he think I also have white father, he thought I might be able to help." She took a knife from the table and ran it between the groove where the dead turtle's upper and lower shells joined. Gwennie obviously loved turtles in a different way than I did.

"Why is it so unusual that his mother was a Mingo?"

"I never see a half-breed Mingo before. Seneca, Huron, yes, but not Mingo. Only few Mingo left, especially here, and they hide from white people, who mad because no Mingo ever sign treaty. That mean many Mingo killed by white people, and the rest fled years ago to Virginia or Ohio Territory." As she spoke, she rummaged around the table until she found a long, narrow wedge carved from wood.

"But why was he by himself?"

Gwennie's expression softened. "I got idea from boy that he and his mother live alone. I think maybe they get left behind when tribe move. That happen sometimes if person sick, or if someone too old to move, someone stay behind until they die. Maybe boy's mother not able to find tribe again. Maybe also tribe upset she have child and not married. Maybe make her leave tribe."

I thought of Gwennie's rejection by her tribe.

"Do you ever wish you could be with your tribe again?" I asked softly, momentarily thinking of Lucy and Elizabeth and my other brothers and sisters.

"No," she said, sliding the wedge under the turtle's shell. She grabbed a mallet and delivered a single solid blow. The upper shell sprang free with a wet popping sound not unlike the noise my grandfather made when he sucked on his teeth. She quickly did the same to the lower, though it was more difficult to get free. "Maybe I miss tribe sometimes. Maybe when I smell Indian fire welcoming spring or someone, as payment, leaves bracelet made of certain kind of seashells. Most of time, I don't, though."

We both looked down at the turtle, smaller and naked without its shell. Gwennie took a wooden spoon, ran it along the inside of the top shell, and held the spoon out to me. A greenish, jellylike substance filled it.

"It called calipash," Gwennie said. "It's the best part. Go ahead."

"Thanks, Gwennie. I'll pass."

She shrugged, ate it, then what was left in the shell as well.

"So now that you're not a Christian," I said, "does that mean you believe in Man . . . ni . . . Man . . ."

"Manitto." She quickly cleaned, gutted, and cut up the turtle.

"Thank you. Do you believe in Manitto again?"

"No."

"Then what do you believe in?"

"I believe in Apple Woman. The meat needs to dry." She stood and took the turtle meat outside.

It was interesting, I thought as I waited. Gwennie and I were so different, and yet we weren't.

My eyes came to rest on the now empty turtle shells. I looked away.

A moment later Gwennie returned with a plateful of dried fish to which she added a handful of dried apples and several slices of bread.

"Eat," she said, handing me a plate.

Looking at the food, I recalled how awful the last meal of fish she'd prepared had tasted. Hesitantly, I took a bite. The fish jerk was tough and dry, but to my surprise it had an unusual, savory flavor that was a relief from the salty taste of most dried meat.

"It's good," I said.

Her dark eyes watched me as she bit into a piece of apple.

"It's too bad you weren't able to help the boy," I said. "Maybe then he wouldn't have killed the McWhirters' little girl and been killed himself."

She chewed thoughtfully for a moment, then said, "Boy not kill little girl."

"What?"

"I said, boy not kill girl."

"Then who did?"

"Her father."

"What? That's absurd, Gwennie! Who told you such a thing?"

"George tell me."

"George? But William told me that the boy killed the girl while he was trying to get away. He said he did it to distract the others, to keep them from following him."

"Kill girl to keep others from following him?" she said skeptically.

"Well . . ."

"Who you believe tell truth—William or George?"

I thought for a moment. "George, I guess."

"Did William say how girl is killed?"

"Well, no. He never did actually say how she died."

"George said she shot in face with rifle. You say you saw boy?"

I nodded.

"You see boy carrying rifle?"

"No."

"So how boy shoot girl?"

"But I don't understand. Why would Ian shoot his own child?"

"George said it was accident, that in the dark with all the noise, man didn't know girl had run in same direction as boy. She was scared and confused, and I guess she started running back at wrong time. Man shoot at boy, but ball hit his own girl. Since she shot in face, girl never scream and man not even know what he done."

What Gwennie said made sense, and even more, it sounded like the truth. I didn't know Ian McWhirter, but it wasn't difficult to imagine how hard it would be to admit killing your own child—even if it was an accident.

An image of the boy flashed through my mind. Starving, he must have been making his way through the woods when he stumbled onto the meadow. Who could blame him for going through the leftovers? And William had claimed he was stealing belongings.

"Is George the only one that knows the truth?"

She shook her head. "George says everybody knew truth by next day, but is easier if everyone pretends it was Indian."

"Gwennie, I'm sorry the boy was killed like that."

"You not sorry girl killed?"

"Well, yes, that too."

"But you more sorry about boy than girl?"

"No," I said hesitantly. "I'm sorry that either of them were killed."

"So why you tell me you sorry boy killed?"

"Well, because he was an Indian."

She fixed her expressionless gaze on me. "No need apologize, John. I not sorry boy killed. I not sorry girl killed. Apple Woman not care either way."

TWELVE

By the time I was fourteen, life in Longmeadow had become unbearable for the entire family: the ever-deepening poverty, the sneering of our neighbors, Father's drunken tirades. By looking at Lucy or Elizabeth or even myself in the looking glass, I could tell our hearts were shriveling into hard, black nuts that tainted our very blood with every beat.

Lucy had bore ten children, which left her permanently bedridden and meant Elizabeth had to take over the care of the children. One morning on my way to school, I found myself unable to face the usual taunts from the boys, and I decided to stay home for the day. Entering our house, I surprised a disheveled Elizabeth, who sat weeping in the middle of the floor, an infant in her arms, two squalling toddlers nearby.

"What are you doing here?" she demanded.

"I'm sorry," I stammered, the smell of spit-up and soiled diapers turning the air rank. "Let me help, Elizabeth."

She struggled to her feet. "You should be gone by now. I don't understand why you haven't gone."

"I couldn't face school today, that's all. I don't feel well."

Her eyes bore into me. "You're fourteen now, John. Why are you still here?" Each word carried the weight of her misery.

We stared at each other for a moment, then I stepped toward her. "I'll hold Penny while you—"

"Go away!" Elizabeth screamed. "Get out!" She advanced toward me menacingly.

Hesitantly, I stepped backward, then stopped. Without warning, she flung a cup at me.

"Go on!" she hollered.

I turned and fled out into the yard. When I looked back, Elizabeth stood on the porch, staring after me. Her hand clutched the railing, her knuckles white, and I saw how hard she fought to not run away with me.

"Go on," she whispered. "And don't ever come back." She whirled around, vanished inside, and slammed the door behind her.

That afternoon, I left Longmeadow for good.

June 1798

I'D JUST FINISHED EATING A LIGHT SUPPER WHEN THREE SHARP RAPS came from the door. No matter how long I lived alone, I doubted I would ever completely get rid of the stab of fear I felt each time someone called unexpectedly.

Picking up a tomahawk, I went to the door, peered through the slit, and saw a tense-looking Thomas peering about. A week had passed since I'd last seen anybody, so I was glad for, if leery of, the company.

"John, are you home?" Thomas called out just as I opened the door. "There you are," he said, seeming a bit taken aback.

"Here I am indeed." Having only spoken on a few occasions, we still didn't have a real sense of each other. "Would you like to come in?"

"Do you want me to?" he asked in a prickly tone that I suspected he used to deal with most of the world. I doubted I need worry about his becoming too friendly.

Looking at his dour expression, I hesitated, then said, "Why not? I haven't talked to a soul since Gwennie a week ago." Even more, I welcomed anything that would take my mind off Palmer. Not more than a few minutes would pass without my thinking of him.

Thomas laughed, and much to my surprise, his face transformed to something almost warm. "She told me what happened when you tried to follow her. Elk shit and hiding in bushes."

"So," I said, annoyed and embarrassed at the memory. "What brings you here?"

Sensing my irritation, he immediately looked and sounded chagrined. "Nothing really. Maybe this is a bad time."

I caught him by the arm as he turned to leave. "Oh, come on in, Thomas. Just don't say anything more about elk shit."

"I won't," he promised with a sheepish smile.

"Would you like some cider?"

"Yes, thanks." I went to pour it. "So, John, how do you like it here so far?"

"Here being this claim or Franklin?" Handing him the cider, I sat.

"The border country in general. Are you glad you came?"

"Yes," I said, drawing the word out. "I suppose so."

"I don't. I hate it."

"Then why are you here?"

"Would you like to know where I'd rather be?"

"If you want to tell me."

"You'll think me peculiar."

"No, I won't."

"Africa."

"Where?" I asked in surprise.

"See, I told you you'd think me odd."

"Where did you ever get such a notion?" I hadn't known what Thomas had come to say, but I certainly hadn't expected this.

"From our slave, Abel."

"You have a slave?"

"Not me. My father did."

"So what on earth did a slave have to say that could make you want to go to Africa? That it was a veritable nirvana, filled with ambrosia and juicy lotus?"

Thomas lowered his eyes and said, "It doesn't matter."

I heard the disappointment in his voice. Something was going on here that I'd missed. Most white people had heard slaves carrying on about Africa being almost like Eden, but for some reason, this story seemed to mean more to Thomas than just silly, wishful thinking. "I'm sorry, Thomas. I really would like to know."

He shrugged. "He just told me a little about the place where he came from—a place in the southern part of Africa."

"Did he miss it?" I asked skeptically. I doubted a slave would miss Africa any more than a cow missed the barn in which it was birthed.

Nodding, Thomas said, "Terribly. Abel wanted to go back there more than anything. Even if it was only to die. He wanted to see the sand dunes again."

"Sand dunes?" Somehow I'd never associated Africa with sand.

"Nothing but," Thomas said, his voice perking up as he spoke. "He said there were mountains of sand—league after league of them. Then at the very edge of the desert, appearing without any warning, was mile after mile of empty beaches with waves crashing one after another onto the shore. He told me the sunsets were like the very sky itself catching on fire. He even said there were lions that slept right there on the beaches and went swimming in the ocean. Lions swimming—doesn't that sound amazing?"

The awe and longing in Thomas's voice was moving. "I've never heard of anything like it before," I told him, and I hadn't.

"I want to see that—beautiful, empty beaches with no one else but me and the lions and the waves."

"I hope you do, Thomas."

He smiled bashfully. "Oh, I'm not stupid. I've as much chance as Abel does."

"I suppose it's possible for him, too."

"Abel's dead."

"Oh. Well, it could still happen for you. You could go to sea if you wanted."

"I'm about as likely to visit the moon as I am Africa."

"Africa's a hell of a lot closer than the moon will ever be, Thomas."

"No, it isn't, John," he said with a sigh. "I don't think it's one little bit closer at all. Listen, there is a reason I came here. Besides chatting about my stupid dreams."

"What is it?"

"Well, before I get to that, there are a few things I need to explain first." Standing, he walked to the fireplace and cleared his throat. "Abel, the man I just mentioned, wasn't just a slave. He was my great-grandfather."

I frowned in puzzlement. "But I thought he was owned by your father."

"That's right."

"I don't understand. How could your father own your great-grandfather as a slave, unless he . . . Oh, my God." All but open-mouthed, I stared at Thomas. He was the son of a slave? "But you look and talk so white." Yet hadn't I noted his dark complexion and curly hair when I first met him?

"I know."

"So," I said hesitantly, "your mother was a slave?"

He nodded.

"And your father was the slave owner."

"Right."

"She must have been awfully light-skinned."

"She was, but given that my father was also her father, her being light-skinned was to be expected."

"Excuse me?"

"My mother's father is also my father. My mother and I are also brother and sister."

I stared dumbly at Thomas for a moment as I tried to sort out what he was telling me. "Let me understand this. Your father got a slave pregnant. She had a daughter, and then when that daughter was old enough, your grandfather got her pregnant with you?"

When he nodded, I felt ill.

"My God, Thomas," I said, horrified, "no wonder you're out here." I'd never given much thought to slaves before. They were just there. But Thomas wasn't a slave, he wasn't even mostly black.

"The reason I'm here is because my father—my *master*—has a bounty on me as a runaway slave."

"But you're three-fourths white. I thought I'd heard that three-fourths is enough to overcome most of the inferior fourth? At least enough for you to be a free man?"

He shook his head. "In Georgia, any black blood makes you black. That's the law. And I consider myself black. I hate every drop of white blood that's in me. No offense."

I thought I understood his anger. "No offense taken. So there's really a bounty on you?" It didn't seem fair.

"Yes."

"Who knows about this?"

"Gwennie. George. One other person."

"Is this why you don't own a real claim?"

Thomas nodded. "George lets me stay in Franklin, but he says he can't risk letting a runaway slave own land or do much of anything else for that matter. It might endanger his plans for Franklin."

"I see. How long has this been going on?"

"A year and a half now. You see, I had been living in the north where Father had sent me when I got older. He refused to acknowledge me, but since I was too white-looking to keep around, he sent me to live with his sister and get an education."

"So what happened?"

"One day, after I'd become a man, I went to Georgia to demand Father let my mother come live with me. Furious at my audacity, he said no nigger of his ever demanded anything from him. He set the bounty hunters on me then and there. It's no small miracle I escaped and made it out here."

"What are you going to do now?"

"Well, John, that's what I wanted to talk to you about. I've got a plan, but I need your help."

"My help? Thomas, I don't think there's much I can do. I don't have any money, and I don't know any powerful men."

"You can pose as Samantha's beau."

"What? Why?"

"Because if you don't, her father is going to send her to Virginia to help his widowed sister take care of her children."

"It's you. You're the one she wants to marry, but can't."

He nodded. "George will tell William I'm a runaway if Samantha and I try to marry."

"So how does my posing as her beau help you out?"

"We're going to run away together, head north to Lower Canada. Blacks are free there. But we can't leave until closer to fall, or her father might track us. But he'd never leave his family with winter coming on."

"So William won't send her away if he thinks I'm going to marry her?"

"That's right."

"But, Thomas, William was practically pronouncing us man and wife when they came calling a couple of weeks ago. How am I going to put him off until fall?"

"You can tell him you want to make sure you can provide for a family, that you want to work all summer on the claim and then you'll be ready to marry."

"I don't know, Thomas. It sounds awfully thin to me. What makes you think William will go along?"

"What choice does the man have? There isn't anyone else other than you. Since I know his wife doesn't want Samantha to go all the way back to Virginia, he'll have to go along with what you say.

"John, there's nothing in this for you, other than helping us to get a fresh start. But if I can ever do anything for you, you have my word that I will."

"Let me think about it, Thomas."

"Fair enough," he said, rising. "Thanks for even doing that." We shook hands and he left. As I watched him ride away, I struggled with whether or not I really wanted to risk everything helping Thomas, a runaway *slave*, escape to Canada.

I thought of Palmer and me, and how I'd been treated all these years for being different. Being black suddenly didn't seem like such a pernicious thing. Hell, if the truth be told, I probably wasn't any more desirable to the other settlers than Thomas was.

How could I not help him?

∧ ∧ ∧

One morning, a week later, I was awakened by three sharp raps on the door. Not Thomas again, I groaned, pulling the bearskin over my head. He'd come by three times in the past seven days, each time ostensibly just to present me an extra hare he'd trapped or to give me a hand with the watering. I hadn't yet told him I'd go through with his plan. I was going to help him, I'd decided that. I wanted to be sure, that's all.

He again knocked at the door, this time louder. Annoyed, and despite being naked, I jumped from the bed, yanked open the door, and said angrily, "Thomas, this has to . . . stop . . ."

"Hello, John." Palmer glanced up and down my bare body. "Mind if I come in?"

Dazed, I stepped back and let him enter. Guilt, shame, arousal, all washed over me as I contemplated his return. Suddenly realizing I was naked, I hurriedly pulled on a pair of pants. Part of me wanted to pull him into my bed; part of me wanted to make him leave. I felt that if I touched him even once, I'd never get the feel of his skin from my mind again.

"Have you eaten yet this morning?" he asked.

"What?"

"Eaten—have you eaten?"

"No." I didn't seem to be capable of more than one-word replies.

"Why don't you sit while I fix us something to eat."

"I didn't think I'd see you again," I blurted out. Why have you come back? I wanted to ask, but didn't. I didn't want him knowing how much I'd missed him.

"I guess you thought wrong then."

"How long are you here for?"

He shrugged. "I don't know."

"Where are you staying?"

He fixed his eyes on mine. "I don't know that either."

The words "stay here" tried to push their way out of my mouth, but I clenched my jaws shut. Didn't I already have enough problems with Thomas and Samantha and William?

After we ate, Palmer insisted on helping me water the truck patch.

"It hasn't rained since I left?" he asked as we labored.

"Not a drop." He worked without his shirt. It was all I could do not to reach over and stroke his smooth, tanned skin.

"And Gwennie's been helping you water?"

"And Thomas a little." Judging from the way I kept catching Palmer looking at me, I wasn't the only one who wanted to do some touching.

"Thomas? Why him?"

"Well, he's trying to convince me to pose as Samantha's beau."

"You're shitting me! I warned you that they'd find a way to get you to marry her."

"I'm not going to marry her. He just wants me to pretend I'm going to."

"Why on earth does he want you to do such a thing?"

I told him everything I'd learned.

"And are you going to do it?" he asked when I'd finished the tale.

"Maybe. I'm not even sure it would work."

"Poor Thomas—he hasn't had much of a life, has he? His plan might work, for a little while at least, mostly because William really doesn't have much choice but to agree to what you say."

Finished with the watering, we began to weed.

"So where have you been for the past two weeks?" I finally asked.

"Here and there. I wasn't sure where I wanted to go, so I let Maizie"—he nodded at his horse—"pick the way. She took us all the way to the end of the valley. I visited and stayed with a few people I know along the way."

As he spoke, I recalled George's accusation that Palmer free-loaded off others.

Palmer grunted as he pulled a stubborn weed from within a row of corn. "I helped one family rebuild a cabin that burned, and another with their hoeing. Oh, and I saw that Gwennie woman at an apple orchard, of all things, in the middle of nowhere."

"She told me about those. She's got six or seven scattered around. She trades apples with settlers and other Indians."

"You don't say? Clever. Anyway, after that, we rode north again along a valley that runs parallel to this one. Next thing I knew, Maizie had brought us back here." He smiled and said, "I reckon

maybe she heard you talking about the kwenaskat being all gold and
tall come the end of summer and decided she had to see it for herself, maybe even try a couple of mouthfuls and see how it tastes."

I laughed. "Thomas didn't say anything about its appeal to
horses, so we'll just have to wait and see."

The weeding finished, we both sat amongst the shade cast by the
Indian corn, exhausted. Dirt and sweat streaked Palmer's face, and
with a start I realized how wrong George was. Palmer didn't free-
load, far from it. This wasn't the first time he'd worked like a horse
and asked nothing in return. I needed to listen to others a little less
and pay more attention to what people actually did.

I asked Palmer to stay for dinner.

"I was hoping you'd ask," he said. "But first I was thinking about
going to the creek for a bath. Would you like to join me?" he asked,
waggling his eyebrows.

My dick hardened at the suggestion, but then a cold splash of
guilt washed over me and I said, "No. I've a few things to tend to
here."

"Might I borrow some soap then?"

"Of course." He waited outside while I went in to fetch it.

When I returned a moment later, he'd already stripped naked.
The late-afternoon sun perched in the sky at that low angle that
brought out the luminescence in everything, including Palmer. His
blond hair, tanned flesh—even his blue eyes—all glowed in the
light.

"Here you are," I said, and our hands brushed.

He took the soap, grinned, then took off running through the
grass, whooping and carrying on like a kid. I smiled as his white ass
flashed down to the creek. It was all I could do not to shed my
clothes and follow.

Shortly before twilight, we sat out on the porch eating, hoping to
catch whatever cool breeze the evening might offer as relief.
Palmer's damp hair lay flat against his head, further bringing out the
sharpness of his features. Wearing only his pants, he sat with his
hands laced behind his head, his feet up on the railing, his plate balanced on his bare stomach—the entire image stirring in me a feeling
of intimacy and desire.

His gaze rested in the west, taking in a spectacular sunset. Tongues of orange and copper, scarlet and saffron, leapt up from behind the mountains, licking at the gradually darkening dome of the sky.

"The sunset almost looks as if the mountains are on fire," I said, "and those clouds are flames leaping upward."

He sighed, as if bringing his thoughts back from somewhere far away. "Odd you should say that, John. When I was at the very southern end of the valley, I met some Indians who'd ventured from across the Ohio. They said there were huge forest fires burning on the other side because of the drought. So in a sense you're almost right." He looked down toward Franklin and shook his head. "With so many trees here dead thanks to George and my brother, I'm damned grateful the fires are so far away."

We watched the sunset in silence, until it had begun to fade away to dark, and I asked, "What are you going to do now?"

"Those Indians I mentioned that told me about the fire? Well, I spent some time talking with them about where they come from, and they told me that many days' ride further west of the Ohio is an ocean of grass that even they don't know how far it goes, or even what's on the other side. I'm curious to see it."

"But what about a claim? Or a wife?"

"What about them?"

"Don't you want them?"

"Don't talk such rubbish, John. You know I don't want a wife."

"I've heard about men who cozen their wives by having relations with men."

"You think I'm the sort of man to do that?" he asked with a hurt edge in his voice.

"No, but you can't be certain." I paused. "I didn't mean to imply you were duplicitous, Palmer. Truth be told, I think you're the most forthright man I've ever met."

"Thanks. I think men who lie to their wives like that ought to have their balls laid twixt two large rocks until they can decide who it is they want to roger."

"What about your family and George and everyone else who thinks you should be married?"

"To hell with them," he said with a wave of his hand. "They're the same people who want to cut down every forest and convert every Indian—without a single thought about whether it's right or not. Even then, they only do it because their precious Bible tells them to." He was quiet for a moment. "It wasn't supposed to be like this."

"What?"

He gestured to the valley. "Border country. The frontier. I thought out here there wouldn't be people trying to tell me what to do. I figured they would be so busy worrying about Indians and bears and floods that they wouldn't have so much time to poke their nose into other people's private affairs. Turns out, it's the only diversion they have from their own miserable lives."

"Well, you have to admit, it's not as bad as back east."

He set his plate down. "I suppose." He fixed his gaze on me. "I've joshed you about it before, but I'm curious to know—would you consider marrying?"

"No. I know that for certain." I weighed how much to tell Palmer, then decided I should keep my own counsel—a smart decision—and one that I promptly ignored. "I tried to want to. I don't mean that I ever slept with a woman, but I tried awfully hard to want to."

"When did you know you were different?"

Palmer's question both frightened and thrilled me. Neither the Major nor Zach had ever spoken of how we were different from most men. "I suppose I've always known. But I didn't admit it to myself until a few years ago."

"Why then?"

"It's not exactly my proudest moment."

"I didn't mean to pry. You don't need to tell me anything."

"It's all right. I want to tell you. I met this woman, almost four years ago now. Her name was Patience, and one day, as I was buying flour from her, she said something that made me laugh. She seemed smart and funny, and it had been so long since I'd known anyone interesting that I allowed myself to spend time with her.

"We'd go for long walks and have picnics. I even liked her family and let myself be talked into taking my Sunday repast with them. I don't know what in the hell I was thinking." Palmer said nothing as I remained quiet for a long moment. "I knew damned good and well she was falling in love with me. I also knew who it was I couldn't stop looking at when he walked past, and who I dreamt about at night. It sure as hell wasn't her.

"It went on for several months. I suppose I let it continue because I was flattered and lonely, and I truly wanted to feel about her the way she did about me. I was sick of being different. All I wanted was to fit in somewhere, to belong to somebody. As I said, she was smart and strong and not unattractive, but for some reason didn't interest many men. In fact, she told me I was the first."

"What happened?"

"One day we were sitting on a riverbank—I remember there were swans nearby—and she leaned over and kissed me. And even though I tried so hard to feel something, I didn't, and she knew it. The look on her face was terrible, like she thought there was something wrong with her. I couldn't bear knowing I'd broken her heart. Without saying so much as good-bye to her, I left the next day. I figure that makes me one of the sorriest sons of bitches God ever made." Palmer had hardly moved, much less said a word, as I spoke. "Other than hurting Patience, that happens to be the thing I hate most about myself—that I'm forever picking up and leaving. Running is what it is. It's why I have to stay here and make this work. Otherwise, I'll never stop."

Hesitantly, I glanced over at Palmer, trying to read what he was feeling. "You're probably thinking how awful I am for leaving her, aren't you?"

"I got a girl with child," he said softly, "so I'm hardly one to be judging what you might have done."

Palmer had been with a woman? But the day we had sex, he'd told me hadn't.

"Her name was Iphigenia—I called her Iffy, and I slept with her a couple times. I thought it might change me, and I was desperate to change before somebody found me out. It didn't change me, of course. I suppose I knew it wouldn't, but I did it anyway. When Iffy knew she was going to have a baby—my baby—she went to see a crone who lived up in the mountains. She'd heard the woman could take care of things. I let her go. Hell, I *wanted* her to go!" He sounded as if he were about to sob. "I hated myself for what happened. I suppose I still do."

Now I understood why he had lied to me. I hesitated, not wanting to force Palmer to talk if he didn't want to. I decided if he wanted to tell me, he would.

"Whatever the woman gave her took care of it but almost killed her as well. When Iffy hadn't come back by sunset, I set out to look for her. She'd collapsed a mile from her cabin, bleeding and in terrible pain. It's a wonder bears hadn't set upon her. I carried her back home to her mother. After that, I couldn't face her or anyone else in town. The next day, I set out for Caleb's without saying anything to anybody."

I knew there was nothing Palmer could say to make me feel better about Patience, so I doubted there was much I could say to him.

He surprised me when after a few silent moments he asked, "Have you ever seen the moon rise from the top of the mountain ridge?"

"No."

"Come on then. Let me show you a place I know."

"I can't, Palmer. It's late, and I've a long day tomorrow."

"You mean you won't come. You're afraid of me."

"Of course I'm not afraid of you, Palmer." I didn't sound convincing even to myself.

"Come with me now, and if nothing has changed by the time we come back, I'll leave and you'll never see me again."

A half hour later, I found myself jouncing along on top of Maizie as we passed by the pine trees that marked the arid, upper forest from the leafy valley forest below. Maizie trotted along at a pace I thought too fast, given how dark it was amongst the trees. Palmer rode as if in a hurry to get away, and I suppose he was. We both were.

At first I tried to hold on only with my legs, but after I nearly slipped off twice, Palmer reached behind, took my arms, and wrapped them around his middle. It was all I could do to keep from laying my head on his shoulder.

After another half hour passed, we emerged from the forest and onto the rocky spine of a ridge that crept forward and upward. The great swath of the Milky Way stretched overhead like a flag blowing in a celestial wind. The higher we went, the better I felt.

"Do you know what some Indians believe about the night sky?" Palmer asked.

"No," I said, looking up at the vault of dark purple embedded with sparkling stars. A shooting star briefly but brilliantly leapt across the sky.

"That each star stands for one Indian."

I studied the thousands upon thousands of glittering lights. I liked that. "Maybe they represent white people, too."

"Do you know what they reckon a shooting star means?"

"No."

"That an Indian has died and is passing over to the afterlife. Every winter, when life is hardest, there is a week that is the coldest and has the least food, and that's always the week the sky is filled with falling stars all night long."

I looked for another falling star, but didn't see one.

"Want to know what I believe about falling stars?" Palmer asked.

"Sure."

"I reckon every time a star falls, it means someone didn't do what was in their heart."

I stopped looking at the stars.

"Do you believe in hell, Palmer?"

"No, nor heaven."

"Are you saying you don't believe in the Bible?"

"That's right. Do you?"

"I don't know," I said, even though I did believe. "What do you believe in?"

"I don't know. John, I reckon I've seen no more reason to believe my soul goes to heaven than I do to believe it flashes across the sky when I die. I can believe that shooting star we saw a little bit ago was the soul of the Indian boy by the creek just as easily as I can that Jesus came back to life, and his body rose up to heaven."

Palmer's odd ways of thinking both excited and frightened me. "Do George and Caleb and the others know your feelings?" I asked.

He laughed. "They already think I'm a heretic. If they knew that

I thought the Indians were more Christianlike than Christians, there's no telling what they might do. Anyway, enough theology for one night. We're almost there."

Leaning forward, I peered around his shoulder and saw that the trail abruptly zigzagged sharply upward. Maizie, propelled by thrusts from her powerful back legs, nearly reared backward as she scrambled her way up the slope. My stomach lurched and plunged with her every jump forward. I held Palmer even tighter.

Maizie surged forward a final time, and we were there.

The spiny ridge up which we'd ascended topped out on a rocky outcropping perhaps twice the size of my cabin. Nothing but darkness surrounded us, and I felt as if I were floating in the sky.

"Watch out for the edges," Palmer warned as we dismounted. "We're pretty high up, and it's a steep drop on all sides." I was suddenly glad I couldn't see down.

No longer pressed against Palmer's bare skin, I realized it was chilly. Palmer must have felt the chill as well, because he was pulling a shirt from his saddle pack.

"John, if you're cold, I've a blanket. But we'll have to share."

A hooting owl swooped by overhead, startling Maizie. She abruptly backed up, bumping into Palmer, who appeared to stumble, lose his balance, and before I could react, vanish over the edge of the precipice.

Struck dumb, I stood with my mouth open, staring at the spot where he had disappeared without a sound.

"Palmer," I managed to whisper at last. Against my will, afraid of what I would see, I forced myself toward the edge. He can't be gone, I pleaded with God. He'd only just come back.

Kneeling down, I worked my way closer until I could peer out over the edge. Except for the glint of the creek below, I saw only darkness.

Then Palmer popped up from a ledge on which he'd been hiding. "I was beginning to think you hadn't even noticed I'd gone!"

My first instinct upon seeing him was to scream, but I was too stunned to do anything but stare.

"Gotcha," he said.

I staggered away.

"John?" Palmer called out from the ledge. A moment later, he was next to me. "John? Are you all right?"

I wasn't, but I nodded anyway.

"I'm sorry. I just meant it as a joke."

"I thought you were dead," I said emotionlessly. "When you vanished, I thought that God must truly hate us. I thought I was being punished for what I did to Patience, and you to Iffy." And for how I feel about you, I wanted to add.

"Jesus. John, forgive me."

"You're peeved with me, aren't you?"

"What are you talking about?"

"You're mad because I won't ask you to stay with me. Why else would you make me think you're dead?"

"I'm sorry, John. Here. He handed me a flask. "This will steady you."

I took the flask. "Maybe you've a right to be mad." Cold whiskey burned my throat. I shivered. "I don't know what to do, Palmer. I never have. Running away was always the best I could do."

He ignored my lament. "You're cold, aren't you? Come here then. I'll warm you up."

Silent, we sat facing east, our backs propped against a cold slab of granite, the blanket held tight around us. Vigorously he massaged my fingers and arms and legs.

"Palmer, don't be so hard on yourself for what happened to Iffy," I said softly. "You made a mistake. *We* made mistakes."

"It was a serious mistake, John. She almost died. After what happened, I know no one else will ever marry her. I ruined her life."

I thought of Patience.

Surprising myself, I pulled Palmer close. All I knew was that I wanted to comfort him, to offer him what relief I could. We began to kiss. He was tender as he ran his fingers across my face. My lips gently brushed over his eyes, his cheeks, his mouth.

We made love. Despite everything, it felt right and pure. It felt like forgiveness.

Later, we lay under the blanket, watching the stars. I hooked my bare leg over Palmer's; he squeezed my arm, then slipped his around me. I couldn't believe how different this sex was from the first time. Where there had been guilt from being intimate with Palmer, I now only felt peace. Where there had been shame about what I wanted, there was now happiness.

And Palmer behaved as if he felt the same way.

I could never go back to the way things had been with the Major, or with Zach before I'd discovered his secret. Lying with the formal and stodgy Major had felt more like a military parley than sex. Afterward, the Major had cleaned himself up, straightened his clothes, and never said more than "Good-bye. Wait till you hear from me again." Even Zach had acted afterward as if we'd done nothing more intimate than share a shot of whiskey.

"Here comes the moon," Palmer whispered.

The glowing lip of the moon rose into the blue summer night, steadily revealing itself bit by bit, like a violet blossoming. Rather than silver, though, this moon shone almost red or orange, as if somehow the colors of the sunset still lingered in the sky, waiting only for the light of the sun—or the moon—to make them perceptible again.

"This is beautiful, Palmer."

"I'm glad you like it. Even George can't spoil this."

"You hate that man, don't you?"

"I'd like to believe I don't *hate* anybody, except I'm not that self-deluded. Yes, I hate him."

"Why?"

"Because he wants to recast everything to fit his vision of the world—whether that's good for who, or what, he changes. I reckon that's a dangerous way to go through life."

"Aren't you being a little harsh? He's only trying to establish a town."

"And who knows what harm will come from it?" Palmer asked bitterly as he plucked an amaranth blossom.

"What sort of harm, Palmer?"

"Have I told you how my brother, Millard, died six years ago?" he asked, smelling the flower.

"No."

"Back when we lived in Kentucky, my pa wanted to hunt bear, but to do that you need dogs that are savage fighters—dogs that we couldn't afford. So Pa got a puppy, nothing more than a mutt, from some folks in our hollow. I got to play with him the first day we had him. He was a sweet, gentle animal who would have made a fine companion."

Palmer began yanking purplish petals from the blossom.

"That first night Pa locked the dog in a pen and, for the next two years, beat and starved and vexed that animal in every way he could think of. He was trying to make it so mean and pissed and vicious it wouldn't hesitate to take on a bear."

Palmer yanked the last petal and threw the stem to the ground.

"Then one day Millard, who was four, let himself into the pen to play with the dog. He reckoned it would be fun. The dog plunged straight for his throat, and even though I was only ten feet away, there wasn't a thing I could do. That dog wasn't meant to be a killer, John. And turning him into one forfeited my brother's life."

Palmer wiped at his eyes.

"And this valley"—Palmer gestured to the dark land below us— "wasn't meant to be stripped and gutted like some deer. Mark my words, maybe not today or next year, but someday George's blind devotion to making Franklin as big as possible will cause other Millards to be killed."

Palmer cried freely now, and I pulled him to me. He lay curled against me a long time without speaking.

"Palmer?" I whispered.

"Yes." He sounded so serious.

"It's just that I've got to pee."

We both laughed out loud, and I struggled up to go relieve myself.

In the moonlight, I was able to see more clearly the ledge that Palmer had used to hide. It was wider than I'd thought, but the way the lip of the ledge on which I stood jutted out made it difficult to see the one below.

Going back, I lay down, curling up next to Palmer. Being next to him still felt good—wonderful, even—but not as perfect as it had before I'd stood up. His talk of Millard and George reminded me of the world below and the difficulties it held. No matter how much I loved Palmer, a life together would never be easy.

"What are you thinking about?" Palmer asked as if he sensed the change as well.

Thoughts of the dead Major, of Zach raping me, flashed through my mind. "Why things have to be the way they are."

"Who says they have to be a certain way?"

"Everybody."

"But you're wrong. Things for me aren't the way my father said they had to be. And they're not the way your father told you they would be either."

I bristled at what sounded like criticism. "Maybe. But hell and the devil confound me, things aren't the way I want them to be."

"It's not hell or the devil that confounds us, John. Mostly, I think, it's ourselves. We tell ourselves that we can't do this or that. If we want something to be different, then I believe it's up to us to make it that way."

"That's such bullshit, Palmer," I said, pushing myself upright. "Would you say that to Iffy?" Immediately I regretted my words. How quickly we had gone from a feeling of such closeness to one of such frightening discord!

Shadows played across his face as pale moonlight illumined his sharp, proud features. "Don't bring her up."

"What about that Indian boy then? He wanted to find his father, so he went to look for him. And what did he get? His head spiked on top of a pole, all because he ate some garbage. Are you trying to say he did that to himself?"

"No, of course not."

"Well, you just said that people confound themselves."

"John, you're being childish. I didn't say it was always that way."

"Well, it's not fair."

"No, it's not."

"We didn't ask . . ." I let my voice trail off, then said, "That boy didn't ask to be born an Indian."

"I know."

"So why did he end up dead?"

"Aren't you the one who believes in God, John? What would he say?"

"I don't know. The preachers in Longmeadow would say God's will is unknowable."

"And that seems more reasonable, more fair to you than my saying it's up to people to make the changes they want?"

"No. I hate both answers. I'm not sure what I believe. I just know that boy's dying wasn't his fault."

"No, it wasn't. But sometimes people die for no reason. You have to make the best out of whatever you've got, do whatever you can. Otherwise, what's the point? You sit around complaining until you die anyway, and nothing, not a single thing, has changed."

"I'm scared, Palmer."

"That you'll end up with your head on a spike?"

"No. That *you* will."

We rose shortly before dawn, descending into the woods as the sun bloomed in the east. With an unspoken agreement, I unstrapped Palmer's few belongings from Maizie while he watered and fed her. I didn't have to tell him I wanted him to stay, and he didn't have to ask. I felt no hesitation about what was happening, nor did I care about the consequences of what others might think.

Once inside, we both collapsed into bed, sleeping until early afternoon. At last, though, I rose, knowing I had to tend to the truck patch. I'd just emerged from the outhouse when I heard Thomas calling out to me.

"John!" he said as his skinny nag maneuvered through the grass. "Good afternoon."

"Good afternoon, Thomas," I said, my stomach sinking. Despite myself, I suddenly cared about what others might think. Or maybe it wasn't so much that as it was what the others might *do* if they found out.

My eyes darted to the cabin to make sure Palmer hadn't emerged.

"Just getting up?" Thomas asked, glancing skyward.

"I didn't feel so good last night." Where was Palmer's horse? I didn't want Thomas asking any questions.

"Sorry to hear that. Not the best time to have company then."

"It's all right. You couldn't have known."

To my dismay, Thomas began to slide down from his horse. "If you're sick, then you'll be needing someone to tend to your truck patch. I can even come in and fix you something to eat if you'd like."

"Thomas, I've made up my mind. I'll pose as Samantha's beau."

"You will?"

I nodded and thought, Now go away!

"That's great, John. I don't know how to thank you."

By leaving, I wanted to say. Instead, I only glanced over my shoulder.

"Are you looking for something?"

"No. I thought I saw something." Just then Maizie loped around the corner, giving truth to my lie.

"I thought you didn't have a horse."

"I didn't."

"But you do now?"

"Yes. I bought it. From Palmer Baxter just before he left."

"Oh." Thomas stared at me strangely. "I see. So tell me, does Sam know yet that you've agreed to our plan?"

"No, not yet."

"I'd like to tell her right away. She's been worried sick over it." Thomas settled back into his saddle as he turned his horse around. "Would you like me to come back later? I'd still be happy . . ."

"No, Thomas. It's really not necessary."

"All right then. We'll come by soon to settle the details. And thanks again."

Eager to tell Samantha, he dug his heels into the sides of his horse, who took off with such surprising speed that Thomas barely seemed to be in control. Which I found ironic, given that it felt as if I were the one with no control.

THIRTEEN

A year after I left Longmeadow, I found work cutting tobacco on a farm in Virginia with a farmer and his son. The man's son, Tobias, was my age, and together we cut and trimmed the tobacco, then laid it out under the hot sun.

"Say, John," said Tobias as we worked alone, "have you eyed Charlotte Wright at the store? I reckon she's filled out nicer than a Christmas duck."

I'd taken no more notice of this Charlotte than I had the slaves hauling away the dried tobacco, but I knew better than to say so.

"Of course," I said.

Without warning, Tobias appeared beside me, pressing me backward into the uncut tobacco. The cool leaves reached just over my head, meaning we were hidden from sight.

"Aye, Charlotte's a beaut, all right," he said, breathing heavily. "I've always wanted to touch her here," he said, caressing my bare chest. I dropped the cuttoe I'd been using to trim the plants.

"Would you like to do that?" he asked, then added, "To her?"

I nodded, and he placed my hand on his warm flesh.

"Then I'd like to touch her here." His hand slid toward my waist, then slipped inside my breeches as he took me in his *hand. Without warning, he guided my hand inside his trousers as well.*

Hardly able to draw a breath, I stared into eyes as green as the tobacco surrounding us. By now our pants had been pushed down our hips so we could silently watch as we stroked each other. A mixture of horror and wonder engulfed me, until both were overwhelmed by the more physical sense of impending release. Trying to stifle our moans, we climaxed within moments of each other, wiped our hands on the tobacco, and without a word, went back to work.

I fled that night.

July 1798

PALMER AND GWENNIE AND I WATERED THE TRUCK PATCH. SEVERAL times I'd all but caught Gwennie smirking at me as she looked from me to Palmer and then back again.

Once, when Palmer went down to the creek to fetch more water, she said, "So you've agreed to help out Thomas and Samantha, have you? Probably not a bad idea now that he's here."

"What are you talking about, Gwennie?"

Gwennie smiled. "You think I blind as a mole, don't you?"

I thought about protesting, then said, "Is it that obvious?"

"Is what that obvious?" Palmer asked as he returned.

"Nothing," I said abruptly.

"That you two stuck on each other like sap on tree trunk," Gwennie said.

Palmer said, "It probably is obvious, but I told her as well."

"You did!" I exclaimed. "Why?"

"Calm down, John. I told Gwennie because she's nobody's fool. I suspected she knew, and she did. I figured, why pretend with her?"

"Great! Just great!" I exclaimed, kicking over a bucket. "Do you know what happens if anyone in Franklin finds out? They hang people for this, or flog you to a bloody pulp so you're never right again." Pacing back and forth, I thought of the Major. "They might even do worse than that. You don't think George—or anybody else—is going to stand by while you and I . . . And what about Caleb? He's your brother and a preacher for Christ's sake! Shit! And have you thought ab—"

Catching up to me, Palmer clamped his hand over my mouth. "Lord, you're as excitable as a blue jay around a wild cat. Relax, John. Take a deep breath."

Deep breath, my balls, I thought, tempted to bite him.

Palmer continued, "Now listen to me. Everything will be fine. Most people aren't a tenth as perceptive as Gwennie, and we'll be very careful around others."

I pushed his hand from my mouth. "I think Thomas suspects."

"You do? Why?"

"He saw your horse the other morning. I told him I'd bought her, but he still looked suspicious."

"Did he say or do anything else?"

"No."

"Don't forget, Thomas needs you, John. Even if he were to suspect, and I doubt he does, he wouldn't say anything. Do you feel better now?"

"John," Gwennie said, "did Thomas tell you everything about him and George?"

"That depends on how much he had to tell. What he did tell me was that George won't let him have a claim or get married because he's an escaped slave."

"Did he tell you about the gunpowder?"

"Gunpowder? No."

"Thomas storing gunpowder for George."

"He is, huh?" Glancing at Palmer, I shrugged. "And why is that important?"

"Because George storing it for French."

"What?" Palmer and I asked simultaneously.

"George storing gunpowder for French army."

"But the French are helping the Indians. If George is helping the French, that would be treason," I said, stunned.

"Gwennie, are you sure?" Palmer asked.

She nodded.

"But why is he doing it?" I asked.

"He need the money. He tell Thomas that with what the French are paying him, he can make Franklin as big as he wants. He also owes money to people back east."

"Why is Thomas doing it?" Palmer asked.

"Because George knows Thomas is an escaped slave," I said. "It's just like his not being able to have a claim or marry Samantha. Thomas doesn't have any choice but to do what George tells him."

"Not true, John," Gwennie interjected. "George may not let Thomas do some things, but he also not force him to do things he not want to. Storing gunpowder was Thomas's idea. And George paying him well to do it. Thomas do it because he need money for he and Samantha to start claim in Canada. Of course, George not know about he and Samantha."

"Why are you telling us this, Gwennie?" I asked.

"Because I think everybody better off if they know something. This way nobody tempted to cheat anybody else."

"I'm not so sure I reckon this is such a good idea," Palmer said.

I wasn't either, but I could see her point. On the other hand, I felt as if I were trapped in a house of cards. All it would take was a mistake by any one of us to bring the whole thing down.

Two days later, Gwennie dropped by to invite Palmer and me to come have dinner with her that night.

"She lives in a what?" Palmer asked as we made our way through the woods.

"A cave. And wait until you see the things she has in there—a real bed. And beautiful dresses. Things she got from trading apples with Indians and settlers. She must drive a hard bargain."

"Actually she doesn't."

"How would you know?"

"I heard George talking about it one night with Caleb. Most of those fancy things she took from people as a favor."

"How is trading apples for an expensive bed doing someone a favor?" I asked.

"Instead of making people pay real money or trade something useful, Gwennie was willing to take things they were either going to have to throw away anyway or that they could never use on the frontier. And if they were poor, she wouldn't make them pay at all."

"I see," I said, chagrined at having thought Gwennie greedy. Especially after all of the help she'd given me.

All of a sudden Palmer stopped.

"What's wrong?"

Holding a finger to his lips, he glanced around the woods, and I felt the hair on the back of my neck rise. Woods that just a moment ago had felt lively and harmless had in an instant become menacing and foreboding.

"I thought I heard something," Palmer whispered.

"What?"

"I'm not sure."

"A bear? An Indian?"

Palmer shrugged. "Maybe it's nothing."

"Should we keep going?"

"How much further is it?"

"Not much. The other side of the ridge. Ten minutes, no more."

He nodded. We walked on in silence, Palmer listening intently, while I, in turn, watched him with as much intensity.

"We're here," I said as we stepped into the clearing.

Immediately, I caught sight of Gwennie's drying rack. Or what was left of it.

"What's wrong, John?" Palmer asked, noticing the disturbed look on my face.

I motioned to the center of the clearing. Where the drying rack had stood, only a pile of splintered wood now remained. Not far from that were the smoking remains of a fire, the stones around it now scattered about. Even the kettle that had reminded me of a hen lay on its side, its iron legs twisted every which way, the kettle itself badly dented.

"Maybe a bear's been through here." Palmer knelt to inspect the ground.

I eyed the woods nervously, especially the thick brambles of blackberries.

"Gwennie!" I called out, going to the opening of the cave. "Gwennie, are you all right?"

"Wait for me, John," Palmer said, following me in. "Whatever happened wasn't done by a bear or any other animal. There are nothing but human footprints out there. Let's be careful."

The crevice through which we entered seemed even longer and narrower than it had before, and I shivered when the top closed over us. "Gwennie?" I called out into darkness that only swallowed my words.

"Wait here," Palmer said. "I saw a torch outside. I'll fetch it."

Unable to make myself wait, I continued forward, trying to recall where her table and bed and other items had been. My shin smacked against something with a sharp crack, and I cried out in pain.

Behind me, light flickered on the wall.

"I thought I told you to wait."

Ignoring Palmer, I took the light and held it out in front of me. "What the hell?"

Palmer whistled. "Either she was one hell of a lousy housekeeper, or there's been a fight in here."

The shelves along the wall had all been knocked down, the jars laying shattered on the floor, their contents scattered about. Her table had been flipped onto its side, then someone had taken an ax and hacked away at it. Even the legs and frame of her bed had been shattered. In the center of the room lay a pile of dresses, blankets, bearskins, and a painting, all violently shredded.

There was no sign of Gwennie.

"Looks like the black devil himself has been here," said Palmer nervously. "Do you have any idea who might have done this?"

I shook my head. "She told me that neither the Indians nor the settlers were particularly fond of her, but she said nothing about anybody threatening her."

"Who knew she lived here?"

"George. Thomas. Samantha, I suppose."

"But they're her friends. At least George and Thomas are, and I can't see any reason for Samantha to do something like this."

"Neither can I," I said. "But what if Thomas found out Gwennie had told us about the gunpowder?"

"And he was so angry that he did this?"

I held up my hands helplessly. "It's possible. What do we really know about him?"

Palmer shrugged. "Nah. He doesn't seem the type." Palmer's eyes took in the room again. "It doesn't look like she was robbed. Whoever did this wasn't interested in taking much with them. It looks more like they were angry about something."

"But was Gwennie here when it happened?"

"Well, she was expecting us for dinner, and the fire was going. I think she must have been here, John. Maybe we should scout the woods."

My stomach constricted with worry over what we might find.

For a half hour we scoured the woods, but the only sign we found were more footprints.

"Those were made by a white man," Palmer said. "Probably George or Thomas, but the fact is they could've been any settler."

We followed the clearest footprints until Palmer lost them in a nearby creek.

"What do we do now?" I asked.

"Go to Franklin and tell the others?" Palmer said doubtfully. "Maybe they'll help us to organize a search party."

"Like hell they will, Palmer. You know how those people feel about Indians, including Gwennie. The only thing they'll organize would be a raid on her belongings."

"What about George? Don't we at least have to tell him? Perhaps he might even know something."

"All right." But I'd become leery of George and his plans. I suspected if he knew anything about this, he wouldn't tell us.

George knelt on the floor with his back to me as he sorted through a small crate of highly prized iron nails.

"But, George," I pleaded, "she's your *friend*."

"No, not my friend, John. She's an Indian, and I just did the Christian thing in helping her out. I'd appreciate it if you'd keep that in mind. I don't want people going around saying I'm friends with Indians."

"But as a Christian, aren't you worried about her?"

Standing, George turned to face me. "She's an Indian, John. And a strange one at that. Everyone knows she's prone to take off for long stretches of time."

"George, her cave has been ransacked! She didn't just take off."

"It was probably some other Indians then. They never have been very fond of her."

"Like anybody in Franklin is. Won't you do anything to help me look for her?"

"Look where, John? These Indians are nomadic. They're not capable of staying in one place for more than a week or two. We'd never find her."

"So what should I do?"

"Work on your claim if you know what's good for you. Look, I've a town and a business to run. But," he said, cutting off my protest, "I will put out the word and see if anybody knows anything."

"All right," I said, mollified only a little.

"Now if you don't mind," he said with barely hidden exasperation, "I've work to tend to."

In the fervid afternoon heat, Palmer and I listlessly sat on the porch. Everything in the valley had grown still and quiet, except for the sound of the cicadas hidden deep in the grass—their relentless thrum seeming to be the very essence of heat itself. It was almost as if the creek and trees and even the earth had fallen into an uneasy, restless sleep beneath the blazing sun.

"I can't believe how indifferent he was, Palmer," I said. "When I first arrived, he talked about how Gwennie had helped Alexander and Catherine and how . . ." My voice trailed off as I noticed Palmer staring at something in the distance.

"Isn't that Thomas?" he asked as I turned to look.

"Shit," I groaned. "What are we going to tell him about you?"

"Nothing. It's none of his business. What do you think he wants?"

"It's probably more nonsense about my posing as Samantha's beau."

"Hello, John," Thomas said as he rode up. Then to Palmer, "You're Palmer Baxter, aren't you?"

Palmer nodded. "Pleased to meet you."

"Me as well, but I was given to understand that you'd left."

"I reckon I had. But now I'm back."

"I see." Thomas transferred his gaze from Palmer to me. "So, is Sam here yet?"

"No. Should she be?" I asked.

"I told her to meet me here, and I'm late, so she should've been here by now."

"Well, we haven't seen her."

Thomas slid down from his horse. "Odd. Maybe she got hampered with something at home. Anyway, I came as soon as George told me about Gwennie. How long has it been now?" With a sigh, he lowered himself into a chair on the porch.

"Three days. I've spent most of every day looking for her, but so far not a single sign."

"Three days, huh?" Thomas said. "I wish I'd known sooner so I could've helped—I owe Gwennie a lot. This valley's so big, though. And after three days, God only knows how far away she might be."

"I'm not sure how much more we can do," said Palmer. "Maybe she did—"

He was cut off as a breathless Samantha burst around the corner, her forehead freshly scraped.

"Sam! There you are," said Thomas. "What happened?"

He stepped forward to look, but she brushed his hand away. "I fell, that's all."

"Well, where have you been?" he asked.

"Clarissa and I were out picking berries, and I lost track of time." When she caught sight of Palmer, her eyes widened in surprise. "But I thought you 'ad left?"

"Does everybody in Franklin keep track of my movements?" Palmer asked.

Her eyes darted from Palmer to me and back again. Thomas took Samantha's hand in his own, absentmindedly stroking it as he said, "John, what did George say about Gwennie?"

"He said he wouldn't help. He says she's nomadic."

"He's probably glad she's gone," Palmer said. "After all, her living in the valley aggravated a number of folks."

"You was close to Gwennie, weren't you, John?" Samantha asked.

"Yes. She's been very kind to me, and I owe her a lot. I couldn't bear it if something has befallen her."

A smile briefly crossed Samantha's face.

"When did you last see Gwennie, Thomas?" Palmer asked casually.

Thomas furrowed his brow. "I suppose it would have been the day before you found her missing. She said she'd come from up here visiting." Palmer glanced knowingly at me.

"Did she stay long?" I asked.

He shook his head. "No. Just stopped by to chat for a little, then she left."

"Did she say where she was headed?"

"Nope. Just said it was getting late and time to go."

"Are you friends with her, Samantha?" I asked, hoping she might have a clue.

"She was tolerable for an Injun woman, but we ain't friends."

"I know you've got your claim to tend to, John. First thing tomorrow, I'll start scouting for her. God only knows what I'll find."

For a long moment, the four of us sat there in silence, and I wished they would go, that I had never met them or had anything to do with their schemes.

A cool breeze sprang up from the north and I luxuriated in it.

"Look at that," Palmer said, pointing to the horizon. "I think I see actual storm clouds."

"Really!" I exclaimed, so excited at the prospect of the drought's breaking that Gwennie was momentarily forgotten. "Palmer, if you're having me on, I hope you never piss again."

"I'm not. Look there."

Shading my eyes, I stared into the distance. Sure enough, from behind the mountains, dark clouds the color of blood pudding roiled upward, towering over the valley like a threat. Each looked as heavy with water as a pregnant cow about to deliver her calf.

I felt like dancing for joy.

Apparently Samantha did to, because she clapped her hands together and said, "Pa's going to be so pleased." Then doubt flickered across her face. "I hope it's not like an Englishman in bed—all bluster and swagger and no dirty deed."

"Sam," Thomas said. "Watch your mouth. Where did you pick up such an expression?"

"It *has* to rain," I said, thinking of all the hours spent hauling water.

"We'll have to wait and see," said Palmer.

Thomas cleared his throat. "John, I don't mean to impose, but if you don't mind, can we talk a minute about your posing as Sam's beau?"

"All right," I said.

"Sam told her father yesterday about your 'change of heart,' and he's planning on coming up to see you tomorrow. Is that all right?"

I glanced at Palmer. "That's fine," I said hesitantly. "Though just what is he coming for?"

"Mostly to make sure I'm not lying," Samantha said. "I 'eard 'im telling Ma 'e wouldn't be the least bit surprised to learn I'd made the whole thing up. 'E's also coming to talk about when the wedding will be."

Palmer held up a hand before I could protest. "Don't worry, John. Sam's already told him you want to wait until fall."

"And?" I asked.

"And," Samantha said, "'e's going to try and browbeat you into 'aving it sooner. But I 'eard 'im tell Ma that 'e won't push you too 'ard, or 'e's afraid you'll change yer mind."

"Damn right, I will."

Thomas practically beamed at me. "See, I told you how well it would work."

"And then come fall, you two will sneak away to wherever you're going?" I asked.

Thomas nodded. "And Sam will leave a note saying she misled you all along. That way everyone will be sympathetic toward you."

As thunder rolled up from the distance, all four of us turned to look at the approaching clouds. A cool breeze swirled around me, bringing another moment of welcome respite.

"They're still headed this way," Thomas said.

Palmer shook his head. "But look. There aren't any old men's beards."

Peering into the sky, I could see there were no signs of beards—falling rain—trailing down from the dark underbellies of the clouds.

"Well, then," said Samantha, "that just means all the more for us when it gets 'ere." Rising from where she sat, she walked along the porch, running her hand along the rail. "Catherine and I sat out 'ere last summer. It rained a lot then." She paused, then said more to herself than anyone else, "I was so jealous of 'er. I wanted 'er cabin, 'er 'usband, 'er baby. It wasn't fair."

Thomas looked pained as he listened. "This time next year, Sam, I promise we'll have a place like this. Maybe even a baby of our own. You'll see."

Samantha looked at him, smiled, and said, "I know." Then she turned to me. "If it weren't for Thomas, I'd be jealous that Palmer seduced you and not me."

"For God's sake, Sam!" Thomas exclaimed.

"What? What do I care that they're sodomites?"

Somehow she'd found out about Palmer and me! But how? Had she spied on us? Intuition? However the hell she knew, I had to make sure she didn't try to use it to her advantage.

"We know about the gunpowder, Thomas," I said resolutely.

Palmer rose from where he sat. "John!"

Thomas looked stunned, then angry. "Gwennie told you, didn't she?"

"That's right," I said. "We know about George and the French and the gunpowder."

"John, you idiot!" said Palmer.

"She threatened us, Palmer!"

"No, she didn't," Palmer said. "She just says too much."

Palmer didn't know what he was talking about. I knew a veiled threat when I heard it. Especially since Palmer hadn't been with me and heard Samantha say she would do anything to get what she wanted.

"John, I'm sorry," Samantha said contritely. "I didn't mean nothing by what I said."

Maybe I had overreacted.

"She'll say no more foolishness, John," Thomas said. "Not to anyone. I promise that. Come on, Sam."

Within minutes, they had vanished into the woods at the far end of the meadow. The wind picked up as the thunderheads bore down on us while I studiously ignored a glaring Palmer. At any moment I expected a cloud of curtains to be drawn across the sun.

"By all that's infamous, John Chapman, what the hell were you thinking?"

"I thought she was threatening us, Palmer."

"She's not especially bright. She probably didn't even know what she was saying."

"Maybe. Maybe not. But I don't goddamned trust her, Palmer. Or anyone else."

"Even me?"

"Don't be an ass," I snapped. "Of course I trust you."

"Why are you so angry?"

For a moment I said nothing, unable to articulate my feelings. "Because I'm frightened. Because I feel vulnerable. I don't like pretending that I'm going to marry her. I don't like pretending that you're just staying here."

"But we have to, John."

"Of course we have to! I know that as well as you, Palmer—I know it better." I hated that we were sniping at each other. It was wrong, especially since neither of us had anyone else we could trust.

Lightning flashed against the darkening sky, giving me an excuse to turn away. Already dark clouds the color of ugly bruises and hateful intentions were closer, bearing down on us as surely as winter on autumn. Occasional gusts of wind rumbled down the valley rippling through the treetops, their leaves trembling suddenly in the sunlight like a million green-winged birds in flight.

"That," said Palmer, "is going to be one holy hell of a boomer. I hope Caleb has the little ones gathered up."

Stepping next to Palmer, I hesitantly touched his face, then slipped my hand inside his already undone shirt.

"I'm sorry for snapping at you that way, Palmer." Sunlight fell across his bare arms, making his fine blond hair shimmer against his tan skin. When he didn't draw away, I pulled him close, and we kissed. His face was rough and scratchy, but his lips were warm and soft.

"Aren't you worried someone might—"

"Shh," I whispered, pulling his mouth back to mine. This time, though, I used my tongue. Despite being lost in the hot, wet feel of him, somewhere my mind registered the low rumble that came from the dark clouds now above us. Without speaking, we began pulling at each other's clothes, only stopping our kissing long enough to take off a shirt or undo a belt.

Soon we were naked on the porch, embracing. Cool breezes swirled over my hot skin as my hands slid over his wide shoulders, across his chest and stomach, then circled down along the curves of his ass. He groaned when I cupped his balls in my palm; I fondled them gently, amazed both at how they felt in my hand—heavy, exquisite—and at the fact that I held them at all.

Using both hands, I lowered him onto the porch, then for a long moment stood there watching him. He lay on his back smiling shyly up at me.

As I crouched next to him, lightning flashed closer, the thunder rolling over us a few seconds later. I glanced out over the meadow as the entire field of tall, spiky grass bowed down as one, crushed to the earth as if the weight of my gaze were too much to bear, though I knew it was only the wind. I sat back on my heels, pulled Palmer to me, and we began kissing again.

A mighty gust of wind slammed into the porch, actually knocking me back a step. Fat drops of rain began pelting the ground with loud smacking sounds that drowned out the sound of my own moans. All at once the rain fell in frenzied sheets while waves of thunder rolled down from the clouds.

The bolt of lightning struck terrifyingly nearby. A blinding-white effulgence washed over us, followed an instant later by an explosion louder than any I'd ever heard. The next thing I knew, I lay sprawled on the other side of the porch, stunned, while an eerie light pulsed all around me once, twice, three times.

It was beautiful.

Someone screamed nearby.

"In! In! Get inside, John!" It was Palmer, panicky, naked, his face bloodied, stumbling wild-eyed for the cabin door.

Still unable to move, I lay on the porch. Soaked and chilled to the bone, I shivered uncontrollably, marveling at how easily the seemingly insurmountable heat had been vanquished by the storm. I knew I should be inside, away from the storm, but I couldn't tear my eyes away as the lightning stabbed the earth again and again, while the wind and rain lashed the trees and the meadow.

Then, without warning, it was over—or all but. Lightning-studded clouds drifted away to the south, the thunder fading to booms, then distant rumbles. The rain tapered off; the wind's frenzied howling gave way to gusts that hurried the storm away. Blue sky returned, reclaiming with ease what the dark clouds had just so furiously occupied. Moments later, the sun reappeared, flooding the valley with warmth and bright light, and still naked, I was grateful to be warm again.

A strange odor lingered in the air—acrid and sour, which made my eyes narrow. I lay motionless, but shaken, as my mind, like the sky, tried to clear and calm.

Palmer stepped out onto the porch, his eyes warily searching the sky as if he didn't quite trust that the storm had gone. A bearskin hung over his shoulders. A streak of blood ran from his forehead and over his cheek. I tried to speak, but my mind still churned with the sights and sounds of the storm, and I couldn't.

He hobbled to my side and with a tremor in his voice asked, "You all right, John?"

"I think so. You're bleeding." I reached over to touch the gash in his forehead, but he brushed my hand away.

"I reckon we should check for a fire. Stop it now, before it's too late."

"Fire?"

"You know, from the lightning? It hit somewhere nearby. It might've sparked a fire."

"Shit, you're right." I yanked myself to my feet. Without even grabbing my clothes, I vaulted from the porch and raced around the cabin.

I didn't have far to go. Fifteen feet behind the cabin, I found the shattered, smoking stump of what had been a large oak. And fifteen feet beyond the stump lay the rest of the smoldering tree, most of the green leaves having burnt and crumbled to ash, the bark scorched and still burning in some places. Somehow none of the other trees or surrounding brush had caught fire. Barefoot, I stepped carefully among the smoldering bits of wood, imagining what would've happened if the trunk had been thrown in the other direction, onto the cabin.

Palmer came up behind me. "It doesn't look too bad."

Crouching down, I scooped up handfuls of dirt, tossing them onto the trunk.

"Stand back." Palmer pulled the bearskin off his shoulders, using it to beat out the flames while I continued to kick dirt onto the smoking patches. The fires were out after a few minutes' work, and we stood there naked and dazed, staring at the dead trunk.

"What about the rest of the valley?" I asked nervously. "There were a lot of lightning strikes."

Palmer nodded. "I didn't see any smoke yet, but we should keep an eye out. The valley is awfully dry." He tried to wipe away some of the blood from the gash on his forehead.

I took him by the hand. "Come on. Let's go inside and tend to that."

Once inside, after I had cleaned and bandaged his head, I was overcome by a sudden enervation. "Palmer, I'm exhausted. I need to lie down."

To my surprise, he lay down with me. Resting with my eyes closed, I felt purged by the storm. After seeing such a display, the problems I had didn't seem so significant.

Outside, meadowlarks called out as if to reassure each other that they, too, had weathered the storm. As I grew more sleepy, a calm settled over me.

Palmer pulled my body close to his so that we lay together like spoons. The hairs on his chest tickled my back, while the press of his warm flesh against mine only relaxed me even more. He kissed the nape of my neck, and while I still wasn't sure he was right about Samantha, it was a relief to know that Palmer had forgiven me.

The squeak of the door woke me. I opened my eyes just in time to catch sight of Palmer's rosy ass disappearing outside. His clothes still lay on the floor, and I knew he had gone to the necessary.

I drifted back to sleep, then woke up a short time later. Palmer hadn't returned, and without his warm body pressed against mine, I noticed the chill that touched the cabin. I began to wonder what was taking him so long. Only a few shafts of weak, watery daylight still filtered through the holes in the wall, and I realized that dusk wasn't far off. Finally, I pulled on my pants and went outside to see what Palmer was up to.

"Palmer!" I called out as I stepped off the porch. I approached the necessary and called out again. Even after I knocked, he didn't answer. I opened the door. It was empty inside. Had he gone to check on the truck patch? Anxious, I turned and walked back around the cabin, but saw no sign of him there either.

"Palmer?" I called out, louder this time. I heard nothing but the silence of the valley. Even the meadowlarks seemed to have fallen quiet. This was ridiculous. He'd been naked when he left. How far could he have gone?

Something was wrong. Something had happened to Palmer.

Heading for the creek, I waded through the kwenaskat—growing so fast that it now reached halfway up my thighs. He wasn't down by the creek, and I was running out of places he could have gone. I wondered if perhaps he'd been taken ill and fallen and lay hidden by the grass.

"Palmer!" I called repeatedly as I crisscrossed the meadow again and again. "Palmer, if you're hiding, it isn't funny." Little by little, I turned in a small circle, my eyes searching the meadow, the woods, the shadows, but I saw nothing.

Perhaps, I thought, he'd taken Maizie and ridden somewhere, though the thought of him doing so naked was absurd. I checked anyway.

At first I didn't see her in the shadows of the woods, but then I spotted her lying down, something I'd only seen her do once before. My nails bit into the palm of my hand.

"Maizie?" I said softly as I approached her from behind. I nudged her glossy back with my foot. "Maizie?" I reached down to stroke her neck. Something warm and sticky matted her fur, and I knew she was dead. Wanting to be certain, I stepped over her unmoving body, nearly slipping as I trod on her slick entrails. Not only had her throat been slit, but she'd been gutted like a fish as well. The warm blood told me she hadn't been dead long.

My first thought was that Indians had struck and any moment I, too, would feel a flash of hot pain as my gut was slit open. Convinced that Palmer also lay nearby, his throat slit, his guts spilled like a burst tomato, I nearly froze in terror and grief. Finally, when nothing happened, I forced myself to move and comb the nearby brush for his body. But he wasn't there.

Returning to Maizie, I stared at her body, bewildered. Frantic with worry, I tried to think of an explanation. If this was the work of Indians, where were they now and why hadn't they attacked the cabin? Maybe this had something to do with the gunpowder Thomas was storing. Or had Palmer done this? That made no sense. None of this did. Then with a sense of dread, it hit me that whatever had happened to Palmer had happened to Gwennie, too.

Although night would soon fall, I decided to get the hell out of here and make my way to Franklin. I wasn't safe here alone and knew I'd be better off with George and the others helping me search for Palmer. Bounding up the stairs to get dressed, I nearly missed what lay on the steps. But something did catch my eye, and I turned back to look.

A snake lay coiled on the middle step, and I sprang away. Naked and breathless, I stared at the thick, glossy snake until I realized it neither moved nor made a sound. In fact, it wasn't a snake.

Coming closer, I saw that whatever was lying there was long and thick and black. I crouched down, and without realizing it, stretched out my hand to touch it. The texture was fine and silky, though one end was shredded from where it had been hacked off with a knife.

I gently picked up Gwennie's ponytail, and in a flash I understood everything.

Zach had come. And he'd taken Palmer.

FOURTEEN

When I was twenty-one, and working at a gristmill in upstate New York, two men were caught committing sodomy. Each was flogged twenty times, then, bloody and beaten, cast out of town by a jeering mob. Despite my unceasing wariness, I'd been friendly with one of the men and had wanted to be more. It could easily have been me crawling down that dusty road.

I left before it was. I found an abandoned cabin several days walk from the town, and there I spent my eighth year away from Longmeadow living as a hermit. Seven years of wandering from place to place had left me feeling as rootless as a boulder. Hiding away in my cabin for weeks on end meant I spoke to no one but myself. Even for someone as used to solitude as I was, the loneliness was miserable.

One morning as I walked to the river for water, I stumbled upon an orphaned fawn. Her mother had died from an arrow she'd taken through the chest, though apparently she eluded the hunter before collapsing in a heap. I found the fawn bleating as she tried to nurse from her mother's stiff body. I took her back to my cabin and called her Elizabeth.

She kept me company for the rest of the year.

July 1798

TRAVELING THROUGH THE WOODS AT NIGHT—ESPECIALLY IN A FRANTIC state—was more treacherous than I realized. But I had no choice. Somewhere in the valley, Zach had Gwennie and Palmer, and I knew I had no choice but to go for help. After falling twice in the first fifteen minutes, I knew I had to slow down or risk breaking a leg and being of no use to anyone. But going slower was hard: the certainty that Zach was either watching nearby, enjoying my torment, or far worse, terrorizing Palmer and Gwennie, only goaded me to go faster.

For hours I marched on in darkness, until the first notes of the unseen thrushes' matins swelled up from the dark, telling me dawn was at hand. Soon larks and nightingales joined in the musical clamor, and their songs managed to comfort me some, though I took far greater comfort in spotting Thomas's nag quiescently standing by his cabin. During my journey, it had occurred to me that Zach might have struck here as well.

"Thomas, wake up!" I called out, banging on the door. "It's me, John Chapman!" I paused for a moment, listened, then banged again. "Thomas, something has happened. Please open—"

The door swung open, replaced by a groggy Thomas, his rifle pointed at my chest. "What the hell?"

"Thomas, it's me, John! Put down the gun and let me in!" Despite the cool morning air, sweat dotted my face.

"John? By all the devils, what are you doing here?"

"I know what's happened to Gwennie! And now it's happened to Palmer! I need your help!"

He blinked several times, turned, and staggered inside.

"I need your help, Thomas," I repeated, following behind. "You said you'd help me anytime I needed it." I became aware of a second person in the room. Samantha sat huddled in Thomas's bed, a bearskin practically pulled up to her eyes.

"Hello, Samantha," I said self-consciously. She said nothing, but only looked at me oddly, almost as if—what? Excited? Nervous? Unable to quite read her, and too pressed to particularly care, I turned my attention back to Thomas.

"What's this all about, John?"

When I finished explaining, he looked at me as if I'd suggested he move back to his father's plantation. "This Zach person, you really think he kidnapped Gwennie and Palmer?"

"I know he did. He wants revenge on me."

"When did Palmer disappear?"

"Last night. He went out to the necessary and never came back."

"How do you know it was this Zach? Did you see him? There are still occasionally Indians out here, you know."

"No, I didn't see him. But he left this." I gently placed the hacked-off ponytail onto the table.

"What the hell is it?" Thomas asked, flinching as if I'd dropped a copperhead in front of him.

"It's Gwennie's ponytail." I told him about Zach's sick collection of souvenirs from his hobby.

Looking both fascinated and repulsed, Thomas leaned forward, gently touching the hair.

"'E cut off Gwennie's 'air?" Samantha asked with a whimper from the bed.

Thomas turned to stroke her arm reassuringly, then asked me, "And he keeps the girls' ponytails after he kills them?"

I nodded again.

"My God, that's hideous. And you think that's what he's done with Gwennie?"

"Yes. Several times over the past few weeks I've sensed someone watching me. Even Palmer noticed it the day Gwennie went missing."

"And what do you think he's done with Palmer?" Thomas asked.

Before I could answer, Samantha sat upright in bed. The bearskin fell away, revealing two enormous breasts. "John, you should leave Franklin before something 'appens to you next!"

"What are you talking about, Sam?" asked Thomas. "He can't leave his friends. And I'm going to help John."

Sam leaned forward, clutching at Thomas. "No! You can't! I won't let you!"

Thomas looked at her as if she were crazed, which was about what I thought. "By St. Christopher's whiskers, Samantha Connolly, what are carrying on this way for?"

"You can't 'elp John! I won't let you!"

"Why on earth not?" Thomas asked.

Samantha's eyes leapt from Thomas to me and back again.

"Because 'e'll 'urt you," she whispered. "Maybe even kill you." She crumpled forward, burying her face in the bearskin.

"What are you going on about, girl?" Thomas demanded.

Samantha said nothing, only shaking her head as she sobbed.

Thomas grabbed her by the wrist and yanked her naked from the bed. "You know something you're not telling, and I want to know what it is!"

"Thomas, yer 'urting me," she squealed, trying to wrench her wrist free.

"Not half as much as I'm about to. Tell me what's going on?"

"I know 'im."

"Who?"

"The one you been talking about. I met 'im one day on my way up 'ere. At first I thought 'e was from town since 'e knew about John."

My stomach sank.

Samantha continued, "I didn't know what 'e was like at first. 'E was nice to me and listened to what I 'ad to say. It was only later I began to suspect that 'e was bad."

"Oh, Lord," muttered Thomas.

"I did it for us, Thomas," Samantha sobbed. "I didn't think 'e would 'urt anybody. I'm sorry, John. I truly meant no 'arm."

"What did he want from you?" Thomas asked.

Samantha wiped away her tears. "'E wanted to know about John, specially who he was friendly with."

Damn Zach! I thought. Damn him to hell! I should have burned down the blockhouse with him in it when I had the chance.

"What did you tell him?" I asked.

"Where Gwennie lived, and I told 'im Palmer 'ad come back and was with you, John. He swore 'e was only going to take 'em away fer a while, until John left. That way we could 'ave the claim and not 'ave to move to Canada. I swear 'e said nothing about cutting off 'air or 'urting them."

My knees went weak.

"Later I get scared of 'is plan and told 'im I didn't want to go through with it. 'E 'it me and said 'e would kill Thomas and my sisters if I told anybody 'e was 'ere or what 'e was up to."

Thomas glared at her. "You realize you may have killed two people?"

"I know!" she wailed. "I'm sorry!"

For a moment I thought Thomas might strike her, and I doubted I'd try to stop him.

"But maybe it's not too late," Samantha sobbed. "I think I might know where 'e took them."

"Then why the hell didn't you say so, girl!" snapped Thomas.

I leapt to attention. "It's all right, Samantha. Just tell us where we can find Palmer and Gwennie."

Somehow Thomas's hoary horse managed to bear the weight of both of us as we ascended the ridge to where Palmer had brought me the night he returned. I pictured the rocky outcropping on which we had lain, the steep drop-offs on all sides. It was just like Zach to choose such a shrewd place to hole up.

The ash and birch and cedar of the lower reaches of the forest still stood thickly around us, telling me we had a ways to go.

We rode on in silence for a few more minutes, then Thomas said, "So what are we going to do once we get up there?"

"I haven't the faintest idea."

"You don't have a plan?"

A plan! I thought with disgust. I've never had a plan! Not once in my damnable life. Maybe that had been my problem all along.

I sighed. "No, I don't, Thomas. We've got your rifle, and we outnumber him two to one. I guess we just go up there and try to overpower him."

"Somebody will probably get killed."

"Somebody will."

"Did Palmer have his rifle with him?"

"No, I told you he'd only gone to the necessary."

"And you didn't bring the rifle with you?"

Thomas's words were like a slap. How could I have been so dense? Hadn't I learned anything on the frontier?

"No," I whispered, cursing myself for my stupidity. "I didn't bring it."

"We could go back."

"It would take us all day to fetch it. Palmer and Gwennie don't have that much time." I wasn't sure they had any.

Thomas shrugged. "It doesn't matter anyway. We still have mine."

"Of course it matters! With two rifles we would have had a real advantage!" Even I could hear the hysterical edge to my voice.

"We'll make do, John."

I again pictured the rocky outcropping above us. It was the perfect place for Zach to wait. If he was watching—and he would be—there was no way to surprise him.

The worst part of this, the hardest part to bear, was my deep conviction that the blame for everyone's misfortune rested on me. If only I'd compromised somewhere along the way. If only I had married some woman in Longmeadow, taken a job in a mill, maybe even had children . . . If I had, none of this would be happening.

"Thomas, I think I should go up alone. After all, I'm the one he wants. Maybe he'll let Gwennie and Palmer go."

"He won't be expecting both of us. I think we should use that to our advantage."

"How?"

"I'm not sure." Thomas thought for a moment. "Zach has obviously done all of this to lure you up the mountain—his telling Samantha was no accident. I assume he wants to kill you."

"I'm sure he does." I had an idea. "What if he thought I was already dead? What if *you* told him that?"

"Not bad. It would certainly throw him off stride. How did you die, though?"

"You killed me."

"Me! Why?"

"Because I killed Samantha."

"Which you did because she's the one who helped Zach get Gwennie and Palmer."

"Right." I was pleased with my plan.

"But how does that help Gwennie and Palmer?"

"Because your telling him will distract him, and maybe I can sneak up the trail and get off a shot."

"It sounds risky." Before I could protest, Thomas continued, "But I can't think of anything better. We'll give it a shot. Or should I say, we'll give Zach a shot?"

I tried to laugh, but nothing came out.

Shafts of light sluiced down over the mountaintops. Here and there, sunlight struck the landscape, brilliantly lighting up verdant tree-tops and lush, rolling meadows, before finally glinting off the creek.

Near the top of the mountain, but still out of Zach's sight, I slipped off Thomas's horse at the last spot that afforded cover. Without a word, Thomas continued on to hopefully distract Zach. Only a moment or two passed before I heard Thomas holler "No!" followed by the sound of a gunshot that echoed down the valley. Silence ensued.

I slumped against a boulder. Just like that our plan had failed: Thomas was dead, as dead as I would be in another minute. I considered turning and fleeing back to the valley, then leaving Franklin altogether for somewhere else. But running away yet again would be even worse than death.

As swiftly and silently as possible, I scrambled my way up the ridge, all the while expecting Zach's face to peer down over the edge, his rifle aimed at me. How, I wondered, would a bullet feel as it ripped into me? Hot, I imagined.

Halfway up, I encountered Thomas's horse on its side, its face all but obliterated by a lead ball. Thomas was nowhere to be seen, and I felt a flicker of hope. Then I spotted the barrel of Thomas's rifle poking out from some scrub.

Thanking God, I quietly slid it free, made sure it was still loaded and primed, then continued on up.

A few feet from the top, I heard the unmistakable voice of Zach cursing as he scuffed about in the rocky scree that covered the out-cropping. "I told that whore's spawn she was a fool to be running away with a darkie!" Zach thundered. "You're even more useless than I imagined."

"I killed him," Thomas said. "Chapman lost control when he found out what Sam had done. He tried to stab her and I had to kill him."

I peered up over the edge as Zach buried his foot in Thomas's gut.

"He was mine to kill, you filthy bunghole!" Zach shouted as Thomas writhed on the ground. "I wanted to see the look on that simpleton's face when I shoved his catamite over the edge."

I spotted Palmer, still naked, and now bound and gagged, poised on the edge of the cliff. I froze. Even from here, I could see the cuts and bruises that scored his body. What the hell had Zach done to him? Gwennie lay next to Palmer, her arms and legs similarly lashed, her head and shoulders already hanging out over the edge. I couldn't tell if she was alive or dead.

Raising the primed and loaded rifle, I drew a bead on Zach. Just as I pulled back on the trigger, Thomas staggered to his feet. I jerked the gun upward as the rifle went off, missing Thomas by no more than inches.

Zach spun toward me, his voluminous red hunting shirt billow-ing out behind him. His feral eyes didn't look so much at me as through me, and his mouth hung open in a snarl as savage looking as a meat ax. "Well, fry me in bear fat," he said in an eerily calm tone that didn't match the demented look on his face. "If it isn't Johnny Chapman—*frontiersman!* How's the claim? You're not missing some-thing, are you?" he sneered, actually smiling before rushing at me like a bull elk in heat. Despite bracing myself to absorb his blow, we slammed to the ground in a tangled heap.

Zach's size gave him an immediate advantage. Before I realized what was happening, he had me pinned on my back, jagged bits of rock digging into my flesh. I looked up into his leering face just as he spit in mine.

"Surprised to see me, John-ny? You forgot to say good-bye when you left."

I struggled to free myself, but he only laughed.

"After what you did to me in Warren, did you really think I was going to let you go?" Before I realized it, he had let go of my arm long enough to smash my face with his fist.

Under his weight and dazed by the punch, it was a struggle to speak, but I managed to say, "I didn't do anything to you."

"You beat me insensible, then left me for dead. That's what you did, you pathetic squit!"

"After you raped me, you beshitted bastard!" I screamed.

"I saw how you looked at me every day. I couldn't take off my shirt without your roger practically ripping your breeches in two. You wanted everything I did to you from the day you arrived."

I closed my eyes and turned away.

He laughed again.

"Let them go, Zach," I whispered. "I'm here now."

"Is that your plan—to beg me for their lives? You are worthless." Without warning, he reached between my legs and seized me by the balls. "Well, not completely worthless. What do you say, John-ny— you want it once more, so you can die a contented man?" He squeezed so hard it became difficult to think or breathe. Flashes of light exploded in front of my eyes until I thought I would pass out.

A shadow passed over us, followed by the crack of wood against bone. Bellowing like a beaten mule, clutching his head, Zach rolled away. Behind him stood Thomas groggily clutching his rifle by the barrel. Before I could get to my feet, Zach sprang to his, grabbed the rifle by its gunstock, and viciously clubbed Thomas upside the head. Thomas staggered backward, and for one horrible moment I thought he was going to stumble over the edge. Instead, he collapsed in a heap.

Moaning, Zach himself sank to the ground, giving me a chance to finish him off, but I could barely think through the waves of pain engulfing me, much less move. Zach struggled back to his feet. He looked at me before his eyes jumped to Palmer, then Gwennie, then Thomas. He smiled.

I managed to rise to my knees. Even though the outcropping was small, there was no way I could protect everyone. All it would take was a single push for any one of them to vanish over the edge.

"Who you gonna save, Chapman?" Zach asked. Without warning, he darted toward Gwennie. I struggled toward her, but then Zach veered toward Thomas. I threw myself in that direction, falling face-first to the ground.

Zach howled with laughter. "What's poor Chapman to do? Such a difficult decision!"

He feinted toward Palmer. I lunged that way, only to watch Zach turn about and come within a foot of Gwennie.

"Oh, Chapman, this is *too* much fun!" Zach said with glee.

God how I wanted to see his decapitated head on top of a pole. On hands and knees, I scrambled in Gwennie's direction as fast as I could.

Laughing, Zach leapt over me, charged toward Palmer, and I knew I couldn't reach him in time.

Until Zach tripped. "Son of a shitten bitch!" he howled, tumbling into the dirt.

In a flash, I lunged forward and grabbed Zach's ankle. Pulling as hard as I could, I dragged him backward a yard until he rolled onto his side, drew back his free foot, and smashed it into my mouth. I tasted dirt from his boot as blood and pain and nausea welled up inside me. I let go, and through a haze of pain, I watched him crawl ahead until only a few feet remained between him and Palmer.

I staggered to my feet, stumbled forward, and threw myself on top of Zach. Enraged, I grabbed him by the shirt collar and rolled backward, somehow throwing him up and over me.

Despite the pain that racked my body and the dizziness that blurred my vision, I managed to rise. Zach already stood, sucking in rasping mouthfuls of air. There was fire in his eyes.

"You can't beat me, you sorry excuse for a man!" he yelled, rushing forward, burying his fist in my gut. "You're not a tenth the man I am! I want you to know that before you die!" He caught me with an uppercut, then shoved me as hard as he could.

Staggering backward, I sensed the edge of the precipice before I actually tumbled over it. In my instant of free fall, I had only enough time to feel relief that I had died trying to help, grateful that at least it was over, and after one final blow, I would suffer no more.

I slammed into a rocky ledge like a sack of potatoes thrown from a wagon. For a moment, I lay there not certain what had happened. My tongue ran over my bloodied lips, which were covered with hard bits of something, either grit or fragments of my teeth.

Despite the pain and the shock, I realized I'd landed on the same hidden ledge that Palmer had used to frighten me with when he'd pretended to fall.

Above me, Zach bellowed, "See! *See!* Nobody gets the best of Zachariah Griffin! I told you, Palmer, your precious Johnny wouldn't be able to help you! Want to see his body before I do the same with you?"

My mind swam with pain and fear as I sat up, pushing myself away from the edge, thinking only that I needed to get off the narrow ledge before I did fall. With my back against the rock, I scanned the ledge overhead, searching for a rock or tree root to use to pull myself upright.

"Where the hell did Chapman's lily-livered ass land?" Zach growled from above. I froze as something red swung down in front of me. Somewhere in the dazed and battered recesses of my mind, I recognized Zach's hunting shirt.

"This time," Zach continued, "I want to see the bastard's broken neck."

Because of the way the upper ledge jutted out and shielded me, he had no idea I was there.

Literally without thinking, I simply reached up, grabbed a handful of the red shirt, and yanked as hard as I could.

Zach sailed out over me, his arms and legs flung wide as he fell. There was, however, one instant when I was able to see the look of utter stupefaction on his face before he vanished from view without so much as making a sound.

A sweeter sight I had never seen.

Dizzy, I pressed my back against the rock and closed my eyes. Feeling as if at any moment I might pass out and follow Zach over the edge, I took several deep breaths to steady myself. When I felt a little more stable, I dragged myself upright and somehow managed to climb back on top of the outcropping. Unable to stand, I crawled to where Palmer lay, dragging him away from the ledge before untying him.

"What happened?" he asked, bewildered. "I saw you fall. Then Zach disappeared. I thought you were dead."

"Gotcha," I croaked, and even managed a weak smile. Palmer smiled a little, then laughed out loud, and such relief swept through me I thought I might cry. "Now help me move Gwennie," I said.

Together we rolled her to safety. As I watched Palmer undo her bindings, I realized she, too, was naked. "Is she alive?" I asked, suddenly ashamed.

Palmer pressed his ear to her chest. "I think so. But she hasn't had water in three days."

I noticed a pile of supplies that must have belonged to Zach. Rifling through them, searching for water, I glanced to where Thomas still lay in a heap.

"What about Thomas?" I asked.

As Palmer reached Thomas, he began to stir. Palmer helped him sit up, then came back to me. "He's confused, but I think he'll be all right."

Every one of us was badly hurt, but we had survived. I had stayed and protected what mattered most to me. I had beaten Zach.

I stumbled across a leather flask fat with water. "Here. Give this to Gwennie."

As Palmer forced the flask between her lips, she began to cough. I slipped off my shirt, draping it over her shoulders. Palmer said, "She's coming to. Everything will be all right now, John."

Watching Palmer tend to her, I spotted the ragged gap where her hair had been hacked away. Anger flooded through me. Going to the edge, I stared down into the trees below wanting to spot Zach's broken body.

"Do you see him?" Palmer asked, coming up behind me.

"No."

"Where would he have landed?"

I tried to remember exactly which way he had fallen. I'd been in so much pain, so confused, that I wasn't sure. "There," I said, pointing to the most likely spot.

Palmer studied the area for a moment and said, "Well, the trees are pretty thick down there. Even with that red shirt of his, it would be hard to see him. We'll find his body later. We should go."

I nodded but remained rooted to the ground. My thoughts came slowly, as if my mind were shutting down. Now that Zach was dead, I seemed unable to move.

"It's over, John," Palmer said, trying to soothe me. He said something else that didn't penetrate my mind, then shook my arm and asked, "Are you listening?"

I was, but only just. His voice seemed to come from too far away.

I was to blame for all of this. The least I could do now was to help as best I could, but I continued only to stare into the distance. Palmer took my face in his hands and gently said, "John, we have to get down from here. We're all hurt and need help. I need you to get ahold of yourself."

His words brought me back almost immediately.

"You're naked," I said, and for some reason, began to laugh.

Palmer laughed as well. "You just noticed now, did you? Remember, I was expecting only to go as far as the necessary."

"Ow!" I said, clutching my side. Each time I laughed—in fact, each time I breathed—it felt as if someone were scraping a knife over my insides. I suspected I had at least one broken rib.

"Are you all right?" Palmer asked.

Trying to nod, I realized how blurry my vision had become. I became aware of how dizzy I felt, not to mention nauseated. Suddenly, it was hard to stand.

"John?" Palmer asked, stepping toward me.

Wanting to sit, I only tried to wave him away, but everything began going dark. The last thing I recalled was the sensation of falling.

I awoke in the cool darkness of a cabin.

"There you are," said Palmer. He sat next to me, a tiny candle flickering nearby.

"Where am I?"

"Thomas's cabin. You passed out, and we carried you back."

"You did?" I mentally groaned at the thought of him, after all he'd been through, having to carry me down that entire mountain.

His left hand held a rag that he dipped in a bowl, then ran over my face. Cool water trickled down my skin. "Well, Thomas and I did. And Gwennie."

"Gwennie? Gwennie carried me back?" This time I groaned out loud. "Some help I turned out to be. You'd have been better off if I'd never come."

"You killed him, John."

"How long have I been asleep?"

"I reckon eighteen hours or so."

"Is it night then?"

"Yes."

"How is Gwennie?"

Palmer shrugged. "She hasn't said much. In truth, she hasn't said anything. She's over there in the corner."

"Is she sleeping?"

"I don't think so. The last time I checked, she just lay there staring at the ceiling. I think Zach did some pretty awful things to her."

"How did you know his name?"

"He told me. That's about all he told me, though, damn his soul to hell."

So Palmer didn't know Zach had done all of this to get even with me. I wasn't sure if I felt relieved or not. "Where's Thomas? How is he?"

Palmer furrowed his brow. "Well, he left to take Samantha home yesterday after we got here. He said he planned on coming right back, but so far there's been no sign of him."

"How was Samantha?"

"Scared. Relieved." Palmer paused. "I'm worried her family figured out what was going on between him and Sam, and that's why he's not back."

"Could be. Palmer?"

"Yes."

I hesitated before asking, "Did Zach say anything at all while he had you?"

"About what?"

"I don't know. What he wanted."

Palmer was quiet so long, I thought he wasn't going to answer. "He wouldn't tell me. Watching him, I reckoned he enjoyed hurting others. At the beginning, when I still thought I could reason with him, I asked if it didn't bother him to hurt people so much. He laughed and said, 'About as much as it bothers me to kill a flea.'"

"Oh." I was afraid to hear any more. "It's cold in here."

"I know. Thomas had only one blanket, and I gave it to Gwennie."

"Why isn't there a fire?"

"There wasn't any chopped wood, and I didn't want to leave you alone. I wasn't sure how badly you were hurt."

"Let a plague rot me for all I care."

"Well, I care."

I asked the question I was most afraid of. "How are you?"

He smiled and said, "Better than a barrel of apple butter."

I glanced toward the window, then said, "Liar." I ached for whatever he had suffered at Zach's hands.

It hadn't yet begun to lighten outside, but because of the cool freshness of the air and the depth of darkness, I said, "It must be close to morning."

"I reckon so."

"Why don't I fix us something to eat."

"I'll take care of it."

"No, let me. I'm already embarrassed you had to carry me down when I was supposed to be rescuing you. I'd like to do it."

"All right. Now that you're awake, I'll go chop some kindling."

After Palmer went outside, I lay there for a moment. It was over and I'd won, and I *hadn't* run away. That meant so much to me.

I struggled to my feet. Hobbling, I went to where Gwennie lay, hoping I could offer her some comfort. "Gwennie," I whispered, kneeling next to her. "It's me. John." I wanted to touch her, but something in her vacant gaze told me to just let her be. Her blanket had slipped a bit from her body. I gently reached over to pull it back up to her shoulders.

As I looked at her inert form, the guilt poured back over me. After all, none of this would have happened if I hadn't been running from myself in the first place. I turned to go start breakfast.

"You came back for me," she whispered.

I returned to her side and knelt.

"Of course I did, Gwennie."

"Most people wouldn't have. But you did. You are a good man, John Chapman."

I closed my eyes to keep from crying.

Palmer came back in. "Odd, but I would've sworn I saw an ax out by the woodpile as we came in. But it's not there now."

"You must have been mistaken," I said, stifling a groan as I rose. Every time I moved, I again felt each blow Zach had landed on my body.

Palmer shrugged. "Anyway, I think I found enough odds and ends for you to cook with."

Soon a small fire crackled in the fireplace, but it turned out there wasn't much to cook either.

"Look at this, Palmer," I said, pointing to what passed as Thomas's pantry supplies. "He's got nothing but a half full jug of bear oil and some cornmeal." I scanned the interior of the cabin, spotting six or seven stacks of wooden crates. There had to be three dozen of them. "Is there anything to eat in any of those?"

Palmer laughed and said, "Depends. Can you make anything edible out of gunpowder?"

I whistled. I'd forgotten about George's scheme and Thomas's part in it. "That's a lot of gunpowder. I hope George knows what he's doing. At any rate, I've got cornmeal. At least I can make us some johnnycakes." I held up Thomas's sole cooking utensil—a frying pan—and said, "Can you believe this is all he has to cook with?"

"I'm not surprised. Look how skinny Thomas is. And this place is a Scotch cabin if I ever saw one. The floor is nothing but loose dirt. There are more gaps in these walls than in a crone's mouth. And how about the fireplace? It's just creek stones piled up without so much as mud or patching to keep the heat in."

"It must be freezing in here in winter. This place is a drafty, leaky dump. No wonder Thomas was willing to go to Canada for a chance at something better."

Palmer nodded. "And outside is even worse. Thomas built this place in a ravine with only the one way in and out. Not to mention the fact there's nowhere for him to grow any crops."

Bear oil sizzled as I dropped in the first of the johnnycakes. "Will you watch the griddle, Thomas? I've got to piss."

Strands of early-morning mist clung to tree branches like spirits to just-deceased bodies. Diffuse light from the burgeoning dawn flowed through the forest as I headed for Thomas's crude necessary, and for the first time in days, I felt myself relax. And why not? Palmer was back, and Zach was dead.

Stepping from the necessary, I relished the brisk morning air, ripe with the rich, earthy smell of a forest in the throes of riotous summer growth. But something was amiss. The woods were too quiet for this early in the day. Instead of the usual musical cacophony of nightingales and thrushes and tanagers all trying to drown each other out, there was only silence.

And I still had that unsettling feeling I was being watched.

"Thomas?" I called out hesitantly. "Is that you?"

The forest stayed silent.

"You're being foolish, John Chapman," I said aloud, making my way back toward the cabin. It was understandable, I told myself, that my nerves were yet a bit on edge. It was probably only a hungry bobcat that had scared the birds quiet.

Inside, Palmer was just dishing up a johnnycake. "Here you go, John. I gave the first one to Gwennie." He motioned to where she sat against the wall, and I was so glad to see her sitting up eating that I forgot all about having felt unnerved a moment ago.

"I'm famished," I said. "I'll give Thomas back twice whatever we use."

"I found some apple cider as well," Palmer said, pouring me a cup.

"I ate so many of these when I was at Zach's," I said through a mouthful of johnnycake, "that I swore I could never eat another. I guess I was wrong." I chewed, swallowed, then realized Palmer was staring at me.

"What did you just say?"

I glanced at my plate and said, "That I ate so many of these at Zach's . . ." My voice trailed off as I realized what I'd done.

"You *knew* him?"

"Palmer, I can explain. I was going to." But before I could, we both heard the sound of scuffling from out front.

We froze, our eyes darting to the door.

"Hello?" said Palmer.

A horse gently nickered outside.

"It's only Thomas," said Palmer, and I nodded, letting out the breath I'd held. Rising from the table, he opened the door. "It is him," he said to me, then called out, "There you are! We were worried about you." As I watched, the relieved expression on Palmer's face grew puzzled. I rose, joining him at the door as he said, "Thomas? Is everything all right?"

Sure enough, that was Thomas's gangly form on top of the horse. "Is he injured?" I asked, noticing that the horse kept pawing the ground and twisting its neck back and forth.

Together we went out to him. "Do you need a hand?" Palmer asked, reaching out to him. Then urgently, "Christ, John, he's bleeding. Help me get him down. What did that bastard William do to him?"

As soon as we tugged on his sleeve, he slumped over, sliding off the horse like a bag of peat. He thudded onto the ground before we could catch him. Palmer crouched down to help him just as the sound of a rifle firing blasted through the still morning air. Hot blood splattered my face as a gaping hole opened in the animal's left haunch where Palmer had been. A terrified squeal erupted from the horse just as I heard myself begin screaming, "In! Get inside!"

Without thinking, I gripped Thomas's inert form under the shoulders and dragged him toward the cabin. Thank God Thomas was so skinny. As I reached the door, I looked up to see Palmer standing in a daze, watching the poor animal try to rear upward, only to have its ravaged leg give way underneath it. The horse crashed to the ground, where it lay thrashing and crying out.

"Goddamn it, Palmer!" I bellowed. "Move!"

He turned and bolted into the cabin, shutting the door as another blast from the rifle tore into the cabin wall. Shaking, I fumbled a moment before slamming the wooden bar down into the latches. We each took a step backward as we stared at the door.

"It's Zach, isn't it?" Palmer asked. "He's not human. He's the fallen angel himself."

I nodded, terrified and off-kilter. I desperately wanted to believe this was a nightmare, but I knew damned well it wasn't.

"How?" moaned Palmer. "He's dead! He has to be!" Palmer turned and pressed his face against the wall. He turned to face me, and I saw he was crying. "What does he want, John? You don't know what he did to me!"

"He wants me, Palmer. And I do know."

"He wants you? Why?"

"I'll tell you everything, but first we've got to find something to defend ourselves with."

A panicked look leapt into his eyes. "There's nothing. I looked while you were sleeping."

"Where's Thomas's gun? You didn't leave it on the mountain, did you?"

"Of course not," Gwennie said, speaking for the first time. I turned to look at her as she knelt by Thomas's body. "Thomas took gun with him and Samantha."

"Son of a bitch. That must be what Zach is using now. At least he's only got the one. Even he can't reload it any faster than once a minute."

"Thomas dead," Gwennie said softly.

Palmer and I knelt down next to her.

"Are you sure?" Palmer asked in a quavering voice.

"Yes."

Something pink protruded from Thomas's mouth and I said, "What the hell is that?"

Gingerly taking the pink edge of whatever it was, Gwennie began to tug it out.

"Damnation," hissed Palmer as a bloody scalp slid free.

Without thinking, I reached over and removed Thomas's hat. Streaks of ghostly white skull shone through the blood. A ragged line of skin marked where the hair had been ripped away.

Staggering away, I slumped against a wall. I'd been so wrong on the mountaintop to foolishly believe I had won. I should've known by now that I could never win.

"What do we do now?" Palmer asked hoarsely.

I turned around to find Gwennie and Palmer staring at me expectantly.

Why, I wondered, was I supposed to know?

FIFTEEN

Without my realizing it, Elizabeth grew into a fat, slovenly creature—Elizabeth the deer, that is, not Elizabeth my sister. A year before, she had been a frisky fawn given to nudging me awake too early in the morning. Now she was a pudgy creature that slept much of the day and was given to nipping my bare flesh when she wanted more corn mash to eat, which was much of the time.

I wasn't faring much better myself.

One day while returning from one of my rare forays into town for supplies, I heard a desperate bleating as I neared the cabin. Hurrying up the path, I emerged to find Elizabeth, her haunches already bloodied, cornered by an adolescent luzern—a French-Canadian lynx. Luzerns, while ferocious and fearless, were much smaller than most dogs and normally preyed upon squirrels, possums, and birds, but never deer. Too fat to bolt and too tame to fight back, Elizabeth would soon have been dead if I hadn't returned.

Grabbing several rocks, I quickly drove off the hissing cat. Hurrying to Elizabeth, I stroked her head until she calmed. I was ashamed at what I had done to her. For the next several months, I attempted to wean her from the corn mash I'd been feeding her and encouraged her to eat the grass and leaves she was supposed to eat. I also played chasing games with her, trying to reduce her unnatural bulk and return to the poor creature her innate grace. I was marginally successful at best.

I didn't see what took her that final morning, though I assume it was a panther. All I heard was her sudden cry abruptly cut off, some scuffling in the bushes, then silence. By the time I got outside, the only sign of her was some blood in the dirt.

Staring into the dark woods into which she had vanished, I realized my life had become every bit as unnatural as hers. With that recognition came anger. To hell with those who had mocked or despised me. I refused to accept their judgment, or that my fate was to live hidden away, ashamed and alone. I deserved better.

I set forth to find it.

July 1798

"IT'S NOT THAT BAD," I SAID TO MYSELF OVER AND OVER.

If only I believed it.

"Shit a turd in my bed," Palmer suddenly growled. "All of this damned gunpowder and nothing to use it with. You know what else? There *was* an ax when we got here. That bastard has got that as well. Jesus, what are we going to do?"

"Calm down, Palmer," I said. "Let's think about this for a minute. It's not that bad."

Palmer laughed bitterly. "How do you reckon that?"

"First of all, there are three of us. Second, Zach has to be injured—Thomas and I gave him a thrashing, even before he fell. I don't know how he survived the fall, but it had to have hurt him."

Palmer glanced at Thomas's body. "Fat lot of good that did Thomas. I think we should make a run for it."

"I don't know," I said hesitantly. "I don't think we should leave. I think Zach will try and wait us—"

I was cut off by the sound of something clattering against the roof. The three of us froze, staring at the ceiling.

Palmer looked at me and said, "What the hell was—?"

This time the clattering was louder.

"He's throwing stones," Gwennie said.

Again something bounced on the roof, and I realized she was right. What was he up to throwing stones when he had us trapped? Then I remembered what Zach had said about cornering prey while hunting.

"I was wrong," I said. "He won't wait us out. He told me once to never let your prey have time to gather its wits. He said to press your—"

Another stone hit. And another.

I looked up. "He's trying to lure us out. If he can't, then he'll come after us."

"What do we do?" Palmer asked.

"I don't know," I said frankly. "We don't—"

And another.

"We don't panic," I continued. "He's trying to unnerve us so we'll bolt. He must be badly hurt if this is the best he can do."

We stared upward in anticipation of the next stone. It didn't come, and that made me even more nervous.

"He's demented!" Palmer said, then demanded, "John, what's possessed him to do all of this?"

As quickly as I could, I filled Palmer in about how and why I'd wound up wintering with Zach, about Zach's murderous past, his hunt for his half-breed son, and how I'd literally uncovered the truth about Daniel McQuay.

When I'd finished, I felt relieved and, oddly, a little triumphant. Surely, Palmer would now understand I was right to feel the way I did. "Now you see it really is my fault," I said firmly.

Palmer and I both jumped as two more stones hit in quick succession.

"What's your fault exactly?" Palmer didn't even try to keep the skepticism from his voice.

"Everything: that the Major was killed and I had to flee. The fact Zach kidnapped you and Gwennie. The fact that Thomas is dead. The fact that Zach has us trapped in here like animals he's hunting. Don't you see?"

Another stone bounced off the roof. So much tension filled the cabin that it felt as if an actual person were pressed right up behind me, peering frantically over my shoulder.

"Zach won't rest," I continued, "until he gets even with me. God's punishing me for what I did with the Major, for loving you."

Palmer's eyes met mine, and I wondered what he was thinking.

The rocks seemed to have stopped. Of course, that might only mean Zach had indeed thought of another plan. Perhaps he was advancing on the cabin even as we stood there.

"John, ten sows and their babies couldn't swill that much hogwash," Palmer said, and I knew he was talking about my believing I was being punished by God. "People would have died whether you loved me or not. I hate thinking like that. It makes no sense."

"Palmer, I'm tired of having to worry about bringing misery down onto others."

"Now I understand why you live so far up the valley and why you kept pushing me away."

The roof of the cabin creaked. Palmer and I turned almost as one, our eyes darting to the logs overhead. In the silence, I only heard the nervous sound of our quick breathing.

"Is it him?" Palmer whispered.

"I don't think so. Thomas's roof doesn't look too strong. I think it would make a lot more noise if he were on it. But we have to do something soon."

"Like what?" Palmer asked.

I studied the cabin, trying to see anything I might've overlooked. My eyes fell on the fireplace. Without a word, I knelt down in front of it. After a few moments of prying, I was able to partially slide free one of the creek rocks that made up the chimney. "He never patched these," I said to Palmer. "You and Gwennie can get out this way."

"Then so can you."

Palmer and I stared at each other, and I knew I'd sooner go to hell than let him die because of me. And he *would* die if I went with them, because Zach was going to follow me until either he or I had taken a last breath.

"No," I said. "Even if Zach didn't see us escaping—and remember, the only way back to Franklin is past him—then we're back where we started from. He's got a gun, and we don't. Even if we did escape right now, he'll keep coming after us. This time he has to be stopped for good. And I'm going to do it."

"I won't let you do this for me, John."

"You! Hell, Palmer, I'm not doing this for you," I lied. "It's for Gwennie. She's the one I owe my life to. Now help me with these stones."

I felt his eyes on my back. Then he knelt next to me and helped to try to pry the stones loose. Palmer wrenched a large stone free and the chimney bulged dangerously inward.

"Stop!" I cried.

"See, John. One more stone and the whole thing will come down. So we can't sneak out. We could get out after it collapses, but Zach will hear it fall even if he doesn't see. Then he'll come after us back here. So unless you've got something else in mind, your plan isn't going to work."

I shrugged noncommittally.

"What?" Palmer demanded. "What are you planning to do?"

I wished I knew. "Palmer, let me be. I need to think." I'd already thought of a way to kill Zach if I could get him inside. It would cost me my life as well, but so be it. How could I lure Zach in? I'd offered myself on top of the mountain, but he'd refused, knowing I valued Palmer and Gwennie more than myself. What I needed was something that Zach valued more than getting even with me.

But what on God's green earth might that be? What if there was nothing else? After all, he had pursued me all the way from Warren to exact his revenge. The only thing he had gone further to get was his son.

His son!

Finding his son was the most important thing in the world to Zach. He'd told me that himself. All I had to do now was to find a way to use it against him. But how? If somehow I knew where the boy was, surely Zach would trade Palmer and Gwennie for that knowledge. But I didn't know. But *maybe* I could make him believe I did know, at least until Palmer and Gwennie had escaped.

It had to work. It was my only shot.

While Palmer watched, I used tongs to gather up the embers of the fire, placing the throbbing orange coals into the frying pan. I set the pan on the table and next to it the half-full jug of bear oil.

"John, what do you think you're doing?"

I had to convince Palmer I had a plan that would let me escape alive.

"Answer me, John," Palmer demanded.

"We need a place to meet, Palmer."

"What?"

"A place to meet after this is over. Somewhere between here and Franklin. I'm no martyr, Palmer. I've got a plan that gets me out of here with my scalp."

"What is it then?"

"We don't have time, dammit! Now where can we meet?"

"By the creek where we saw—"

"Oh, Chapman? Chapman?" Zach's voice slashed through the air. I recalled the hare I'd seen snatched by the eagle on the banks of the frozen Conewango. That was how I felt now.

"There's no time for any more discussion!" I said to Gwennie and Palmer. "We'll meet by the creek. Get ready to knock down the fireplace!"

I grabbed Thomas's body and hoisted it to his lifeless feet. Palmer and Gwennie looked at me as if I were as insane as Zach.

"Well, go on," I said. "Get ready. On the count of three. One, two, three!"

As Palmer shoved free the stone holding up the chimney, I flung open the door, pushing Thomas's body into the opening. Behind me, I heard the sound of the fireplace crashing down, then the scrape of rocks being dragged free. With one hand, I held Thomas's head up as straight as I could. Carefully, I tried to peer over his shoulder, but saw only empty clearing.

"Zach," I called out. "It's me, Jo—" The sound of the gunfire reached me just as Thomas's body leapt backward, tearing free of my grasp as it crashed to the floor. I'd been counting on Zach's poor eyesight to trick him into wasting his shot. I had one minute before he could reload and fire again.

"John!" Palmer called, and I turned to face him. Gwennie had already crawled out, and Palmer was poised to follow. "Come with us! We can get—"

"Go, Palmer, you son of a bitch! Before I kick your ass out!" Turning away, I stepped out of the cabin into the clearing. "Zach!" I called. "I know where your son is!"

"Liar!" Zach called out.

"I do. But if you want me to tell you where he is, you're going to have to come and get it from me."

"You've ten seconds to prove it afore I kill those two trying to sneak away!" he hollered.

I thought furiously. The boy's age! Zach had said he'd learned about the boy's existence four years ago and that he'd raped the woman seven years before. So that made the boy eleven now, maybe twelve.

"Time's up!" hollered Zach. "I'm going after—"

"He's twelve! Your boy is twelve! That proves I saw him!"

Zach was silent for a moment, then said, "I told you that. Or you figured it out somehow. I think I'd be better off capturing your precious Palmer. Then you'll tell me everything I want to know."

I had to convince him, to keep him here longer, but how? The only Indian boy I'd ever seen was the one Palmer and I had spotted who'd been looking for Gwennie. He had been eleven or twelve. Could I describe him, convince Zach that way? Something nagged at my mind; something about the boy. My thoughts raced.

Why had the boy been looking for Gwennie? Because his mother had died, and he was looking for his father.

His *white* father! Was it possible? I had to gamble.

"I saw your boy only days ago, Zach! His mother died last winter, and he was looking for you. And I know how he was different, how you planned on being certain which was yours."

"You're a beshitted liar, Chapman. And your time is—"

"He was a Mingo!" I hollered. "And the Mingo had so little to do with whites, and there were so few left, that you knew the only half-breed would have to be yours."

There was a pause, and I wondered how far Palmer and Gwennie had got.

Zach limped from the woods.

Even from this distance, I could see the blood on his face and the way he held his right arm against his chest.

For a moment, he stared off into the distance, then said matter-of-factly, "Where is he, Chapman, you bastard? Where is my son?"

I hated his calling me Chapman.

"If I tell you, do you promise to leave us alone?" I knew Palmer and Gwennie still needed more time to get away.

"I won't promise you a thing. As a matter of fact, I think I'll find out what I want a hell of a lot more quickly if I go catch your catamite and bring—"

Before he could finish, I bolted back into the cabin. As quickly as possible, I splashed the remaining bear oil over the crates of gunpowder and on the walls of the cabin, then flung the embers from the frying pan onto the oil, setting it all ablaze. Small flames, weaving intricate dances, spread outward as delicate spirals of gray smoke curled into the air. I knew it would only be minutes before boxes of gunpowder began exploding like cannons.

Returning to the doorway, I stood just inside and called out, "Zach, if you can't see the smoke already, you will—"

Before I knew what was happening, Zach leapt around the corner, swinging an ax. I dodged to the left as the blade sank into the doorway. He grabbed me by my shirt collar and tried to drag me out of the cabin. Immediately, I fell to the ground, kicking his legs out from underneath him. He tumbled on top of me.

"Where is my boy, you shit-eating bastard?" he bellowed.

Struggling to get away, I got a glimpse of his battered face—his left eye was invisible in a gruesome pulp of blood and flesh and bone. Zach was even more hurt than I'd thought. Yet somehow he fought as fiercely as if uninjured.

Zach pinned me to the ground. Flames spread behind me, crackling and snapping inside the cabin, but Zach seemed to take no notice. If I didn't get him farther inside, he would escape alive.

I spit in his face as I tried to wriggle backward.

"Where is my boy, you son of a bitch? Are you going to tell me?"

I barely managed to shake my head from side to side.

"I swear to God, if you don't tell me, Chapman, I'm going to capture Palmer and cut him apart inch by inch, starting with his feet and working my way up. Now tell me!"

I shook my head again.

"You're a fool, Chapman. You won't stop me from finding my boy. Only slow me down a little." He glanced up at the burning cabin. "That fire's getting a mite too hot. I guess I'll finish you off, then see if your friends want to share what they know."

His hand slid toward my throat, and I knew he was going to choke me to death. I fought as hard as I could. I had to keep him there a little longer—until the flames reached the gunpowder. Then Zach would never hurt Palmer, or anyone, again.

Zach's fingers reached my neck. "Is this all the fight you can put up? Even Daniel, that fat Irish fuck, fought harder than you."

How many times had I heard that as a boy? Each word Zach hurled at me hurt as much as any physical blow, and I felt his fingers close around my throat.

"Depraved sinners like you, Chapman, deserve every rotten thing that ever happens to them. Not one person will miss you when you're dead." Zach's eyes watered from the smoke pouring out the door.

As his fingers squeezed the air from my throat, images— Patience crying, the Major taking his last breath, Zach raping me— flashed through my mind. Surely, Zach was right, or those things wouldn't have happened.

My ears rang as I gasped for air, but I still heard Zach as he said, "You're nothing but a feeble pervert, Chapman, a coward who brings woe and ruin wherever you go. No wonder your father loathed you. No wonder you ran. Running was the one thing you were good at."

At the mention of my father, something inside me snapped. I'd only run in the first place because my father had made my life hell.

How was a boy supposed to fight a man? When the Major died, I had no choice but to run then, too, or die. But hadn't I fought Zach in Warren, then even though I expected to die, climbed the mountain where Zach held Gwennie and Palmer and fought him again? And now, hadn't I stayed behind so that Palmer and Gwennie could get away? I was even willing to die for them.

Those weren't the acts of a coward. Those weren't the acts of someone who ran.

Zach dared to judge me? This monster who lied and stole, who raped and murdered, who was he to call me a sinner?

Zach was wrong. I was wrong. I didn't deserve the scorn and calumny that had been heaped on me all of my life. What I deserved was what I'd felt with Palmer that night on top of the mountain. I deserved to love and be loved. I deserved to live.

I had to escape now or die.

The way Zach straddled me had left his groin open for a merciless blow from my knee. With every bit of strength I had left, I relaxed. I willed my body to slacken, my eyes to stare vacantly upward. Zach's grip relaxed just a bit as he leaned forward to stare into my face.

Now I took that opening. As hard as I could, I drove my knee up into his crotch.

Zach bellowed as he rolled away. Instantly, I was on my feet, racing back into the cabin. If he wanted to learn what I knew about his son, he had to follow me.

The sound of crackling flames filled the air with a roar. Disoriented by the smoke and fire, I just had time to grab the frying pan before Zach charged in after me, grabbing me by the waist. Thrown off-balance, I still managed to slam the pan against his head as we tumbled backward onto the table.

For a moment, I lay on my back watching snakes of flame slither across the roof. Something stung at my skin, tiny pinpricks, and I realized sparks were burning my flesh. Suddenly, Zach's face loomed in front of mine. In one hand, he held the pan I'd hit him with. He brought it down as hard as he could, barely missing my head as I rolled away.

From the corner of my eye, I caught sight of Zach's other arm

hanging limply from his side. The jagged edge of a broken bone protruded through the skin of his forearm. To my amazement, he
seemed not to realize he'd broken it. I reached out, grabbed the
bone, and yanked.

Now he realized it.

Zach screamed, threw the pan at me, and staggered backward.
Continuing to scream, he crashed into a stack of boxes filled with
gunpowder. The top box fell from the stack, bursting as it landed on
the floor. Gunpowder spilled forth, the edge of it coming to rest
inches from flickering flames.

I didn't want to die, not anymore, but I wouldn't run. Zach wasn't
dead yet.

Stumbling through the flames, I searched for the frying pan.
Finding it, I grabbed it, only to have searing pain shoot through my
hand. The pan had been sitting in flames. Ignoring the pain, I held
on to it, and turned to find Zach.

A small explosion came from the other end of the cabin. The
whole place would blow any moment.

Zach tackled me by the knees. Tumbling to the floor face-first, I
felt him climb onto my back. Before I could react, he grabbed me by
the neck, raised my head upward, then smashed it against the floor.
The coppery taste of blood filled my mouth. He raised my head
again, but before he could drive my face downward, I swung the frying pan backward over my head and felt the satisfying smash as it
found his face. He fell off me. Rolling over, I felt possessed with the
same anger I'd had after he'd raped me. Only this time, I didn't swallow it, turn, and run away.

I used it.

Incredibly, Zach again struggled to his knees.

"You want to know where your boy is, Zach?"

He froze.

"I'll tell you. His body has probably been washed all the way
down to the Allegheny by now. But his head is buried in the refuse
heap in Franklin."

A look of horror spread across his disfigured face.

"And guess who killed him, Zach? No, it wasn't me. It was somebody who hated Indians and thought them no better than vermin.

Somebody a lot like you. In fact, he's so much like you, it's almost as if you did it yourself."

"No!" Zach howled as he lunged at me.

As he did so, I smashed the pan against the good side of his face with all of the force I could muster. I heard bones break. He sagged to his left, and before he could move, I slammed the pan down on top of his head with a sickening thud. His one good eye rolled back into his head, leaving only a milky white orb staring back at me. He sprawled backward into a pool of fire. Out of control, I brought the pan down square on his face. When I raised it, I saw his nose had vanished, driven up into his face by the force of my blow.

Gasping for air in the thick smoke, I studied his unmoving form for the slightest twitch. I wasn't going to leave him alive a third time.

His body lay perfectly still as the flames licked around his head like a halo, and I thought of Palmer calling him the fallen angel. Whatever he had been, he was dead, and this time I was certain.

The son of a bitch wouldn't ever call me Chapman again.

The smell of his burning flesh made me gag, and I pulled myself upward and stumbled outside as the first explosion tore through the cabin, tossing me into the air. I tumbled to the earth on the edge of the woods. Somehow I found the strength to drag myself into the shade of the woods.

I looked back in time to see a second, bigger explosion lift off the roof of Thomas's cabin. A third followed a moment later, a gout of flame leaping twenty feet into the air, blowing out the walls. The searing heat forced me to turn away, covering my head with my arms. There I lay, relieved it was over at last.

At least I was relieved until I realized that the heat of the flames wasn't dying down. In fact, it was getting hotter. Raising my head, I stared up into the sky as burning embers and chunks of wood streamed down like some eerie glowing rain. Already flames crackled above me as treetops exploded, fire leapfrogging from leafy crown to leafy crown, each igniting with the sound of a cannon firing. With unbelievable speed, the flames already raced away from me, and I thought of Palmer and Gwennie. How much time had passed since they left? How far had they gotten? Both of them had been injured, and I didn't know whether they could outrun the fire or not.

I had to make sure they got away.

I realized I was already up and running toward the creek. How odd, some small, calm part of my mind thought—I couldn't even recall having risen, much less begun running in any particular direction. But I had. And somehow I kept running despite the terrible stitch that gnawed at my side. All around me sap bubbled and hissed as flames squeezed it from trees. The whole forest sounded alive, crackling and popping, flames leaping and twisting as if trying to escape themselves. Nothing could describe what I saw and heard except to say it was as if the ground had split open and hell had come pouring out.

Then something completely unexpected happened—I ran over the edge of a small cliff. All I knew was that suddenly I was flying through the air, as if I had miraculously sprouted wings that lifted me up into the sky and away from the fire.

Or so I thought until I slammed face-first into the frigid water of the creek.

A meadowlark trilled from somewhere nearby. Somebody caressed my face.

Opening my eyes, I saw a stranger staring back at me. At least I thought him a stranger. With all of the soot that caked his face, it was hard to be sure. But whoever it was had beautiful blue eyes— blue eyes that I recognized.

"Gotcha," Palmer said softly.

"Got . . . you," I managed to reply.

Palmer reached out and touched my forehead. "That's quite a lump you've got there. Do you know who you are?"

I thought for a moment. For the first time in my life, I thought I did. "I'm John Chapman."

Palmer smiled.

"Where are we?" I asked.

He glanced about, shrugged, and said, "North of Franklin, though I'm not sure just how far north."

"What happened?"

"I was just going to ask you that."

An image of Zach lying in the pool of fire filled my mind. I closed my eyes and said, "I remember the fire. Then I was trying to find you and Gwennie to make sure you got away. I ran and ran, and now I'm here."

"You're safe now. The fire's over. What about Zach?"

"He's dead. I saw his body burning." My eyes fluttered open, seeking Palmer's. "It's over. You and Gwennie got away, and Zach is dead."

Palmer stroked my forehead.

"Where is Gwennie?" I asked, struggling to sit up.

"You just take it easy," Palmer admonished. "You look like hell, and under all of that ash and soot, I can't even tell how badly you might be hurt."

"Palmer, where is she?"

"We lost each other in the fire. But don't worry, if I made it, then I'm sure she did, too. Hell, she knew her way far better than I. We'll find her."

"Palmer, it's not your fault."

"What isn't?"

"Whatever might have happened to Gwennie. You didn't cause this to happen."

"Neither did you. You have to believe that."

"I do."

"You do?"

I nodded. "You know, I didn't mean what I said before, about only caring about Gwennie."

"Don't be an ass, John. Of course, I knew that."

Glancing around, I became aware of the smoking skeletons of trees lining the creek, their branches held wide as if they'd burned while pleading for mercy. Ash covered everything like a powdery snow, and in fact, a fine layer of it still fell all around us. The landscape looked more like January than July.

"How far did the fire go?" I asked.

"I'm not sure. I know it went as far north as your cabin."

"No," I moaned.

"It's all right. The cabin survived. Your kwenaskat burned so fast, the fire swept past."

"We should look for Gwennie."

Palmer nodded. "I think we should start in Franklin. That's probably where she went to wait for us."

Leaning against each other, we set off.

Like dazed soldiers whose side has been utterly routed, we staggered along the creek toward town. Eerie silence lay in every direction, while all around us loomed the blackened trunks of trees looking like grotesque, oversize skeletons. I felt as though I trekked through a battlefield rather than a forest.

We reached the Connolly claim, and I had the first inkling of how badly the fire had devastated the valley. Peering through the smoke, I looked for their cabin, their crops, their smokehouse, but they were all gone as thoroughly as if God had wiped them away with the palm of his hand.

"Sweet Jesus," whispered Palmer.

I felt myself stagger from the immensity of the destruction.

"Between the drought and all of the trees that they killed," Palmer said, "the valley never stood a chance once the fire started."

We found Samantha behind the smoldering ashes of the cabin. She lay curled between two boulders, untouched by the flames, so we deduced she'd died from the smoke. Two of her sisters lay beneath her, where she had tried in vain to shield them.

I was speechless.

Palmer said nothing more, and we pushed on.

Hours later, we heard the voices before we actually saw anyone. Sweat ran down my face; I struggled to the top of a hill where I peered out from behind the trunk of a charred pine. The fire had so drastically changed the landscape of the valley that we hadn't realized we were virtually in Franklin—or what was left of it. Where before there had been a collection of rough cabins, a smokehouse, truck patches, the blockhouse, and the pile of trash heaped up by the settlers, there now remained only two stone chimneys, one warped cast-iron stove, the smoldering, foul-smelling remains of the refuse, and of the blockhouse only the remains of the frame, like a skeleton with all of the flesh burned away.

There were, however, people. Perhaps twenty-five or thirty men, women, and children milled around. A few sat on tree stumps; others, apparently injured, lay stretched out on the ash-covered ground. All of them looked dazed, their faces streaked black, their hair the gray of the ash.

When we first approached, no one moved, as if not sure what to make of us. Perhaps they were too stunned to even really see us. At last, however, someone shambled toward us, and I recognized George, but only because of his size and the distinctive way he swayed from side to side as he walked. His right arm hung at his side as if injured. Otherwise he was nearly black from head to foot, and both his hair and sideburns and beard had been burned to a stubble.

"Your shoulder," I said. "You've hurt it."

He nodded. "And I consider myself lucky."

In the distance, I heard one of the smaller children begin to wail. Her mother picked her up.

"It's bad, isn't it?"

He nodded. "Real bad."

"How many?"

"Dead? Thirty that we know of. Maybe more."

"Thirty dead?" I exclaimed, stunned. "That was nearly half of the people who were at the town picnic." A terrible suffocating sensation crowded in on me. Reflexively, I began to blame myself, but I knew now it wasn't my fault. I wasn't responsible: not for Zach, not for the gunpowder, not for the drought or the dead trees that spread the fire.

"John, are you all right?" asked Palmer.

"Yes," I said, then asked, "Was there any warning before the fire hit?"

"Not really. Just this terrible roaring sound, then a wall of flames swept down the valley and took away my town." George wiped his eyes, then said, "Do either of you know what started it?"

Before I could respond, Palmer emphatically said, "No."

"Well, I'm glad you're both all right. Have either of you seen any signs of Thomas or Samantha?"

"They didn't make it," I said. To my relief, George only nodded sadly and didn't ask how they had died.

Instead, he looked at Palmer and said gently, "Your brother's alive—for now. Half of his family died, although we haven't told him that. We'll wait till we know if he's going to make it or not."

"Where are they now?" Palmer asked, and when George told him, he hurried over to them.

This was worse than anything I could have imagined.

"I've never seen a fire move so fast," George said. "It looks as if all of the Connollys were killed, except for two girls who were off picking berries with a neighbor. I've seen no sign of Gwennie."

It was a miracle Palmer and I had survived the fire. Despite Palmer's assurances, the odds of Gwennie, already injured and exhausted, having survived as well weren't good. But she had. Somehow I knew it.

"What happens now?" I asked.

"Most of us are leaving. There's a military fort two days east of here. That's where we're taking the injured and the orphaned children."

"But not everybody's going?"

"No. The fire didn't reach the very end of the valley. There's a couple of families who live there that are going to stay. I know of a couple of other men whose places survived as well. What are you going to do?"

"My place survived. I'm not sure what I'll do. I'd like to stay."

"I hope you do. It might not be until next year, but I'll be back. It would be nice to know you'd be here." He stuck out his hand, and we shook. "Best of luck."

"You, too, George."

I found Palmer talking to Caleb's wife while Caleb sat in the ash, his back against a tree stump. Moaning softly, he held his burnt arms and hands out in front of him while his surviving children took turns slowly dribbling water over them. His face was bright red and blistered, his eyebrows were gone, and the eyes themselves were almost swollen shut.

"Palmer," I said, coming up behind him. "How are they?"

He turned to face me and whispered, "Not good. Six of the children died. Caleb got badly burned saving the rest. I don't think he's going to make it."

"Palmer, I'm sorry."

"You're not blaming yourself, are you?"

"No."

"Zach had to be stopped," he said. "It's possible fewer people died today than would have if Zach had lived."

"How do you figure?"

"Who knows how many more people he might have killed, how much more misery he might have caused in his lifetime?"

Palmer had a point.

"John, I've got to leave. Caleb and his family need my help."

"I'll come with you."

"I think you should stay. This is your home, and I know how important staying here is for you."

"No," I said, trying to object, but Palmer cut me off.

"John, I know you'd come. After what you did for me, I don't doubt that for a minute. But to tell you the truth, it's probably better if you don't. I'm going to have to take Caleb's family back to my parents' farm. Having you there would complicate things."

"I understand." Unable to say any more without crying, I stared down at my ash-covered feet. I couldn't believe I was losing him again.

Palmer studied my face. "You do know I'm coming back, don't you?"

"You are?"

He wrapped his arms around me and squeezed as hard as he could. "Of course I am. This is my home, too."

A moment later, George called for everyone leaving to head out.

Palmer released me and said, "Now go and find Gwennie. I'll be back before winter."

"Be careful. While you're gone, I'll help the others. Gwennie and I will be here when you get back."

He smiled. "And next fall the three of us will watch the kwenaskat turn gold together."

"Go, then. Go help your family."

I stood watching as Palmer and the others moved away in a rag-tag column that began walking eastward. They moved at a crawl, and it took them a good half hour to reach the woods. A gray cloud of ash had been stirred up by their feet, making it seem as if they were fading away, rather than leaving. At the edge of the woods Palmer looked back, waved, then dissolved into the gray haze of the day.

I exchanged a few words with the others who were staying. We agreed to meet in a day to plan what we needed to do next.

After they left, I turned and looked north, up the valley.

Despite the devastating aftermath of the fire, I didn't see a ruined town engulfed by a blackened landscape, but my claim a year from now. I pictured a hot sun in a bright blue sky, and my cabin hidden in the cool shadows of the forest. I saw myself step onto the porch, then Palmer following a moment later. And spread out before us, rippling in the soothing wind, shined forth a sea of golden grass.

REFERENCES

Eckert, Alan. *Gateway to Empire*. Boston: Little, Brown, 1983.

Grumet, Robert Steven. *The Lenapes*. New York: Chelsea House, 1989.

Langdon, William Chauncy. *Everyday Things in American Life*. New York: Scribner, 1937–41.

Lederer, Richard M. *Colonial American English*. Essex Conn.: Verbatim Books, 1985.

McKnight, William James. *A Pioneer Outline of the History of Northwestern Pennsylvania*. Philadelphia: Lippincott, 1905.

Micucci, Charles. *The Life and Times of the Apple*. New York: Orchard Press, 1992.

Price, Robert. *Johnny Appleseed: Man and Myth*. Bloomington: Indiana University Press, 1954.

Rohrbaugh, Malcolm J. *The trans-Appalachian Frontier: People, Societies, and Institutions, 1775–1850*. New York: Oxford University Press, 1978.

Sperling, Susan K. *Poplollies and Bellibones: A Celebration of Lost Words*. New York: C. N. Potter: Crown, 1977.

Tunis, Edward. *Frontier Living*. 2nd ed. New York: Crowell, 1976.

Weslager, C. A. *The Delaware Indians: A History.* New Brunswick, N.J.: Rutgers University Press, 1972.

Wright, J. E. *Pioneer Life in Western Pennsylvania.* Pittsburgh: University of Pittsburgh Press, 1940.

ACKNOWLEDGMENTS

First and foremost, I would like to thank my partner, Brent, for his love, encouragement, and willingness to critique, shape, and reread this manuscript. This novel would never have been published without his input in virtually every aspect of its creation. I also want to thank my agent, Pesha Rubinstein, for taking a chance on such an unorthodox manuscript. The best half hour I ever spent on the phone was listening to Pesha explain why she should be my agent. She delivered exactly as promised. Thanks also go to my editor, Mitchell Ivers, for believing in the book and, more important, getting everyone else to believe in it as well. Of course, I'm also deeply appreciative to everyone at Pocket Books for all of their hard work.

The Lenni Lenape words were translated for me by Jim Rementer, who has shown great patience in answering my questions. I'd also like to thank Stan McInnis and Lisa Hake for their comments on the manuscript as well as their willingness to listen to me go on and on about it for years. And many thanks to my family—Mike, Gayle, and Chris Jensen—for all they've done for me.